MOTH FLIGHT'S
VISION

WARRIORS

THE PROPHECIES BEGIN

THE NEW PROPHECY

POWER OF THREE

OMEN OF THE STARS

DAWN OF THE CLANS

EXPLORE THE
WARRIORS
WORLD

MANGA

NOVELLAS

ALSO BY ERIN HUNTER

SEEKERS

SUPER EDITION

MOTH FLIGHT'S VISION

ERIN HUNTER

HARPER

An Imprint of HarperCollins*Publishers*

Special thanks to Kate Cary

Moth Flight's Vision
Copyright © 2015 by Working Partners Limited
Series created by Working Partners Limited
Map art 2015 by Dave Stevenson
Interior art 2015 by Owen Richardson
Manga text copyright © 2015 by Working Partners Limited
Manga art copyright © 2015 by HarperCollins Publishers

Library of Congress Cataloging-in-Publication Data
Hunter, Erin.
    Moth Flight's vision / Erin Hunter. — First edition.
        pages   cm. — (Warriors)
    Summary: "Strange visions drive a young WindClan cat named
Moth Flight to leave her home on a journey that will change the future of
the new warrior Clans forever"— Provided by publisher.
        ISBN 978-0-06-229147-9 (hardcover)
        ISBN 978-0-06-229148-6 (library)
    [1. Cats—Fiction. 2. Visions—Fiction. 3. Voyages and travels—
Fiction. 4. Fantasy.] I. Title.
PZ7.H916625Mq 2015   2014041203
[Fic]—dc23   CIP
                                                         AC

15 16 17 18 19 CG/RRDH 10 9 8 7 6 5 4 3 2 1
❖
First Edition

ALLEGIANCES

WINDCLAN

LEADER

WIND RUNNER—wiry brown she-cat with yellow eyes

GORSE FUR—thin, gray tabby tom

DUST MUZZLE—gray tabby tom with amber eyes

MOTH FLIGHT—white she-cat with green eyes

SLATE—thick-furred gray she-cat with one ear tip missing

WHITE TAIL—dark gray tom-kit with white patches and amber eyes

SILVER STRIPE—pale gray tabby she-kit with blue eyes

BLACK EAR—black-and-white patched tom-kit with amber eyes

SPOTTED FUR—golden-brown tom with amber eyes and a dappled coat

ROCKY—plump orange-and-white tom with green eyes

SWIFT MINNOW—gray-and-white she-cat

REED TAIL—silver tabby tom with a knowledge of herbs

JAGGED PEAK—small gray tabby tom with blue eyes

HOLLY—she-cat with prickly, bushy fur

STORM PELT—mottled gray tom with blue eyes and thick, bushy tail

DEW NOSE—brown splotchy tabby she-cat with white tips on nose and tail, yellow eyes

EAGLE FEATHER—brown tom with yellow eyes, broad shoulders, and striped tail

WILLOW TAIL—pale tabby she-cat with blue eyes

FERN LEAF—black she-cat with green eyes

SKYCLAN

LEADER

CLEAR SKY—light gray tom with blue eyes

STAR FLOWER—golden she-cat with green eyes

TINY BRANCH—tan-and-silver tom

DEW PETAL—silver-and-white she-cat

FLOWER FOOT—she-cat with tan stripes

ACORN FUR—chestnut brown she-cat

THORN—tom with splotchy brown fur

SPARROW FUR—tortoiseshell she-cat with amber eyes

QUICK WATER—gray-and-white she-cat

NETTLE—gray tom

BIRCH—ginger tom with white circles of fur around his eyes

ALDER—gray, brown-and-white she-cat

BLOSSOM—tortoiseshell-and-white she-cat with yellow eyes

RED CLAW—reddish-brown tom

THUNDERCLAN

THUNDER—orange tom with big white paws

VIOLET DAWN—sleek dark gray she-cat with bits of black around her ears and paws

CLOUD SPOTS—long-furred black tom with white ears, white chest, and two white paws

LIGHTNING TAIL—black tom

OWL EYES—gray tom with amber eyes

PINK EYES—white tom with pink eyes

LEAF—black-and-white tom with amber eyes

MILKWEED—splotchy ginger-and-black she-cat with scar on muzzle

CLOVER—ginger-and-white she-cat with yellow eyes

THISTLE—ginger tom with green eyes

GOOSEBERRY—pale yellow tabby she-cat

YEW TAIL—cream-and-brown tom

APPLE BLOSSOM—orange-and-white she-kit

SNAIL SHELL—dappled gray tom-kit

RIVERCLAN

RIVER RIPPLE—long-furred silver tom with amber eyes

DAPPLED PELT—delicate tortoiseshell she-cat with golden eyes

SHATTERED ICE—gray-and-white tom with green eyes

NIGHT—black she-cat

DEW—gray she-cat

DAWN MIST—orange-and-white she-cat with green eyes

MOSS TAIL—dark brown tom with golden eyes

DRIZZLE—gray-and-white she-kit with pale blue eyes

PINE NEEDLE—black tom-kit with yellow eyes

SHADOWCLAN

<u>LEADER</u>　**TALL SHADOW**—black, thick-furred she-cat with green eyes

PEBBLE HEART—dark gray tabby tom with white mark on his chest and amber eyes

SUN SHADOW—black tom with amber eyes

JUNIPER BRANCH—long-furred tortoiseshell she-cat with green eyes

RAVEN PELT—black tom with yellow eyes

MOUSE EAR—big tabby tom with unusually small ears

MUD PAWS—pale brown tom with four black paws

ROGUES

COW—plump black-and-white barn she-cat with green eyes

MOUSE—small brown barn tom with amber eyes

MICAH—yellow tom with green eyes

MOTH FLIGHT'S
VISION

HIGHSTONES

THUNDERPATH

WINDCLAN
CAMP

FOURTREES

FALLS

RIVER

RIVERCLAN
CAMP

CAT VIEW

SHADOWCLAN
CAMP

THUNDERCLAN
CAMP

SKYCLAN
CAMP

NORTH

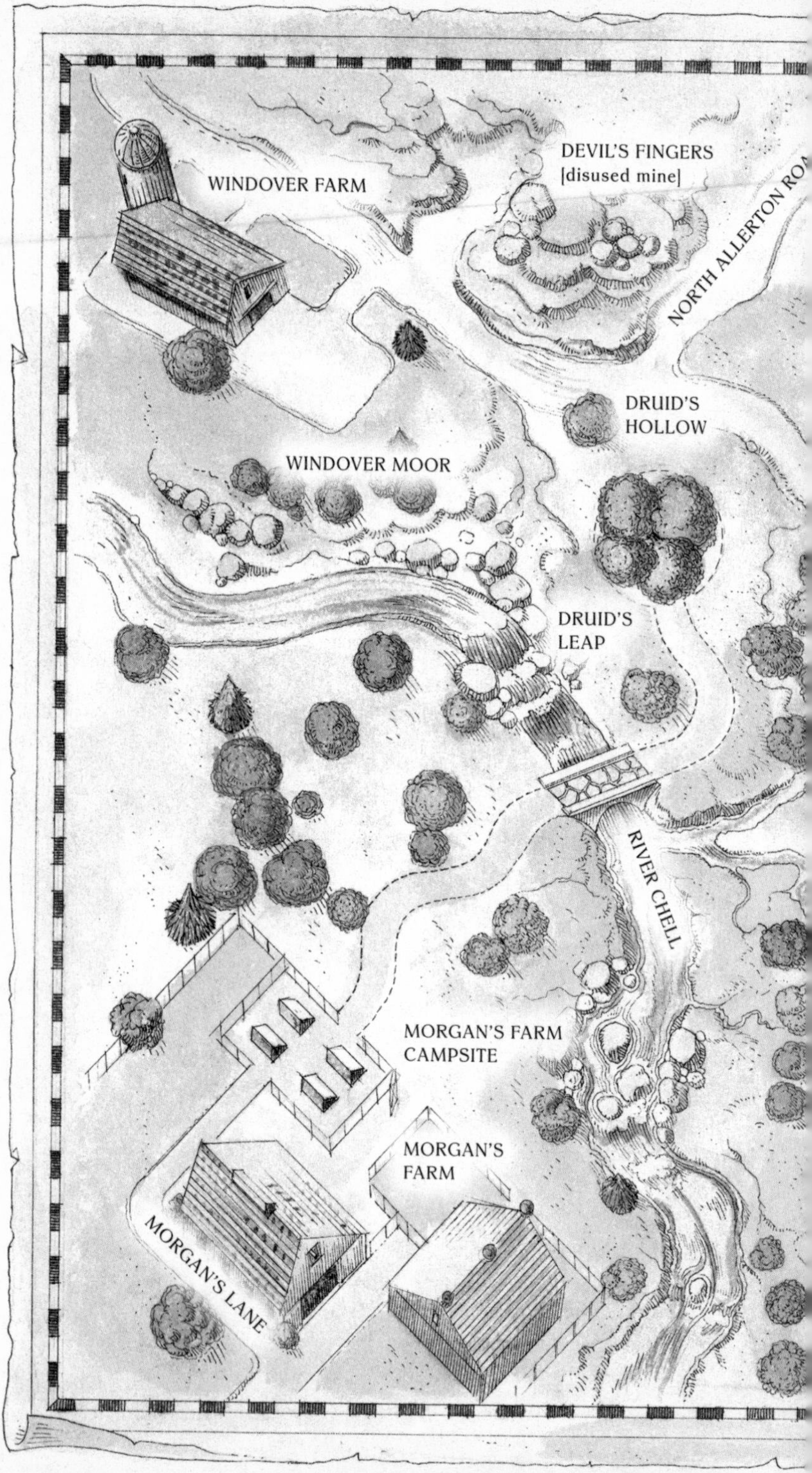

WINDOVER FARM

DEVIL'S FINGERS
[disused mine]

NORTH ALLERTON ROAD

DRUID'S
HOLLOW

WINDOVER MOOR

DRUID'S
LEAP

RIVER CHELL

MORGAN'S FARM
CAMPSITE

MORGAN'S
FARM

MORGAN'S LANE

NORTH ALLERTON
AMENITY TIP

TWOLEG VIEW

WINDOVER ROAD

WHITE HART WOODS

NORTH

PROLOGUE

"Help her!" Horror seared through Moth Flight's body as she spotted the blue-gray she-cat lying in the ditch beside the dirt track. Blood darkened the she-cat's neck, spreading fast through her thick fur. Her flanks trembled as she struggled for each shallow breath.

Other feline shapes moved around Moth Flight, hazy in the pale dawn. She snapped her head around as a hiss sounded beside her. A huge dark tabby reared and smashed his forepaws down onto a smaller black-and-white tom. "Why don't you help her?" Moth Flight begged. But neither cat seemed to hear. The tom scrabbled desperately at the earth as the tabby pinned him down.

Moth Flight's thoughts spun. *Is this a battle?*

But the other cats weren't fighting.

Ginger fur flickered like flame through the ditch as a young tom raced to the she-cat's side and crouched beside her. Two frightened faces peered over the top of the ditch, ears twitching.

Blood was seeping onto the ground from the she-cat's neck.

"She's dying!" Moth Flight yowled to the fighting toms. But they only snarled at one another more viciously.

Dread shadowed her heart. Moth Flight raced toward the injured she-cat, her paws moving soundlessly over the earth. Early sunlight struck her flank, but made no shadow on the earth beyond.

She slid into the ditch and stopped beside the flame-colored tom. "What happened to her?"

The tom didn't answer. He leaned close to the injured she-cat, until his breath stirred her ear fur.

"Don't die!" Moth Flight reached out to touch the she-cat, but her paw passed through the injured cat's flank as if she was cutting through mist.

Dark fur loomed beside her. The great tabby had stopped fighting and come at last. But as he pushed past her, Moth Flight felt no weight. His fur brushed through her as though she weren't there.

The two young cats, watching from the top of the ditch, climbed down into the shadows and stood trembling beside the ginger tom. She saw the tabby's mouth open and close as he spoke, but she couldn't hear his words.

Moth Flight held her breath as she saw the blue-gray cat's flanks grow still.

She's dying!

The sight of death sliced through Moth Flight like an icy wind, and she began to tremble. She remembered Gray Wing's death, just a moon ago. She'd shivered as she'd peered into his open grave, her heart twisting as she saw how small he looked and how dull his fur had become. The warmhearted tom, whose pelt had rippled in the wind, had been lost in death.

Prey seemed to lie in his place. His Clan had buried him, eyes hollow with grief, yet at least the ceremony had given them a chance to say good-bye.

"You must bury her," she breathed shakily.

But the cats did not move. They only stared at their dead friend, hardly blinking as the sun lifted higher into the sky. The black-and-white tom watched from a few tail-lengths away, nervously eyeing the tabby.

"Don't just stand there!" Frustration raged through Moth Flight as she tried to make herself heard. "Show her some respect! Start digging her grave."

No cat turned or even betrayed with an ear twitch that they'd heard her.

The sun lifted higher until its rays spilled into the ditch.

"Are you going to leave her here for crows to pick at?" Moth Flight couldn't believe what she was seeing. *Are these cats heartless?*

Suddenly, the blue-gray she-cat's tail twitched.

Moth Flight gasped, shock jolting through her. Had the wind caught the dead cat's fur?

No!

The blue-gray she-cat was lifting her head, looking blearily at the others.

Moth Flight tried to back away, but the mist seemed to entwine her paws, holding her still. She stared in disbelief as the she-cat spoke to the flame-pelted tom. *She was dead!* Moth Flight couldn't make out the words but she could see, as the cat's blue eyes cleared, authority in her gaze. It reminded her of her own mother's look. Was this she-cat the group's leader? How was she *alive*?

The young cats moved away to let the she-cat stand. As she heaved herself slowly to her paws, relief washed over their faces.

But the tabby only stared. His amber gaze betrayed nothing—neither relief, nor joy. Moth Flight drew in a trembling breath and began to run, clambering out of the ditch, her thoughts spinning as she tried to make sense of what she'd seen.

A pale flash caught her eye and she lifted her head, surprised to see a great, green moth. Its wide translucent wings fluttered in the breeze; dawn sunshine flooded through them so they glowed as bright as new leaves.

She watched the moth dance away, realizing that, beyond it, she could see Highstones. Their towering peaks glittered in the sunshine and Moth Flight narrowed her eyes against the glare, straining to see the moth as it fluttered toward them.

Without thinking, she leaped the ditch and began to follow the moth as it bobbed over the grass, keeping low. *I must reach it!* She bounded after it as it zigzagged like a petal caught on a breeze, staying just beyond paw reach.

It pulled farther ahead until she stumbled to a halt and watched it fly away. Moth Flight was surprised by a fierce longing in her heart. *Wait for me!* A wail caught in her throat. *I want to come with you!*

CHAPTER 1

☙

"What are you mumbling about?"

Dust Muzzle's mew jerked Moth Flight awake. She blinked open her eyes, narrowing them at once as bright afternoon sunshine sliced over the gorse wall of the camp. "Was I mumbling?" The dream of the blue-gray she-cat and the moth were still sharp in her mind. Had she been calling out in her sleep?

Dust Muzzle paced in front of her. "You said you wanted to go with someone."

Spotted Fur stopped beside Dust Muzzle, his eyes warm with affection. "I thought only *old* cats took afternoon naps." He nudged Dust Muzzle. "Your sister has been hanging out with Rocky too long."

Rocky looked up as he heard his name. The old ginger-and-white tom blinked from his nest in the long grass beside the sandy hollow. "She could learn a lot from me," he grunted. "I've seen more moons than the three of you put together." The kittypet had been with the Clan for only a few moons— he'd arrived shortly after Gray Wing had called the groups of cats *Clans* for the first time, a word that had seemed right the moment Gray Wing had said it—but Rocky had taken to

Clan life like a frog to swimming. He didn't hunt as much as the younger cats, complaining that his paws were too slow for chasing. But he loved to help Holly and Eagle Feather with their tunneling. Holly was always planning new tunnels, digging through old rabbit runs to make shortcuts to new ones.

Moth Flight scrambled to her paws. "I didn't mean to fall asleep, but the sun was so warm." Leafbare was finally loosening its grip on the moor and the newleaf sun felt luxurious after hard moons of frost and ice. Panic jolted through her. "Where are Slate's kits?" She scanned the clearing, her heart lurching. Slate had asked Moth Flight to watch White Tail, Silver Stripe, and Black Ear. They'd been playing in the sandy hollow when Moth Flight's eyes had begun to grow heavy. She'd only closed them for a moment and now the kits were nowhere to be seen.

She caught Holly's eye across the camp. The black she-cat was washing dirt from her fur, while Eagle Feather shook out his dusty pelt beside his mother.

Holly frowned. "Is everything okay, Moth Flight?" she called. "You look worried."

Moth Flight forced herself to blink brightly. "I'm fine," she assured Holly.

Dust Muzzle flashed her a look. "Apart from losing Slate's kits," he breathed.

"Hush!" Moth Flight headed across the tussocky grass. "Perhaps they're near the stones." The kits liked to chase one another around the smooth flat rocks near the camp entrance.

"I saw them earlier," Rocky called.

Moth Flight spun to face him. "Where?" Before he could call his answer across the camp for everyone to hear, she dashed to his nest and stopped, panting, beside him. "Where were they?" she begged.

"I saw them playing outside camp when we came out of the tunnel," Rocky told her.

"Whereabouts?" Fear prickled through Moth Flight's pelt.

"Near the RiverClan border."

"You mean the gorge?" Moth Flight's throat tightened. A deep ravine cut through the moor there, a river churning at the bottom. It was a dangerous place for kits.

"Not very near," Rocky reassured her. "They're too sensible to go close to the edge."

"They're only two moons old!" Moth Flight was fighting panic. Slate had trusted her to watch her beloved kits. Still mourning the loss of her mate, Gray Wing, the gray she-cat often rested after sunhigh, weary from her grief. *I've let her down! What if Silver Stripe fell into the gorge? Or a buzzard carried off White Tail? Or Black Ear—stop!* Moth Flight forced her thoughts to slow. "Why didn't you bring them home with you?" She glared at Rocky.

"I thought you'd sent them out there." Rocky blinked at her.

"Why would I *do* that?" Moth Flight lowered her voice to a hiss. "They're too young to be out of camp. They can't look after themselves."

Rocky met her gaze steadily. "I thought that's what *you* were supposed to be doing," he grunted.

A disdainful snort sounded from behind Moth Flight.

She glanced around to where the heather wall of the camp shaded a soft grassy border.

Swift Minnow was eyeing her harshly. "I can tell you haven't been with us long, Rocky," the gray-and-white she-cat meowed. "You clearly don't know Moth Flight very well."

"What does that mean?" Moth Flight glared at the other cat, her belly twisting as she guessed what Swift Minnow was going to say before she'd finished her question.

"You never do what you're supposed to." Swift Minnow sniffed. "Wind Runner sent you out to catch voles yesterday and you came back with leaves from some stinking plant."

"It wasn't stinking!" Moth Flight defended herself. "And I had to bring it back. I'd never smelled leaves like that before."

"Leaves don't feed a Clan," Swift Minnow shot back.

Rocky pushed himself to his paws and gazed gently at the gray-and-white she-cat. "Don't be too harsh, Swift Minnow. Moth Flight's hardly more than a kit herself. Kits get distracted. Everything is new to them." He shrugged and shambled toward a sunny patch of clearing, his pelt twitching along his spine where tunnel mud caked his fur.

"Don't worry." Spotted Fur's mew stirred Moth Flight's ear fur. The golden tom leaned closer, his dappled pelt glowing in the afternoon sun. "The kits will be fine. I'll help you look for them."

Swift Minnow glanced toward the shady hollow in the heather wall where Slate was sleeping. "You'd better find them before their mother wakes up. She's had enough grief."

Moth Flight lifted her chin. "I'll find them!" Wishing she felt as sure as she sounded, she marched toward the camp entrance.

Spotted Fur hurried after her.

Moth Flight glanced back at Dust Muzzle. "Aren't you coming to help?"

Dust Muzzle rolled his eyes. "Not *again*! I'm always helping you out of trouble. You've got Spotted Fur to help you. I'm tired from hunting. Let me rest."

Moth Flight flicked her tail crossly. But he was right. Her brother was always helping her out of scrapes. Last half-moon, Wind Runner had sent her looking for cobwebs to dress Dew Nose's scratched paw, but the night had been so starry, Moth Flight had been distracted by the reflection of the sky glittering in a puddle. It had been Dust Muzzle who'd come to hurry her up and who had finally found a clump of cobwebs among a pile of rocks while she'd been spotting patterns in the stars.

I must learn to focus on what I'm supposed to be doing! Otherwise, I'll never—

"Should we head for the gorge?" Spotted Fur's mew cut into her thoughts.

"The gorge?" she stopped outside the camp entrance and frowned for a moment. Then she hissed, angry with herself. Her thoughts had wandered *again*! Promising herself she would try harder, she nodded. "Of course. That's where Rocky saw the kits last."

She stared across the wide swaths of brown heather

rippling softly in the newleaf breeze. Full moon was in two days, and in another half-moon, the moor would be green with budding leaves, something she had only heard older cats talk about. Moth Flight could hardly wait for the fresh, clean scent of new life. This would be her first newleaf. All she could remember was snow and ice and the slow dying of the moorland in the moons before leafbare. Now it was all going to come back to life again. Excitement fizzed in her paws.

"Moth Flight!" Spotted Fur's mew was stern this time. "We *need* to find the kits!"

She shook out her fur, feeling guiltier than ever. Why did there have to be so many things to distract her? "The kits." She curled her claws into the grass, determined that this time she would stay focused on finding them.

The heather rustled ahead of them and Willow Tail slid out from beneath the bushes, a mouse hanging from her jaws. She dropped it and looked at Spotted Fur. "What's this about kits?"

"I've lost Slate's—"

Spotted Fur cut Moth Flight off before she could finish her confession. "Slate's kits have wandered out of camp and we're going to find them."

Moth Flight glanced gratefully at her friend. "Rocky said he'd seen them near the gorge," she added.

Willow Tail's eyes rounded with worry. "I'd better come with you. Three noses are better than one." Leaving her mouse, she began to hurry down the slope, breaking into a run as she weaved between the clumps of heather. Spotted Fur hurried after her and Moth Flight ran behind.

"Keep your mouths open to taste for their scent," Willow Tail called over her shoulder.

Moth Flight caught up with Spotted Fur, opening her jaws to let the moor scents bathe her tongue. The smell of warm peat filled her mouth. She narrowed her eyes, peering at the slope below, hoping to see a flash of familiar fur. "Can you smell them?" she puffed.

Spotted Fur's gaze was fixed ahead. "Not yet, but with Willow Tail helping we're bound to find them quickly."

Willow Tail had slowed as the slope steepened toward the gorge. She darted this way and that, sniffing the grass around the edge of a gorse patch. "Check that stretch of heather," she called to Spotted Fur.

"Where should *I* look?" Moth Flight called.

"Stay with Spotted Fur," Willow Tail called back. "We don't want *you* getting lost too."

Moth Flight's pelt prickled. Did *every* cat in WindClan think she was as useless as thistledown? Obediently, she slid between the heather bushes after Spotted Fur.

A distant tang touched her nose. "I can smell the river."

"From *here*?" Spotted Fur turned to face her, heather crowding in on either side and arching over their heads.

"I can smell the water plants that line it." Moth Flight felt a pang of longing. "I've always wanted to go and see them up close and pick a few. Water plants are so interesting. Why don't they drown? Don't they need wind like moor plants?"

"You can't go picking plants in RiverClan territory,"

Spotted Fur warned her. "Wind Runner says if there's to be peace between the Clans, then we have to stay on our own lands."

Moth Flight felt a prickle of frustration. "How will we learn anything if we just stick to what we know?"

As she spoke, she saw Spotted Fur stiffen. Alarm sparked in his gaze.

"What's wrong?" Fear pricked her paws.

"Listen!" Spotted Fur's ears were stretched.

Moth Flight stretched hers too, straining to hear what he had heard.

The faint wail of a kit sounded through the heather.

Then Willow Tail's frightened yowl sounded from downslope. "Spotted Fur! Come quickly!"

"The kits are in trouble!" Spotted Fur plunged through the heather.

Heart pounding in her ears, Moth Flight raced after him.

CHAPTER 2

She crashed through the heather, hardly feeling the branches scrape her flanks, and exploded onto the grass a moment after Spotted Fur. He was already scanning the slope and she followed his gaze.

Willow Tail crouched in a dip near the edge of the gorse patch. The pale tabby she-cat was peering into a narrow rabbit burrow. "It's all right, Silver Stripe. We'll get you out."

A plaintive wail answered her. "Hurry! Please! I'm scared!"

White Tail—no bigger than a rabbit-kit—appeared, nosing past Willow Tail and peering into the burrow. "She's been there for *ages!*"

Black Ear paced around them, his fluffy black-and-white fur bushed out. "We tried to reach her but she's too far down."

They're okay! Relief swelled in Moth Flight's chest, then she froze. Black Ear and White Tail were safe, but what about Silver Stripe?

Spotted Fur charged toward his Clanmate. "What happened?"

Willow Tail's ears twitched. "Looks like Silver Stripe fell into a tunnel and she can't get out, the poor kit. She's scared half to death but the hole's too narrow for me to squeeze through."

Moth Flight caught up, skidding to a halt and peering into the small gap in the grass where Silver Stripe's wails were growing louder. "Are you hurt?" she called down.

"Not yet," Silver Stripe squeaked nervously. "But I'm sure I can hear paw steps coming up the tunnel toward me!"

Black Ear's eyes widened. "A badger!"

White Tail unsheathed his tiny claws. "I'll save her." He stuck his head into the hole and began to burrow into the tunnel.

"No you don't!" Spotted Fur grabbed his tail between his teeth and hauled the kit backward. "We're not losing two of you."

Black Ear tried to scrabble free. "But what about the badger?"

"That tunnel's too small for a badger," Willow Tail assured him.

White Tail blinked at the tom. "What about rats?"

Moth Flight's heart quickened, her fear spilling into anger. "Why didn't you just stay in camp?" she snapped at the kits.

Black Ear met her gaze innocently. "We were going to ask you if we could leave, but you were asleep."

Willow Tail flashed her a look. "Were you supposed to be watching them?"

Moth Flight dropped her gaze guiltily. "Yes," she confessed, her fur rippling with irritation. Why did Slate have to ask *her* to watch her kits? *Everyone knows I'm a featherbrain!*

Spotted Fur pushed past her and began tearing at the grass around the narrow tunnel entrance. "Let's just get Silver Stripe out. I can't smell rat scent down there, but she must be cold and hungry."

Willow Tail nodded and hooked her claws into the earth, ripping away another clump. Together they dug out soil around the rim. Moth Flight found herself watching the grassy clods as her Clanmates flung them aside. They exploded as they hit the ground; the soil here wasn't as dark and wet as it was on the high moor. And she noticed that the grass was softer too, nothing like the stiff grass around camp; it smelled lusher too.

"Stop staring and help!" Willow Tail's sharp mew broke into her thoughts.

Moth Flight hopped forward, tripping over Black Ear. He squeaked as her paw squashed his tail, then dragged it free and glared at her indignantly.

"Sorry!" Moth Flight plunged her forepaws into the hole beside Spotted Fur's and began scraping out soil. She could see Silver Stripe's muzzle, lit by the late sunshine that broke into the widening hole. The earth was easy to scrape away—lighter and crumblier than the heavy peat higher on the moor. Moth Flight wondered if different plants grew here and, as she helped Willow Tail and Spotted Fur dig, glanced furtively around, looking for unusual leaf shapes showing in the grass nearby.

"That should be big enough." Willow Tail sat back on her haunches.

Spotted Fur frowned. "It's too small for me to fit in."

Silver Stripe was already trying to scrabble up the steep sides of the hole, yowling with frustration each time she slid down as the earth crumbled beneath her claws.

"*You're* small enough to squeeze in." Willow Tail stared at Moth Flight. "Jump down and give him a boost."

Moth Flight hesitated. She knew that some of the Wind-Clan cats liked running though the rabbit tunnels. Holly often took Eagle Feather and Dew Nose hunting there. But Moth Flight preferred to feel the wind in her fur.

Spotted Fur nudged her shoulder with his muzzle. "Don't think about the dark," he urged gently. "Silver Stripe needs help."

Steadying her breath, Moth Flight slithered into the hole. Her paws slipped as she reached the bottom, and she nearly fell. A cold musky smell swirled around her. She shivered, the darkness of the tunnel pressing around her until her belly tightened with fear.

"You saved me!" Silver Stripe flung herself against Moth Flight, purring loudly. Moth Flight suddenly realized how brave the young kit had been, trapped alone down here for so long.

She peered, blinking, into the blackness beyond the kit, wondering with a shiver how far the tunnel stretched and what might be at the end of it. She sniffed for rat scent, pricking her ears to listen for the slither of tails. *Nothing.* The tunnel was clear. "I'm sorry I fell asleep," she whispered into Silver Stripe's soft ear. "I should have been watching you."

Silver Stripe's cold muzzle brushed her cheek. "I'm sorry we ran off," she apologized, her mew thick.

"Let's get you out of here." Moth Flight ducked and tucked her nose beneath the kit's haunches. "Jump!" she ordered, her mew muffled by fur. As Silver Stripe leaped, Moth Flight heaved her upward. She smelled Spotted Fur's warm breath as he reached down and grabbed the kit's scruff, scooping her into the light.

"Silver Stripe!" White Tail squeaked happily.

Black Ear mewled with excitement. "We thought rats would get you for sure."

Spotted Fur purred. "Are you coming, Moth Flight?"

Moth Flight hardly heard him. As she stared at the ring of light above her, a sharp tang touched her nose. She opened her mouth, intrigued. There was an unfamiliar sour scent mingled in with the heavy smell of earth. She glanced down the tunnel, widening her eyes to adjust to the gloom. White roots dangled from the roof of the tunnel a tail-length away. They didn't smell like *grass* roots. Or heather. Or gorse. *I knew there must be special plants growing in this sandy soil!* Her heart quickening, Moth Flight padded deeper into the darkness until her face brushed the roots. Sticking out her tongue, she licked them gingerly, intrigued by their sweet flavor. *I wonder what the leaves of this plant look like?* Moth Flight knew that she wasn't far from the surface. Leaning back on her haunches, she began to dig upward, through the earth around the roots. If she could just claw away a few pawfuls of soil, she'd be able to drag the whole plant down and look at it properly.

"Moth Flight?" Spotted Fur's mew echoed along the tunnel. "Where are you?"

"Coming," she called back absently. Dirt spilled onto her tongue as she spoke, and she coughed, spitting it out.

"Hurry *up*!" Willow Tail's mew was sharper than Spotted Fur's. "We need to get these kits back to their mother. They're tired and hungry!"

"I won't be long!" Moth Flight scrabbled harder at the soil above her head, screwing up her eyes against the earth, which showered her face. The roots were thicker, higher up, and she curled her claws into their flesh and tugged. They slid free, bringing pawfuls of dirt with them as Moth Flight dragged the plant down into the tunnel. Laying it on the ground, she tried to make out the shape of the leaves.

"Moth Flight!" Willow Tail sounded angry. "We need you up here!"

Moth Flight grasped the plant between her jaws and raced back along the tunnel. Reaching up, she scrambled out, thankful to feel Spotted Fur's teeth in her scruff as he helped haul her free of the crumbling earth.

"What, in all the stars, is *that*?" Willow Tail stared at the plant dangling from Moth Flight's jaws.

Moth Flight dropped it, spitting out dirt. "I don't know," she spluttered. "But I want to find out."

Willow Tail glared at her. "You're not bringing it with you," she snapped. "These kits are two moons old and too tired to walk back to camp. They need carrying."

Moth Flight's heart sank. She glanced at the plant she'd

unearthed. Its bright green leaves had scalloped edges and it smelled pungent—almost how she imagined RiverClan water plants would smell. "I can't leave it behind!" She knew all the plants on the high moor. This was *new*! She looked hopefully at Spotted Fur. "Can't one of the kits ride on your back?"

"I'll ride," Black Ear offered. His eyes were dull with tiredness. "It's better than being carried."

Willow Tail snorted at Moth Flight. "Do you *really* think he'll have the strength to hang on to Spotted Fur's back all the way to camp?"

Spotted Fur glanced apologetically at Moth Flight. "Willow Tail's right. These kits need to be carried."

"I can make it," Black Ear promised. "I know I can."

"Of course you can." Spotted Fur soothed the young kit. "But it'll be easier for *me* if you let Moth Flight carry you."

Moth Flight sighed. "Okay." The plant would have to wait. "I guess I can come back and fetch this later." She stroked the soft leaves with her paw. They felt furry.

Willow Tail's ears twitched impatiently. "What do you want with a dead weed anyway?"

Moth Flight shrugged. "It's *interesting*."

Willow Tail shook her head, sighing. "Cats are meant to hunt prey, not *plants*."

Spotted Fur nosed Black Ear gently toward Moth Flight. "If all cats were the same, life would be dull," he meowed softly.

Willow Tail huffed disapprovingly and scooped up Silver Stripe by her scruff.

Spotted Fur lifted White Tail and Moth Flight grasped Black Ear gently between her jaws and lifted him off the ground. He was as light as prey and she suddenly realized how vulnerable the kits had been out here on their own. A fresh flash of guilt shot though her as she followed Willow Tail and Spotted Fur up the slope toward camp.

Black Ear swung limply from her jaws. He didn't scrabble or fidget like he did when she was trying to get him into his nest in the evenings. *He must be exhausted.* She quickened her pace, falling into step beside Spotted Fur.

They slid into single file as they approached a thick swath of heather. Willow Tail pushed into it first. Spotted Fur waited for Moth Flight to duck in front of him. She followed Willow Tail through the branches to where an old sheep trail cut through the bushes. Spotted Fur's breath tickled her tail as he traced her paw steps.

As they neared the far edge of the heather patch, Willow Tail slowed. The pale tabby's ears pricked and Moth Flight stiffened. Had Willow Tail heard something? A badger? A dog? Moth Flight breathed deeply, but all she could taste was Black Ear's warm scent. Willow Tail put Silver Stripe down and pushed her way out of the heather.

"What's wrong?" Spotted Fur slid past Moth Flight and dropped White Tail beside Silver Stripe.

Black Ear began to struggle. "What's that smell?"

As Moth Flight placed him gently beside his littermates, she smelled the strong tang of a strange tom.

Spotted Fur's hackles lifted. "Wait here with the kits." He

slid out of the heather after Willow Tail.

"It's just a SkyClan tom!" Moth Flight could smell the fragrant scent of bark mingling with the tom's own scent. It was completely different from the heathery scent of her Clanmates. RiverClan smelled fishy, ShadowClan like pine. And ThunderClan always carried the musty scent of the leaf litter that softened the floor of their ravine.

Why were Willow Tail and Spotted Fur so edgy?

Moth Flight shooed the kits ahead of her as she nosed her way out of the heather. A large reddish-brown tom was stretching languorously on a sunlit patch of grass. She recognized him at once. She'd seen him at Gatherings. He was Red Claw. Willow Tail must know him well—they'd been rogues together before they'd chosen different Clans.

Then why was she snarling at him, her ears flat against her head?

"What are you doing on WindClan land?" Willow Tail hissed accusingly.

Moth Flight glanced questioningly toward Spotted Fur. The tabby she-cat sounded *furious*. Why was she so bothered about the tom? He was doing no harm.

As Spotted Fur shrugged in reply, Red Claw lifted his head and blinked at them lazily. "I came up here to enjoy the sunshine. It's too shady in the woods."

Willow Tail spat. "You shouldn't be here! This is *our* land."

Black Ear began to march forward, showing his teeth. "Yeah, this is *our* land!" he squeaked.

Red Claw glanced at the kit, amusement brightening his

gaze. "I'm not hunting. So where's the harm?"

Spotted Tail cocked his head. "How do we know you're not hunting?" he asked.

Willow Tail bared her teeth at Red Claw. "We don't! Listen, I don't want you on WindClan land. You'll bring trouble. You always do!"

Moth Flight pricked her ears. Did Willow Tail know something about Red Claw the rest of the Clan didn't? Was he dangerous? Moth Flight instinctively moved closer to the kits, sweeping her tail around them to draw them near.

Black Ear tried to wriggle free, but Spotted Fur froze him with a warning look.

Pushing himself to his paws, Red Claw faced Willow Tail, his eyes glittering. "You're not WindClan's leader," he growled. "Or SkyClan's. You can't tell me what to do."

Willow Tail unsheathed her claws.

Spotted Fur padded between the bristling cats. "This isn't worth fighting over," he mewed softly. "We may not be Wind Runner, but we can certainly take this back to her and ask what she thinks. Is that what you want?"

Moth Flight shifted her paws uneasily. *What* would *Wind Runner say?* Wind Runner claimed that the borders had been established to make sure each Clan had enough prey to feed themselves, but there was more than enough prey on the moor and in the forests to feed every cat. Besides, Red Claw wasn't even hunting. Still . . . Wind Runner seemed especially edgy where Clear Sky, and SkyClan, were concerned.

Red Claw was eyeing Spotted Fur with annoyance. "I'm

just a tired cat enjoying a rest in a sunny clearing that happens to be a few tail-lengths across the border. Do you think your leader would care?"

Spotted Fur narrowed his eyes. "Again, I could go and ask her, if you'd like." Red Claw scowled, and Spotted Fur went on. "Look, I don't want any trouble. You chose to join Sky-Clan. There must be a sunny clearing somewhere in your own territory."

Red Claw's tail flicked angrily. "Fine." Turning away, he stalked toward the heather.

Silver Stripe stared at Moth Flight. "Who was he?"

"Just a SkyClan cat," she said. She wasn't entirely sure why things had gotten so tense, but she didn't want the kits to worry.

Black Ear hopped over her tail and padded a few steps toward the grass Red Claw had flattened. His small nose was twitching with curiosity. "Are SkyClan cats bad?"

Moth Flight felt a prickle of irritation. "Of course not. They're just like you and me." She didn't understand why there had to be lines scratched between the Clans. Borders just seemed to make everyone suspicious of each other. What if there was a harsh leafbare or a dry greenleaf? Would one Clan let another starve or go thirsty rather than share their hunting lands?

Willow Tail's pelt was still bristling. "We should follow him to make sure he leaves. You can't trust SkyClan cats."

Moth Flight glanced crossly at Willow Tail. "Don't say that in front of the kits!" There was enough gossip in camp about ThunderClan cats being reckless, ShadowClan cats being unfriendly, and RiverClan cats being odd. Making up differences between the Clans was just planting trouble for the future. A new thought struck her, making her pelt prick warily. *I wonder what the other Clans say about us?*

"We should get the kits back to Slate," Spotted Fur meowed.

Moth Flight was suddenly aware that White Tail was shivering against her belly. "He's right. They're getting cold."

"You didn't seem worried about that while you were digging out your precious weed." Willow Tail stared fiercely at the heather where Red Claw had disappeared. "What if he stays on our land?"

"Who cares?" Moth Flight grasped White Tail's scruff and began to pad toward camp, annoyed at the older she-cat. *It's not a weed, it's a plant! And* she *made me leave it behind for the sake of the kits. Now she wants to go chasing after a SkyClan cat.*

"I'm sure he'll leave," Spotted Fur assured Willow Tail, gathering her in with his tail. "Even SkyClan cats know better than to tangle with Wind Runner. Now let's get the kits home."

Willow Tail watched the heather for a few moments more, then sighed and began walking back toward camp. "All right."

Soon, Moth Flight could see the dip where their camp nestled into the hillside and, after a few more paw steps, its heather walls showed against the windswept grass. They were nearly home.

Spotted Fur fell in beside her, Black Ear dangling from his jaws.

She frowned, wondering why he'd been so tough on Red Claw, then she heard a yowl.

Slate was bounding from the camp, Wind Runner at her heels.

"Are they okay? Are they safe?" Slate skidded to a halt, her eyes round with fear.

Spotted Fur placed Black Ear at her paws. "They're a bit cold and hungry, but no harm done."

Moth Flight put White Tail gently down. The kit ran at once to his mother and nuzzled into her soft gray flank.

Silver Stripe wailed, struggling in Willow Tail's jaws. "I fell down a rabbit hole!" Willow Tail dropped her and she raced toward Slate. "Moth Flight had to climb down and push me out."

"She was in there for ages!" White Tail told Slate.

"We thought a badger was going to eat her!" Black Ear added.

Slate pulled her kits to her belly, her eyes glistening even brighter with worry.

Spotted Fur brushed Moth Flight's flank with his tail. "It was just a rabbit hole," he told Slate. "Too small for badgers. We had to dig it open before Moth Flight could squeeze in and rescue her."

Moth Flight felt a wave of gratitude toward her friend. *Spotted Fur always defends me.* But then she caught Wind Runner's eye and her belly tightened.

Her mother was glaring at her. "You were asked to watch them, Moth Flight."

Moth Flight stared at her paws, shame worming beneath her pelt. "I'm sorry."

Slate began lapping her kits furiously. "It was my fault," she murmured between licks. "I was in a hurry to lie down. I should have asked someone more reliable to keep an eye on them, like Fern Leaf, but she was hunting."

Her words raked Moth Flight like claws. She glanced nervously at her mother. Wind Runner's eyes were burning with rage.

The WindClan leader growled. "Moth Flight is old enough to know better. Her Clanmates *should* be able to rely on her."

Moth Flight shifted her paws. "It won't happen again," she mumbled.

"I wish I could believe you," Wind Runner hissed. "How does it look to the Clan if my own kit can't be trusted?"

Moth Flight flinched. Why did her mother have to be the Clan leader? *Everything I do must be an example to the Clan!* And if she got anything wrong, she was letting the whole Clan down. Resentment burned in her belly as she watched Slate fussing over her kits. *I bet she doesn't expect them to be perfect all the time!*

Gray fur flashed at the camp entrance. Her father, Gorse Fur, was hurrying toward them, Dust Muzzle and Fern Leaf at his heels. "You found them!" He stared proudly at Moth Flight.

"She *lost* them!" Wind Runner snapped.

Dust Muzzle's eyes rounded with sympathy as he caught sight of Moth Flight. She saw him exchange glances with Spotted Fur. This was so humiliating. Did Wind Runner have to scold her in front of *every* cat?

Spotted Fur seemed to guess her thoughts. "Let's get the kits into camp," he suggested. "It's more sheltered there." Wind was tugging at their fur. He began to nose Silver Stripe, Black Ear, and White Tail toward the camp entrance, then glanced at Willow Tail. "Are you coming?"

The pale tabby shook her head. "I'm going to follow Red Claw's scent," she growled. "I want to make sure he crossed the border."

Wind Runner narrowed her eyes. "Was Red Claw on our land?"

Moth Flight lifted her head sharply. "He wasn't hunting. He just wanted to lie in the sun."

"They have sun in SkyClan," Wind Runner answered sharply. She nodded toward Willow Tail. "Go make sure he's left our territory."

"I'll go with you," Fern Leaf offered, following Willow Tail.

"Why do we have to have all this fuss about borders?" Moth Flight blurted.

Wind Runner silenced her with a look. "You weren't around for the great battle. If you had been, you'd understand." There was darkness in her gaze.

Moth Flight curled her claws into the ground. *I don't know why I bother opening my mouth.* Her fur pricked angrily along her spine as Willow Tail headed away. Then she remembered her plant. She had to fetch it before a rabbit ate it or the wind blew it away. She turned and began to pad downslope.

"Where are you going?" Wind Runner snapped.

Moth Flight halted. What was wrong now? "I have to fetch a new plant I discovered."

"No you don't." Wind Runner's mew was hard with anger.

Gorse Fur nosed past the Clan leader and met Moth Flight's gaze. "Your mother wants us to go hunting together."

But my plant! Moth Flight's heart sank. What was the point in arguing? Wind Runner would never understand.

Dust Muzzle weaved around her. "Come on," he murmured to her softly. "Hunting will put us all in a good mood." He snatched a glance at Wind Runner.

Moth Flight huffed. "Yeah, right."

Gorse Fur sniffed the air. "I smell rabbit!" Lifting his tail, he raced across the grass. Wind Runner shot Moth Flight a final searing look, and bounded after him.

Dust Muzzle nudged Moth Flight with his shoulder. "Come on. She can't be angry forever."

Moth Flight stared after her mother. The lithe tabby moved with expert speed across the grass, her tail low, and her shoulders pumping rhythmically. Why did Wind Runner have to be so *good* at everything?

Dust Muzzle darted away. "I'll race you!" he called over his shoulder.

Moth Flight hurried after him, her heart like a stone in her chest. Her brother's words rang in her ears as her paws thrummed the earth. *She can't be angry forever.* Wind streamed through her fur.

With a daughter like me, she probably can.

CHAPTER 3

❧

Gorse Fur pulled up sharply as the slope steepened toward the moortop. Moth Flight was out of breath and relieved to see Wind Runner halt beside her mate. Dust Muzzle reached them first. She couldn't help noticing that he was hardly panting as she scrambled to a halt beside him.

Wind Runner surveyed the moor, her pelt rippling the chilly breeze. Moth Flight gazed past her, staring across the wide valley that dipped behind them to Highstones. The sun burned orange in the pale blue sky and, as it sank toward the craggy peaks, Moth Flight watched their vast shadow fall across the moor and fold it in darkness. She suddenly felt very small.

"Moth Flight!" Her mother's stern mew made her jump.

"What?"

"Didn't you hear me?"

Moth Flight stared in dismay. *No.*

"I told you to go with Dust Muzzle and hunt out the prey around that gorse patch." Wind Runner nodded toward a clump of prickly bushes downslope. "Gorse Fur and I will check the high burrows for rabbits."

Dust Muzzle frowned. "Can't I hunt rabbits too?"

"Stay with your sister," Wind Runner told him. "She's not

fast enough for rabbits and if I let her hunt alone, she'll probably end up bringing home nothing but leaves." She stared at Moth Flight. "And leaves don't fill empty bellies."

Moth Flight turned away and stomped down the slope.

Dust Muzzle quickly caught up. "Ignore her," he advised. "Her bad mood won't last."

"It's my fault she's in a bad mood in the first place." Moth Flight padded on, not looking at her brother. "She's going to torture me all day just because I fell asleep."

"You *were* supposed to be looking after Slate's kits," Dust Muzzle reminded her gently.

"They were okay, weren't they? I rescued them!" Moth Flight lashed her tail. It wasn't like she didn't *try* to be a good cat. "Why can't Wind Runner be pleased with that?"

Dust Muzzle didn't answer, but walked closer to Moth Flight, his pelt brushing hers. "Let's forget about it and catch something tasty." He slowed as they neared the gorse.

The grass around the prickly bushes rippled like water in the wind. Moth Flight flattened her ears to block out the sound of the breeze. She tasted the air, hoping for prey scent. Dust Muzzle was right. If she could take home some prey, Wind Runner would be pleased, surely?

Dust Muzzle halted. "I wonder if Willow Tail caught up with Red Claw?"

"I hope not." Moth Flight remembered Willow Tail's anger at the SkyClan cat. "What if she starts a fight? She might get hurt."

"She wouldn't attack him on her own." Dust Muzzle lifted

his muzzle, tasting the air. "She's not a rabbit-brain."

"But she seemed so angry with him." Moth Flight fretted. "I *know* he was on our land, but he wasn't hunting. It was like Willow Tail *wanted* to pick a fight with him."

"Maybe." Dust Muzzle's gaze was fixed on the shadows beneath the gorse. "But she and Wind Runner were right, too: They have sunny clearings on SkyClan territory. Maybe he *was* up to something."

"Maybe," Moth Flight murmured. But she didn't believe it. *Am I crazy to trust Red Claw?*

"Anyway," Dust Muzzle went on, "the next Gathering's the day after tomorrow. We can see if she causes more trouble then."

Moth Flight was still thinking. "They were rogues together," she began, relishing the gossip. It was a nice change from worrying about Wind Runner. But as she spoke, Dust Muzzle dropped into a crouch.

Moth Flight froze and followed his gaze. A shrew was rooting in the grass below a gorse branch.

Her paws itched with excitement. "Let me catch it!" she whispered.

Dust Muzzle gave a tiny nod, his gaze still on the shrew.

Sinking low, Moth Flight crept forward. The shrew buried its snout deep into the grass. *It has no idea I'm here.* Delighted, Moth Flight leaped, pushing hard with her hind legs. Too hard! She sailed into the gorse, crashing through the branches. The prickles stabbed her nose and she screwed up her eyes to protect them. Recoiling with a yowl, she tripped over Dust

Muzzle as he darted past her.

Finding her paws, she rubbed her nose, wincing at the sting.

A moment later Dust Muzzle scrambled from beneath the bush. The shrew dangled from his jaws, dead.

"You got it!" Moth Flight blinked at him proudly. "I wish I was as good at hunting as you."

Dust Muzzle laid the shrew at her paws. "You will be one day. Until then, why don't we tell Wind Runner you caught this?"

Moth Flight bristled. "I don't need your help!" she snapped, then felt instantly guilty as hurt flashed in her brother's eyes. "I'm sorry. That's really kind of you. But I'm not going to pretend to be something I'm not. I'm useless at hunting."

"You just need practice." Dust Muzzle leaned forward and licked her nose. "You're bleeding," he mewed as he pulled away.

"I am?" Moth Flight sighed. Wind Runner would guess she'd crashed into the gorse bush.

"Give it a wash," Dust Muzzle suggested. "It'll hardly show." He scooped up the shrew and headed upslope.

"Aren't we hunting anymore?" Moth Flight called after him.

"I think we've frightened away all the prey around here." Dust Muzzle's mew was muffled by the shrew. "Let's help Wind Runner and Gorse Fur hunt rabbits."

Moth Flight followed him, her ears twitching. She'd ruined the hunt.

As they neared the burrows dotting the high moor, Moth

Flight was surprised to see her parents sitting side by side. Why weren't they hunting? They faced Highstones, their backs to Moth Flight and Dust Muzzle. Wind ruffled their fur, and their heads were bent in conversation.

Their words caught on the wind as she and Dust Muzzle neared.

"Don't be so hard on her." Gorse Fur was pleading.

Moth Flight slowed, Dust Muzzle slowing with her.

"It's about time she grew up and took responsibility," Wind Runner snapped. "She's not a kit anymore. I don't make allowances for the rest of my Clan! Why should I make them for her?"

Moth Flight felt Dust Muzzle glance at her. Her pelt prickled uncomfortably along her spine and she didn't return his gaze. Her parents were talking about *her*!

"She's not irresponsible," Gorse Fur argued, his tone hardening. "She just notices things other cats don't. She gets distracted, that's all."

"When there are mouths to feed and kits to protect, she shouldn't *be* distracted," Wind Runner's tail lashed behind her. "Dust Muzzle isn't always getting into trouble. Why can't she be more like him?"

"Dust Muzzle will make a fine hunter one day, but Moth Flight is special," Gorse Fur pressed. "Can't you see that?"

Wind Runner stared at her mate, blankly. "WindClan doesn't *need* special cats. It needs hunters and fighters!"

Special! Moth Flight growled. "They think I'm rabbit-brained!" she said softly.

Dust Muzzle dropped the shrew. "Gorse Fur is just trying to explain that you're different from other cats."

Moth Flight glared at him. "*You* think I'm different, too?"

"Not in a bad way." Dust Muzzle blinked at her uneasily.

"I don't *want* to be different!" Moth Flight hissed.

"Moth Flight!" Gorse Fur turned. "Are you two back already?" His mew was sharp with surprise.

Wind Runner was staring at the shrew. "Is that all you caught?"

"That's all there was," Dust Muzzle dipped his head.

Wind Runner snorted. "I suppose Moth Flight tripped over her tail and scared the other prey away."

Moth Flight couldn't meet her mother's gaze. She'd guessed right away that it was her fault, without even noticing the scratch on her nose. Moth Flight clenched her teeth, anger and hurt pulsing through her. *I can be just as good as any other Clan cat!* Determined to impress her mother, she scanned the moortop desperately for something she could catch. With a rush of relief she spotted a lapwing, stalking through the rippling grass beyond the rise. She dropped into a crouch and padded toward it.

Just watch me!

The lapwing was stabbing its beak into the earth, twitching as it caught something and began to tug.

Moth Flight's breathing quickened as she willed the bird's prey to resist and keep the lapwing distracted. *Just for a few moments!* She was a fox-length away now, her tail swishing over the grass with excitement.

The lapwing froze, its eye catching sight of her and sparking with panic.

Moth Flight leaped, stretching out her paws wildly as the lapwing flapped into the air. She tried to reach up, twisting. Her claw grazed a talon as the wind from its wings blasted her face and she landed with a *whump* on her side.

Embarrassed, she scrambled to her paws. *I nearly had it!* Disappointment swamped her as she looked around to see Wind Runner shaking her head sadly.

Gorse Fur hurried toward her. "Great try, Moth Flight."

Dust Muzzle followed close at his father's paws. "Lapwings are hard to catch," he sympathized.

Gorse Fur stopped beside her. "Your tail gave you away," he told her gently. "No matter how excited you feel, you must keep it still and lift it just above the ground so you can move silently. We might be smarter than prey, but prey knows what to listen for and, if it hears anything unusual, instinct will send it fleeing in the blink of an eye."

Moth Flight hung her head. "I let it get away."

"Don't worry," Gorse Fur told her cheerfully. "You've *learned* something. That's what's important. You'll be catching lapwings before long."

"Dust Muzzle caught one a few days ago," Moth Flight mumbled miserably.

"Dust Muzzle's had more practice than you," Gorse Fur reassured her.

I'm so sorry. Moth Flight knew that Gorse Fur must feel as disappointed in her as Wind Runner, despite his kind words.

She shook out her fur and looked at him as brightly as she could manage. "I'll get better, I promise."

He purred. "Of course you will."

She glanced toward Wind Runner, but her mother was crouching beside a burrow entrance, her ears pricked and her gaze fixed on the dark opening.

Gorse Fur followed her gaze. "I'd better go and help," he meowed. "Why don't you join me?" He glanced from Moth Flight to Dust Muzzle, but Dust Muzzle's attention was fixed on the grassy slope. His ears were pricked and he opened his mouth as though tasting for prey.

"I'll be back after I've caught that vole," he whispered, heading downslope. He crossed the grass, his paw steps silent, his tail still.

Gorse Fur nudged Moth Flight toward the rabbit burrows. "If you see a rabbit running, do you remember what to do?"

Moth Flight frowned. "Chase it?" she offered hopefully.

Gorse Fur's ear twitched. "Head where it's looking and cut off its escape route. Outrunning a rabbit is hard. Outthinking it is easy."

He quickened his pace, breaking into a trot. Moth Flight followed slowly, sighing as her father caught up with Wind Runner. The Clan leader beckoned her mate on with a flick of her muzzle and he raced away to another hole farther along the rise.

Moth Flight wound her way around the burrows dotting the rise. She wanted to keep her distance from Wind Runner. If her mother managed to flush out a young rabbit, she didn't want to scare it down another hole.

The sun was touching Highstones, turning the peaks orange. Moth Flight shivered as the evening chill reached through her fur. She remembered her dream. It had been so vivid it was hard to believe that she hadn't actually been there while the blue-gray cat died beside her friends. *But she didn't die!* Moth Flight frowned. *She came back to life . . . after she looked so lifeless.* She remembered the fear in the eyes of the flame-pelted tom and the dark, unreadable gaze of the tabby. She could almost believe that these cats were real, not just figments of her imagination. When the blue-gray cat had suddenly twitched after such stillness, none of the cats had seemed shocked— only relieved. *It was as if they knew it would happen!*

"Moth Flight!"

Wind Runner's cry sounded at the edge of her thoughts, no more than the rushing of the wind. She hardly heard her mother. Her thoughts were filled with her dream. The blood on the blue-gray cat's fur had spread so quickly through her matted pelt. How could any cat have survived such a wound?

"*Moth Flight!*" Wind Runner's angry yowl pierced her ear fur. A rabbit pelted past her, then her mother's pelt flashed at the edge of her vision and she heard grass tear beneath skidding claws as Wind Runner slowed to a halt a tail-length away. The rabbit veered downslope, easily avoiding Gorse Fur, who was crouched beyond the rise, and darted down a hole.

"You birdbrain!" Wind Runner turned on Moth Flight, her mew hot with rage. She seemed to be swallowing back a snarl. "If you weren't going to catch it, you should have gotten out of my way so I could have driven it into Gorse Fur's paws!"

Moth Flight stared at her, stricken with horror. *I've done it again!* Panic flashed through her. *Why do I always get it wrong?* "I'm so sorry!"

Wind Runner seemed to be trying to stop herself from shaking as she glared at her daughter. "You were supposed to be *helping*," she meowed slowly, her words clipped.

"I know." Moth Flight stared dejectedly at her paws. "I was just remembering a dream I had. It was so vivid, I sort of . . ." She searched for words, knowing that no matter what she said, her mother wouldn't understand. ". . . I sort of got lost in it."

Gorse Fur galloped toward them. "Moth Flight." There was more pity than anger in his mew. "You need to *try* to pay attention."

"How many times do I have to remind you?" As Wind Runner started another lecture, Moth Flight's shoulders sank. "A hungry clan is a vulnerable clan. With empty bellies, we are prey to disease and attacks from rogues. What if a dog is loose on the moor? Our cats need the strength to outrun it."

Moth Flight lifted her head to meet her mother's gaze. "I'm sorr—" She stopped, her breath catching in her throat. Wide, green wings were fluttering a tail-length away.

The moth!

There it was! Dancing over the grass, whipped one way then the other by the buffeting wind. *Just like the one in my dream!* Moth Flight's heart soared. Suddenly she was swamped by the same longing to follow the beautiful moth that had filled her dream. Her paws itched to run after it. *I have to catch up with it!*

With a purr of delight, she pelted after it.

"Moth Flight!"

She hardly heard her mother's yowl. Wind rushed past her ears as she chased the moth across the grass.

CHAPTER 4

Moth Flight ran. She could hear Wind Runner and Gorse Fur calling, but her eyes were fixed on the moth's great, green wings. She *had* to chase it. The moth wanted to show her something. She just knew it!

The ground sloped steeply beneath her paws and she skidded, straining to keep her balance as she bounded down the hillside where the moor dropped into the valley.

The sun, burning orange on the peaks of Highstones, made a halo around the moth, illuminating its great wings as it fluttered above the ground.

The coarse grass of the moor turned soft as it dipped toward the valley, growing lush as the land flattened. Suddenly Moth Flight felt hard stone beneath her paws; the stench of the Thunderpath touched her nose. She paused, wary.

The moth paused too, wheeling in the air and flying back toward her. It swooped above her head.

It's beckoning to me! She knew the moth wanted her to keep following.

"I'm coming!"

The moth began to head away, moving toward fields beyond the Thunderpath. A breeze lifted it, swirling it sideways.

Moth Flight leaped, paws outstretched, hoping to touch its soft wings.

As she arched her back, straining to reach it, hard muscle slammed into her flank and knocked her rolling across the black stone of the Thunderpath.

Surprise flared through her as she tumbled onto the grass verge on the far side. A roar exploded in her ears and wind tore at her fur. The foul stench of a monster swept over her, burning her throat, as grit pelted her flank. Wailing in terror, she screwed up her eyes and flinched from the stinging shower.

"Moth Flight!" Gorse Fur's voice sounded in her ear as the monster's roar faded.

She scrambled to her paws, blinking open her eyes.

Gorse Fur stood beside her, his gaze almost black with shock. "You could have been killed!"

She stared at him, numb.

"You were standing in the middle of the Thunderpath!" Fury flared in Gorse Fur's eyes. "Didn't you hear the monster coming?"

Moth Flight blinked at him, struggling to make sense of what had happened. "I was chasing the moth." Hadn't he seen it? She turned her head, scanning the hedge beside them. Where had it gone?

Paws thudded over the Thunderpath. Moth Flight glimpsed her mother and Dust Muzzle racing toward them.

"You rabbit-brained fool!" Wind Runner scrambled to a halt, bristling with rage.

Dust Muzzle's eyes glittered with horror. "If Gorse Fur

hadn't knocked you out of the way—"

Wind Runner didn't let him finish. "You could have *both* been killed!"

Moth Flight saw fear in her mother's gaze. She stiffened, cold dread rippling beneath her pelt. She had never seen her mother *frightened* before.

"Are you hurt?" Dust Muzzle leaned forward, sniffing at Moth Flight's pelt. The young tom's gaze flicked toward Gorse Fur. "Are you both okay?"

Gorse Fur blinked reassuringly. "We're fine," he promised.

Wind Runner's gaze burned into Moth Flight's. "No thanks to you!"

Moth Flight backed away, suddenly scared. "I'm sorry." She began to tremble. *Gorse Fur and I both could have died! And it was my fault!*

The ground swayed beneath her paws.

"You've *always* been irresponsible!" Wind Runner's sharp words cut through her jumbled thoughts. "Losing Slate's kits, getting lost collecting plants when you should have been hunting. We're used to *that*. But you've never been this reckless! You're not just a danger to yourself! You're a danger to your *Clan!*"

"I'm s-sorry." Guilt welled inside Moth Flight, rising in her throat until she could hardly speak.

"You've worn that word out today!" Every hair on Wind Runner's pelt stood on end. "*Sorry* doesn't bring back cats from the dead! WindClan would be better off without you!"

Moth Flight hardly heard Dust Muzzle's gasp or the gentle

words of Gorse Fur as he tried to calm his mate.

"No one was actually hurt," he soothed.

Moth Flight's heart seemed to crack in her chest. *Wind Runner is right.* She was a danger to her Clan. What if Silver Stripe *had* been killed by a badger? Or Black Ear carried away by a buzzard? *What if Gorse Fur had been killed by a monster as he tried to save me?*

As she backed away, her vision blurred. *What have I done?* She stared at her family, her chest too tight to breathe.

"Where are you going?" Wind Runner yowled.

"I need time to think," Moth Flight struggled to speak. "I need to be by myself for a while." Unsteadily, she turned and headed for the hedge beyond the grass verge.

Gorse Fur's mew rang behind her. "You can't just go off by yourself!"

"Don't try and stop me!" she wailed. She slid beneath the hedge and began running. Shallow ridges of soil stretched before her and she raced over them, her paws slipping into the furrows and tripping over ridges. But she *had* to keep going. She had to get away!

"Come back!" Wind Runner's call echoed from beyond the hedge. "Sulking won't help!"

I'm not sulking! Moth Flight's thoughts whirled as grief stormed inside her. *But you're right! I am a danger to my Clan.*

I don't deserve to be with you.

CHAPTER 5

Moth Flight raced blindly across the field until golden branches loomed ahead, forcing her to a stop. She pulled up, heart lurching, her paws sinking into the soft soil. A beech hedge blocked her way. She glanced back across the ridged earth. No one had followed. *Good!* Her throat tightened. *Are they relieved I've left?*

She gazed bleakly around. Beyond the hedge top, rooks whirled like dark leaves around the canopy of a large elm. They shouted at one another while a monster howled along the Thunderpath behind and, somewhere far away, dogs barked.

Moth Flight shivered. A cold wind was tugging at her pelt. Down here, in the valley, shadow swathed the fields. The sun was hidden by Highstones now, but its rays still bathed the moortop in soft orange light. Slinking beneath the beech hedge, she pressed her belly to the earth and tucked her nose between her paws.

What now?

She was of no use to her Clan. And the moth had disappeared. As she'd chased it, she had been so sure she'd been heading the right way. Now she didn't know where to go. The beech leaves rattled around her and she drew her paws in tighter.

Her belly growled. She hadn't eaten all day and even her misery couldn't hide her hunger.

I should hunt.

She lifted her head and gazed halfheartedly through the shadows, hoping to spot a mouse scuttling among the roots.

Only the leaves stirred. She peered from under the branches at the field. Birds swooped across the furrows, trawling for insects, before swooping out of reach. Moth Flight's tail drooped. Wind Runner would catch one easily. She'd crouch in a dip, invisible against the earth, and hook one as it dived. *But not me.* Even if she was any good at hunting, Moth Flight knew her white pelt would give her away.

Wind ruffled the surface of a puddle a few tail-lengths away. At least she could drink. Moth Flight slid out from beneath the hedge and padded toward it. As she neared, movement caught her eye. A dark brown toad was slithering along the edge.

Could I eat a toad? Moth Flight frowned. She knew RiverClan cats ate frogs. And ShadowClan boasted of eating lizards. *At least it'll be easy to catch.* The toad hopped clumsily and landed with a thump on the side of a furrow, its hind legs flapping as it tried to find its feet. Moth Flight dropped into a hunting crouch and waited for it to jump again.

As it leaped, she lunged toward it, flinging out her forepaws and knocking it to the ground. It fell onto its back, showing a pale belly. Moth Flight screwed up her face and ducked to give a killing bite.

Its flesh was squidgy between her teeth and she shuddered as she crunched through its spine. As it twitched and fell limp, Moth Flight felt relieved. Its blood wasn't as sweet as rabbit blood, but at least it didn't taste like pond water.

Grasping her catch between her jaws, she carried it back to the hedge and squeezed into the shadows once more.

Hungry and cold, she began to eat, queasy as she tore at the toad's flabby flank. *Perhaps the legs are meatier.* She gnawed at one, trying to ignore the muddy taste of the creature's flesh. Once she'd swallowed a few mouthfuls, her aching hunger eased, and she pushed the toad away. She imagined Wind Runner telling her not to be wasteful and that hungry bellies couldn't be choosy. But Wind Runner wasn't here. *I can do what I like.*

Her heart quickened. *Am I really going to stay out here all night?* She'd never slept away from her Clan. She was used to Dust Muzzle's pelt pressed against hers and the sound of her Clanmates snoring. She suddenly realized how safe she'd always felt in camp.

Nervously, she peered from the hedge. The afternoon shadow had turned to night. The birds had stopped swooping. The rooks had stilled and grown quiet. Moth Flight blinked up at the sky, where stars were beginning to show. She glanced toward the puddle, hoping to see their reflection sparkle like familiar friends in the muddy water.

Something moved in the field.

Moth Flight tensed. A shape was creeping along the hedge

toward her. Its dark shadow rippled across the leaves, making them rustle as it passed.

A fox? The creature was skulking low to the ground. She opened her mouth to taste the air, but toad stench still soured her tongue. Belly tightening, she backed deeper into the hedge, hoping it wouldn't see her. The creature had stopped and was sniffing the furrows. It paused and lifted its head. Moth Flight froze as its eyes flashed toward her. As it darted forward, she unsheathed her claws. Bracing her hind paws against a root, she prepared to defend herself.

Blood roared in her ears as the creature neared. She could hear its paws thrumming the earth. Its gaze darted this way and that, as though it was scanning the hedgerow.

It knows I'm here. Panic flared through her. *Should I run away?*

"Moth Flight!"

Moth Flight blinked in surprise. The creature was calling her name. And she recognized the mew!

"Spotted Fur?" Relief swamped her as she made out the familiar shape of his shoulders. His dappled, golden pelt was pale in the moonlight.

"I've *found* you!" He pulled up beside the hedge. "What are you doing in there? Are you okay? You smell scared."

"I'm fine." Moth Flight ducked out, limp with gratitude. Heather scent pulsed from Spotted Fur's pelt, smelling of their home. "I thought you were a fox!"

"What if I had been?" His eyes darkened with worry.

"You weren't." Moth Flight flicked her ear. She didn't want to think about the answer.

"Dust Muzzle said you'd run off."

"I did."

"Well, you can't stay out here all night just because you had an argument with Wind Runner. Let's get you home."

Moth Flight stared at him. Hadn't Dust Muzzle explained? "I'm not *going* home. I'm a danger to my Clan."

Spotted Fur swished his tail. "Don't be silly. You're not a danger to any cat. Wind Runner's upset, but it'll all be forgotten by the morning."

Moth Flight dug her claws into the earth. "She said the Clan would be better off without me, and she's right. I'm not coming home."

"You can't stay here!" Spotted Fur stared at her. "It's not safe. Besides, you must be starving."

Moth Flight lifted her muzzle indignantly. "I caught a toad." She reached under the hedge and hauled it out.

Spotted Fur backed away, screwing up his muzzle. "You can't eat that!"

"I already have," Moth Flight told him proudly. "You see? I ate some of its leg. You think I can't look after myself, but I can!"

Spotted Fur's gaze softened. "Oh, Moth Flight. Of course you can." He leaned forward to brush his cheek against hers but she flinched away.

"Don't treat me like a kit!" She'd heard him talk to Black Ear in the same tone earlier. "I'm *not* going home!"

Spotted Fur sat down. "Well, in that case, we'd better make a nest for the night."

"You're staying with me?" Moth Flight shifted her paws uneasily. She was desperate to prove she could look after herself. But it *would* feel safer to have Spotted Fur sleeping beside her.

"I'm not leaving you out here by yourself," he answered. "Besides, you'll have changed your mind by the morning. After a good night's rest, you'll be ready to go home."

No I won't. But Moth Flight bit back her answer, frightened that he might be right.

Spotted Fur nodded toward the dead beech leaves lying in drifts along the hedge. "Why don't we push some of those underneath the hedge to make a nest?"

"Let's dig a hollow first," Moth Flight suggested. "It'll be warmer."

"Good idea." Spotted Fur sniffed beneath the branches, then began scraping among the roots with his forepaws.

Moth Flight pushed in beside him and helped. Before long they'd dug a shallow dip between two gnarled roots. Spotted Fur fetched pawfuls of leaves and Moth Flight patted them into a soft, if slightly crunchy, lining for their nest.

"I'm hungry," Spotted Fur mewed when they'd finished. He sat down in the nest and sniffed the air. "Have you seen any mice?"

"If I had, do you think I'd be eating a toad?" Moth Flight sat beside him, the leaves crunching beneath her. His pelt felt warm against hers.

Spotted Fur purred. "I could go and hunt."

"There might be dogs around. I heard them barking

earlier," Moth Flight warned. She didn't want to be left alone in the dark. Suddenly, she wondered how she could ever have thought of sleeping out here by herself.

Spotted Fur gazed at her fondly. "Okay." He dipped his head. "I'll eat your stinky toad."

"The legs aren't that bad." Moth Flight reached out and, hooking the toad with a claw, dragged it into the nest. She dropped it at Spotted Fur's paws.

"You haven't eaten much of it," he commented.

"I wasn't hungry."

"Have some with me now," he urged. "It'll be a cold night and a full belly will keep you warm."

The toad didn't taste so bad when she was sharing it, but it still wasn't as good as rabbit.

Moth Flight purred as Spotted Fur screwed up his face. "RiverClan cats eat frogs all the time," she reminded him.

"RiverClan cats *swim* too," Spotted Fur answered, chewing. "That doesn't mean we should go throw ourselves into the river."

They ate as much as they could and kicked the remains out of the nest. "You never know—" Spotted Fur stopped to stifle a yawn. "A bird might come pecking around it in the morning. Then I can catch a *decent* meal."

"It wasn't that bad," Moth Flight lied defensively. Why did he have to act as though he was better than she was? Crossly, she curled down into the nest, snuggling as deep into the leaves as she could, and closed her eyes. Spotted Fur's rough tongue lapped her ear.

"I know you've had a hard day," he murmured. "But we were all really worried about you. The others will be so relieved to see you tomorrow."

"Even Wind Runner?" Moth Flight kept her eyes closed.

Spotted Fur touched his muzzle to her head. "*Especially* Wind Runner."

Her heart swelled and she lifted her head, blinking at him gratefully. He was such a kind friend. She *should* go home in the morning. She'd been a rabbit-brain to stay out here by herself. She felt him settle beside her, and relished the warmth of his pelt against hers. *How could I live without my Clan? I just need to try harder.* She ignored the unease tugging in her belly. *If I just practice my hunting and concentrate more on what I'm doing . . .* Letting tiredness sweep over her, she slid into sleep.

CHAPTER 6

Moth Flight opened her eyes, stiffening as darkness pressed around her. It wasn't the glittering darkness of a starlit night, but a stifling gloom. The air smelled dank, sharp with the mineral taste of stone. She blinked, surprised to find herself standing, cold rock beneath her paws.

Where am I? Where's Spotted Fur?

She glanced around, looking for her Clanmate and wondering what had happened to the beech hedge. All she could make out in the shadows was stone. Above her, a small opening let starlight filter in. It pooled on a large rock jutting from the floor.

I'm in a cave! With a start, she realized that she was dreaming. *But it feels so real!* The cold stone made her paws ache. The damp air chilled her pelt. Moth Flight shivered as she gazed at the rock, looming at the center of the cave. Padding forward, she sniffed it. Her whiskers tingled and her heart quickened. *What is this place?* Something about the stone seemed to carry the promise of a coming storm, thickening the air around it so that Moth Flight expected, any moment, to feel the cave shudder with thunder.

Someone's coming!

Her ears twitched as she heard the sound of paw steps echoing toward her. She turned and saw a dark shadow on the side of the cave. A tunnel! Two cats emerged, their fur pale as weak starlight lit their pelts.

Moth Flight could make out the shapes of a gray tom and a long-furred she-cat. *I know her!* Her heart leaped as she recognized the cat she'd watched struggle back from the brink of death. She darted forward, excited to see the she-cat healthy and strong. Her thick fur looked well-groomed; her eyes shone brightly in the half-light. *She looks younger!* Moth Flight tipped her head, confused.

Why was she dreaming about the same cat? And why did it feel vivid enough to be real?

"Who are you?" Her mew echoed across the cave, but the cats didn't seem to hear. Their gaze was fixed on the great rock as they padded toward it, the gray she-cat slowing as she approached.

"Please talk to me!" Moth Flight hurried to their side, reaching out a paw to touch the gray she-cat. But, as in her last dream, her paw passed through the other cat as though she were mist.

The tom's mouth moved. The gray she-cat dragged her gaze from the rock and nodded.

Why can't I hear them? Moth Flight burned with frustration.

Unease seemed to glitter in the she-cat's gaze as she approached the rock and lay down before it. She glanced up and Moth Flight followed her gaze.

Through the hole in the roof, she could see the moon rising. Delight fizzed through Moth Flight's pelt as its rays turned the stone silver. *It's so beautiful here!*

The she-cat closed her eyes.

Moth Flight leaned closer. *What now?*

Suddenly, the cave exploded with light—a flash more blinding than lightning. Moth Flight's eyes—stretched wide for the darkness—burned. She screwed them shut, shaking. Then, slowly she opened them to narrow slits.

Through the glare, she saw the gray she-cat reach forward and touch her nose to the glittering stone.

What's happening? Moth Flight leaned forward, desperate to understand. Curiosity seared through her pelt. The gray she-cat grew as still as the rock itself. A tail-length away, the tom had curled on the floor, his eyes closed.

Moth Flight padded around the gray-she cat, her belly fluttering with excitement. Then pelts moved around her. Moth Flight gasped. The cave was suddenly filled with cats.

Where had they come from?

She blinked in shock as she realized their pelts were translucent and shimmered as though water rippled through their fur, reflecting starlight.

Spirit-cats! Moth Flight had heard tales of ghostly ancestors appearing at Fourtrees after the great battle. They had shared tongues with the Clan leaders and brought peace to the warring cats. They had appeared in the moons since, but she had never seen them herself.

She stiffened. If they *were* ancestors, Gray Wing might be

among them. Eagerly, she scanned the starry pelts. There was no sign of him.

A great tom padded to the gray she-cat's side. Leaning down, he touched his nose to the top of her head.

The she-cat flinched as though pain flared through her, but she did not move from her spot, or open her eyes. The tom's mouth moved as he spoke but Moth Flight couldn't make out the words. Then he backed away and the gray-she cat grew limp once more.

With a rush of hope, Moth Flight wondered if the spirit-cat could see her. The dead could speak to the living, after all. Why shouldn't they be able to see a dream-cat? She lifted her chin challengingly. "What's happening? Why are you here?" Her mew hung in the air. No echo rang from the walls. No cat looked at her.

Disappointed, she weaved among them, longing to feel their pelts brush hers. But it was like she wasn't there!

A small brown tom padded forward, his sparkling pelt camouflaged against the shimmering of the stone as he stopped beside the gray she-cat. He touched his nose to the she-cat's head, and once more she flinched violently.

Moth Flight gazed sadly at the ranks of starry cats. "I wish you could hear me." Suddenly she felt very alone and small. For a moment she wanted to escape this dream and return to her warm nest beside Spotted Fur. Then a familiar color flashed at the edge of the cave. The pale green of the moth's wings fluttered beyond the starry cats. It was hovering at the tunnel entrance, where the gray tom and she-cat had entered.

Moth Flight's breath caught in her throat. She knew she must follow it. Passing through the circle of starry cats, she hurried into the darkness beyond.

The smell of damp leaves filled her nose. As her eyes blinked open, she heard Spotted Fur's gentle snoring. Disappointment dropped like a stone in her chest. *I'm awake!* She was back in her nest, lying beside Spotted Fur. The beech leaves rattled overhead. An owl called from close by. Moth Flight lifted her nose from her paws and peeked out across the moonlit field. Frost sparkled on the furrows. *Where is my moth now?* With a flash of understanding, Moth Flight knew. *It's waiting to lead me!* But where? And when? Why did it always seem to disappear just as she was starting to follow it?

Determination hardened in Moth Flight's belly. *This isn't supposed to be easy. It doesn't want me to give up!* She stood up and slid from beneath the hedge, fluffing her fur against the cold. Dawn was lighting the sky beyond the looming moor-top. Spotted Fur would be awake soon. There was no time to waste.

How could she even think of returning to her Clan now? Perhaps she was being foolish; perhaps she was wrong; perhaps the moth was nothing but a dream. But if Moth Flight went home now, she'd never stop wondering whether something important was waiting for her far from home.

I can't leave Spotted Fur without telling him. If she was going to send him home without her, he had a right to know why. She dropped onto her belly and leaned into the nest, the warm smell of him filling her nose. Her heart ached. She was going to miss her Clan. But she had to follow her heart. Stretching forward a paw, she prodded Spotted Fur.

Grunting, he lifted his head.

"I have to go," Moth Flight whispered.

Struggling to open his eyes, he peered at her blearily.

"I'm sorry," she apologized. "I know it seems crazy but I *know* that there's something I need to do. I can't go home until I've done it. And if I don't leave now, I may never have the chance again."

Spotted Fur licked his lips, as though he was still lost in a dream. "No more toads," he mumbled, his eyes slipping shut. With a sigh, he rested his nose back onto his paws.

Moth Flight gazed at him, wondering if he'd even heard her. She leaned forward and touched her nose to his cheek. "I'm sorry, Spotted Fur," she repeated. Guilt pricked her heart as she wriggled backward, out of the hedge. "Good-bye. I hope we'll see each other again." She straightened, shaking leaf dust from her pelt. Glancing across the field, she wondered which way to head.

The moor lay behind her, Highstones ahead. Lifting her tail she padded forward, following the hedgerow until it turned, and then squeezed under it onto a dirt track beyond. A ditch ran beside the track, water swirling along the bottom. Moth Flight jumped into it, flinching as the cold water swallowed her paws. Then she waded downstream, pleased that the narrow brook would wash away all scent of her. Spotted Fur wouldn't be able to follow her trail. Whatever she was supposed to do, she knew that she must do it *alone*.

CHAPTER 7

When she felt sure that she'd disguised her trail completely, Moth Flight hopped out of the ditch, shaking water from her paws, and followed the dirt track. It turned suddenly, rising toward a Twoleg nest. Moth Flight halted. She didn't want to stray close to Twolegs. They were unpredictable and kept dogs. Instead, she nosed her way through a patch of bracken and found herself in an overgrown meadow.

Pushing through the long grass, she paused to sniff the stems, excited by how many unfamiliar plants grew here. There were flowers budding, and soft grass, rising taller than her tail. It was so different from the moor, where the weather scoured the landscape so that only the toughest plants could survive and the few that did seemed to cling to the earth, keeping low for fear of being torn away by the relentless wind.

Here, plants grew fearlessly, as if they had no memory of cruel weather. Moth Flight's nose filled with their pungent scent until she felt dizzy. She followed the valley, Highstones rising in the distance on one side, the moor looming on the other. Until she knew where she was meant to be going, she wanted both to be close.

What if her journey lay beyond the valley? Past Highstones? Out of sight of the moor? Her belly tightened at the thought. It felt strange enough to be so far from her Clan, and heading away from Spotted Fur. As the sun rose and began to cross the wide, blue newleaf sky, she found herself slowing, unsure of her next paw steps. Perhaps this was where the moth had wanted to lead her; perhaps it had only wanted to show her the rich foliage growing so close to her home.

Her belly growled and she realized how hungry she was. And thirsty. She licked her lips, tasting the air for water. If she could find another dirt track, there might be a ditch beside it. If she were lucky it would provide water and perhaps a vole. *Or a toad, at least.* She shuddered.

Pushing through a hedge, she found herself at the edge of a wide field. The grass here was short. Sheep grazed, eyes blank, clumped in small groups like clouds dotting a green sky. A few tail-lengths away, where the hedge gave way to fence, water pooled in muddy dips where monsters had left paw marks.

Ears pricked warily, Moth Flight padded toward the puddles and crouched beside the nearest one. She lapped the brown water, trying to ignore the bitter taste. She heard hooves pattering across the grass and looked up to see sheep moving toward her. Unsure of them, she backed away. They ambled aimlessly, their attention fixed on the grass, buffeting each other clumsily. Such dumb animals might trample her without even noticing. She headed around them, keeping a safe distance, her nose twitching at the warm, sour smell of them.

Suddenly movement flashed at the corner of her eye. A small brown shape was darting through the grass.

Mouse!

Heart leaping, Moth Flight dropped into a crouch.

The mouse was scampering toward the hedge, its nose twitching nervously.

Prey will smell you before they see you, so keep the wind behind you. Moth Flight remembered one of Gorse Fur's lessons and lifted her tail, letting the breeze stream through it. She was in luck; the mouse was upwind. It would never smell her. All she needed to do was creep up on it without it hearing her.

Treading delicately, she pulled herself over the grass. She made sure that her tail didn't brush against the grass, grateful for Gorse Fur's training and surprised that she suddenly remembered so much of it. Why couldn't she remember it when she was trying to impress Wind Runner?

The mouse was moving fast, its gaze fixed on the hedge. If she wanted to catch it before it found the safety of the shadows, she would have to run. Holding her breath, Moth Flight quickened her pace, trying to keep her paw steps as light as feathers falling. With any luck, the pattering of the sheep's hooves a few tail-lengths away would disguise any noise she made.

The mouse kept running, but she was almost close enough to pounce. Her chest tightened with excitement. *Keep your eyes on it*, she reminded herself as she stiffened for her leap. She had to land on it the first time or she'd lose it.

Ready . . .

Green wings fluttered beside her. Moth Flight scrambled to a halt.

The moth!

Forgetting the mouse in a moment, she turned to stare at the moth. It was right in front of her, its great wings brilliant in the sunshine.

Reaching up with her forepaw, she tried to touch it. But it whisked away and began heading across the field.

Delight surged through Moth Flight's pelt. She chased the moth, a purr rumbling in her throat. *It's come to show me the way!*

It flitted past a group of sheep. Moth Flight veered around them. The moth lifted higher into the air. *No! Don't leave me!* Fear flashed through her. What if it climbed so high she lost sight of it? She ran faster, desperation pricking in her paws.

I'm not losing you this time!

A bark cut through the air. Moth Flight's pelt bushed.

Dog!

Dragging her gaze from the moth, she glanced around.

The bark sounded again, louder this time. Then the dog burst into excited yapping. Fear shrilled through Moth Flight.

It's seen me!

She twisted, scanning the field desperately, her senses confused by the earthy meadow scents.

The sheep began to run, panic showing in their eyes. They closed into a flock, and headed for Moth Flight.

Still she couldn't see the dog.

But its jubilant barking was getting closer every moment.

Suddenly the flock opened. The terrified sheep scattered

as a black-and-white shape surged among them. They shied away, bleating with fear, as it raced toward Moth Flight.

She froze for a moment, horror gripping her, then spun and pelted for the edge of the field.

The hedge there was thick. If she could squeeze through it, the dog might not be able to follow.

Blood roared in her ears as she pushed hard against the earth.

But the dog's paws were thrumming closer.

I can't outrun it! Unaware of everything but terror, Moth Flight ran onward. Teeth nipped her tail tip. Too scared to look back, she felt her fur spike. The dog's hot breath billowed over her haunches. Its yelping dropped to a vicious growl.

If it got a grip on her hind legs, she'd be lost.

I must face it. The only way to escape was to wound it first.

Her paws slithering on the grass, she turned and reared. With a yowl, she lashed out with her forepaws.

Yellow fur flashed between her and the dog.

Moth Flight froze in surprise, drawing back her paws as a cat pelted past.

Stumbling, her heart in her throat, she watched as the dog swerved and began to chase the yellow tom across the field.

Where did he come from?

Moth Flight stood and watched, numb with shock.

"Quick!" A mew sounded behind her. She snapped her gaze around, amazed to see two cats pulling up on either side of her.

A plump black-and-white she-cat stared at her urgently. "We've got to get out of here."

A small tom with graying whiskers around his brown muzzle nudged her toward the hedge. "Now!"

Moth Flight stared across the grass. The yellow tom was zigzagging, the dog at his heels. "But what about him?"

"Who, Micah?" The brown tom swapped amused glances with the black-and-white she-cat.

Moth Flight stiffened as Micah veered suddenly and plunged between the legs of the startled sheep. Bleating with surprise, they scattered as the dog raced after the tom, knocking them aside if they weren't quick enough to get out of the way.

The she-cat purred beside her. "Micah doesn't need any help."

"Come on." The tom nudged her again. "We can show you somewhere safe."

The black-and-white she-cat was already hurrying toward the hedge, her plump belly swinging beneath her.

Heart swelling with gratitude, Moth Flight followed after her. Behind them the dog's bark grew shrill with fury. The brown tom fell into step beside her, slowing to let her push through the hedge first. As the stems scraped her flanks, relief swamped her. She just hoped that these cats were right and the yellow tom who had saved her didn't need any help.

CHAPTER 8

♣

"Follow me!" The plump she-cat was climbing a steep slope, scrambling up the wooden slats that crisscrossed it.

Moth Flight hurried toward her, crossing the straw-covered floor, nervous at finding herself inside a huge Twoleg den. It towered around her, the roof high above her head. The brown tom trotted after them, not even glancing at the large black-and-white creatures that shifted and huffed at one end of the den.

"Are they dangerous?" Moth Flight whispered, eying them warily.

"Cows? Dangerous?" The tom shrugged. "They're clumsy, but not mean. Stay away from their hooves and you'll be okay."

The she-cat had already made it to the top of the slope and peered down from a broad ledge where big lumps of dried grass were stacked.

Moth Flight paused at the bottom of the slatted slope, paws twitching with unease. "What is this place? Are there Twolegs here?"

The tom nudged her onto the first rung. "This is the barn. The Twolegs store their hay in the loft and keep their cows below. But they're used to us being here and they don't bother us."

Are these cats kittypets? Moth Flight clung onto the next slat and pulled herself up. One of her hind paws slipped and hit the tom on the muzzle. "Sorry!" She hauled herself up. "I've never seen a slope like this before."

The tom snorted and shook his fur out. "Ladders are only hard to climb the first time," he assured her. "Just keep going."

Moth Flight scrambled over the top, onto the ledge where the she-cat waited. She sneezed, hay dust filling her nose. *This must be the loft.*

As Moth Flight sniffled, the she-cat purred with amusement. "You'll get used to that too."

Moth Flight wasn't so sure. Her eyes stung. The air was thick with dust; she could see it clouding in the shafts of sunlight that sliced through every gap in the high wooden walls of the barn. The loft stretched into shadow where it reached to the back wall of the huge den. Stacks of hay crowded every side.

The tom landed next to her. "You're safe up here. Dogs can't climb ladders. They're all paws and no sense."

"What about Micah?" She could still hear the dog barking angrily in the distance.

"Micah is the fastest and cleverest cat I know." The plump she-cat sat down and began licking her belly fur.

"No dog ever gets near him," the tom assured her.

The she-cat looked up from her washing. "What are you called, dear?"

"Moth Flight." She glanced around the stacks of hay, her nose twitching as she smelled prey in the shadows. Her belly growled. She was hungry.

"*Moth Flight?*" The she-cat blinked at her. "Is that a kittypet name?"

Moth Flight lifted her chin sharply. "I'm no kittypet!" She snorted indignantly. Then she hesitated, guilt pricking her pelt. Were these cats kittypets? The tom hadn't answered her question. She didn't want to offend them after they'd been so kind. She tipped her head apologetically. "Are *you?*"

The tom lay down and stretched in a strip of sunshine. "We're farm cats. We share our territory with Twolegs, but we look after ourselves." He yawned.

The black-and-white she-cat straightened. "My name's Cow and that's Mouse."

Moth Flight swallowed back a purr. Such odd names!

"Where are you from, dear?" Cow pressed.

Moth Flight's purr caught in her throat as she remembered the WindClan camp. "I come from the moor. I live there with my Clan." Homesickness swept her so fiercely, she swayed on her paws.

Cow leaned forward to steady her with a soft shoulder. "You must be hungry, you poor thing. You've strayed a long way from home." She glanced at Mouse. "The moor's that great hill looming in front of the sunrise, isn't it?"

Mouse nodded. "Is your Clan your family?" he asked Moth Flight.

"Kind of." Her heart ached as she remembered Dust

Muzzle and Gorse Fur, and even harder as she pictured Wind Runner. *I wish I could make her proud of me.*

Moth Flight heard paws pattering over the ground below. She turned in time to catch sight of yellow fur, then heard scrabbling on the ladder. Moments later Micah jumped into the loft. His striped pelt gleamed in a streak of sunlight and his green eyes flashed as he met Cow's gaze. "That dog will be picking thorns out of its paws for days." A purr rumbled in his throat.

"Did you lead it through the bramble patch again?" Cow's whiskers twitched with amusement.

"Of course!"

Moth Flight stared at him. "You sound like you do this a lot!"

"There's not a dog in the whole valley that can catch me." Micah whisked his tail in the air. "And if they did, I'd give them such a clawing, they'd regret it."

Mouse rolled onto his back, drowsily. "It must be a new one. The old farm dogs know better than to chase you, Micah."

Moth Flight gazed in admiration at the yellow tom. He stared back at her, his eyes widening.

She shifted her paws uneasily. He was staring at her as though she had green fur. "What's wrong?" Self-consciously, she smoothed a paw over her ears, wondering if one of them was bent inside out.

"It's *you*!" Micah's pelt ruffled along his spine. His mew was thick with disbelief. "What are you doing *here*? This isn't where you belong!"

Cow blinked at him. "What are you talking about, Micah? She's a stranger."

"But I know her!" Micah insisted.

Mouse pushed himself to his paws. "You've been on this farm since you were a kit. *How* can you know her? She's never been here before."

"I've seen her in my dreams!" Micah murmured, half breathless, his eyes wide.

Cow whisked her tail over her paws. "Don't be mouse-brained. She's real!"

Moth Flight hardly heard the she-cat. She was staring at Micah. "Do you have dreams too?"

Mouse sniffed. "Every cat has dreams."

Micah glanced at him. "I've heard you talking about *your* dreams, Mouse. You do nothing but chase mice and rats."

"That's not true," Mouse sniffed. "Sometimes I dream that they're chasing *me*!"

"But my dreams feel like they're real!" Micah insisted.

"Mine too!" Moth Flight's belly tightened with excitement.

Cow weaved between them, tail high. "Poor Moth Flight is starving. Let's eat first and talk later." She nodded toward the shadows at the back of the loft. "Shall I catch a mouse for you? There are plenty!"

Moth Flight shook her head. She had a long journey ahead. The moth still had something to show her, she was sure of it. And if her dreams could be trusted, she assumed it had something to do with the spirit-cats. She must prove that she was strong enough for the task. "I'll catch my own prey, thanks."

She glanced past Cow, snatching a look at Micah. *I don't want him thinking that I can't hunt for myself,* she thought, her pelt growing hot.

Cow jerked her nose toward the shadows. "Help yourself."

Micah padded past her. "Let's hunt together," he suggested. "That chase has made me hungry."

"We'll all hunt." Cow stood up.

Moth Flight felt a jab of disappointment. She wanted a moment alone with Micah to ask about his dreams. Were they like hers?

"Come on!" Cow marched toward the back of the loft.

Micah leaped onto one of the stacks of hay and disappeared down the other side.

Moth Flight wondered whether to follow him, but Cow was beckoning her into the shadows.

"Here's a great spot," Cow lowered her voice. "There are always plenty of mice who can't resist a nibble on the straw, even up here."

She dropped into a crouch. Moth Flight sank down beside her and stared into the gloom. Dust filled her nose but, through it, she could taste the musky scent of prey.

Her belly growled again.

Cow stifled a purr. "I'll let you go first," she whispered.

"Thanks." Moth Flight crept forward, her eyes adjusting to the gloom. Between two lumps of hay, movement flickered. Concentrating, Moth Flight remembered Gorse Fur's advice, realizing as she did how many times he'd told her the same thing. *Move slowly. Lift your tail. Put your pads down softly.* Her father's words ringing in her mind, she stalked forward, ears pricked. Excitement tingled in her belly. As she neared the hay lumps, she could make out the small, round haunches of a mouse. Holding her breath, she padded closer, then halted. Bunching the muscles in her hind legs, she prepared to pounce. For a moment, she was aware of absolute stillness and silence. Then she leaped.

The mouse darted away, but Moth Flight was quick. She landed a whisker away from the hay lump and thrust her paw into it, moving faster than she'd ever moved in her life. Triumph flared through her as her claws sank into warm flesh. Quick as a flash, she hooked the mouse out and killed it with a single bite.

Black-and-white fur pelted past her. Hay dust exploded around her as Cow thumped against one of the lumps, scrabbling under it for a moment before dragging out her own catch.

Her eyes shone at Moth Flight as she killed the mouse she'd caught, then nodded approvingly at Moth Flight's. "There's no better place to live than a barn," she purred loudly.

Moth Flight met her gaze, grateful for this cat's warmth. But she couldn't agree. For a moment she imagined the wind on the high moor, sweeping through her fur as she chased rabbits with Dust Muzzle. *One day I'll catch one.* Happiness swelled in her chest as she imagined the impressed look on her brother's face.

"Come on." Cow was padding back to the sunny opening of the loft, her mew muffled by her mouse.

Moth Flight scooped up her own catch and followed.

Mouse was already eating. Micah appeared a moment later, scrambling over the stack of hay and landing lightly beside them, a mouse dangling from his jaws.

Moth Flight bit into her mouse, relishing the sweet flavor. She remembered, with a grimace, last night's toad. How could RiverClan eat frogs every day? Perhaps they didn't. Perhaps they saved them as a *treat*! She shuddered.

Soft breath brushed her ear. "You said you dream as well." Micah's mew broke into Moth Flight's thoughts. He'd moved close, laying his mouse beside hers.

"Yes," she murmured.

Cow was busy eating. Mouse had already finished and was starting a leisurely wash a tail-length away.

Micah took a bite of his mouse. "What do you dream about?" he asked, his mouth full. "Me?"

Moth Flight shook her head, trying not to purr. Micah clearly was not a modest cat. "I dream about a moth, and spirit-cats. They're so vivid it's like they're real."

"*Spirit*-cats?" Micah stared at her.

"Dead cats who visit the living." Moth Flight wondered suddenly if farm cats were visited by their ancestors too? By the puzzled look on Micah's face, she guessed not. She pressed on. "Do you dream the same? About moths and other cats?" Perhaps he didn't know that the cats in his dreams were dead. She stared at him eagerly, hardly smelling the warm scent of prey wafting from her mouse. Hope sparked in her chest. Would Micah know what the moth meant and who the gray she-cat was?

He shook his head, then swallowed. "I just dream about you." A frown wrinkled his brow. "Just you. Playing with a young gray tabby tom—"

"Dust Muzzle?" Moth Flight interrupted.

"I don't know his name. Sometimes you're playing Catch the Tail, sometimes you're out on a wide stretch of grass, hunting. Sometimes you're with different cats—another gray tom, thinner and older than the Muzzle one."

"Gorse Fur!" Moth Flight's pelt stood up along her spine. This cat had really seen her in his dreams!

Micah shrugged. "If you say so. And there's a wiry brown she-cat. She always looks cross."

"That's Wind Runner, my mother," Moth Flight told him.

Micah took another mouthful of mouse. "I was taken from my mother when I was a kit. But if mothers are that stern, I'm happy I had Cow instead." He glanced fondly toward the plump she-cat. Her eyes were glazed with contentment as she chewed the last of her catch. Micah's whiskers twitched suddenly. "Why are you always taking plants back to your den?"

"You saw that?" Moth Flight stared at him.

"The other cats tease you, but every hunting trip, you bring back a plant instead of prey. It drives your mother crazy."

Moth Flight purred loudly. Micah made it sound funny. Then she paused. "Are you surprised to see me in real life?"

He narrowed his eyes, as though thinking. "My dreams have always seemed real, so it seems natural that I'd meet you one day."

Moth Flight nodded eagerly. "I know just what you mean.

My dreams aren't about you, but they seem so *real*. They have to *be* real, right?"

Micah eyed her, dubiously. "Green moths and spirit-cats?"

Moth Flight gazed into his bright green eyes. "You dreamed of me when you'd never met me," she told him. "So anything's possible."

Micah's ear twitched. "I guess." He held her gaze and warmth flooded her pelt.

She stared back, feeling suddenly as if she had always known him. Her fur tingled. *Is this cat part of my journey?*

CHAPTER 9

✿

Moth Flight sneezed herself awake. Sniffling, she blinked open her eyes and saw the stacks of hay towering around her. She could see the flattened nests of straw where Cow, Mouse, and Micah had slept. Warmth still radiated from them.

She sat up, wondering where they'd gone. It was light, but no direct sunshine sliced through the barn walls. Moth Flight tasted the air and, through the musty scent of hay dust, smelled rain. She stood and stretched, feeling energy surging through her muscles. She had slept soundly and comfortably, her belly full. As she pressed her chest to the floor, her tail quivered with satisfaction and she straightened and fluffed out her sleep-flattened fur.

She suddenly realized that she hadn't dreamed at all and wondered, stiffening, if the farm was where the moth had been leading her. She'd found Micah here, hadn't she? He had dreamed of her. Perhaps the moth had just wanted them to meet. She frowned, pushing the idea away. That didn't explain her dreams of the gray she-cat, or the glittering stone, and the spirit-cats who'd gathered around it.

She had to move on. There was still more to discover.

She padded to the top of the ladder and peered down. Tentatively, she put her front paws on the top slat, then let them bump down to the next. Her heart lurched and she dug in her claws, gripping anxiously to the rough wood. Clumsily, she slithered down to the next slat, then the next, her hind paws trying desperately to catch up so that, in a moment, she was half scrambling, half falling, toward the ground. She leaped clear as soon as she saw the ground was close enough for her to land comfortably, relieved that the farm cats hadn't been here to see her ungainly descent.

The cows in the shadows behind her swished their hooves through the straw. Hurrying past them, she headed for the small crack in the wall where Mouse and Cow had led her into the barn the day before.

Drizzle sprayed her face as she padded cautiously onto the stretch of stone beyond. She narrowed her eyes, relishing the light rain. It felt refreshing after the dusty air inside. A mild breeze swirled newleaf scents around her. Beyond the stone clearing, the trees were turning green, their branches glowing with fresh leaf buds, ready to unfurl.

"You're awake!" Cow's call made her turn. The black-and-white cat was padding across the stone toward her.

Mouse hurried at his friend's heels. "Did you sleep well?"

"Yes." Moth Flight purred as they halted beside her.

"You must be hungry," Cow guessed.

"I'll catch something on my way," Moth Flight told her.

"On your *way*?" Cow tipped her head, frowning.

Moth Flight gazed back at her, searching for words. How

could she explain that her dreams were leading her onward? "There's just somewhere I need to go." As Moth Flight finished, green wings fluttered at the far end of the stone clearing.

My moth! Her heart leaped. It was swooping back and forth over a stone wall, as though beckoning her.

She headed toward it, fluffing out her pelt against the drizzle.

Cow swerved in front of her. "You can't just leave!"

"I *have* to." Moth Flight tried to duck around her but Mouse blocked her way.

The tom's eyes glittered with worry. "You're too young to be wandering around the valley alone!"

"I'll be okay." Moth Flight tried to push past him, but Cow nudged her back.

"Just stay for a few days, until you've eaten and rested properly." There was concern in the she-cat's yellow gaze.

"I can't." Moth Flight glanced anxiously at the moth. It swooped faster, as though impatient. She couldn't let it get away again! "I have to go *now*!"

"You nearly got caught by a dog!" Mouse reminded her.

"I'll be more careful from now on," Moth Flight promised.

"You're no more than skin and bone." Cow blinked at her. "Stay and let us fatten you up a bit before you leave."

Moth Flight bit back frustration. *I'm only skin and bone compared to you!*

The moth flitted suddenly away, heading for the trees beyond the wall. Moth Flight strained frantically, trying to see past Mouse and Cow, who were backing her toward the barn. *It'll go without me!* Anger surged in Moth Flight's belly. She unsheathed her claws. Was she going to have to fight her way out of here?

The moth fluttered toward the wall once more. *I'm coming!* Moth Flight promised silently. "Please let me go!" she begged. It might disappear at any moment, just like it had done before.

"Let her go if she wants." Micah's deep mew echoed across the stone. He slid out from beneath a monster that was sleeping on the far side of the clearing and strode toward them, tail high. Moth Flight felt a surge of joy, tinged with admiration. Wasn't Micah scared of the monster? It could wake up at any moment!

Micah stopped beside his friends and shook the rain from his whiskers. "Can't you see that she's desperate to leave?"

Moth Flight looked at him gratefully. "The moth from my dreams is trying to show me something."

Micah nodded solemnly, as though he understood.

Cow looked startled. "What if something happens to her?" she fretted. "I'll never forgive myself."

"You can't protect every cat, Cow," Micah reasoned. "She's old enough to look after herself. She was traveling alone when we found her."

"She was nearly ripped to shreds by a dog," Cow pointed out.

Micah looked at Moth Flight. His bright green gaze burned into hers. "She *has* to go."

Moth Flight nodded, her gaze flicking toward the moth. "I have to go *now!*"

Micah turned his gaze, softening, onto his friends. "I could go with her."

Mouse's eyes widened. "Go with her?"

Micah met the old tom's gaze. "Then Cow won't have to worry." He turned to Moth Flight. "Can I come?"

But this is my journey! She opened her mouth, expecting the words to come out, but they froze on her tongue. "Come with me?" was all she could manage.

"You've been in my dreams since I can remember," Micah told her. "I need to find out *why* as much as you need to find out about the moth and the spirit-cats."

Moth Flight shifted her paws. "I think I'm supposed to do this alone."

"Then why did you appear in my dreams?" Micah stared at her pleadingly until she felt caught in his green gaze. "Please let me come."

She knew what he was feeling—the tug in his belly as his dreams called out to him. Now that he'd seen his dreams become reality, he couldn't just go on with his life as though nothing had happened. Besides, she felt deep beneath her fur that they were connected in some way. Micah must be linked with the moth and the spirit-cats. Slowly she nodded. "Okay." The moth lifted into the air and began to zigzag toward the trees. "But we have to leave *now*."

"You can't go, Micah!" Cow's eyes shimmered with sadness. "You've grown up here."

Micah touched his muzzle to hers. "And you've been like a mother to me. I will always remember you. And you'll see me again."

Mouse's eyes were dark. He dipped his graying muzzle. "I've heard many cats say that, but once a cat wanders, they rarely come back."

Moth Flight's heart ached for the farm cats, but her paws itched to race after the moth. "I can't wait," she told Micah. "Cow and Mouse, thank you for everything, but I need to go. Micah, catch up with me." She glanced at the moth. Its bright green wings were nearly camouflaged against the budding trees. Bounding away, she chased after it, crossing the stretch of stone and leaping onto the wall at the end.

She dropped down into soft grass on the other side and began tracking the moth. She could just make it out as it flitted through the woods. She ducked into their shadow, relieved to be out of the rain.

The moth dropped low to bob over ferns that were just starting to unfurl among the trunks.

Paw steps sounded behind Moth Flight and she glanced over her shoulder. A striped yellow pelt showed between the trees. Micah was racing after her.

He caught up to her, panting. "What's the rush?"

Moth Flight nodded toward the moth. It had stopped, resting for a moment against the bark of a beech. "Can you see it?"

Micah followed her gaze and his eyes widened. "It's beautiful! Is that the moth you dreamed about?"

"Yes!" Joy sparked beneath Moth Flight's pelt. She hadn't been sure if the moth was real, or just a trick of her imagination. But Micah could see it too!

Micah purred. "So you *know* what it's like when your dreams suddenly show up while you're awake?" His green eyes shone as they met hers.

Before she could answer, the moth took off again, and began to weave once more among the trees. Moth Flight followed.

"Where do these woods lead?" she asked as Micah fell in beside her.

"They open onto a slope where a track leads past another Twoleg farm," Micah told her.

Moth Flight stiffened. "More dogs?"

Micah's pelt brushed hers as he trotted beside her. "Don't worry," he purred. "I can handle dogs."

CHAPTER 10

❧

The moth avoided the Twoleg farm, much to Moth Flight's relief. As she and Micah emerged from the woods, it veered deeper into the valley. Overhead, the clouds were clearing and the drizzle eased. By sunhigh, the sky showed patches of blue, and by late afternoon, the sun shone in a cloudless, blue sky.

A chilly breeze whisked around Moth Flight and, despite the sun burning her pelt, she began to feel cold. They hadn't eaten all day, but Moth Flight was frightened to stop and hunt in case they lost sight of the moth. Her belly rumbled and she fluffed out her fur to keep warm. As if sensing her discomfort, Micah padded closer and they shared each other's warmth as they followed the moth.

It led them over field after field and, following the setting sun, headed closer to Highstones.

Weariness dragged at Moth Flight's paws as they padded into the shadow of the great peaks. As the sun disappeared behind them, Moth Flight blinked, trying to adjust from bright sunshine to shade. The grass was becoming coarser beneath her paws. As they approached the foot of Highstones, it gave way to bare, rocky soil dotted with patches of heather.

The land sloped steeply ahead of them and the moth lifted higher, swooping toward the sheer cliffs above.

Micah halted and shook out his pelt. "We can't keep following it without rest."

Moth Flight glanced back at him. "But we have to! What if we lose it?"

Micah climbed onto a smooth, wide rock and sat down. His pale pelt looked colorless in the dusky gloom. "It'll come back in the morning. It's come back before."

Moth Flight's hackles lifted. "We can't stop *now*!"

Micah looked toward the moth. It was fluttering against the cliff face. "How are we going to follow it up there? We don't have wings."

"We'll find a path." Moth Flight scanned the sheer rock anxiously, looking for ledges and tracks they could follow. Her heart sank as she saw nothing but the steep face of Highstones. "There must be a way."

The moth's wings were hardly visible against the shadowed stone. Moth Flight had to squint to make them out. "It's stopped moving!" Her pelt rippled with surprise as she realized it had settled. Was it tired too?

Micah jumped from his rock and followed her gaze. His breath billowed in the chilly evening air. "Is that a hole in the cliff face?" he murmured.

Moth Flight narrowed her eyes. Blackness surrounded the moth, as though it had settled on the lip of a gaping mouth. The opening was square, with sharp corners like the holes in Twoleg nests. Excitement fizzed beneath her fur. "It's an entrance!"

"An entrance to what?" Micah sounded wary.

"I don't know, but this must be what it wants to show me!" Moth Flight scrambled quickly up the slope, loose stones cracking beneath her paws. As she neared the entrance, the moth lifted once more into the air and began to spiral upward. "Wait!" Moth Flight called to it, her belly tightening. "Aren't you going to show me what's inside?"

But the moth kept circling upward until Moth Flight saw it lift above Highstones, where the purple sky was streaked orange by the setting sun. Moth Flight strained to see the moth as it flitted higher until it was no more than a speck against the evening sky. Then it disappeared. She curled her claws against the stony ground, her heart aching. "Can you see it?" she called desperately to Micah.

"It's gone." Stones rattled behind her as Micah climbed the slope.

"It *can't* be!" Moth Flight stared at him as he reached her, bereft.

He smoothed his tail across her spine. "It's shown you what it wanted to show you," he murmured gently. "You don't need it anymore."

Slowly Moth Flight turned her gaze toward the gaping mouth in the cliff. "I think I have to go in there." Dread hollowed her belly. She remembered the choking fear she felt in the moorland tunnels. "I don't like the dark," she whispered shakily.

"I'll be with you," Micah promised.

Moth Flight shook her head. "You dreamed of *me*," she reminded him. "You didn't dream of moths. I must go alone."

"Why?" Micah blinked at her.

Moth Flight felt her paws trembling. "I'm not sure, I just know I must." Certainty sat in her belly like hunger.

Micah's ear twitched. "Okay," he meowed briskly. "But you're not going in there until you've had something to eat."

Moth Flight dipped her head, grateful to have him with her. She was starving. Perhaps that was why her paws were trembling so much. As he turned, she followed him down the slope.

"I'm sure I smelled mouse dung around here." Micah began sniffing around the edge of the smooth, wide rock he'd stopped on. His ears pricked. "This is going to be easy." As he spoke, a small shape darted from beneath the rock and raced across the stony ground. *Mouse!* Micah leaped, landing on it before it had run a tail-length. He snapped its neck and Moth Flight smelled the warm scent of blood.

Her mouth watered and she began to scan the slope, looking for her own prey.

"You eat this one." Micah dropped the mouse at her paws.

"I can catch my own," Moth Flight protested.

"I know," Micah agreed. "But not now. Save your strength for whatever's inside that cave."

As he padded quietly away, his nose twitching, Moth Flight glanced up at the gaping mouth in the cliff face. She swallowed. The moth wouldn't have led her anywhere dangerous, surely? She pushed the thought away. *I'm meant to do this,* she told herself, *no matter what.* Crouching, she ate Micah's mouse, her belly growling for more as she finished. She was pleased to see Micah heading back with two more mice swinging from his jaws. He glanced at the bloodstained rock where her meal had been and dropped his fresh catch on the space. "You *were* hungry," he purred. He pushed one of the mice toward her and hooked the other toward himself.

"Are you sure?" Moth Flight felt a prick of guilt. He'd walked just as far as she had today. He must be starving too.

"I can catch more while you're exploring your cave." He took a mouthful, his whiskers twitching with pleasure.

"You'll wait for me?" she asked tentatively. The sky was dark now. Stars were showing in the blackness. The chilly wind had grown colder. Frost was beginning to sparkle on the rocks and the stone beneath her pads was so cold that it made her paws ache.

"Of course I'll wait for you!" He looked up from his mouse sharply. "Why would I leave?"

She shrugged. "It's cold. I thought you might want to find shelter."

"We'll find shelter together, once you get back."

Moth Flight felt her throat tighten with gratitude. "Thank you," she croaked.

She took longer to finish her second mouse. She wanted desperately to see inside the cave, but fear was tugging her back. Her heart pounded in her chest. *It'll be so dark!* Swallowing her final mouthful, she tried to steady her breathing. Micah was washing beside her, his mouse long gone. She felt soothed by the easy, rhythmic strokes of his tongue. *He'll be waiting for me.* The thought comforted her as she glanced up at the cave.

"Are you ready?" His mew made her jump.

Moth Flight nodded, her eyes wide.

"You'll be fine," Micah promised. They stood up together and he padded beside her as she climbed up the slope. Scrabbling the last few tail-lengths, she leaped onto the lip of the cave. The stone was smooth beneath her paws. Micah jumped up next to her and peered inside. "It's a good thing you've got whiskers," he muttered. "You're going to need them to tell where you're going."

She glanced into the darkness. "I've got a nose too, and ears," she murmured, trying to reassure herself. "I'll be okay."

"I know." Micah caught her eye, his gaze solemn. She felt his breath on her muzzle as he leaned forward and touched his nose to hers. "But be careful."

"I will." Turning away, Moth Flight padded into the cave.

It felt huge—high and wide enough for a Twoleg. She sniffed the air tentatively, but there was no living creature in here except her. All she could smell was stone and stagnant water. She padded deeper into the gloom, straining to see how far it reached into Highstones. Blackness lay ahead and, as she padded onward and the weak starlight faded behind her, she realized that this was a tunnel, not a cave. As darkness swallowed her, she waited for fear to flare in her belly, but none came. She felt curiously calm, her paw steps steady on the smooth stone floor.

A chill reached through her pelt. This sunless place felt colder than a snowbound night on the moor. She opened her mouth and let the damp air bathe her tongue, tasting the tang of stone as freezing air filled her chest.

The ground sloped beneath her paws. Stone touched her whiskers on one side and she let it guide her as the tunnel began to bend. She was blind here, though her eyes were wide open, straining to see any glimpse of light. But, with blackness on every side, she could only follow the twists and turns by touch as the tunnel spiraled down into the earth. She was surprised to feel peace spread from her belly through every hair on her pelt. It was as though the stone welcomed her and was leading her deeper into its heart. She listened, ears stretched, and heard a distant drop of water resound on hard rock.

How far must I go? As she began to wonder if the tunnel would lead on forever, her whiskers suddenly tingled and she smelled crispness in the dank air. She quickened her step. Fresh air lay ahead! Had she reached the other side of Highstones? Or perhaps she had circled back to the hole where Micah was waiting. Expecting any moment to turn a corner and find herself beneath a wide moonlit sky, she stepped instead into a cavern glimmering with watery starlight. She could hardly make out the walls, but she recognized it at once. Heart quickening, she scanned the cave and saw the huge rock jutting at its center.

Just like my dream!

She looked up and saw the hole in the roof. Stars flickered beyond and she could see the moon sliding into sight.

Moth Flight glanced expectantly at the rock. She knew what would happen next.

As the moon lifted higher, the rock suddenly sparked into light.

Moth Flight narrowed her eyes against the glare.

The great stone was glittering like countless dewdrops sparkling in sunlight. The cave shimmered in its glow.

Are the spirit-cats here? Moth Flight glanced around eagerly. But nothing moved in the cave. She was the only cat there.

Pushing away disappointment, she padded to the spot where the gray she-cat had lain, and pressed her belly to the icy floor. Tucking her paws beneath her, she tried to imagine the she-cat's warmth still lingering in the stone. Her pelt tingled with excitement. *This is where I was meant to come!* Closing her eyes, she stretched her muzzle forward and touched her nose to the sparkling rock.

CHAPTER 11

Light flared through her, tingling in every hair. Moth Flight opened her eyes, aware of paws scuffing the stone floor around her. She sat up, blinking. She was no longer alone. By the light of the moonlit stone, she could see the shimmering pelts of spirit-cats all around her. They were staring at her.

They can see me! Joy swelled in Moth Flight's chest. *At last! They can see me!*

She met the gaze of a tabby tom, who dipped his head to her, then looked at the tortoiseshell she-cat beside him, who closed her eyes slowly, nodding a greeting. Moth Flight's fur pricked along her spine. These cats were showing respect! Didn't they know she was just a young WindClan cat who hadn't even learned to hunt properly yet?

A glittering gray pelt moved toward her and she recognized the face of Gray Wing. "You're here!" she breathed, excitement fizzing in her paws.

Gray Wing stopped a muzzle-length from her nose. "Welcome, Moth Flight." His eyes glowed with pride. "You've come at last."

"Welcome."

"Welcome."

"You've come at last."

Murmurs of greeting rippled through the gathered cats.

What did they mean? Moth Flight's heart quickened. "Come at last?" she echoed, puzzled.

A white she-cat padded forward and stopped beside Gray Wing. Her pelt glistened with starlight and her green eyes glowed emerald as though lit by ancient wisdom. Moth Flight found herself drawn into the white cat's gaze, breath catching in her throat.

"I'm Half Moon." Affection warmed the she-cat's mew. "We've been waiting for you."

"For *me*?" Moth Flight stepped back, surprised. "Do you *know* me?" The spirit-cats had looked straight through her in her dreams; they never even saw her.

Half Moon seemed to read her thoughts. "We know every cat."

"How?" Moth Flight blinked at her.

"We watch over you." She gazed wistfully at the hole in the roof.

Moth Flight glanced at the stars twinkling outside. Did the spirit-cats live up there like some kind of . . . Clan?

Half Moon's gaze flashed toward her once more. "Like the stars, we light your way when it grows dark. We know what is in your hearts and your dreams."

"Then why couldn't you see me in my dreams about the blue-gray she-cat?" Moth Flight glanced around the glittering cats. Was the she-cat here? There was no sign of her. "You were right in this cave with her. I saw you!"

Half Moon dipped her head. "Some dreams you must dream alone."

Moth Flight narrowed her eyes. "But my dreams led me here."

"The moth led you here," Half Moon reminded her.

"Did you send it?" Moth Flight didn't wait for a reply. Of course they sent it! "How did you know I'd follow it?"

"We didn't," Half Moon told her. "We only hoped. It was the only way we could be sure that you were the one."

"The *one*?" Moth Flight's tail tip twitched anxiously. She suddenly felt very far from home. She glanced at Gray Wing's familiar face, hungry for reassurance.

But Gray Wing dipped his head and stepped back. "Half Moon will explain."

The white she-cat sat down and tucked her tail over her paws. "We brought you here for a reason," she began.

"Why me? I'm not special. I'm just a—"

Half Moon silenced her with a look. "You *are* special."

Moth Flight remembered Gorse Fur's words on the moortop. *Dust Muzzle will make a fine hunter one day, but Moth Flight is special.* She stared at her paws. "I can't hunt as well as the others. I keep getting distracted." Had the spirit-cats brought her all this way to tell her she wasn't good enough to be a Clan cat?

"We know," Half Moon meowed softly. "But that's not a bad thing. We want you to carry on being yourself."

"Being *myself*?" What did that *mean*?

"Honor the qualities that make you who you are," Half

Moon went on gently. "Your curiosity, your dreams, your openness to the world around you."

Moth Flight blinked at her in surprise. "But they are useless qualities in a Clan. Curiosity and dreams don't feed hungry bellies." Moth Flight could hear her mother's voice as she spoke.

Half Moon's tail twitched. "Let your Clanmates fill empty bellies. They will always be better hunters than you."

Moth Flight's pelt burned with shame.

"You have strengths no other cat has," Half Moon went on. "Of course curiosity is no good for a hunter, nor is an open mind. A hunter must focus on the prey in front of his nose. He misses the things that *you* notice."

Moth Flight struggled to understand. "But all I see are stars in puddles and interesting plants!"

"You saw this cave in your dreams," Half Moon pointed out. "You clearly have a stronger connection with us than any other cat has."

"But other cats have seen you!" Moth Flight argued.

"That was at the beginning. Before the Clans had found their way. Now things must change." Half Moon glanced around her starry companions. "The Clans need more than leadership and strength; they need nurture and care. But it must come from within. We can't guide their paws in everything. That is why we have chosen you to be the first medicine cat."

Moth Flight's pelt rippled along her spine. "*Medicine* cat? What do you mean?"

Half Moon tipped her head. "You will learn to heal your

Clanmates when they are sick or wounded using plants from the moor, forest, and river."

Moth Flight remembered each of the leaves she'd brought back to camp over the past few moons. Could some of them be used to heal? How would she know? She shifted her paws, her thoughts quickening. When she'd been a kit, her littermate, Morning Whisker, had died from the sickness that had swept through the Clans. Then Cloud Spots had figured out that an herb—the Blazing Star—could fight the illness, and the sick cats were cured. And there were *already* cats skilled in helping others. Last leafbare, when every cat had been coughing and many became so sick they could not hunt, Pebble Heart from ShadowClan had brought herbs to cure them. Dappled Pelt had come from RiverClan and helped Slate birth her kits. She could start by learning from these cats.

Enthusiasm pulsed through her paws. Then she could discover new herbs. One day, she might find her own Blazing Star—an herb that would save her Clanmates! Moth Flight's heart quickened. She imagined Wind Runner watching her heal a sick cat. She could already see the surprise in her mother's eyes. *She won't be angry with me anymore! And my Clanmates will stop thinking I'm useless!*

A purr sounded in Half Moon's throat and Moth Flight's attention snapped back to the starry she-cat. Half Moon was gazing at her fondly. "You look like you relish the challenge."

"I do." Moth Flight met her green gaze, suddenly aware that she could feel her paws trembling. "I just hope I'm good enough."

A brown tabby she-cat pushed past Half Moon. Moth Flight backed away, unnerved by the fierceness in the tabby's starry gaze.

"You must devote yourself to your Clan," the she-cat growled.

Moth Flight stiffened crossly. *I already do!*

Half Moon brushed her tail soothingly along the tabby's spine. "She will come to know that, Rainswept Flower. In time."

An orange tabby she-cat called from the far side of the rock. "You must learn the way of healing herbs."

"And you must learn to recognize the omens we send you!" A tom, his pelt dark as night sky and glittering with stars, padded closer. His gaze was stern. "Only you will know what our omens mean. You must use such knowledge to advise your leader."

Advise Wind Runner? Moth Flight blinked. "She'll never listen to *me!*"

The black tom didn't blink. "Then you must be strong. You must *make* her listen."

Half Moon nodded. "Moon Shadow is right. This is not an easy task we give you. But we are relying on you to keep your Clan safe."

Moth Flight's mouth grew dry. "I'll try," she promised softly. "But what about the other Clans? Do I have to I keep *them* safe as well?"

Moon Shadow answered her. "Each Clan will have its own medicine cat."

Moth Flight blinked. "Have you spoken with them already?"

"*You* must tell them," Moon Shadow ordered.

"But how will I know who they are?" Moth Flight felt dizzy. How could she tell other cats how they must live their lives? And was she ready to change her *own* life—to spend it healing rather than hunting? She would be *responsible* for her Clanmates!

Half Moon shifted, gently shooing Moon Shadow and Rainswept Flower backward with her tail. She glanced at the empty stone in front of Moth Flight. "Watch."

Moth Flight followed her gaze, gasping as a shape shimmered into view. "Dappled Pelt!" She recognized the RiverClan she-cat, curled in a nest fast asleep, and wondered how she could be here in the cave. Tentatively, she reached out and tried to touch the she-cat's pelt. Her paw passed through air.

"She is at home, dreaming in her nest," Half Moon glanced over her shoulder and beckoned a brown-and-white tabby she-cat closer with a flick of her tail. "Bright Stream. Come and share your blessing with Dappled Pelt."

Bright Stream padded toward the vision, her gaze warm as she leaned close. She touched her nose to the sleeping head. "Protect them," she whispered.

Moth Flight half expected Dappled Pelt to wake, but she faded from view and another cat took her place.

Cloud Spots!

As Moth Flight blinked at the sleeping ThunderClan tom,

Half Moon called to another of her companions. "Jackdaw's Cry!"

A black tom hurried forward. He looked fondly at the black-and-white cat. "Take care of your Clan." Jackdaw's Cry stretched his muzzle to touch his old Tribemate with his nose.

Cloud Spots flashed out of sight and a gray tom replaced him.

Pebble Heart. Moth Flight wasn't surprised to see the ShadowClan tom appear. He'd always known more about herbs than any cat.

A tortoiseshell she-cat padded past Half Moon. Her pelt shimmered as she stopped beside the vision of Pebble Heart. Moth Flight guessed who she was before Half Moon said her name.

"Be quick, Turtle Tail. The moon is passing." Half Moon's mew was thick.

Moth Flight knew that Turtle Tail was Pebble Heart's mother. She'd been killed by a monster while trying to rescue her kits. *She died the day I was born.* Moth Flight felt weak with anguish as she saw joy and grief glisten like sunshine through rain in the tortoiseshell's green gaze.

Turtle Tail touched her nose to her kit's head. "I always knew you were special," she murmured. "Take care of them all, my dear."

Pebble Heart stirred, his ear twitching as his mother's muzzle grazed it. Then he huffed and turned in his sleep, and the vision faded.

Gray Wing moved to Turtle Tail's side and guided her

away, his tail curled protectively across her spine.

Moth Flight watched the pair take their place among their companions. *Who next?* Medicine cats had been chosen for every Clan except SkyClan. She looked back at the stone and blinked as yellow fur shimmered into view. *There's no yellow cat in SkyClan.* She stiffened as she recognized the slender shoulders and smooth back of the tom. "Micah!"

Shock pulsed through her. Unlike the others, Micah wasn't asleep. He sat, alert, gazing ahead, as though waiting.

He's waiting for me.

A small tabby she-cat brushed in front of Half Moon.

"Petal." Half Moon purred fondly as she passed.

Moth Flight stared as Petal approached the vision of Micah. "How can *he* be a medicine cat?" she gasped. "He doesn't belong to any Clan!"

"Nor did I, once." Petal blinked at her, her eyes glittering in the light from the stone. She leaned forward and brushed her muzzle against Micah's cheek. "Protect your Clan as though they had raised you."

Micah didn't flinch, but carried on staring, serenely unaware that spirit-cats were watching him. Moth Flight wanted to call out to him that she was safe and she could see him. But she knew he wouldn't hear.

As Micah faded away, Half Moon stepped forward once more. "You must return to your Clan now, Moth Flight. Tell the cats what we have shown you."

Moth Flight stiffened. "All of them?" She'd have to convince every cat that what she'd seen was real. How would she make them believe her?

"Just speak your truth, Moth Flight." Half Moon's mew was firm. "Have faith in who and what you are."

I am a medicine cat. Moth Flight lifted her chin as the white cat went on.

"Next half-moon, and every half-moon after that, you and the other medicine cats must return here and we'll speak again."

"Next *half-moon*? I'll need more time that that!" Moth Flight spluttered. She pictured Tall Shadow sitting sternly in her bramble den, and Clear Sky's thick tail flicking scornfully. And Thunder! He was the most powerful tom she'd ever seen. She'd never even spoken to the mysterious River Ripple. And Wind Runner . . .

Her paws felt suddenly hot against the icy stone. *I don't even know if I'll be able to convince my own mother!* "I can't do it!" Her heart pounded in her chest. "I'll never be able to do it!"

CHAPTER 12

❦

Half Moon whisked her tail irritably. "Have faith in yourself!"

Moth Flight's hackles lifted. That was easy for *her* to say! *You're dead! What do you have to lose?* "My Clan thinks I'm feather-headed enough," she snapped. "If I go back with stories about talking to spirit-cats and telling them that they're supposed to have medicine cats and I should be one, they'll think I'm a complete birdbrain!"

"The moonlight will be gone soon. We don't have long," Half Moon warned. "This is your destiny, whether you want it or not. You have no choice but to follow it. Every Clan's destiny depends on *you*, though they don't know it yet. But they will. And there will come a time when they will listen to you and you alone. I can tell you this, but it's up to *you* to earn their respect."

"*How?*" Moth Flight felt frantic. At any moment the moon might pass over the hole and the cave would be plunged into darkness. She'd be alone, to face the Clans by herself. "I haven't managed to earn any cat's respect so far! Wind Runner told me I was a danger to my Clan. I lost Slate's kits. I nearly got Gorse Fur killed by a monster. I'm useless!" Her mew broke as hopelessness overwhelmed her. She dropped her gaze to the moon-washed stone.

Downy fur moved in front of her. She lifted her head to see a tom-kit nosing past Half Moon. He was tiny, and looked hardly more than a day old, although his eyes were open and bright. A she-kit stopped beside him, a little bigger, but less than a moon old. Moth Flight blinked at them, shocked to see kits among the spirit-cats, but then her nose twitched. She recognized their scent. For a moment she was back in Wind Runner's nest, nuzzling for milk at her mother's belly beside Dust Muzzle. "Morning Whisker? Is that you?" She stared at the she-kit. Morning Whisker had died in the sickness that swept the Clans. She looked well now, her starry pelt fluffed out, her eyes sparkling.

Morning Whisker nodded. "It's good to see you, Moth Flight."

Moth Flight's gaze flicked to the tom-kit. He'd died before she could know him, on the day they were born. "Emberkit?"

"Hello, Moth Flight," he purred.

Morning Whisker padded closer. "You have to do this, Moth Flight," she urged. "The Clans need you."

"But I don't know how," Moth Flight answered bleakly. "Wind Runner's never going to listen to me."

"She will," Morning Whisker insisted.

"You don't know that."

Morning Whisker's gaze hardened. "We share three things, Moth Flight."

"What?" How could she share anything with these dead kits?

"Isn't it obvious?" Emberkit pushed in front, fur spiking. "We share a history, a future, and—"

Morning Whisker interrupted her brother. "Let Moth Flight tell us the third thing."

Moth Flight frowned, trying to guess. "I don't kno—" Then she realized. "A *mother*!" She paused, breathless with anguish. She'd never wondered before about her brother who'd died. And yet, here he was, as bright and strong as a living kit. Their sister stood beside him. She hadn't thought about Morning Whisker for moons. Her pelt pricked along her spine. Wind Runner was *their* mother too! Moth Flight was used to sharing Wind Runner with Dust Muzzle, but Dust Muzzle had always seemed independent; he'd never worried about Wind Runner's approval. He'd never had to; everything came naturally to him. But these kits had been Wind Runner's too, before they'd been taken from her. Did Wind Runner still think about them? Of course she did! She must *miss* them! *Is Wind Runner missing me too?* With a pang, she remembered her mother's angry words as they'd parted. "I just wish I could please her," she murmured sadly.

"You will," Morning Whisker mewed.

"Of course you will!" Emberkit's tail was twitching excitedly. "In time she will understand everything. Until then, she will support you because you are her kit."

Moth Flight wasn't convinced. "She thinks I'm useless."

"She can be harsh," Morning Whisker conceded. "But are you surprised? The moor is a harsh place. She lost *us* there. If she's strict, it's because she worries about you, not because she thinks you're useless."

Emberkit stepped forward and lifted his muzzle close to Moth Flight's. His breath felt warm on her nose. "She just wants to protect you. It's a mother's strongest instinct. When you're medicine cat and your Clanmates are relying on you, you will feel the same way."

Moth Flight's ear twitched uneasily. *Will I have to be mother to the whole Clan?*

Around her, the starry cats began to fade, becoming so translucent that she could only see the stars in their pelts.

Emberkit was no more than shimmering light before her.

"Don't go!" Panic blazed beneath her pelt. She called to Half Moon, whose green gaze was growing pale. "You haven't told me how I can convince the Clans to listen to me! Won't you come to the full moon Gathering and tell them yourself?"

"No." Half Moon's mew was barely an echo. "But we will send a sign when you tell them, to let them know that we speak through *you* now."

"A sign?" How would she know it? What should she look for? The cats were disappearing one by one. "What sign?" she mewed desperately as the moon passed out of sight and the cave was swallowed by shadow.

A voice echoed from the blackness. "We will split the sky. And later, stars will rise."

Split the sky? What did it mean? Moth Flight struggled for breath. The darkness seemed suddenly suffocating. *Later, stars will rise. . . .*

What could it possibly mean?

CHAPTER 13

❧

Moth Flight followed the tunnel upward, her paws trembling. Was she really going to be responsible for any sick cats in her Clan? How would she explain it all to Wind Runner? Why did the spirit-cats want to speak through *her*?

Your curiosity, your dreams, your openness to the world around you.

She remembered Half Moon's words.

The spirit-cats believe in me. . . . Joy surged beneath her pelt, pushing her doubts away. Suddenly, the cold stone beneath her paws felt like it belonged to her. This was *her* place. She'd found it. Determination hardened in her belly. *I won't let you down,* she promised silently.

Starlight showed through the darkness ahead, seeping like water into the tunnel. Moth Flight quickened her pace, breaking into a run as she neared the opening. She leaped from the ledge, sending stones clattering down the steep slope.

Micah, sitting on the wide stone below, turned, his eyes flashing in the moonlight. "What happened?" He bounded toward her and met her, breathless, halfway up the slope.

She skidded to a halt and stared into his starlit eyes. "It was amazing," she breathed.

"I was worried. You were gone so long." His gaze flitted over her pelt, as though he was checking that she wasn't hurt.

"I'm fine," she reassured him. She shuddered, realizing how cold she was. The dampness of the tunnel had reached to her bones. She fluffed out her pelt.

Micah began to steer her gently down the slope. "There's still a little warmth from the sun left in the rock." Nudging her up onto the wide stone where he'd been waiting, he joined her.

A dead mouse was lying in the middle. "I thought you might be hungry."

"Thanks." Moth Flight blinked at him gratefully. "But I don't think I could eat anything right now. I'm too excited." She could feel faint warmth beneath her paws and crouched, pressing her belly to the rock. Micah crouched beside her, his fur barely brushing hers, just close enough for her to feel the heat from his pelt.

"Do you want to talk about it?" Micah asked softly.

Moth Flight stared at him. "Of course. It was the most amazing thing that ever happened to me!"

Micah gazed at her eagerly.

"There was a cave at the end of the tunnel. Just like the one I saw in my dream. It has a big rock at the center and a hole in the roof and when the moonlight hit the rock, it blazed like a fire! And then the spirit-cats appeared."

"You saw them for real?" Micah widened his eyes.

Moth Flight nodded. "Even Gray Wing this time."

Micah gazed at her blankly.

"He was part of our Clan until he died a moon ago," she

explained. "It was good to see him again."

"Were all these spirit-cats once alive?" Micah asked.

"Yes!" Moth Flight could still hardly believe she'd spoken with them. "I didn't recognize many." The memory of Morning Whisker and Emberkit burned brightly in her mind. "I saw my dead littermates."

Micah blinked. "I'm sorry! I didn't know you'd lost—"

Moth Flight interrupted him. She didn't need sympathy. "I'm glad I saw them. They were so *wise*. They looked like kits still but they acted like grown cats."

"You spoke to them?"

"They told me not to be scared of Wind Runner. She's only stern because she cares about me."

Micah's breath stirred her cheek fur. "Didn't you know that already?"

Moth Flight hunched her shoulders. "I always thought she was disappointed in me because I couldn't hunt as well as Dust Muzzle."

Micah's eyes flashed teasingly. "I guess she wishes you'd bring *prey* home instead of plants," he joked. "But how could she *not* love you?"

Moth Flight shifted self-consciously. Micah's stare seemed suddenly too intense to bear. Was he just humoring her? Did he think she was crazy? She was talking about dead cats! "You believe me, don't you?"

"I've dreamed about you since I was a kit." Micah's ears twitched. "Now that I've met you for real, I can believe anything."

Moth Flight felt relief sweep over her. She was lucky to have someone to share this with, someone who believed her. She suddenly pictured her Clanmates. What would they say when she told them that the spirit-cats had told her she was special? *But you're a featherbrain!* She imagined Swift Minnow's scornful mew.

"Tell me what they said." Micah's voice jerked her from her thoughts.

"They told me I was to become a medicine cat and learn about herbs and healing and that they would send me omens and I had to explain the omens to Wind Runner." Moth Flight's chest tightened. "They said it was my destiny." She gazed deep into Micah's eyes, expecting uncertainty, but he stared back solemnly. "Do you think I can do it?" she asked anxiously.

"You have dreams about moths and spirit-cats and you love to collect plants instead of prey." Micah sat up and stretched. "You'll do it brilliantly."

"Do you really think so?" She jumped to her paws.

"Do you *want* to do it?"

Moth Flight imagined herself treating cats, collecting herbs, advising Wind Runner and searching the stars for omens. Anticipation prickled beneath her pelt. "Yes!" Her tail quivered. "But it's not just me," she went on. "They want Cloud Spots to be a medicine cat too. And Pebble Heart and Dappled Pelt and—" She stopped herself. Was Micah ready to be told of *his* destiny? He'd only agreed to follow the moth with her, not to give up his life on the farm to live with the

Clans. "I have to tell them. I have to tell *all of them* what I've seen." She felt her paws begin to tremble again.

"Of course!" Micah swished his tail, excitedly. "They'll want to know."

Moth Flight dropped her gaze, feeling suddenly small beneath the wide starry sky. Could she really do this? As she tried to imagine telling her Clan that she'd spoken with Gray Wing and Half Moon and Emberkit, her paws pricked with alarm. "They already think I'm a birdbrain. This will just prove it."

"Why?" Micah frowned, puzzled.

Hopelessness swamped Moth Flight. "I've done so many dumb things," she confessed. "They won't believe me."

"They *have* to believe you!" Micah puffed out his chest. "*I* believe you."

"You don't know how dumb I can be."

Micah padded around her, impatiently. "You're not dumb."

"You don't know me."

"Yes, I do!" Micah stopped and stared at her. "I've never met a cat who goes off chasing moths or disappears into strange tunnels in the middle of the night or tells me that she's going to learn how to heal and read omens." He paused, his gaze sparkling so intensely that her heart seemed to miss a beat. "You're wonderful!"

Moth Flight shifted her paws nervously. Would he think she was so wonderful when she told him about *his* destiny? "You're part of it," she blurted.

Micah stiffened. "Part of what?"

"You're meant to be a medicine cat too."

"On the farm?" He tipped his head, puzzled.

"No!" Moth Flight paced across the stone and looked over the trees to the distant moor, curving like a cat's spine against the glittering sky. "You're to be SkyClan's medicine cat."

"That's your Clan, right?" Micah stopped beside her.

"No." Moth Flight steadied her breath. "I'm from Wind-Clan. SkyClan is Clear Sky's group. They live in the forest, not on the moor." She felt Micah shift uneasily beside her.

"So I'll live *there*, and not with you?"

Her heart lifted. He hadn't said no. She turned sharply and faced him. "Do you mean you'll do it? Become a medicine cat for the Clans?"

Micah returned her gaze, but she could read nothing in his eyes. "The leader of SkyClan," he began. "He's a tom, right? Fierce. He likes bossing other cats around."

Moth Flight's mouth grew dry as he went on.

"Is he suspicious of other cats? And proud? Gray with blue eyes?"

Moth Flight backed away, startled. He was describing Clear Sky exactly. "How do you know?"

"I've dreamed of him," he murmured. "I dream I'm bringing him catmint to help a sick kit."

"Catmint?" Moth Flight pricked her ears.

"It's an herb that grows behind the barn. It looks a bit like nettles but the leaves are smaller and they don't sting. You'll know if you ever see some. It smells great. And it helps coughs." Micah whisked his tail impatiently. "I keep having the same dream. The kit's always sick and the gray tom's ordering me to hurry with the catmint." He blinked at her. "But I can see now—it *wasn't* a dream! *None* of my dreams have been dreams. I've been seeing my destiny!" His fur rippled with surprise. He lifted his gaze toward the moor.

Moth Flight shifted her paws nervously. He'd just discovered that the life he'd planned was not the life that had been planned for him. "Do you mind?"

"Why should I mind?" Micah shrugged. "It's pointless to mind your own destiny. You just have to face it."

Moth Flight wondered how he could be so calm. Fear hollowed her belly as she tried to imagine the moons that lay head of her. "Aren't you scared?"

"No," he meowed softly. "One path is as good as another. It's not knowing which one to take that's scary. Now that I know where I'm meant to be going, there's nothing to fear." He looked at her. "For *either* of us."

"Do you promise?" Her mew quavered.

"I promise." His green gaze was steady. Starlight sparkled in its depths.

Moth Flight reached out her muzzle and touched his. Her heart slowed as his nose brushed her cheek. She felt soothed by his stillness, aware of the moonlight washing their pelts.

CHAPTER 14

"Wake up."

Moth Flight felt a muzzle nudging her shoulder. She lifted her head, blinking at the bright sunshine. *Where am I?* Confused for a moment, she saw Micah, standing beside her on the smooth, wide rock at the foot of Highstones.

Memories flooded her. The night before! *The spirit-cats! The moonlit stone!*

Heart leaping, she scrambled to her paws. "We have to get back and tell Wind Runner!" They'd talked until dawn had crept over the moortop, and then slept. Now the sun was sinking behind them. "Come on!"

"There's no hurry. We can eat first." Micah jumped off the rock and sniffed for prey underneath.

"There isn't time. It's full moon tonight. We have to get back and tell her before the Gathering. Then she can let the others know." Moth Flight leaped from the rock and headed across the stony ground, toward the fields. If she could convince Wind Runner that the Clans needed to have medicine cats, then Wind Runner could explain everything to the other leaders. *They might not believe me, but they'll believe the WindClan leader.*

She heard Micah's paw steps hurry after her. "What's the *Gathering*?"

"The Clans meet every full moon to share tongues," Moth Flight explained quickly, her eyes fixed on the meadow ahead. "They swap information about dangers, like Twolegs or dogs, and how the prey's running. It helps keep the peace."

"Do the Clans *fight*?" Micah sounded surprised.

"They did once," Moth Flight told him. "Now we meet and share so that we'll never fight again."

She quickened her pace. The moor looked a long way off. They'd be lucky to get there before dusk.

"We'll travel faster on full bellies," Micah scanned the land around them as stones gave way to grass beneath their paws.

Moth Flight kept her gaze firmly ahead. "If you see prey as we travel, then catch it. But I'm not stopping."

Evening was flooding the valley by the time they neared the steep hill that climbed to the moor. Micah had caught a shrew he'd spotted as they leaped a ditch. He'd killed it and they'd quickly shared it between them. It hadn't stopped Moth Flight's hunger. Her belly was rumbling as she caught sight of the Thunderpath, but she ignored it. She must concentrate on crossing. The wide strip of black stone cut across their trail and Moth Flight stopped at the edge. Her ear fur tingled, picking up the distant roar of a monster. Stale monster scent soured her tongue.

"Come on." Micah hurried onto the flat stone. He stopped in the middle and turned as she hung back on the verge. She remembered the last time she was here. Fear wormed in her belly. She'd nearly got Gorse Fur killed. What if he'd died? *I was so rabbit-brained!* Had Wind Runner forgiven her?

You're a danger to your Clan.

Moth Flight stared at the Thunderpath, her mouth suddenly dry. Spotted Fur had promised everything would be fine by the morning. That had been two days ago. Would it really be fine?

It has to be! I'm going to be a medicine cat. She forced herself to remember Morning Whisker's words. *If she's strict, it's because she worries about you, not because she thinks you're useless.* A spirit-cat couldn't be wrong, could she?

"Moth Flight!" Micah's yowl made her jump. She blinked, focusing on him. The roaring of the monster was louder. Its silhouette loomed on the horizon. Glaring eyes blazed through the twilight, blanching Micah's yellow pelt.

I'm not risking another cat's life!

Moth Flight pelted forward, whisking past Micah. "Come on!" She glanced over her shoulder, relieved to see him hare after her as she made for the far side of the Thunderpath. She skidded to a halt, grass snagging between her claws. Micah slowed beside her. Foul wind tugged her fur as the monster roared past, honking like a goose.

"That was close!" Micah panted.

Moth Flight blinked at him anxiously. His pelt was bushed. "I didn't expect you to wait for me in the middle."

"I didn't expect you to stand daydreaming at the side!"

"Next time, don't wait for me," she told him. "I get distracted."

Micah's ears twitched uneasily. "Are there any Thunder-paths on the moor?"

"No."

"Good."

They climbed the slope in silence. As they reached the top, the setting sun warmed Moth Flight's back for a moment before it slipped behind Highstones. She stopped and blinked through the dusky half-light. She could smell WindClan scents clinging to the gorse ahead. And the heather, fragrant with evening dew. Her paws pricked with happiness. She was home!

She glanced at Micah. It was strange to have him beside her. She was used to crossing this grass with her Clanmates. Was he nervous? He was entering unknown territory. "Are you ready?"

Micah gazed across the moor sloping away in front of them. The forest stood beyond, no more than a shadow against the purpling sky now. He lifted his tail. "I'm ready."

"Follow me." Moth Flight headed toward the gorse, weaving between the thickly clustered bushes. Flower buds had begun to unfurl since she'd left and their sweet perfume filled her nose. She quickened her pace as they reached an open stretch of grass.

"How long have the Clans lived here?" Micah trotted at her side.

"Not too long. We were one big group once," Moth Flight explained. "But we split into Clans moons ago. Some preferred the pine forest, some preferred the oaks. Some wanted to live beside the river." She glanced sideways at Micah. "They *swim*."

"They *swim*?" Micah's ears twitched. "Why?"

"Only the stars know." Moth Flight had never understood any cat who enjoyed getting their fur wet. "Wind Runner and Gorse Fur have always been moor cats. So that's where we live." She pointed her muzzle toward the shadowy dip in the hillside that enclosed the camp.

Micah narrowed his eyes. Moth Flight wished she could tell what he was thinking.

She broke into a run. She didn't want him to lose his nerve. "Come on." The full moon was rising into a clear sky. "They'll be heading to Fourtrees soon. I have to speak to Wind Runner before she leaves."

She smelled Spotted Fur's scent as she ducked into a swath of heather. The golden-brown tom had followed this path through the bushes earlier and, by the smell of it, Dust Muzzle had been with him. Their scents rose from the earth. *Wait till I tell them where I've been!* Excitement buzzed beneath her pelt. *Wind Runner will have to believe me!* She suddenly felt sure that she could convince her mother she'd spoken to Half Moon. *She may think I'm a featherbrain but she knows I wouldn't lie.* She could hear Micah panting behind her and the heather swishing against their pelts as she led him zigzagging through it.

"Are we nearly there?" he puffed.

"It's not far." She burst out onto open grass and saw the gorse wall of the camp ahead. Circling around it, she led Micah to the entrance.

Above them, stars were beginning to glitter as the sky

darkened. *Is Half Moon up there watching?* Moth Flight's paws prickled. She was determined to prove that the spirit-cats had put their faith in the right cat.

She ducked through the camp entrance, Micah on her tail.

Storm Pelt was sitting among the tussocks, Dew Nose at his side. They leaped to their paws as they saw Moth Flight.

"You're back!" Joy sparked in Storm Pelt's eyes. Then he saw Micah and raised his hackles. "Who's *he*?"

"He's a friend." Moth Flight pulled up in front of the mottled gray tom. "He saved me from a dog two days ago."

Micah stiffened as Dew Nose sniffed him, suspicious, but kept his hackles smooth.

"What's he doing here?" she demanded.

"I'll tell you later." Moth Flight scanned the camp, her heart thumping. *Where's Wind Runner?* Unease fluttered in her belly. Slate was playing with her kits at one edge of the camp while Rocky lay nearby, watching lazily. No one else was in camp.

"Moth Flight! You're back!" Silver Stripe spotted her and came bouncing across the grass. Black Ear chased after his sister excitedly.

Slate looked up from White Tail, who was rolling on his back trying to swipe her mother's tail. "You're safe!" she called happily. "Wind Runner will be relieved."

"Where *is* Wind Runner?" Moth Flight's heart quickened.

Rocky heaved himself slowly to his paws. "She's left with the others."

Dew Nose was still watching Micah warily. "They've gone

to the full-moon Gathering."

"Already?" Moth Flight stared at him, her heart dropping like a stone. "But I wanted to speak to her."

Micah padded to her side, ignoring Dew Nose's curiosity. "When did she leave?"

"Not long ago," Storm Pelt told him.

Dew Nose stalked around her brother and glared at Micah. "We stayed behind to guard the kits."

Silver Stripe raced around Micah and Moth Flight. "You smell funny!" she squeaked.

"Where have you been?" Black Ear stared at her with wide eyes. "You're all dusty!"

Micah looked at the kit, his whiskers twitching with amusement. "We've been to Highstones."

"Highstones!" Slate was crossing the grass toward them, White Tail at her heels. "That's a long way from here."

"I know." Moth Flight suddenly realized how tired her paws were. But she couldn't stop now. "We have to catch up with Wind Runner. I've got something important to tell her."

Slate narrowed her eyes. "Is everything okay?"

Moth Flight met her gaze. "Everything's fine," she promised.

"Why the rush?" Rocky was shambling toward them too. But there wasn't time to talk.

"You'll hear about it later!" Moth Flight turned and headed for the entrance. "I have to catch up with Wind Runner."

"You're not taking him to a Gathering, are you?" Dew Nose called after Moth Flight. Micah was following her.

"Gatherings are for *Clan* cats!"

"He'll be a Clan cat soon!" she called over her shoulder.

She burst out of camp and headed downslope. Opening her mouth, she tasted the air. WindClan scent bathed her tongue, so fresh she struggled to make out which way they'd gone. Micah was already sniffing the ground. He whipped his tail eagerly as he reached a spot of trampled grass a few tail-lengths ahead. "They went this way."

Moth Flight rushed to his side and checked the scents. He was right. Fresh paw-scents coated the tussocks here, and headed toward a wide clump of heather. She followed the trail, nose low, pushing through the bushes onto the grassy slope beyond. It led past the outcrop of rocks she used to hunt on with Dust Muzzle. Wind Runner must be leading her Clan along the old sheep track that went through deep heather and ended at the top of Fourtrees. Checking to see that Micah was still following, Moth Flight broke into a run.

He caught up and fell in step beside her. "Do you think we'll catch her in time?"

"I think so," Moth Flight puffed. "The scents are very fresh."

They slid into single file as heather rose around them and the sheep track meandered among the bushes, finally opening at the top of the hollow.

Moth Flight halted and scanned the ridge. Her belly tightened. She couldn't see Wind Runner or the WindClan cats. But she could smell their scents rising from the hollow. "We're too late," she whispered. "They're down there."

The tops of the oaks loomed in front of them, the huge branches softened by a haze of leaf buds. Moth Flight gazed into the valley and saw pelts moving below.

She shifted her paws. "Let's wait until they've finished the Gathering. Then I can tell Wind Runner about the medicine cats."

Micah looked at her. "All the Clan leaders are going to be down there tonight, right?"

Moth Flight avoided his gaze. She could guess what he was thinking. "You want me to go down there and tell *every cat*."

"They have to know," he reasoned.

"But I wanted to tell Wind Runner first," Moth Flight argued.

"Why?" Micah's green gaze didn't waver.

Moth Flight felt hot. "Because it's easier," she admitted.

"Moth Flight." Micah moved his muzzle closer until she could feel his warm breath billow around her nose. "You can *do* this."

"You want me to walk into the middle of a Gathering and tell all of them that some spirit-cats told me they should have medicine cats?" Fear tightened her belly.

"The spirit-cats believe you can do it." Micah didn't move.

Moth Flight nodded stiffly. "They told me to be strong." She tried to ignore the panic flashing beneath her pelt.

"Then, be strong." Gently, Micah nudged her toward the top of the hollow.

Paws numb with terror, Moth Flight let him steer her into the thick bracken that crowded the slope. Pressing against her, he guided her among the thick stems. Her ears twitched as she heard the murmur of the cats below. *I can't do this!* The bracken rustled around her as they neared the bottom of the slope. She felt sick. "Wait." She paused, desperately trying to think of what she was going to say.

Micah halted beside her and peered through the bracken. She followed his gaze.

"Who's that gray cat?" he whispered.

"That's Clear Sky."

Micah nodded. "I thought so."

"Did he look like that in your dream?"

"Yes." His gaze scanned the gathered cats. "Who are the cats standing beside him?"

Moth Flight narrowed her eyes, trying to tell who was who. Bright moonlight shone through the budding oak branches, turning the pelts of the Clan cats silver. "That's Jagged Peak." She nodded toward the small gray tabby tom who paced beside Clear Sky. "He's Clear Sky's brother but he lives with WindClan now. And Thunder is the big tom next to them."

"Thunder is leader of ThunderClan." Micah was clearly trying to learn as much as he could.

"He's also Clear Sky's son."

Micah stared at her. "They all live in different Clans even though they share the same blood?"

"Clan connections are stronger than blood ties now," Moth Flight told him. She glanced back at the cats milling in the clearing among the trees. Where was Wind Runner? Her gaze flitted from pelt to pelt until she recognized the narrow stripes of her mother. Wind Runner was pacing restlessly between Gorse Fur and Dust Muzzle. Spotted Fur, Fern Leaf, and Willow Tail sat nearby.

The grass on the far side of the clearing swished as River Ripple led his cats into the clearing. Dappled Pelt was with him, and Shattered Ice, Night, and Pine Needle.

River Ripple nodded a polite greeting to the other leaders and settled on an arching root beneath one of the oaks. As his cats gathered around him, Tall Shadow led Pebble Heart, Raven Pelt, Juniper Branch, Mud Paws, and Mouse Ear into the clearing.

"We're all here." Clear Sky's mew rang out loudly in the chilly night air.

Wind Runner crossed the clearing and stopped in front of the SkyClan leader, dipping her head politely first to him, then to Thunder, River Ripple, and Tall Shadow. "What news do you bring?"

"Newleaf has brought fresh prey to our part of the forest," Clear Sky told her.

"And to ours," Thunder added.

River Ripple hopped from the root and joined the other leaders. "The river is still swollen with snowmelt, and the fishing is good."

Moth Flight felt Micah shift beside her. He was watching the Clan cats with wide eyes.

Wind Runner offered her report. "There are rabbits on the moor and the lapwings are beginning to nest. There will be plenty of prey by greenleaf."

A hiss sounded behind her. "There won't be if SkyClan keeps hunting on our land." Willow Tail stalked across the clearing.

Wind Runner looked sharply at her Clanmate.

Clear Sky stiffened. "Are you accusing us of prey-stealing?"

Willow Tail faced the SkyClan leader. "Just *one* of you." Her gaze flashed to the reddish-brown tom sitting behind Clear Sky.

Moth Flight recognized Red Claw. She tensed. Was Willow Tail still determined to start a fight with the SkyClan tom?

Red Claw got to his paws, his tail flicking ominously behind him. He padded toward Willow Tail, showing his teeth. "Why would a forest cat want to steal moor prey? We've got rabbits of our own—fatter than your scrawny vermin."

Willow Tail's hackles lifted. "The only scrawny vermin on our territory lately is *you!*"

Red Claw flattened his ears.

Wind Runner pushed between them. She looked at Clear Sky. "You need to keep your Clan under control."

Clear Sky narrowed his eyes. "It's your cat who's trying to start a battle."

"She is just defending our borders," Wind Runner snapped back. "Besides, it isn't only Willow Tail who's noticed. Slate found rabbit bones just on our side of the SkyClan border. None of my cats enjoyed that meal. Which of *yours* did?" She glared at Red Claw.

Moth Flight's fur prickled nervously. Slate *found evidence*?

Still, one rabbit didn't seem worth fighting about. The Gathering was meant to be a time of peace. The Clans weren't supposed to quarrel here.

Micah shifted beside her. "Are they going to fight?"

"I hope not." Moth Flight watched uneasily as Clear Sky nudged Red Claw aside and glared at Wind Runner.

"Any animal could have killed that rabbit. What other proof do you have my cats are on your territory?" he growled.

"Willow Tail saw Red Claw on the moor a few days ago," Wind Runner hissed.

"Is she telling the truth?" Clear Sky's tail twitched irritably as he turned to the SkyClan tom.

Red Claw lifted his chin. "I was there. I don't need to hide it. I wasn't hunting. Can't we even set paw on another Clan's land now?"

Willow Tail glared at him. "Not when you're a fox-hearted traitor."

"How dare you!" Red Claw's eyes flashed in the half-light. Willow Tail let out a low warning growl.

They mustn't fight! Blood roared in Moth Flight's ears. The spirit-cats wanted her to share her news with the other Clans. How could she if they were at war? "Wait here!" She left Micah and bounded from the bracken.

The cats turned, eyes glittering with surprise as they saw her. She skidded to a halt in the clearing, suddenly conscious that everyone was staring at her.

"Moth Flight?" Wind Runner stared across the dappled clearing, her eyes round with dread. "Is that you?"

Moth Flight blinked at her. "Of course." Why did her mother look so scared?

Wind Runner flattened her ears. "Are you *dead*?" Fear edged her mew.

Moth Flight frowned, struggling to understand. *Dead? Why would I be dead?* She glanced at her paws, noticing how the moonlight was making her white fur glow. Then she realized, shocked. She'd appeared at a Gathering like a spirit-cat! Did Wind Runner think she'd been killed on her journey? Alarm spiked in her belly. "No!" She hurried toward Wind Runner. "I'm alive. I've come home!" She pressed her muzzle against her mother's cheek.

Wind Runner was trembling.

Gorse Fur shouldered his way through the watching cats, his gaze glittering with anger. "Where have you been? We've been worried sick!"

Moth Flight dipped her head apologetically. "I'm sorry," she mewed. "But I had to go. There was something I needed to find."

"What?" Wind Runner lifted her head sharply. Her grief seemed to evaporate.

Moth Flight backed away. Clear Sky was staring at her. River Ripple padded closer, his eyes round with interest.

Tall Shadow tipped her head to one side thoughtfully.

Moth Flight's belly fluttered with fear. She lifted her chin. "I bring news from the spirit-cats," she began.

"Really?" Clear Sky huffed, clearly unconvinced. Tall Shadow rolled her eyes.

Moth Flight glanced toward her Clanmates, hoping to find support.

But Swift Minnow was staring at her accusingly. "Have you been daydreaming again, Moth Flight?"

Jagged Peak exchanged glances with Holly. Spotted Fur blinked at her sympathetically.

They don't believe me. Moth Flight fought the panic rising in her chest.

A low growl sounded in Red Claw's throat. "She's just trying to distract us." He turned his gaze back to Willow Tail. "No cat accuses me of stealing."

Wind Runner hissed. "No cat steals from WindClan."

Frustration surged beneath Moth Flight's pelt. Did they really think their dumb fight was more important than a message from their ancestors? She lashed her tail. "You *have* to listen to me!"

Red Claw flashed her a look. "Did Wind Runner put you up to this, Moth Flight?" He growled. "Is she scared her Clan is going to look like a bunch of liars?"

Wind Runner's hackles lifted. "Clear Sky." She glared at the SkyClan leader. "You seem to make a habit of taking in troublemakers. I thought you'd have learned after One Eye turned on you. But you're still filling your Clan with thieves and bullies."

Clear Sky's blue gaze turned to ice. "My cats are brave and honest."

Star Flower pushed past Blossom and Acorn Fur and stood beside her mate. "Clear Sky is a great leader. He knows his cats and he knows they would never lie!"

Wind Runner curled her lip. "Then why did Slate find rabbit bones at the border?"

Red Claw snorted. "How do we know Slate is telling the truth?"

"Slate is not a liar!" Wind Runner hissed.

"Stop it!" Frustration flared through Moth Flight. "I'm trying to tell you the most important news you'll ever hear. The future of the Clans depends on it!" She stiffened, surprised by her own boldness.

Dust Muzzle blinked at her.

Before any cat could interrupt, she went on. "I *spoke* with the spirit-cats. They told me that each Clan should have a medicine cat to care for their sick. Dappled Pelt will be RiverClan's medicine cat and Pebble Heart will be medicine cat for ShadowClan. I'm to be WindClan's and Cloud Spots will be ThunderClan's." She paused. It wasn't time yet to tell them about Micah. They needed to get used to the idea of medicine cats first. She dug her claws into the ground, bracing herself for the Clans' reactions.

Tall Shadow stepped forward. "Why would the spirit-cats tell *you* this? Why not tell us?" She glanced at Clear Sky and River Ripple. "We're the Clan *leaders*."

"They said that they would speak through me from now on," Moth Flight told her.

Clear Sky spluttered. "*You*? You're hardly more than a kit!"

Moth Flight tried to ignore him, but her paws began to tremble. "They said they will send omens, and that I must tell Wind Runner what the omens mean." She noticed Dappled Pelt staring at her, eyes bright with starlight. "I guess each medicine cat will see omens and interpret them for their leader." That was what Half Moon had meant, surely?

Wind Runner padded closer, her pelt rippling along her spine. "Moth Flight?" Her mew was gentle. "I know you think you're doing the right thing. But is this just another one of your dreams?"

"It's *real!*" Moth Flight dug her claws harder into the cold earth. "I followed a tunnel into Highstones and I found a stone filled with moonlight and I saw the spirit-cats." She knew she must sound crazy and she saw some of the Clan cat's eyes soften into pity as she went on. *I knew it! They don't believe me.*

Clear Sky sniffed. "You forgot to tell us who SkyClan's medicine cat would be."

Moth Flight stared at him uncertainly, words frozen on her tongue. Was he taking her seriously?

"The spirit-cats told you so much," Blossom yowled mockingly. "Did they forget to mention *us*?"

"She's making it up!" Mud Paws accused.

"She just wants attention." A ShadowClan tortoiseshell padded forward.

Pebble Heart nosed past her. "Give her a chance, Juniper Branch!" He gazed softly at Moth Flight. "Do you know who SkyClan's medicine cat will be?"

Moth Flight glanced over her shoulder toward the bracken where Micah was hiding among the shadow stems. How would these cats react when she told them the spirit-cats had named a stranger?

The bracken rustled and Micah pushed his way out. "They said that I would be SkyClan's medicine cat," he said.

Shocked mews rose among the Clan cats.

"Who's he?"

"He's not one of us!"

"Who said he could come here?"

"This is Micah." Moth Flight pressed her flank against Micah's as he stopped beside her. "He saved me from a dog and came with me on my journey to Highstones."

River Ripple narrowed his eyes. "Did he see the spirit-cats too?"

Moth Flight shook her head. "The moth led *me* to the cave, not him."

Wind Runner had stiffened. "Is this the moth you're always dreaming about?"

"Yes." Moth Flight watched the cats exchange glances. Thunder stared at Micah through slitted eyes. Clear Sky's pelt rippled uneasily along his spine. Tall Shadow was watching, her ears twitching. Helplessness swept over Moth Flight. How could she convince them? Only River Ripple looked calm. "I didn't *dream it*!" she mewed desperately. "It was *real*."

"I saw the moth." Micah lifted his chin.

"You might just be saying that so you can be our medicine cat," Clear Sky growled.

"The moth was real. It led us to Highstones." He met Clear Sky's gaze steadily. "I want to be your medicine cat, but I wouldn't lie to you."

"What do you know about healing?" Clear Sky demanded.

"Nothing, yet," Micah told him calmly. "But I will learn."

"We'll all learn!" Moth Flight added. "There are cats who already know healing herbs. If we can learn some, we can learn *more*! The Clans will depend on their medicine cats one day. Half Moon told me!"

"*Half Moon?*" Clear Sky stiffened.

Tall Shadow stepped closer.

Dappled Pelt blinked. "You spoke with *Stoneteller?*"

Quick Water hurried to Clear Sky's side. "She must have seen Stoneteller," the old mountain cat whispered. "How else would she know her name?"

Clear Sky was still staring at Micah. "She probably heard Jagged Peak or Gray Wing talking about her."

Moth Flight heart's leaped. They knew who Half Moon was! Were they going to believe her after all?

Dappled Pelt's eyes shone with excitement. "My dreams must have been a sign!"

River Ripple looked at his Clanmate. "What dreams?"

"I've been dreaming about teaching cats about herbs and healing for the past moon," Dappled Pelt told him. Her gaze flitted to Micah. "I think one of the cats in my dream might have been *him*."

"Why didn't you say anything?" River Ripple asked quietly.

"I thought they were just ordinary dreams," Dappled Pelt answered.

Clear Sky padded toward Micah, opening his mouth to taste his scent. "You smell strange."

"I smell like the farm I was raised on." Micah stood still while Clear Sky circled him.

Cloud Spots nosed his way to the front. "I've had a dream too," he admitted. "I saw the moonlit stone." He looked at Moth Flight. "Was it in a cave?"

Moth Flight nodded, swallowing back excitement. "Inside Highstones."

"And there was a hole in the roof?"

"You've *seen* it?" Moth Flight could hardly keep her paws still.

"I dreamed I was there with you, Dappled Pelt, and Pebble Heart." Cloud Spots nodded toward Micah. "And him."

Tall Shadow turned to Pebble Heart. "Have you had any dreams?"

"Only last night." His eyes glowed like stars. "I dreamed Turtle Tail was leaning over me. She said she always knew I was special."

Moth Flight's tail quivered. "And she told you to take care of them all, didn't she?"

"Yes!" Pebble Heart blinked. "That's exactly what she said!"

Juniper Branch looked at Tall Shadow. "Are we actually going to believe this hare-brained WindClan cat?"

Gorse Fur flicked his tail angrily. "She's not hare-brained."

"So why does Spotted Fur always joke that one day she'll find the end of a rainbow and try to climb up it?" Juniper Branch scoffed.

"I was *joking*!" Spotted Fur caught Moth Flight's eye apologetically.

Fern Leaf brushed past him and stared at Moth Flight.

"What if you're wrong about this, Moth Flight? You might have misunderstood the spirit-cats' message. You can't even tell the difference between plants and prey."

Wind Runner faced the gray-and-white she-cat. "She can tell the difference. Perhaps she brings home plants because that's what medicine cats do."

Moth Flight felt a rush of gratitude. She glanced at Micah. "I think they're going to believe me," she whispered.

Clear Sky's tail was still twitching impatiently. "So Sky-Clan is going to be stuck with an extra mouth to feed." He glared at Micah resentfully.

"I can hunt," Micah told him.

"Won't you be too busy looking after sick cats?" Clear Sky sneered.

Star Flower stood beside her mate. "Perhaps we should wait for the spirit-cats to tell us themselves before we start making any changes."

Juniper Branch and Swift Minnow murmured in agreement.

"The spirit-cats have spoken to us before," Tall Shadow reasoned. "If they're not speaking to us now, it's because they have nothing to say."

"But they *do!*" Alarm buzzed beneath Moth Flight's pelt. *You have to listen to me!* What more could she say? She suddenly remembered Half Moon's parting words. *We will split the sky. And later, stars will rise.* The spirit-cats had promised to send a sign when she told the Clans.

Where was it? She stared up through the branches to the stars beyond.

"What are you looking for?" Clear Sky asked her, his mew thick with scorn. "Do you think you can call them whenever you want?"

Moth Flight blinked at him. "They promised to split the sky when I told you."

Clear Sky's whiskers twitched with amusement. Purrs echoed around the clearing.

"Split the sky?" Juniper Branch shook her head. "What nonsense!"

Moth Flight squared her shoulders. "They said they'd split the sky and later stars would rise."

Clear Sky sat down. "Okay." He looked up. "Let's wait."

Silence gripped the clearing. Above, the sky stretched cloudless and black.

Moth Flight's pelt burned with shame. *Perhaps I dreamed it after all! I've thought dreams were real before. Perhaps I've been wrong all along!*

She could feel the eyes of the Clan cats on her. "What have I done?" she whispered to Micah. "I'm such a rabbit-brain!" She shrank beneath her pelt.

Suddenly, a flash lit the clearing. A bolt of lightning cracked the sky and, for a moment, the Clans were drenched in blinding white light.

Terror ripped through Moth Flight. She dropped to the earth.

On the far side of the hollow a tree exploded into flame as the lightning hit it. It shuddered and split. One half fell, blazing, to the ground.

Moth Flight stared in amazement. *They did it! They split the sky!* Her heart leaped into her throat. *They have to believe me now.* She glanced around the clearing.

The Clan cats gaped at the flaming tree. Then, one by one, they turned toward Moth Flight.

CHAPTER 15

The roar of the flames died away as the fire burned itself out. Moth Flight felt Micah shift beside her. The Clan cats stared at her in silence.

She froze, her breath catching in her throat, when River Ripple padded forward and dipped his head low. "Moth Flight, you were brave to speak up. Come with me." He headed for the huge stone that rose from the soil as though it had been growing for countless moons from the heart of the earth.

Moth Flight glanced nervously at Micah as River Ripple leaped onto the great rock.

"Go on." He nudged her forward with a flick of his muzzle. "You've done the hardest part."

Self-consciously, Moth Flight padded into the shadow of the rock and scrabbled onto a ledge, then leaped into the moonlight. She landed beside River Ripple, who was gazing at the Clan cats below.

She peered over the edge. What a long way down! Her Clanmates seemed suddenly small. Moth Flight glanced at the sky. A thick band of stars stretched like a silver pelt across the indigo blackness. Was that where the spirit-cats lived? A star Clan? She remembered their star-flecked pelts, glittering in the darkness of the cave. How small the Clans must look to the spirit-cats. They were so powerful they could command lightning! And yet they cared about these cats, enough to watch over them and guide them.

"There can be no disagreement now." River Ripple's mew jerked her back into the moment. The Clan cats were watching her expectantly.

Thunder lifted his tail, his orange pelt pale in the moonlight. "The spirit-cats have spoken. Each Clan will have a medicine cat."

Quick Water called from among the SkyClan cats. "If we'd had medicine cats earlier, the sickness might not have taken so many."

Moth Flight shook her head. "We don't know any more now than we did then," she pointed out. "We can't change the past. But we can change the future. Somehow we must discover new herbs and new cures."

"How?" Pebble Heart looked up at her. "It will take moons to test out every plant."

"Yes," Moth Flight agreed. "In the meantime, we can learn from each other. Each Clan has cats who know a little about healing."

Swift Minnow lifted her muzzle. "Reed Tail knows plenty." She glanced proudly at her mate.

The silver tabby dipped his head modestly. "I am happy to share the little I know with Moth Flight."

"And I'll share whatever you teach me with the other

medicine cats." Moth Flight nodded to Pebble Heart. "Will you learn all you can from the cats in ShadowClan?"

Pebble Heart nodded.

Cloud Spots whisked his tail. "I will gather all the knowledge in ThunderClan."

"The medicine cats are to meet at Highstones every half-moon," Moth Flight told them.

Dappled Pelt blinked. "That's a long way to travel!"

Moth Flight met her wide-eyed gaze. "Once you have seen the moonlit stone for real, you'll be glad you made the journey." She suddenly realized that she was addressing the Clan like a leader. She backed away from the edge, butterflies rising in her belly once more.

"Don't be afraid," River Ripple whispered in her ear. "The spirit-cats chose you. This is your destiny."

She stared at the mysterious RiverClan leader, wondering if the star Clan ever shared with him. He seemed so wise.

An angry mew rang in the clearing.

Moth Flight stiffened as Clear Sky glared up at her. "You talk as though everything has been decided." He fluffed out his pelt. "We shouldn't have to take medicine cats who have been chosen for us! We should decide our Clan's future for ourselves!"

Moth Flight forced herself to meet his gaze. "We can't ignore the spirit-cats."

"You must have misinterpreted what they told you!" Clear Sky was eyeing Micah. "Why would they choose a stranger for SkyClan?"

"Are you saying she's a liar?" Wind Runner turned on Clear Sky, hackles up.

Clear Sky held his ground. "I'm just saying she might be mistaken."

"If she were mistaken, would the spirit-cats have sent a sign?" Wind Runner snapped. "Micah is your medicine cat! Stop complaining!"

Clear Sky's gaze flashed with fury. "That's easy for you to say. You don't have to take in a rogue."

Wind Runner's tail twitched irritably. "You've taken in plenty of rogues before, Clear Sky. You just don't like being told what to do."

Clear Sky glared at the WindClan leader. "Neither do you."

"At least if I'm wrong, I'll admit it," Wind Runner flashed back.

"I'm never wrong!" Clear Sky's ears twitched.

Moth Flight felt a sudden rush of pity for Micah. What if Clear Sky *did* agree to take him? The SkyClan leader had never let any cat tell him what to do. The spirit-cats wanted the medicine cats to advise their leaders. How could Micah advise Clear Sky if he wouldn't listen? She glanced at Micah, who watched silently, moonlight silvering his pelt. His gaze seemed so sure and steady. *He'll find a way.*

She stepped to the front of the great rock once more. "Micah may be a stranger to the Clans, but he shares a bond with us. He always has."

Clear Sky lifted his muzzle to stare at her. "What?"

Mews of surprise rippled around the cats. Micah stiffened

as they stared at him, their gazes sharp with curiosity.

"Tell them, Micah," Moth Flight encouraged.

Micah's tail quivered. "I've dreamed of you." He nodded toward Clear Sky. "I dreamed I was bringing you catmint to treat a sick kit."

Star Flower pricked her ears. "What's catmint?"

"It's an herb that grows on the farm," Micah told her. "We use it to treat coughs."

Star Flower turned to Clear Sky, her purple gaze glittering. "He could help Tiny Branch!"

Clear Sky's fur lifted along his spine. He looked uneasily from Star Flower to Micah. "Can you get some of this catmint?"

"Of course." Micah tipped his head to one side. "Who is Tiny Branch?"

Clear Sky narrowed his eyes. "He's my kit."

Micah lifted his tail. Moth Flight could see he was excited. He was clearly keen to start work.

River Ripple moved beside Moth Flight. "Are we all agreed?" he called to the cats below. His gaze fixed on Clear Sky.

Clear Sky hesitated. "Are you sure this catmint will help?" he asked Micah.

"It helped me when I was a kit."

"We have to try it!" Star Flower urged.

"Okay." Clear Sky dipped his head. "If you can heal Tiny Branch, you can stay with SkyClan."

Tall Shadow lifted her muzzle. "From now on, Pebble

Heart will be ShadowClan's medicine cat."

"And Cloud Spots will be ThunderClan's," Thunder agreed.

"Dappled Pelt will be medicine cat for RiverClan." River Ripple sat down and tucked his tail over his paws.

Moth Flight looked toward Wind Runner. She met her mother's gaze, surprised at its warmth.

"Moth Flight will be medicine cat for WindClan."

Her heart swelled with pride and joy as her mother spoke. Quickly, she slithered down the side of the rock and leaped to the ground. She hurried toward Wind Runner. "I'm sorry I scared you," she blurted as she reached her.

Wind Runner touched her nose gently to Moth Flight's cheek. "I understand now why you went." She pulled back, meeting Moth Flight's gaze. "I'm sorry I was so hard on you. Gorse Fur was right. You *are* special. I've been rabbit-brained not to see it."

Gorse Fur reached them, Dust Muzzle at his heels. "I'm so proud of you!" His eyes shone as he looked at Moth Flight.

She purred loudly, hesitating as memories of Emberkit and Morning Whisker flashed in her thoughts. "I saw my littermates," she told Wind Runner. "They were with the spirit-cats and they spoke to me."

Wind Runner's eyes glistened with emotion. "Are they okay?" Her mew caught in her throat.

"They are still kits," Moth Flight told her. "But they look well and happy, and they have grown wise."

Wind Runner jerked her muzzle toward Gorse Fur. "They

are happy." The words were no more than a breath but they were filled with joy.

Gorse Fur pressed his cheek against his mate's. "They will always be safe," he murmured.

The ShadowClan cats were starting to climb the slope toward the pine forest. Thunder was leading his cats away through the trees.

"We should go too." Wind Runner signaled to her cats with a flick of her tail and began to head for the moor.

Clear Sky and Star Flower led SkyClan into the brambles as RiverClan disappeared into the long grass that reached toward the reed beds.

Dust Muzzle nudged Moth Flight's shoulder. "Are you coming?"

Moth Flight scanned the empty clearing, relieved to see Micah hanging back at the bottom of the slope. "I'll catch up with you," she told Dust Muzzle.

Her brother glanced quizzically at Micah, then headed after their Clan.

Moth Flight hurried toward Micah. "We did it!" she mewed excitedly.

Sadness clouded his gaze.

"What's wrong?" Wasn't he happy that they'd convinced the Clans?

"I'm going to miss you," he mewed softly.

Her heart quickened. She'd forgotten! He was going to live in SkyClan's camp. They'd only been together a few days, yet leaving without him seemed strange. "I'll miss you too."

He leaned forward and touched his muzzle to hers. "I'll see you at half-moon."

"We can travel to the Moonstone together," Moth Flight murmured.

Eyes flashed from the top of the slope. "Micah! Hurry up!" Clear Sky's mew rang around the hollow.

"I'd better go." Micah headed for the undergrowth. "I don't want to start off on the wrong paw."

Moth Flight watched him disappear. The pricking sadness in her heart was suddenly swept away by excitement. She'd changed the future of the Clans! Nothing would ever be the same again. She glanced up at the sky, wondering if Half Moon was proud of her.

Green wings flitted in the moonlight overhead.

The moth!

It fluttered toward her, dancing closer until it settled on her muzzle. Her whiskers twitched as it tickled her nose. Her breath stirred its wings, then the moth swooped away, circling higher and higher until it was lost among the oak branches.

Had it come to say good-bye?

Thank you! Moth Flight heard the bracken rustle at the top of the slope. Her Clan was heading onto the moor. She hurried after them, pushing through the stiff stems. Her life was going to be different now. Her heart quickened. *Half Moon,* she whispered into the chilly night air. *Help me be strong enough to fulfill my destiny.*

CHAPTER 16

❧

"Moth Flight, look at me!"

Silver Stripe's mew sounded behind her. Shaking leaf crumbs from her paws, Moth Flight turned impatiently to watch the pale gray she-kit.

Silver Stripe was wedged into the prickly gorse halfway up the wall of her den. Black Ear was tugging at his sister's tail, while White Tail was trying to climb up beside her.

"Please, get down!" Moth Flight marched across the freshly dug floor of her den and snatched Silver Stripe's scruff in her teeth.

It was Wind Runner who had suggested hollowing out a den especially for Moth Flight. Storm Pelt, Reed Tail, Fern Leaf, Holly, and Dew Nose had spent days digging out a dip beneath the stems and tearing away branches to shape a cave in the heart of the thickest part of the gorse wall. The floor was wide enough for three nests. One for herself, and two for any sick cats who might need to be watched. The branches would make a great place to store the plants she collected. She could slot her herbs among the spiny stems and keep them sheltered from the weather.

Moth Flight dropped the kit on the ground. "If you want to climb, go outside."

Silver Stripe blinked at her. "But Slate told us to stay with you."

Moth Flight glanced back at the piles of leaves she'd collected. She was hoping to sort them and store them among the gorse stems at the back of her den before sunhigh.

Black Ear followed her gaze and hurried toward the piles. He began sniffing them, sneezing as he reached a pungent heap and scattering leaves across the floor of the den. "Sorry!"

Moth Flight swallowed back frustration. *I have to tell Slate that she needs to find another cat to watch her kits now that I'm a medicine cat.* Moth Flight loved the kits, but she had new responsibilities now.

In the days since the full-moon Gathering, she'd gradually become used to the strange new way her Clanmates treated her. When she disappeared into thought, Swift Minnow no longer teased her. When she brought plants back to camp, Wind Runner was the first to ask her if she'd found something interesting. Jagged Peak nodded a respectful greeting whenever she passed him. Only Slate didn't seem to have noticed the change, still lost in her grief for Gray Wing.

The entrance rustled as Reed Tail poked his head in. "Do you need any help?"

"Can you look after these three?" Moth Flight grabbed Black Ear's tail and hauled him away from the herbs.

"Swift Minnow's just back from hunting," Reed Tail told her. "I'll see if she can watch them."

White Tail frowned. "But we want to stay in Moth Flight's cave!"

"Kits need fresh air and sunshine." Reed Tail slid into the den and nosed the gray-and-white tom-kit toward the entrance.

"Wait!" Black Ear was sniffing the herb piles again. "What's this?" He wrinkled his nose at a lush green leaf.

Moth Flight's ears twitched. "Horsetail." *I think.* She was having trouble remembering all the names.

Silver Stripe pushed past her brother and sniffed it. "What's it for?"

Moth Flight frowned. "It cures twisted tails," she guessed.

Reed Tail blinked at her sympathetically. "It's chervil and it's good for bellyache." He padded past Silver Stripe and hooked a leaf with his claw. "But the root is better than the leaves. They aren't really strong enough."

Moth Flight's pelt grew hot. "Of course!" She remembered now. Reed Tail had told her yesterday when he'd taken her out collecting herbs. Why couldn't she remember the simplest things?

White Tail stared at her with wide eyes. "I thought you were our medicine cat?"

"Maybe Reed Tail should be the medicine cat," Silver Stripe suggested.

Moth Flight shifted her paws uneasily. Perhaps the kit was right. How was she ever going to learn everything she'd need to know? She wondered for a moment if the spirit-cats had made a mistake choosing her. *I'm too featherbrained.*

Reed Tail shooed White Tail toward the entrance and nudged Silver Stripe and Black Ear after them. "Go and find Swift Minnow. Tell her I sent you."

"It's not fair," Silver Stripe complained.

"We were only helping," added Black Ear.

As the kits disappeared, grumbling, from the cave, Moth Flight looked gratefully at Reed Tail. "You know so much more than me about herbs and healing. Perhaps they're right. Perhaps you should be WindClan's medicine cat."

Reed Tail gazed at her fondly. "The spirit-cats chose you for a reason. I think they wanted someone who could do more than remember herbs."

"Like what?" Moth Flight felt lost. She was up to her ears in plants and names and had no idea how she'd ever know the right herb in an emergency. What if a Clanmate died because she couldn't remember? Panic sparked in her paws.

"You've only just begun," Reed Tail told her softly.

Outside, Holly's yowl rang across the clearing. "Where do you three think you're going?"

"The kits!" Reed Tail headed for the entrance. "They're probably trying to sneak out of camp again." The gorse swished as he squeezed out of the den.

Moth Flight looked back at her herb piles, and began pushing the scattered leaves back together.

A cough sounded outside.

Rocky.

The old tom had been coughing for a few days. Moth Flight glanced at the empty nest at the side of the den, freshly woven from heather by Storm Pelt and Eagle Feather. It would be cozier than Rocky's nest in the long grass. Even though new-leaf was warming the moor, the nights were still chilly and the wind relentless. Perhaps a few nights' sleep in the shelter of her den was all Rocky needed to recover. She hoped so; the tansy she'd given him last night clearly hadn't worked and she didn't know any other herb that might cure him.

"Rocky!" Moth Flight slid out of her den and crossed the clearing.

Rocky was weaving slowly among the tussocks, heading for the prey pile. He paused as she stopped beside him.

"How are you feeling?"

"Not bad. I thought I might feel better if I had something to eat—" Rocky broke off, coughing. His shaggy shoulders heaved with the effort. Struggling to catch his breath, he looked at her, his gaze clouded with exhaustion.

Moth Flight pushed away worry. She must focus on *curing* Rocky; fretting wouldn't help. Her thoughts quickened. He'd been heading for food. *A hungry cat is a healthy cat.* Her mother used to say that when she returned home with prey for Moth Flight and Dust Muzzle. "Are you hungry?"

"Not really." Rocky shrugged. "I just thought a small bite of shrew might help." He gazed at her bleakly.

"I think you'd better move into my den," Moth Flight mewed briskly. "There's a nice, clean nest for you and it'll be warm." *And I can keep an eye on you.* His lack of appetite worried her. *Perhaps I need to give him more tansy.* She wished Dappled Pelt were here. Or Pebble Heart. They might know what to do.

I bet even Micah knows more than me. As she steered Rocky gently toward her den, she thought of the yellow tom. Her pelt prickled with warmth. She'd be seeing him before long, at the half-moon gathering at Highstones. She paused and waited for Rocky to squeeze into her den. Following, she pointed her muzzle to the heather nest. "Rest there while I fetch you more tansy."

As Rocky climbed in and began to knead the heather, Moth Flight turned toward her herbs. *Perhaps I gave him the wrong one.* She sniffed at the curly green leaves she'd shredded for him last night. It was definitely tansy. She felt sure. She grabbed a bunch between her jaws and crossed the den. Dropping it on the edge of Rocky's nest, she leaned close and felt heat pulsing from his pelt. *He has a fever.* "Eat these." She pushed the tansy closer and headed back to her herbs. Frustration tightened her belly. She *knew* there must be something here to help his fever, but what?

Rocky lapped at the leaves, swallowing, then coughing harder than ever.

Moth Flight stared at him anxiously. The tansy wasn't helping!

Catmint. The name flashed in her mind. Micah had mentioned it! He'd said it would help Tiny Branch's cough! *It looks a bit like nettles but the leaves are smaller and they don't sting. You'll know if you ever see some. It smells great.* He'd said it grew by the Twoleg barn. Rocky began to wheeze. The farm was too far to travel. She needed to find some quickly. Would there be any around the Twoleg nests beyond the forest?

"Try to rest," she told Rocky. "I'm going to hunt for herbs." She watched the old tom settle stiffly into his nest. His pelt was clumped and his gaze dull. *I wish I knew how to make him feel better.* "Shall I fetch you something from the prey pile before I go?"

Rocky grunted. "I don't think I can swallow."

"Is your throat sore?"

"Like I swallowed hot nettles." Rocky laid his muzzle on the edge of his nest and shook as he fought back a cough.

"I won't be long!" Moth Flight raced from her den. She'd be lucky if she made it to Twolegplace before sunhigh. She bounded over the tussocky clearing.

"Moth Flight!" Dust Muzzle called from rocks near the entrance. He was chewing on a vole. Spotted Fur lay beside him, washing his face.

She slewed to a halt. "What?"

"Where are you going?" Dust Muzzle padded toward her.

"I need to find catmint."

"For Rocky?" Dust Muzzle looked toward her den. "I saw you take him to your den."

"It will help his cough," Moth Flight explained.

Spotted Fur crossed the grass toward them. "Where are you going to look?"

"Twolegplace," Moth Flight told him.

An excited squeak sounded from behind the rocks and Black Ear scrambled onto the highest stone. "Can we come?"

Moth Flight blinked at him. "No! It's too far."

"But I'm bored," the kit complained.

Reed Tail stuck his head up from behind the rocks and nudged the kit with his muzzle. "I'll take you out on the moor when Slate wakes up," he promised.

Moth Flight blinked at him. "Was Swift Minnow busy?"

"She was tired from hunting," Reed Tail told her. "She said a tom was as good as a—"

Black Ear interrupted. "Perhaps Slate will come with us!"

"No way. She's always too tired." Silver Stripe scrambled up beside her brother. "Can we hunt on the moor?"

"Teach us some hunting moves!" White Tail leaped onto the rock. "I want to catch a rabbit."

"They're bigger than you!" Reed Tail teased.

"Reed Tail!" Holly called from the prey pile. "There are three fat mice here. Do you know any cat who might want one?"

"Me!" Silver Stripe leaped from the rock and began scrambling over the tussocks.

"I want the fattest one!" Black Ear chased after his sister.

"You *are* the fattest one!" White Tail hared after them.

Reed Tail glanced at Moth Flight. "I hope Slate says it's okay to take them out of camp. They have more energy than a nest of squirrels."

Moth Flight watched him trudge after the kits, grateful that he'd taken them off her paws. She turned back to Spotted Fur. The tom's amber gaze clouded with worry.

"Twolegplace is a long way. You'll have to cross Clear Sky's forest."

"I'll be okay," Moth Flight reassured him. "Clear Sky doesn't mind cats crossing his borders anymore. Besides, I'm a medicine cat now. I'm only hunting for herbs."

Dust Muzzle frowned. "What if you run into rogues in Twolegplace?"

"And there are Thunderpaths," Spotted Fur added anxiously.

"We'd better come with you." Dust Muzzle shook out his pelt.

Moth Flight blinked at him. "Aren't you supposed to be hunting today?"

Spotted Fur paced around her. "We can hunt on the way back."

Moth Flight wondered if she'd travel faster alone, but it made sense to take help. When she reached Twolegplace, she'd have to sniff out catmint, and three noses would be better than one. "Okay!" She whisked her tail. "Thanks." Heading for the entrance, she broke into a run.

As she burst out of camp, relishing the fresh breeze that streamed through her whiskers, heather scent filled her nose. Happiness surged beneath Moth Flight's pelt as she raced downslope. She would find catmint and cure Rocky! She pushed harder against the grass. Paw steps thumped behind her as Spotted Fur and Dust Muzzle caught up.

"Slow down!" Dust Muzzle called. "You can't run all the way!"

"We'll have to walk in the forest." Moth Flight kept her gaze fixed ahead. The roots and brambles under the trees would slow them down. They might as well make good time here, where they knew the terrain well. She ducked into a swath of heather, heading down a rabbit trail she'd followed countless times before.

Racing out the other side of the heather, she headed for the forest, Dust Muzzle and Spotted Fur following her.

They crossed the border gingerly, exchanging glances. The whole Clan told tales of the days when Clear Sky had challenged any cat he'd found in his forest. *We'll be fine.* Moth Flight lifted her chin. Since the great battle, cats had crossed each other's territory freely, but it was understood that no cat would hunt on another cat's land. *We're not hunting.* As the trees blocked the sun's warmth, she shivered. What if a SkyClan cat challenged them the same way Willow Tail had challenged Red Claw about his "theft"? She pushed the thought away. Rocky needed catmint.

Dust Muzzle was staring between the towering trunks, eyes wide as he adjusted to the gloom. "SkyClan cats must have eyes like owls."

Birdsong echoed eerily from the tree trunks, closed in by the canopy of branches. Sunshine filtered through the bright new leaves and dappled the forest floor. Brambles spilled from between the trees, and ferns unfurled in wide clumps.

Moth Flight tasted the air. The musty flavor of old leaves and damp wood bathed her tongue. "Don't SkyClan and ThunderClan miss the sunshine?" she whispered.

"They must." Spotted Fur fluffed out his pelt. "It's weird not hearing the wind."

Moth Flight realized that the pressing hum in her ears was the sound of stillness. High overhead the leaves swished, but down here, among the roots, no breeze stirred.

"This way." Dust Muzzle padded forward, heading up a rise where the forest sloped toward a small clearing and sunlight broke through the canopy.

Tiny paws scuttled across the leaves to one side. Spotted Fur jerked his head around.

"Ignore it," Dust Muzzle warned. "We can catch bigger prey when we're back on the moor."

Spotted Fur huffed and followed Dust Muzzle as he jumped over a fallen log. Moth Flight scrambled behind them, yelping as a bramble snagged her paw.

Dust Muzzle glanced back. "Are you okay?"

"Yes." Moth Flight tugged herself free, wincing. "How do they hunt here?"

Spotted Fur shrugged. "Perhaps they wait for their prey to trip."

At the top of the rise, Moth Flight relished the warmth of the sun for a moment before shadow swallowed it again. "Do you know which way to go?" she called to Dust Muzzle, who had pulled into the lead. He was following a trail smoothed by rabbit tracks, by the smell of them.

"I'm trying to find the Thunderpath," he answered.

Spotted Fur fell in beside her. "It runs between SkyClan and ShadowClan territory."

Dust Muzzle glanced over his shoulder. "And it leads straight to Twolegplace."

Moth Flight shuddered. "I don't want to follow a Thunderpath. It stinks."

"Do you want to get lost among these trees?" Dust Muzzle argued.

"Can't we just head away from the sun?" Moth Flight reasoned.

"We could if we could see it." Dust Muzzle veered from the trail as brambles cut across it.

Spotted Fur paused. "Is that a gap in the trees over there?" He pointed his nose toward a lighter stretch of forest.

Dust Muzzle headed toward it.

Moth Flight padded beside Spotted Fur, her nose twitching as the sour scent of monsters touched it. She could see light spilling between the trunks. They cleared another log, leaped a ditch, and climbed another rise. Ahead, the trees opened onto a wide gap that cut through the forest like a claw mark. Black stone lined the gash, stinking of Twoleg stench and, on the far side, the trees turned from oak to pine.

Moth Flight felt dizzy from the scents washing over her. The sharp tang of pinesap and monsters made her queasy. "Let's stay in the trees," she begged.

"It'll be easier to walk along the verge." Dust Muzzle headed out onto the grass.

Spotted Fur followed. "It's sunny here."

Moth Flight peered at the black stone as a monster howled past. Dust Muzzle hardly flinched. Spotted Fur only narrowed his eyes against the stinking wind that billowed in its wake.

Moth Flight ducked back among the trees. She could still remember Gorse Fur's close brush with death. "I'm staying here."

"Walk where I can see you!" Dust Muzzle trekked along the grass verge, keeping pace with her as she pushed through a clump of bracken.

"I'll keep an eye on her." Spotted Fur bounded into the forest and fell in beside Moth Flight.

"You can walk with Dust Muzzle," she told him. "I'm okay by myself."

"I'd rather walk with you."

She ignored the meaningful glance he gave her and wondered if Micah was nearby. Had the farm cat explored this part of the forest yet, or had Clear Sky been keeping him busy in camp?

She opened her mouth, tasting the air for a trace of his scent. But the stench of the Thunderpath drowned out any other smell. Tail drooping, she padded on, scanning the trees ahead for some sign of Twoleg nests beyond.

The forest grew warm as the sun climbed higher, until Dust Muzzle called from the verge. "I can see Twolegplace!"

Moth Flight's heart lifted. "Is it far?"

"No!"

She quickened her pace, Spotted Fur breaking into a trot beside her. Picking her way past a bramble patch, she scanned the trees ahead. Sharp-cornered walls showed behind the trunks.

She broke into a run as she reached the edge of the woods. Dust Muzzle left the verge and hurried to catch up with her as she zigzagged through the undergrowth until she reached a sheer wooden wall. She stopped at the bottom, judging the height. Taking a breath, she leaped. She hooked her claws into the rough wood and scrambled like a squirrel to the top. Balancing on the narrow ridge, she gazed across the jumble of Twoleg nests and patches of grass, crisscrossed by a maze of wooden walls. The ridge wobbled as Dust Muzzle and Spotted Fur jumped up beside her.

"We should split up," Moth Flight told them.

Dust Muzzle narrowed his eyes as he scanned the nests. "We don't know what we're looking for."

"Micah says catmint looks like nettles," Moth Flight told him. "Its leaves are smaller and don't sting. He said that it smells so great, you'll *know* if you find it."

Spotted Fur's pelt ruffled. "Does Micah know *every* herb?" There was an edge in his mew.

"Just catmint." Moth Flight gazed down into the grassy clearing below. Unusual plants crowded the edge. She opened her mouth and let their scent touch her tongue. Nothing smelled *great*. She nodded toward the wooden walls farther along. "You search there, I'll head the other way," she told Dust Muzzle.

"I'm sticking with you," Spotted Fur told her.

Moth Flight dug her claws into the ridge. "We'll find it quicker if we split up." Spotted Fur was nice but she didn't want him breathing on her tail everywhere she went.

Dust Muzzle whisked his tail, wobbling as he turned on the wall. "Call if you need help," he told her, picking his way along it. "We won't be far away."

Spotted Fur caught Moth Flight's eye. "Are you sure you don't want me to go with you?" he asked hopefully.

"Dust Muzzle will need help searching for herbs. He's used to hunting rabbits." Moth Flight turned her tail on him and headed in the opposite direction.

The wall trembled beneath her and she had to concentrate to keep her balance. In the next clearing between the walls she saw huge white-plumed grasses towering around a patch of grass. The clearing beyond was covered with stone. She sniffed the air as she reached the next one, relieved to see countless plants crammed between the wooden walls. Excited, she jumped down among them and began snuffling through the leaves.

Like nettles. Micah's words rang in her mind. If only she'd met him in the woods; he could have helped her find it. She paused. A wonderful scent was filling her nose. She blinked, gazing around.

There! A leafy plant, just like Micah had described, was crammed between a flowering shrub and a spiky grass. She hurried toward it, her pelt pricking as its scent reached inside her. Excitement flared in her belly. She stopped beside it and plunged her muzzle deep into the plant, dizzy as she breathed in the mouthwatering smell. It was just like Micah had said. *You'll know it when you find it!*

She grabbed a clump of stems between her teeth and ripped them away from the plant. Laying them at her paws, she grabbed another mouthful, tearing away as much as she could. Delighted, she patted the broken stems into a tight bunch and bent to pick them up. *Thanks, Micah.*

She paused, remembering their journey to Highstones.

It was still so vivid in her mind: the sun setting behind the stones; the meal Micah had caught for her before she'd gone into the tunnel. She'd been so nervous, and he'd been so reassuring. That had been the best night of her life. She suddenly tasted the scent of damp stone and imagined the spirit-cats shimmering into view around her. Joy warmed her belly as she pictured how kindly they'd greeted her. *You're special—*

A loud yelp broke into her thoughts. She jerked her muzzle around. A Twoleg burst from its nest and raced toward her. It was barking like an angry dog.

Moth Flight's heart seemed to burst. Blind with panic, she snatched up the catmint between her jaws and hared for the wooden wall. Twoleg paws grabbed for her, their clammy flesh pulling her fur as she twisted free. A growl rumbling in her throat, she leaped up the wall and clung to the top. The Twoleg was yowling in rage, its red face only a tail-length away.

Fighting terror, Moth Flight leaped along the wooden ridge, her claws stretched as it wobbled beneath her. In a moment, she was beyond the Twoleg's reach. Another wall blocked its way, and it was clearly too clumsy to climb over. She slowed, finding her balance and made her way shakily back toward Dust Muzzle.

Her brother was already hurrying toward her, his pelt bushed, his gaze flashing toward the barking Twoleg. "Did it hurt you?"

Moth Flight's mouth was too full to speak. Instead she jumped down into the forest. She spat out the catmint and sucked in a deep breath.

Dust Muzzle landed beside her, darting around her anxiously. "Are you okay?"

"Just scared!" she panted. "I didn't see it coming until too late."

Spotted Fur scrambled down the wall. "What happened?"

Dust Muzzle rolled his eyes. "My dreamy sister nearly got caught by a Twoleg."

Moth Flight glared at him furiously. "I can't help being dreamy!" she hissed. *Be yourself.* Half Moon's words flashed in her mind. "It's just the way I am."

"One day it's going to get you into trouble," Dust Muzzle fretted.

"I escaped, didn't I?" Moth Flight lashed her tail. "And *don't* tell Wind Runner! She'll just worry about me!"

Spotted Fur nosed between them and sniffed the catmint. "It *does* smell good!" A purr rumbled in his throat. "Can I chew some?" He was already rubbing his cheek against the stems.

Moth Flight nosed him away sharply. "That's medicine for Rocky!" she snapped, still angry with her brother. "He doesn't want your drool all over it." She snatched up the stems and marched back into the forest.

Paws aching from the journey home, Moth Flight left Dust Muzzle and Spotted Fur to hunt on the moor and hurried back to camp. Holding her head high so she didn't trip over the stems, she scrabbled over the tussocky clearing and headed for her den.

Jagged Peak looked up as she passed. "That smells mouth-watering!"

She dipped her head to him, unable to answer.

Storm Pelt and Eagle Feather fell in beside her, leaning close to sniff the leaves.

"What's that?" A purr rumbled in Storm Pelt's throat.

"Is it for Rocky?" Eagle Feather asked.

Moth Flight dropped the stems at the entrance to her den. The heady scent clouded her thoughts and she shook out her pelt, hoping to clear them. "It's catmint," she told them.

Eagle Feather was crouching, sniffing at the leaves. "Where did you find it?"

"Twolegplace." Moth Flight could hear Rocky coughing inside her den.

"It's a shame it doesn't grow on the moor." Storm Pelt's blue eyes shone. "It smells great."

"It's for curing coughs." Moth Flight shooed Eagle Feather away with a flick of her tail. "It's precious." She glanced toward the sandy dip beside the big stone. Sunlight pooled at the bottom. If she dried the leaves, they wouldn't rot. She hooked two stems from the pile and pushed the rest toward Storm Pelt. "Will you spread these in the hollow so that they dry?" She glanced around. Swift Minnow and Reed Tail were lounging in the late-afternoon sunshine at the edge of the camp. Slate sat blinking at the entrance to her den while Silver Stripe, Black Ear, and White Tail skittered around her, chasing one another's tails. Wind Runner stretched beside the big stone, her belly turned toward the sun and her eyes closed. Moth Flight blinked at Storm Pelt. "Sit and guard them while they dry," she ordered. "I don't want everyone in camp sniffing the leaves. They're for *sick* cats." She wouldn't blame her Clanmates for wanting to taste the tempting leaves. She'd wanted to try one herself, but she worried that, if cats ate catmint while they were healthy, it might not work when they were ill. Besides, she didn't want to travel to Twolegplace every few days to fetch more!

Storm Pelt nodded, grabbing the stems between his jaws. Eagle Feather followed eagerly as he hopped into the hollow and began spreading them over the sandy earth.

Moth Flight ducked into her den. She laid the stems beside Rocky's nest. Heat was still pulsing from his damp pelt.

"Rocky?" She touched him gently with a paw and he blinked his eyes open. "How are you feeling?"

He coughed in reply.

"I've brought you something that might help." Moth Flight tore off a leaf with a claw and placed it beside Rocky's muzzle. "Eat this."

Rocky sniffed the catmint, his eyes brightening. "It smells nice!" He blinked at her gratefully and lapped up the leaf.

She tore off a few more, dropping them beside him. He lapped them up as quickly as she could shred them, until both stems were plucked clean. *Was that enough?* She leaned closer, wondering how long the catmint would take to work.

Rocky purred happily, though he still wheezed with every breath.

"Moth Flight!"

She lifted her head sharply. A familiar voice was calling outside.

Micah! Pelt pricking with excitement, she ducked out of her den. The yellow tom was crossing the clearing, the late sunshine turning his fur golden. She hurried to meet him, hoping her pelt didn't look too dusty after her long trek through the forest. Her heart leaped as she saw him.

He stopped as he reached her, his eyes shining. "How's life as a medicine cat?"

"You should know!" Moth Flight met his gaze, joy surging in her chest. "What's life like with SkyClan?"

Micah swished his tail. "Okay, I guess." He didn't sound sure.

"How's Tiny Branch? Did you cure him?"

"He's charging around camp with his littermates, as healthy as a lark." Micah puffed out his chest proudly.

"Clear Sky and Star Flower must be happy," Moth Flight commented.

"Star Flower is," Micah told her. "I think Clear Sky's wishing he hadn't promised I could stay if I cured his kit."

Worry rippled through Moth Flight's fur. Clear Sky could be cruel. "Is he giving you a hard time?"

"Nothing I can't handle. He meows loudly, but he keeps his claws sheathed. I think—"

"Micah." Wind Runner's mew cut him off. "What are you doing here?"

Moth Flight turned to see her mother approaching. Her fur was still flattened where she'd been lying. Sleepiness clouded her gaze. But Moth Flight recognized her tone of voice. She stiffened, wondering whether the WindClan leader was going to find fault with her or with Micah. "He came to see me," she told Wind Runner. Then she paused, glancing anxiously at Micah. "You did, right?"

Micah purred. "Of course! I've missed you."

Wind Runner's gaze darkened. "I really don't think you should be here," she told the yellow tom. "Clear Sky's not too happy with WindClan at the moment. Not since we accused Red Claw of prey-stealing."

Or since I told him to take a farm cat into his Clan, Moth Flight thought.

Wind Runner narrowed her eyes. "You smell like the forest, Moth Flight," she meowed sharply. "Where have you been?"

"I went to Twolegplace to fetch catmint for Rocky."

Wind Runner bristled. "Did you cross Clear Sky's territory?"

"It's the quickest route."

Micah blinked at her. "I wish I'd known," he told her earnestly. "I would have escorted you."

"It's okay," Moth Flight reassured him. "Dust Muzzle and Spotted Fur came with me."

Wind Runner's tail twitched. "*Three* of you crossed Clear Sky's land?"

Moth Flight faced her. "So what? We weren't hunting. And Rocky needed the leaves."

"But what if—"

Micah cut Wind Runner off, his eager gaze fixed on Moth Flight. "Did you find some?"

Moth Flight nodded. "It was just like you said. Once I smelled it, I knew it was catmint."

"It makes your mouth water, doesn't it?" Micah purred.

"Stop it!" Wind Runner pushed in front of Micah. "You can't come into our camp whenever you want to gossip about herbs!" She turned on Moth Flight. "And *you* can't go wandering into SkyClan territory without telling me."

Moth Flight blinked at her. "But it was for Rocky! You're always going on about the good of the Clan. Well this *was* for the good of the Clan."

Wind Runner's gaze darkened. "It's not for the good of the Clan if it starts a battle."

Moth Flight's pelt pricked. "Surely there wouldn't be a battle over something as dumb as crossing each other's land."

"Clear Sky's started one before," Wind Runner muttered.

Micah's ears twitched. "I think Clear Sky is more interested in being a good father at the moment than fighting battles." Before Wind Runner could reply, he caught Moth Flight's eye. "I'd better go."

"Yes." Wind Runner stared at him. "You'd better."

Moth Flight sniffed indignantly. "I'll walk you to the border."

Wind Runner shot her a look. "Don't cross it."

"I won't!" Moth Flight whisked her tail as she headed for the entrance. Then she paused. "I'd better check on Rocky before I go. I want to see if the catmint's working."

Wind Runner stalked away, growling. "Don't be long. I want Micah back in his own territory by sunset."

Micah glanced at Moth Flight, his eyes glittering with amusement. "She's even sterner than I imagined."

"I warned you." Moth Flight headed for her den, stifling a purr.

Inside, Rocky stretched in his nest, spreading his belly happily. A loud purr throbbed in his chest. He wasn't coughing. Moth Flight blinked at him. "It sounds like the catmint worked."

"I feel great!" Rocky lifted his head and stared blearily at Moth Flight.

Micah padded past her and smelled the old tom's breath. "How much did you give him?" he asked Moth Flight.

"Two stems." Moth Flight hurried to the nest anxiously. "Was that too much?"

Before Micah could answer, Rocky reached out a paw and gave her a playful shove on the muzzle. "It was just the right amount." His tail flicked over his belly. As it flashed past his nose, he grabbed it between his forepaws. "Got you!" Delight shone in his eyes. "Look! I caught my tail!"

Moth Flight stiffened. She'd never seen him act like a kit before. "Have I poisoned him?"

"He'll be fine," Micah reassured her. "He might just be a little playful for a while. But his cough should improve."

"It already has." Rocky flopped onto his side, his head lolling over the edge of his nest.

"Come on." Micah steered Moth Flight toward the

entrance. "Let him sleep it off."

"I'm not sleepy," Rocky called after them.

"Stay in your nest," Micah told him firmly. "We don't want you wandering off and getting lost in the heather. You might feel better but you still need to rest." He nosed Moth Flight from the den.

Outside, in the sunshine, Moth Flight blinked at him. "How much *should* I have given him?" she asked.

"Two or three leaves are enough." Micah headed toward the camp entrance.

Moth Flight hurried to catch up. "Did Tiny Branch act like that when you gave him some?"

"I only gave him one leaf," Micah weaved between the tussocks and headed out of camp.

Moth Flight's pelt prickled hotly along her spine as she followed him. Rocky had been the first cat she'd ever treated. "I'm such a featherbrain," she mewed crossly.

Micah looked at her, surprised. "Why?"

"I should have known it was too much."

"How?" Micah padded at her side. "You'd never seen it before. I'm impressed that you even *found* some."

"Really?" Moth Flight blinked at him.

"Don't be so hard on yourself," Micah told her. "We're all learning."

"Have you made any mistakes?" Moth Flight asked.

"Not yet." Micah gazed across the heather. "But there's so much I don't know yet. Clear Sky seems to think I should have the answer to everything. Most of the time, I'm just guessing."

The breeze tugged Moth Flight's pelt, chilly now as the sun began to set. But she hardly noticed. She was relieved to hear that Micah was feeling overwhelmed by his duties too. "I thought it was just me," she meowed softly.

Micah's flank brushed hers. "It's not just you," he assured her. "I bet Dappled Pelt, Cloud Spots, and Pebble Heart are struggling too."

"Not Pebble Heart," Moth Flight sighed. "Everyone says he's a natural healer." She glanced at her paws. "I wish I was."

"How do you know you're not?" Micah challenged. "Rocky seemed very happy just now."

Moth Flight purred, picturing the old tom. "A bit too happy."

"There's no such thing as 'too happy.'" Micah broke into a run, swerved around a patch of heather and bounded down the slope as it steepened.

Moth Flight chased after him, purring as she ran. She caught up as they neared the border. "Wait!" She didn't want him to go home yet.

He skidded to a halt as he neared the brambles spilling from among the trees. "What?"

"You don't have to get back to camp already, do you?" Moth Flight gazed into his amber eyes.

Micah glanced at the border. "I guess not." He didn't sound sure.

Moth Flight tipped her head. "Is something wrong?"

"No." Micah swished his tail breezily. "Of course not. I just promised Acorn Fur I'd help her mix some herbs."

"Acorn Fur?" Moth Flight frowned. "But *you're* SkyClan's medicine cat."

"Clear Sky wants me to have a helper." Micah avoided her gaze. "I think he wants her to keep an eye on me."

"Clear Sky's never been too trusting." Moth Flight padded closer. "I'm sure he'll get used to having you as a medicine cat soon."

"Yeah." Micah shrugged. "Besides, Acorn Fur's nice. We get along fine. And she's bright. I quite like having her around."

Moth Flight pushed away the jealousy pricking in her belly. "Acorn Fur's okay," she conceded.

"We found a way to treat scratches," Micah told her. "If you chew dock leaves and horsetail stems into a paste, you can smear it deep into a wound."

Moth Flight pricked her ears. "I'll try that next time one of the kits grazes a paw."

"It stings," Micah warned. "They'll make a fuss. But it will stop the wound from getting infected."

The brambles shivered. "Micah!" Acorn Fur padded into the evening sunshine. "I've been looking for you."

Micah dipped his head to the chestnut brown she-cat. "I was just on my way back to camp."

"Clear Sky wants you there now." Acorn Fur eyed Moth Flight warily. "He says Tiny Branch needs more catmint."

Micah frowned. "Tiny Branch is fine."

"Just come!" Acorn Fur glared at him. "Clear Sky is in one of his moods."

"Let me say good-bye to Moth Flight first."

Moth Flight felt Micah's soft breath on her muzzle as he leaned toward her.

"Hurry up!" Acorn Fur crossed the border and padded to Micah's side.

Micah caught Moth Flight's eye, his gaze apologetic. "I've got to go," he whispered.

"See you at half-moon," Moth Flight murmured back.

"Yeah." Micah followed Acorn Fur into the trees.

Moth Flight watched the shadows swallow him, her pelt pricking uneasily. Acorn Fur was treating him more like a hostage than a Clanmate. Was Micah okay in SkyClan? She tore her gaze away, already longing to see him again, and headed back to camp.

CHAPTER 17

Moth Flight glanced at the moon. It rose, a perfect half circle, among the stars. The days since full moon had passed quickly. Moth Flight had been busier than she'd ever been before. Now she was on her way to Highstones.

She paused, her paws chafed from the stony farm tracks.

Micah halted beside her. "Tired?"

"A little," she admitted. She'd normally be curled in her nest by now.

They'd left WindClan as the sun sank toward the horizon. Micah and Cloud Spots had met Moth Flight on the moortop where she'd been waiting, the wind rippling her fur, heart racing in anticipation of their journey to the Moonstone.

Now she glanced at Highstones, looming ahead of them. "We've made good time." Cloud Spots had hurried ahead. She could see him, no more than a shadow tracking back and forth at the bottom of a beech hedge, as though looking for the easiest way through. "What if the spirit-cats don't come?"

Micah touched his muzzle to her shoulder. "You worry too much."

Cloud Spots glanced over his shoulder. "I've picked up Dappled Pelt's trail!"

"At last!" Moth Flight was beginning to wonder whether the RiverClan medicine cat had forgotten the meeting.

"Pebble Heart's with her," Cloud Spots called.

Moth Flight hurried to catch up with the ThunderClan medicine cat. "Is the trail fresh?"

"Yes!" Cloud Spots ducked under the hedge and disappeared.

Moth Flight squeezed after the long-furred black tom, the beech twigs scraping her pelt. Micah wriggled through at her tail.

On the other side, a meadow stretched into the shadow of Highstones. The cliff seemed to swallow half the sky. Cloud Spots was already bounding through the long grass toward two feline shapes moving at the far side.

"Pebble Heart!" Cloud Spots's yowl rang in the cold night air. "Dappled Pelt! Is that you?"

"Yes!" Pebble Heart's call echoed back.

Micah broke into a run. "Come on! We're nearly there!"

Moth Flight hared after him. As the soft grass turned to stones beneath her paws, she reached the RiverClan and ShadowClan medicine cats. "I thought you'd forgotten," she puffed.

Dappled Pelt's tortoiseshell fur rippled along her spine. "How could we forget something as important as this?"

"I can't wait to speak with the spirit-cats!" Pebble Heart's eyes shone with starlight.

Micah paced back and forth, his tail twitching. "Cow and Mouse would never believe this." He looked toward Highstones. The opening was just barely visible, a dark shadow in the face of the rock.

Cloud Spots followed his gaze. "Is that where we're going?"

"Yes." Butterflies fluttered in Moth Flight's belly.

"Is it deep inside?" Pebble Heart's mew trembled.

"There's no need to be scared," Moth Flight reassured him. "Once we've entered, you'll feel the Moonstone calling you." She remembered the strange calm that had enfolded her last time.

"Come on." Micah began to cross the stones.

Moth Flight bounded after him, pebbles crunching beneath her paws as the slope steepened toward the foot of the cliff. "I bet you never thought, a moon ago, that you'd speak with dead cats," she guessed as she caught up.

"I never thought I'd be living in a *forest*," Micah returned.

Moth Flight blinked at him anxiously. Did he resent how much she'd changed his life? "Are you sorry you met me?"

Micah halted and met her gaze solemnly. "No. It's the best thing that ever happened to me."

Joy rippled beneath Moth Flight's pelt. "I feel the same w—"

"Hurry up." Cloud Spots slid past them, his black pelt hardly visible against the dark rock. Only his white ears and paws gave him away.

Dappled Pelt hurried after the black tom. Pebble Heart bounded behind, scattering stones in his wake.

Wincing as one hit her paw, Moth Flight glanced up at the

dark opening. What would the others think when they saw the Moonstone for the first time?

"Come on." Micah nudged her forward.

Pebble Heart had already leaped onto the shadowy ledge. The white spot on his chest glowed like a star. Cloud Spots hopped up beside him and stared blinking into the tunnel. Micah followed Dappled Pelt as Moth Flight scrambled up after them.

The icy stone felt familiar beneath her paws. She sniffed the shadows. The tang of stone and water washed her muzzle and she shivered, excitement swelling in her chest. "Follow me." As she padded into the darkness, cold air flooded over her pelt. Behind her, the starlight faded. "We have to reach the cave by the time moonlight strikes the stone." Her breath billowed, warm around her nose.

She heard the other cats' paws scuff the stone as they followed. Eyes wide, Moth Flight peered into the blackness, relaxing as she let her whiskers guide her. Brushing the wall of the tunnel, she followed it down as it snaked deep into Highstones.

"Do you remember the way?" Cloud Spots's anxious mew echoed behind her.

"What if you take the wrong tunnel?" Dappled Pelt fretted.

"I know where I'm going," Moth Flight promised.

Micah's breath rippled her tail-fur. "I can't believe you came down here alone."

"I wasn't alone." A purr trembled in Moth Flight's throat. "The spirit-cats were waiting for me."

"Are they there now?" Pebble Heart's mew sounded from the blackness.

"We'll see when the moonlight hits the stone." Moth Flight quickened her pace. She didn't want to miss it. Fresh air touched her nose. "We're nearly there!" She rounded a corner and felt the tunnel open around her. Air swirled over her pelt and she blinked as she saw weak starlight rippling on the cave walls ahead. She paused, her heart pounding. Pebble Heart padded past her, nose twitching. Dapple Pelt and Cloud Spots circled the great rock.

Micah stopped beside Moth Flight. He stared at the hole high in the roof. "Who'd have thought starlight could reach down this far?"

Moth Flight purred. "Wait until the *moon*light arrives." She padded toward the rock and settled herself in front of it. "We have to touch our noses to it," she told the others.

"How do you know?" Cloud Spots blinked at her.

"I saw another cat do it in a dream, and last time I came—"

Pebble Heart cut her off. "Look!"

Moth Flight followed his gaze. Through the hole, she could see the clipped edge of the moon. "Hurry!"

Fur brushing rock, the other cats settled around the Moonstone. Dappled Pelt's eyes flashed with excitement. Pebble Heart shifted on his belly, pelt pricking.

Cloud Spots crouched beside him, a whisker from the stone. Micah settled beside Moth Flight. She felt warmth seeping from his pelt and closed her eyes.

Pebble Heart's gasp made her blink them open.

Light blinded her. The rock shimmered in front of her muzzle, brighter than countless stars. Her breath quickened as she touched her nose to it.

The rock seemed to fall away. She was swept through the air, her head spinning, her heart pounding in her ears. And then she felt soft grass beneath her paws.

She blinked open her eyes.

Where was the cave?

She was on top of a hill. Green meadows stretched away on every side. In the distance, a forest lifted its branches to a clear, blue sky. She felt sunlight warm her pelt and smelled the fresh scent of newleaf.

Micah shifted beside her.

She caught his eye. "Where are we?"

"You don't *know*?" He blinked in surprise.

"Last time, I never left the cave."

Cloud Spots looked around, pelt bristling. Dappled Pelt leaped to her paws.

"What is this place?" Pebble Heart's eyes were stretched with wonder.

A silky mew answered him. "These are our hunting grounds."

Half Moon was climbing the slope toward them. More pelts shimmered into view, encircling the hilltop. Starlight shone in their fur.

Joy swelled in Moth Flight's chest. *The spirit-cats!* They'd come!

Half Moon padded past Moth Flight and halted.

As Micah turned his head, surveying the ranks of starry cats, Pebble Heart stretched his muzzle and sniffed at Half Moon.

Dappled Pelt tipped her head, curiosity flashing in her eyes. *"Stoneteller?"*

"It is good to see you settled in your new home," Half Moon purred.

Cloud Spots gazed into Half Moon's dark green gaze. "Is it really you?"

"Of course."

The ThunderClan tom's gaze flitted to the other starry cats. "Jackdaw's Cry! Bright Stream!" He raced from one cat to another, touching muzzles excitedly.

"Rainswept Flower!" Dappled Pelt darted toward a brown she-cat. She greeted her, then jerked her muzzle toward an orange she-cat. "Hawk Swoop!"

Micah shifted his paws, staring blankly at the spirit-cats.

"Turtle Tail!" Pebble Heart's eyes lit up as he saw his mother. He nosed his way between the spirit-cats toward her.

Turtle Tail was already hurrying to meet him. "Pebble Heart!" Her eyes glowed with joy as she touched her muzzle to his head.

Purring, he rubbed against her. "I thought I'd never see you again!"

"We're always close by." Gray Wing slid from the crowd.

Pebble Heart jerked his muzzle around, delighted. "You're *both* here! *Together!*"

Gray Wing purred loudly, his starry pelt shimmering. "It's

good to see you, Pebble Heart."

Half Moon lifted her chin. "Let us gather and share news."

At her words, the starry cats closed the circle around Half Moon, Micah, and Moth Flight. Pebble Heart, Dappled Pelt, and Cloud Spots left their old friends and hurried to the center.

"You did well." Half Moon's green eyes glowed as she gazed at Moth Flight.

"Did I?" Moth Flight blinked at her anxiously.

"Yes." As Half Moon dipped her head to Moth Flight, murmurs of appreciation rippled around the spirit-cats.

Moth Flight glanced at them shyly, pride surging beneath her pelt. "I just told the Clans, like you asked me to." She remembered with a shudder Clear Sky's scorn. And Tall Shadow's disbelieving gaze. Even her Clanmates had thought she'd imagined the spirit-cats. "Thanks for sending the lightning." Without it, the Clans might never have taken her seriously. "When you said you'd split the skies, I never guessed that's what you meant."

Half Moon gazed at her warmly. "You will get better at understanding us."

Moth Flight hoped she was right. "What did you mean when you said *later the stars would rise?*" She tipped her head, waiting for the white she-cat to explain.

"You will know when it happens."

Frustration pricked Moth Flight's paws. Why couldn't Half Moon just say what she meant? "When *what* happens?"

Half Moon narrowed her gaze. "This is your life. We

cannot guide every paw step. If we did, you would only discover *our* path. You must discover your own."

Moth Flight's tail drooped. "I guess." *But it would be easier if you just told us what to do.*

Half Moon seemed to read her thoughts. "It would be easier, but not better." She turned to Micah. "Thank you for leaving your home to join us."

"*Us?*" Micah's ears twitched. He glanced uneasily around the spirit-cats. "I only joined SkyClan."

"You joined the Clans," Half Moon purred. "What are we, if not another Clan?"

Moth Flight's breath caught in her throat. The spirit-cats saw themselves as a Clan. "You're *Star*Clan," she breathed, remembering when she'd looked up at the stars and first thought of the name.

Half Moon's eyes shone. "Yes." She lifted her chin, surveying her starry Clanmates. "That's exactly what we are."

"StarClan!"

"StarClan!"

The word rippled around the sprit cats, their eyes lighting up as they spoke their new name.

Half Moon swished her tail, her dark green gaze returning to Micah. "You bring fresh spirit to the Clans, Micah," she purred.

Moth Flight sniffed. "He would, if Clear Sky let him. He's told Acorn Fur to watch him."

"Clear Sky is the leader," Half Moon reminded her. "He will do what he thinks best for his Clan. But he will see Micah's worth." Her gaze darkened. "I just hope he sees it soon."

"So do I!" Micah fluffed out his fur.

Gray Wing padded forward and stopped beside Half Moon. "We are pleased to see the medicine cats learning skills from each other."

Bright Stream lifted her tail. "We hope you will share more!"

"The Clans must pool their knowledge," Rainswept Flower urged from among her Clanmates.

"But we know so little!" Moth Flight blurted.

Half Moon's gaze flitted around the medicine cats. "You will learn more if you share."

Excitement sparked in Moth Flight's chest. *Of course!* Micah had told her about catmint and she'd used it to cure Rocky. If she knew everything Dappled Pelt, Cloud Spots, Pebble Heart, and Micah knew, she'd be able to help her whole Clan. She blinked at Half Moon. "We *will* share! I promise."

The StarClan cat's pelt began to fade. Around her, the spirit-cats were growing pale.

Alarm flashed through Moth Flight. "Don't go yet!"

"We will return next half-moon," Gray Wing called as he shimmered out of sight.

The green meadows and distant forest grew hazy as Moth Flight desperately tried to fix her gaze on them. She felt dizzy as they began to swirl. Blackness enfolded her and a chill swept her pelt.

She blinked open her eyes. She was in the cave once more, the Moonstone no more than a dull lump of rock.

Micah shivered beside her.

Pebble Heart pushed himself to his paws.

Dappled Pelt lifted her head, blinking. "Did you all see that?"

"We were on a hill!" Cloud Spots eyes gleamed in the weak starlight.

"Stoneteller!" Dappled Pelt jumped up, her pelt bristling. "She wants us to share what we know about healing!"

"Who's Stoneteller?" Moth Flight tipped her head. Why did the older cats keep calling Half Moon by that name?

"She was our healer in the mountains," Cloud Spots explained. "We called her Stoneteller."

Micah sniffed. "If *she's* a healer, why doesn't she share what she knows with us?"

Dappled Pelt padded around him, her pelt pricking excitedly. "Healing was different in the mountains. There weren't many herbs. She must want us to learn new skills."

Pebble Heart's eyes glazed, as though deep in thought. "We have the chance to become better healers than she ever could. She knows that. She *wants* us to be better."

Moth Flight's paws tingled. "We must try our best. We have to share everything we know." She wanted to make Half Moon proud. *She's put so much faith in me.* "A few days ago, Micah told me how to stop cuts from getting infected." She looked at him expectantly.

"I made a poultice of dock and horsetail by chewing up the leaves," Micah told them eagerly. "Blossom had a scratch that was turning sour, so I licked the poultice deep into the wound and it was better by morning."

Cloud Spots's whiskers twitched excitedly. "Clover kept chewing at a wound on her paw, so I smeared some mouse bile on it. She didn't put her nose near it again."

"Shattered Ice got a bellyache from eating a stinking fish," Dappled Pelt put in. "I gave him watermint. He felt a lot better."

"I've been trying to work out if pinesap is good for anything," Pebble Heart mewed thoughtfully. "So far it only seems useful for sticking leaves over wounds to keep dirt out."

As the others looked expectantly at Moth Flight, guilt wormed beneath her pelt. *I haven't discovered anything! Except that too much catmint makes cats crazy!* "I guess I could see if *heather* is good for anything," she mewed tentatively. "But what if it's poisonous?"

"It can't be," Cloud Spots reasoned. "WindClan cats must be covered in heather dust. And you don't get sick when you wash."

Why didn't I think of that? Moth Flight began to feel hot. "Perhaps I should have brought Reed Tail with me," she mumbled. "He knows a lot."

"So does Milkweed," Cloud Spots mewed. "She's the one who suggested mouse bile."

Micah's tail twitched. "Instead of bringing every cat who knows something about healing *here*, why don't we travel to each other's camps?"

Moth Flight frowned. She wasn't sure what he meant.

"It would only take one or two of us to travel around,

learning and sharing knowledge." Micah paced in front of the Moonstone. "What if Moth Flight and I traveled to another Clan's camp and learned everything we could? Then we could move on to another Clan and share what we'd learned and pick up new skills."

"What about the Clan you'd left behind?" Cloud Spots argued. "They'd only learn what you knew."

"We could take turns," Micah suggested. "You could travel with Dappled Pelt, or Pebble Heart. So long as we keep learning and sharing, it doesn't matter who travels where."

Pebble Heart nodded. "It sounds like a good idea."

"How can we leave our Clans?" Dappled Pelt argued. "They need us."

Moth Flight shifted her paws. "I know so little that Wind-Clan would be just as safe with Reed Tail in charge."

"Milkweed knows enough to look after ThunderClan while I'm gone," Cloud Spots added.

"You see?" Micah's eyes glowed in the half-light. "The sooner we get started the better."

Dappled Pelt tipped her head. "Why don't you and Moth Flight come visit RiverClan first? River Ripple will welcome you. He thinks medicine cats are a great idea."

"It might be hard to get Tall Shadow to agree to have strangers in her camp," Pebble Heart murmured.

Micah blinked at him. "Do you think *Clear Sky* is going to let me leave without an argument?" He swished his tail. "We have to persuade our leaders that it's for the good of their Clans."

Pebble Heart nodded slowly. "The more we know, the better we can help our Clanmates," he agreed.

"Then it's settled." Micah turned to Dappled Pelt. "Moth Flight and I will visit you the day after tomorrow."

Moth Flight's ears twitched. "What if Wind Runner stops me?"

"You're WindClan's *medicine cat* now," Micah told her. "She *has* to listen to you."

Moth Flight blinked. He was right. She wasn't a kit anymore. She wasn't even an ordinary Clan cat. "Okay," she agreed. "I'll meet you at the stepping-stones, the day after tomorrow." She'd seen stones dotting the river where the forest gave way to the reed beds of RiverClan's territory.

Micah purred. "Great."

Pebble Heart shook out his pelt. Cloud Spots stretched, shivering, while Dappled Pelt swallowed back a yawn.

Moth Flight guessed they were cold and tired. "Let's go." She headed for the tunnel. "We've got a long way to travel."

Micah fell in beside her as she ducked into the shadows. "How's Rocky's cough? Did the catmint work?"

"Yes." Moth Flight purred. Rocky had slept the whole day away after he'd swallowed the leaves, but he'd woken brighter and his cough was clearing up.

Pebble Heart's mew sounded from the darkness behind. "Is he the only cat in your Clan with a cough? Sun Shadow and Raven Pelt have been coughing for days."

"Dew Nose was a bit wheezy this morning," Moth Flight told him. "But I think it's just pollen making her throat tickle."

"Milkweed and Clover both have coughs," Cloud Spots meowed.

"Shattered Ice has been croaking like a frog these past days," Dappled Pelt's mew echoed around the tunnels walls.

Moth Flight brushed against Micah, frowning. Perhaps newleaf *always* brought coughs. "Is Tiny Branch still okay?"

"He was spluttering a bit this morning," Micah confessed. "I told Acorn Fur to keep an eye on him."

Moth Flight could hear anxiety in his mew. "He'll be okay if you give him catmint, won't he?"

Micah's paws scuffed the rock. "There was a tom on the farm with a cough," he meowed darkly. "We called it redcough because, at the end, he coughed up blood."

At the end? Moth Flight shivered. The darkness suddenly seemed to press against her pelt as she padded on.

"I've never seen a Clan cat cough *blood*," Dappled Spots murmured darkly.

Alarm pricked in Moth Flight's paws. "Didn't catmint help?" she asked Micah. "You said there was some behind the barn."

"Cow tried giving him catmint, but it didn't work," Micah explained.

"I know something more powerful than catmint." Cloud Spots's mew sounded at Moth Flight's tail. She felt his breath stir her fur. "There's a tree on SkyClan's land. It oozes sap from cracks in the bark. The sap can cure any cough."

Moth Flight glanced over her shoulder hopefully. "Even redcough?"

"I've never tested it," Cloud Spots admitted.

Fresh air began to wash Moth Flight's muzzle. A few more paw steps, and starlight showed through the darkness. Crisp air sent a surge of energy through her fur. She hurried onto the ledge and gazed over the valley. Moonlight drenched the distant moor. "We'll be home by dawn." She leaped down, sending stones cracking down the slope, and headed for the meadow.

Paws heavy with weariness, Moth Flight ducked through the gap in the camp wall. Beyond it, the sky showed orange over the forest as dawn pushed the night away. She could hear the gentle snoring of her Clanmates, and make out their pelts, just shadows in the grass as they slept curled in their nests. How good it would feel to slip into her den and snuggle deep into her own nest.

She heard the sound of fur brushing the rocks as she passed them. She turned, blinking, through the half-light. "Who is it?"

Wind Runner's scent bathed her nose as her mother slid from the rocks.

"You're back." The WindClan leader stretched sleepily and touched her nose to Moth Flight's cheek.

"Did you wait up for me?" Warmth glowed in Moth Flight's chest.

"I slept a little," Wind Runner admitted. "But I wanted to make sure you got back safely. It's a long journey to High-stones."

"I had Micah with me," Moth Flight reassured her.

"I know." Wind Runner wrinkled her nose distastefully. "I can smell his scent on you."

Moth Flight felt suddenly self-conscious. "Cloud Spots, Dappled Pelt, and Pebble Heart were there too," she pointed out.

Wind Runner's gaze slid away. "Did you speak with the spirit-cats?"

"Yes!" Moth Flight lifted her tail excitedly. "StarClan told us we must share the knowledge we have with each other."

"*StarClan?*" Wind Runner jerked her gaze back.

"That's what the spirit-cats are called now. They even have their own hunting grounds."

Wind Runner's eyes widened but she didn't comment. Instead she tipped her head. "*Who* has to share knowledge?"

"The medicine cats." Moth Flight squared her shoulders. She might as well tell Wind Runner about Micah's plan now. "I'm meeting Micah at the border tomorrow. We're going to visit RiverClan and learn everything Dappled Pelt knows about healing. All the medicine cats are going to visit each other's camps. It's what StarClan wants."

Wind Runner narrowed her eyes. "Clear Sky won't let Micah visit other Clans. No matter what *StarClan* wants."

"Why not?" Moth Flight met her mother's gaze. "He's angry with WindClan, but that has nothing to do with Micah."

"Clear Sky doesn't like to be told what to do."

"Micah will convince him it's for the good of his Clan," Moth Flight insisted. "Micah can be very persuasive."

Wind Runner's ear twitched uneasily. "I don't doubt it."

"I'm tired." Moth Flight ignored the suspicious glint in her mother's gaze and headed across the clearing. "I'm going to my nest."

"There's a mouse for you on the prey pile," her mother called after her softly.

"Thanks." Moth Flight blinked gratefully over her shoulder. "But I'm too tired to eat."

"Sleep well, then." Wind Runner dipped her head. "I'll make sure you're not disturbed."

Moth Flight slipped quietly into her den. Rocky was purring in his sleep, his whiskers twitching as he dreamed. She climbed into her nest, surprised to find fresh heather lining it. Relishing the sweet scent, she curled down and rested her chin on the edge. Through the den entrance, she could see sunlight drenching the camp wall as the night sky paled into dawn. She wondered whether StarClan watched them during the day. *Or do they fade with the stars?* She pictured the sloping meadows and distant forest of StarClan's hunting grounds; joy warmed her pelt as she thought of Gray Wing and Turtle Tail walking side by side once more. She purred. Tomorrow she'd be traveling with Micah to RiverClan. Was he looking forward to their journey as much as she was?

CHAPTER 18

As sunhigh neared, Moth Flight pulled a mouse from the prey pile. She wasn't very hungry, but she didn't want her belly rumbling when she met Micah. And who knew what they'd be offered to eat in the RiverClan camp? She shuddered, remembering the toad she'd caught, and hoped there'd be more to eat among the reed beds than river prey.

She padded past Swift Minnow, who was washing in the long grass beside Reed Tail. Jagged Peak and Holly were repairing gaps in their den wall by threading heather—which Eagle Feather and Dew Nose had fetched from the moor— tightly between the stems. Gorse Fur and Wind Runner sat at the edge of the sandy hollow, their heads bent close as they talked. Slate sat beside Fern Leaf and Willow Tail, blinking in the sunshine while Black Ear, White Tail, and Silver Stripe climbed the gorse wall behind her.

Warm prey scent bathed Moth Flight's nose as she carried the mouse into the shade of the camp wall where Dust Muzzle and Spotted Fur were lounging in the thick grass, a half-eaten rabbit lying between them. As she dropped her mouse beside them and bent to take a bite, she noticed Spotted Fur's tail twitching crossly from the corner of her eye. She ripped a lump of flesh from the mouse and looked at him. "What's up?" she asked, her mouth full.

He frowned. "Dust Muzzle says you're going to visit River-Clan with Micah."

Moth Flight swallowed. "StarClan wants the medicine cats to learn from each other."

"Can't you visit RiverClan by yourself?" Spotted Fur asked.

"Micah needs to learn too." Moth Flight cocked her head as she chewed. Why was he being so crabby?

"Why can't you travel with Pebble Heart or Cloud Spots?" Spotted Fur asked accusingly.

Dust Muzzle hooked the rabbit closer with a claw. "Moth Flight can travel with whomever she likes," he meowed absently.

Spotted Fur got to his paws and shook out his pelt. "I don't know if spending time with other Clans is a good idea," he meowed loudly.

Holly glanced over her shoulder, a sprig of heather in her paws.

Moth Flight stiffened. The golden tom was attracting attention from their Clanmates.

Fern Leaf jerked her muzzle around. "So it's true! You're really going to visit RiverClan?"

"Yes." Moth Flight shifted her paws uneasily.

Wind Runner looked up, eyes narrowing.

"Is that a good idea?" Holly dropped the sprig of heather and headed across the clearing. "Rocky's still sick."

"Reed Tail's promised to watch him," Moth Flight defended herself.

Swift Minnow flashed her mate a look. "You didn't tell me!"

"He's not that sick." Reed Tail pushed himself to his paws. "He's just enjoying his cozy nest in Moth Flight's den."

Slate's eyes rounded with worry. "What if one of my kits gets ill?"

Silver Stripe called down from the gorse wall. "We never get sick!"

"But what if you do?" Slate fretted.

"Reed Tail will know what to do," Moth Flight promised the queen. *He probably knows more than than I do.* "Besides, I'm only going to RiverClan. Someone can come and fetch me if you need me."

Willow Tail's ears twitched. "It's just asking for trouble, crossing another Clan's borders."

"Dappled Pelt invited me!" Impatience tightened Moth Flight's belly. Willow Tail was only trying to make a point because of Red Claw. She felt a surge of anger toward the pale tabby she-cat; with all this talk of borders, she was getting as bad as Clear Sky! "Besides, I'm a *medicine cat*. I'm going there to *learn*, not to hunt!"

Wind Runner padded to the center of the clearing. "StarClan has told the medicine cats to learn from each other." Her gaze swept the Clan.

Moth Flight felt a ripple of relief. Wind Runner wasn't going to stand in her way.

Gorse Fur nodded solemnly. "What Moth Flight learns

from the other medicine cats will help us."

Jagged Peak stepped out from the shadow of his den, heather sticking out of his pelt. "Mixing with other Clans is dangerous," he growled.

Moth Flight bristled. "Why? *You've* lived with the forest cats *and* on the moor *and* in the pine marsh with Tall Shadow!"

"Which means I've learned how important it is to remain in one place." Jagged Peak met her gaze. "Your loyalty should be with us."

"It *is* with you!" Moth Flight snapped. "Visiting the River-Clan camp won't change that."

"But you're going because *StarClan* ordered you to, not Wind Runner," Holly chipped in. "Are you a WindClan cat or a StarClan cat?"

Moth Flight stared in dismay at her Clanmates. How could any cat doubt her loyalty? Her mother was the Clan leader!

Wind Runner lashed her tail. "Stop all this mouse-brained chatter!" she growled. "I realize that we are not used to having a medicine cat among us. And it feels strange to take orders from spirit-cats. But Moth Flight only has the good of the Clan in her heart. She is going to learn so that she can take care of us better." She fixed her gaze on Slate. "If one of your kits falls ill, wouldn't you want Moth Flight to know as much as she can about healing?" She turned to Jagged Peak, her gaze hardening. "*Never* suggest that Moth Flight's loyalties are divided! She was born a WindClan cat and, whatever happens, her heart will belong with her Clanmates."

Moth Flight felt a surge of gratitude toward her mother.

But Spotted Fur's accusing gaze still burned her pelt. She stared at her paws. *He's jealous of Micah.* Guilt wormed in her belly. Was it disloyal of her to like the SkyClan medicine cat so much?

She left her mouse and padded across the clearing. "I promised I'd meet Micah at sunhigh." She avoided her Clanmates' stares. "I don't know when I'll be back, but if there's an emergency, send for me."

Ignoring the hushed murmurs behind her, she slid out of camp, relieved to feel the cool wind in her fur.

Moth Flight headed for the RiverClan border. As she climbed down the steep path that led to the river, she saw Micah, seated on a stepping-stone. He was silhouetted, still and strong, against the flashing water. He looked up as she neared and she narrowed her eyes against the glare of the sparkling ripples.

Behind him, the river split, cutting through the reed beds to create an island in the middle. She knew from listening to her Clanmates talk that RiverClan made their camp there and she wondered what it would feel like to be entirely surrounded by water.

"It's so peaceful here!" Micah's purr rumbled over the chattering stream.

Moth Flight jumped gingerly onto the first stepping-stone, watching the water as it swirled around her. She flinched as a ripple broke over the edge of the stone and splashed her forepaw.

Micah purred louder. "You might have to get used to getting your paws wet in RiverClan."

"I hope not." She shook the water off.

It felt good to be away from camp. The newleaf sun warmed her pelt. The river was sheltered from the wind by the forest on one side and the cliffs on the other. Pungent scents filled her nose and the birds chattered over the babbling of the river. She blinked happily at Micah. Alone here, with him, she didn't need to impress Wind Runner, or know how to treat Black Ear's bellyache or Storm Pelt's itchy ears.

She crossed the stepping-stones until she reached Micah, then lifted her face to the sun and half closed her eyes. The wind whisked the reed beds on the far shore, stirring the rushes until they rippled like water.

Downstream, a black she-cat padded onto the shore. An orange she-cat passed her, wading into the shallows until the water streamed through her belly fur. She dipped her head, then plunged beneath the surface.

Moth Flight froze. "She sank!"

Micah leaned forward, ears pricked. "Wait." He watched the water until suddenly, with a splash, the RiverClan she-cat broke the surface a few tail-lengths away, a fish clamped between her jaws. She swam back to shore, then hauled herself out and disappeared among the reeds. Her Clanmate gave a *mrrow* of approval, then followed.

Moth Flight shivered. "I hope Dappled Pelt doesn't try to teach us to do *that*!"

Micah purred. "If she does, you can threaten to teach her

how to hunt in your tunnels."

"I hate tunnel-hunting," Moth Flight confessed. "It's Dust Muzzle's specialty, not mine."

"You're a medicine cat," Micah reminded her. "You have your own special skills."

"I *wish*."

"That's why we came here." Micah jumped onto the next stone and crossed to the far shore. He glanced back at Moth Flight. "We'll know plenty by the time we leave. But we'd better hurry up. Those cats probably told Dappled Pelt we're on our way."

Ruefully, Moth Flight followed. She wished she could spend all afternoon watching the river with Micah. But he was right. Dappled Pelt would be expecting them. She landed on the sandy shore and followed Micah along a trail that wove among the reeds. The earth was muddy and squelched between her claws. As the trail widened, she caught up with Micah. "What did Clear Sky say when you told him you were visiting RiverClan?"

"He wasn't happy." Micah kept his gaze fixed ahead.

"Did he try and stop you?" Moth Flight scanned Micah's pelt for scratches.

"He wanted to know why," Micah told her. "It took a while to convince him that it was for the good of SkyClan but, in the end, he agreed."

"Wind Runner thought you'd never convince him." Moth Flight felt a glimmer of satisfaction that Micah had proved her mother wrong.

"I think Clear Sky likes cats who stand up to him," Micah told her. "And it helped that Star Flower was there. Since I helped Tiny Branch, she wants me to learn as much as I can— in case Dew Petal or Flower Foot gets sick."

"How's Tiny Branch's cough?"

"It seems to get better one day and worse the next," Micah murmured thoughtfully. "I wonder if there's something in the forest that aggravates it."

"Silver Stripe always sneezes when she's been playing near heather flowers," Moth Flight commented. "Maybe you could follow Tiny Branch for a day and see where he plays."

"I wish I had time for that," Micah meowed. "Clear Sky keeps me busy treating flea bites and gathering herbs."

"But you have Acorn Fur to help you." Moth Flight ignored the jealousy pricking beneath her fur. "Couldn't she take your duties for a day?"

"Clear Sky insists she never leave my side when we're on SkyClan territory."

Moth Flight blinked. "Never?"

Before Micah could answer, the reeds ahead shivered and a black she-cat slid out and blocked the path—the same one they'd seen on the shore downstream. She eyed Micah and Moth Flight suspiciously. "What are you two doing here?"

"Hi!" Micah greeted her cheerfully. "Didn't Dappled Pelt warn you? She invited us to come and learn what she knows about healing."

"Night!" A mew sounded farther along the trail. Dawn Mist appeared from among the rushes. Her orange-and-white pelt was wet, slicked against her slender frame. "Dappled Pelt said that if it's Micah and Moth Flight, you're to escort them to her den."

Night narrowed her eyes. "I *still* think it's a bad idea to let other Clan cats into our camp."

"River Ripple says it's okay," Dawn Mist argued. "And they're only medicine cats. What's the worst they can do? *Cure* you?"

Night snorted and turned her tail on them. "Follow me," she huffed.

Moth Flight padded beside Micah, following the she-cat along the winding path.

Dawn Mist fell in beside her Clanmate and glanced over her shoulder. "I wish I could visit the other Clans," she mewed. "I can't imagine what it's like to live on the moor or in the forest."

Moth Flight's paws slithered on the muddy earth. "It's *dry*," she muttered.

As Dawn Mist purred with amusement, the reeds opened up and Moth Flight saw a clearing ahead. Fish scent washed her muzzle as two kits bounded across the sandy soil and bundled into Dawn Mist.

"Dawn Mist!" The gray-and-white she-kit bounced around the orange queen. "Pine Needle ate more of the trout than me! It's not fair."

The black tom-kit dug his paws into the earth. "I did *not*! She's just being greedy!"

"Poor Drizzle." Dawn Mist licked the gray she-kit's head. "I'll catch another fish soon," she promised.

"Can we have one *each*?" Pine Needle asked.

Drizzle blinked eagerly. "I want the biggest one!"

"You two are greedier than foxes," Dawn Mist purred. She nosed the kits away. "Go and play. I'm helping Night show our guests to Dappled Pelt's den."

Drizzle's eyes opened wide as she spotted Moth Flight and Micah. "What are *they* doing here?"

"Invasion!" Pine Needle fluffed out his fur. "Should I warn River Ripple?"

A deep purr rumbled at the side of the clearing. "There's no need to warn me. I was expecting them."

Moth Flight jerked her nose around and saw the River-Clan leader sitting in the shade of the reed wall.

He stood and crossed the camp, dipping his head as he neared. "I'm glad you're here. Dappled Pelt's in her den." He pointed his muzzle to the foot of a long-dead tree. Its roots snaked into the earth, forming a cave beneath the stump, where countless moons of wind and water had hollowed out the earth.

Night flashed Moth Flight a look. "I hope you can hunt for yourselves," she growled. "I'm not feeding WindClan or SkyClan cats."

River Ripple blinked calmly at his Clanmate. "It doesn't matter what Clan they're from; their hunger is no different from yours."

Night snorted and stalked away.

Dawn Mist whisked her tail. "Don't worry about her," she whispered to Moth Flight. "She enjoys being bad-tempered."

Drizzle pricked her ears. "Yesterday she said that I was as

dumb as a water vole. But I'm not."

"Of course you're not!" Pine Needle's whiskers twitched mischievously. "You're *dumber*."

"Hey!" Fluffing her fur out indignantly, Drizzle leaped at her brother. Pine Needle ducked out of the way and hared across the camp.

"I'll get you for that!" Drizzle hurtled after him.

"When they're not eating, they're fighting." Dawn Mist rolled her eyes. "I'd better fetch them more prey." She headed toward a gap in the reeds where the river lapped the edge of the clearing. Without pausing, she slid into the river and disappeared beneath the surface.

Moth Flight glanced at Micah. The RiverClan cats seemed more like otters than cats. Micah was gazing around the camp. Shattered Ice lay in a patch of sunshine at the far end of the clearing. Swift, a dark brown tom, washed himself beside the camp wall.

River Ripple flicked his tail toward Dappled Pelt's den. "She's been looking forward to your arrival."

Micah dipped his head to the RiverClan leader and headed toward the tree stump. Moth Flight hurried after him, her nose twitching as the stink of fish grew stronger. She could see that the gaps between the roots of Dappled Pelt's den had been woven with reeds. Feathers were threaded between them and fluttered in the soft breeze.

Dappled Pelt stuck her head out from under an arching root. "You're here at last!" she purred. "Come in! I've just finished sorting my herbs."

As the RiverClan medicine cat ducked back into the

shadows, Moth Flight followed her down the short slope that led into the den. She shivered. The reed walls screened out the bright sunshine and the shadows felt cold and damp. Reeds were strewn over the floor. They shifted beneath Moth Flight's paws. She blinked, adjusting her eyes to the half-light. "You've got plenty of space!" She paused in the center and looked around. There was room enough for four nests here, though she could only see two, both woven from rushes. She looked up and saw shadow where the roof disappeared into the rotting stump. A spider was spinning a web at one corner. "You'll always have cobwebs to dress wounds!" she mewed, delighted. *Perhaps I should catch spiders and try to persuade them to nest in my den!*

Micah slid under the root and padded inside. "Does it flood?" He glanced over his shoulder.

"Not unless the whole island floods," Dappled Pelt told him.

Moth Flight blinked, alarmed. "Has that ever happened?"

"It happened once, during a storm that came after moons of rain." Dappled Pelt patted a stray rush into the nest beside her. "River Ripple says if there's rain like that again, we'll shelter in the forest until it passes."

Micah was peering into the shadows behind Dappled Pelt, where an earth wall formed the back of the den. "Is that where you keep your herbs?"

Moth Flight followed his gaze. Small holes had been hollowed from the mud, and green leaves stuck out here and there.

"There's a different hole for each herb." Dappled Pelt's eyes shone proudly.

"Doesn't the damp air make them rot?" Moth Flight was used to the dry winds that scoured the moor.

"It's airy enough," Dappled Pelt told her. "The breeze from the river keeps it cool, which seems to preserve fresh leaves, and I find that fresh leaves are more effective than dried leaves."

Micah frowned. "It's a shame," he murmured. "Leafbare brings more illness. But by then, all we'll have left in our supplies are dried leaves."

"Seeds and berries keep their strength." Dappled Pelt reached into one of the holes and pulled out a pawful of dark berries. She dropped them at Moth Flight's paws.

As Dappled Pelt drew out one herb after another, telling them where they could be gathered and what they treated—juniper for bellyache, poppy to ease pain—Moth Flight tried hard to remember them, sniffing their pungent leaves, rolling their seeds beneath her paw, fixing the scents in her mind. She couldn't wait to get home and start scouring the moor.

Micah nosed past Dappled Pelt and sniffed a wide, furry leaf. "What's this?"

As Dappled Pelt turned to see, a yowl split the air outside the den.

"Help!"

Moth Flight froze as Night skidded down the slope into the den. Her eyes were wide with terror. "You have to come! I just pulled Drizzle from the river—she's not breathing!"

CHAPTER 19

♣

Dappled Pelt darted past her Clanmate. Micah hared after her. Panic flashing beneath her pelt, Moth Flight followed.

Dappled Pelt was already skidding through a gap in the camp wall as Moth Flight reached the clearing. Micah raced at her heels. Moth Flight gave chase, blood roaring in her ears. She leaped through the gap and pulled up sharply as the river loomed in front of her.

Dawn Mist was standing at the water's edge, her eyes hollow with dread. Water dripped from her fur and she trembled like frightened prey. A sodden scrap of fur lay at her paws.

Drizzle! Moth Flight's heart leaped into her throat.

Dappled Pelt dropped into a crouch beside the unmoving kit.

Micah leaned close. "Is she dead?"

Dappled Pelt jerked her nose toward Dawn Mist. "Keep her warm. She's in shock."

Micah hurried to Dawn Mist's side and pressed against her.

Moth Flight's paws seemed frozen to the ground as she stared at Drizzle. The tiny kit's flank wasn't moving. "She's not breathing!" She stared at Dappled Pelt. Why did the

RiverClan medicine cat look so calm?

Dappled Pelt's gaze flitted over Drizzle's body, then she lifted her forepaws and rested them on the she-kit's chest.

Moth Flight watched, eyes stretched wide, as Dappled Pelt began pumping the kit with rapid jerks of her paws. "What are you doing?" How could squashing the poor kit help?

Dappled Pelt ignored her. She paused and leaned down, sniffing at Drizzle's muzzle. Then, straightening, she began to pump the kit's chest again.

Drizzle's body shuddered with each jolt, her paws flapping limply, like the paws of a dead rabbit.

Dappled Pelt paused again and sniffed at Drizzle's nose.

Dawn Mist let out a low moan. "She's dead!"

"No," Dappled Pelt, growled fiercely. "Not yet." Once more she rested her paws on Drizzle's chest and began pumping.

Suddenly, with a splutter, Drizzle jerked and began coughing up water. Dappled Pelt quickly rolled the kit onto her side, stroking her chest fiercely as Drizzle brought up more water.

"Drizzle?" Dawn Mist's mew was no more than a breath.

Drizzle stopped vomiting and blinked at her mother. "What happened?" she croaked weakly.

Pine Needle stuck his nose out from behind a clump of reeds. "Is she okay?" His eyes were bright with terror.

Dawn Mist beckoned him closer. "She's fine." She looked anxiously at Dappled Pelt. "Isn't she?"

"Yes. Now that she's coughed up the water, she'll be able to breathe again," Dappled Pelt told her briskly.

Moth Flight stared at the River Clan medicine cat. She

wasn't even trembling. *How does she stay so calm?*

Pine Needle hurried to his mother's side and pressed against her flank. "She wanted to see if she could catch her own fish. But she disappeared under the water," he mewed shakily. "I called Night when she didn't come up again."

"She needs to learn to swim before she catches a fish." River Ripple brushed past Moth Flight.

She spun, her heart lurching at the sight of the RiverClan leader. She hadn't heard his paw steps.

He touched his muzzle to Dawn Mist's cheek. "Start teaching them as soon as Drizzle has recovered."

Dawn Mist met his gaze, her eyes glistening. "I wanted to wait until they were stronger."

"Fish swim the moment they are born," River Ripple murmured. "It's never too soon for a RiverClan kit to learn."

Drizzle pushed herself uncertainly to her paws.

Dawn Mist leaned down and lapped her cheek. "Let's get you into my nest and warm you up." She nosed the kit toward the clearing.

River Ripple ran his tail along Pine Needle's spiked fur. "You did well to fetch help."

"I only called to Night."

"That was the right thing to do," River Ripple told him.

Pine Needle stared at him uncertainly. "I shouldn't have let her go into the water."

River Ripple touched his muzzle to the kit's head. "Sometimes we can't stop others from making mistakes. But we can help them when they do. And that's what you did." He nosed the kit after his mother, who was lifting Drizzle into a reed nest on the far side of the clearing.

Dappled Pelt watched her leader as he guided Pine Needle away. "He's so good with the kits," she murmured. "It's a shame he doesn't have any of his own."

Moth Flight hardly heard her. "How did you know what to do?"

"River Ripple taught me," she explained. "He's lived near the water all his life and he knows that you can push water out of a cat's chest as easily as a cat can suck it in."

Micah swished his tail through the air. "You were fantastic! I thought Drizzle was dead."

Dappled Pelt gazed at the river as it swirled past. "It's a trick every RiverClan cat should know."

Admiration surged beneath Moth Flight's pelt. *I hope I'm as calm and skilled as Dappled Pelt one day!* How must it feel to save another cat's life? She wondered if Half Moon had been watching. *I'll try to become as good as she is,* she promised silently.

Clouds hid the setting sun. A thin drizzle misted the river and a breeze rustled the reeds around camp.

Moth Flight shifted closer to Micah as the damp wind licked her pelt. She eyed Night, who was watching them warily from the other side of the clearing. Dawn Mist was still curled in her nest, tucked among the rushes. River Ripple had gone hunting for shrews in the reed beds with Dawn Mist's mate, Swift. "Are you sure we should stay the night?" Moth Flight whispered.

"Of course!" Micah looked up from washing his belly.

"Look how much we learned today! Tomorrow we'll learn even more."

Moth Flight was glad he was with her. She liked the River-Clan cats, but it felt strange to be away from the hollow. After she'd returned from the valley, she thought she'd never leave her Clanmates again. "Do you think River Ripple will catch a shrew?" she mewed hopefully.

Dappled Pelt had slipped into the river as the sun began to sink, promising to bring them back a juicy trout.

Micah blinked at her. "Don't you want to taste fish?"

Moth Flight wrinkled her nose. She'd smelled nothing but fish and herbs all afternoon. She was looking forward to tasting the sweet, familiar flesh of prey with legs. Before she could answer, water splashed behind them and Dappled Pelt waded out from the river.

Moth Flight's heart sank as she saw a fish between the tortoiseshell's jaws. It thrashed as she padded onto land, its scales glittering through the rain. Dappled Pelt stopped in front of them and dropped it on the ground.

Moth Flight hopped backward as it wriggled, spattering mud onto her paws.

Purring with amusement, Dappled Pelt stilled it with a forepaw and leaned to give a killing bite. "At least you know it's fresh," she meowed, looking up.

Micah glanced at Moth Flight. "Do you want the first taste?"

She flattened her ears and sniffed uneasily at the fish. "Is this a trout?"

Dappled Pelt's eyes flashed. "It's called a chub."

Moth Flight stifled a shiver. "Does it taste anything like toad?"

"No!" Dappled Pelt snorted. "Who eats *toads*?"

"They taste like mud!" Micah spluttered.

Heat spread beneath Moth Flight's pelt. There was no way she was going to tell Micah and Dappled Pelt that she'd shared one with Spotted Fur. She touched the chub gingerly with a paw.

Micah caught her eye. "Do you want to wait and see if River Ripple brings back a shrew?"

"No." Moth Flight lifted her chin. She wasn't a coward. Besides, it would be rude to refuse Dappled Pelt's gift. "I want to taste fish." She leaned down and sank her teeth into the soft flank of the chub, delighted to find the texture meatier than the rubbery toad flesh. As she tore away a chunk, the flavor sang on her tongue. She blinked at Dappled Pelt in surprise. "It's *nice*!" Chewing, she relished the soft flesh. It tasted of fresh water. "It's *delicious*!"

"Don't tell Wind Runner you like RiverClan food," Micah joked. He took a mouthful, his eyes brightening as he chewed. "Oh, you're right! It's great!"

As he spoke, River Ripple nosed his way through the reed wall of the camp, a water vole dangling from his jaws. Swift followed him, carrying a shrew. They stopped when they saw Moth Flight and Micah.

River Ripple dropped the vole. "You're eating fish!"

"It's tasty!" Moth Flight ripped off another mouthful.

River Ripple nodded toward the shrew dangling from

Swift's jaws. "You might as well share that with the kits."

The dark brown tom dipped his head and carried his catch toward the nest where Dawn Mist was curled with Drizzle and Pine Needle. Placing it beside the tightly woven bundle of reeds, he stuck his nose in and nudged Dawn Mist's pelt.

She jerked her head up, blinking.

"How's Drizzle?" Swift asked.

"I'm fine!" Drizzle sat up, ears pricked.

"I smell *vole!*" Pine Needle clambered onto his mother's back and peered from the nest. Nose twitching, his gaze flashed toward River Ripple's catch. He scrambled out of the nest and raced toward it. "Can I taste it?" He glanced at the RiverClan leader.

"Of course." As River Ripple pushed the vole toward Pine Needle, Drizzle leaped from the nest and hurried to her brother's side.

"I want to taste it too!"

River Ripple purred. "It's good to see you looking better."

Drizzle stuck her tail up indignantly. "I wasn't sick. I only went for a swim!"

River Ripple's whiskers twitched. Water beaded along them as the rain grew heavier. He glanced up at the darkening sky. "I'm going to my nest." He headed toward a den, woven among the roots of another tree stump.

Moth Flight felt rain seeping through her pelt. "Where should we sleep?" she called after the RiverClan leader.

He paused and nodded toward Dappled Pelt's den. "Is there room enough there?"

Dappled Leaf nodded. "They can share the spare nest."

As River Ripple disappeared inside his den, Moth Flight glanced shyly at Micah. She'd only shared a nest with her brother before. Dust Muzzle had always teased her that it was like sleeping next to a badger. "I'm afraid I snore."

"Good." He took another bite of fish. "I snore too."

Dappled Pelt rolled her eyes. "Great," she muttered.

When they'd finished the chub, she led them to her den. Rain was thrumming the earth as dusk gave way to night, and Moth Flight was relieved to slip into the shelter of the tree stump. She crossed the dark den and climbed into the reed nest on the far side, surprised to find the stems silky beneath her paws. All the sharp ends had been carefully tucked underneath so that curling into it felt almost as good as curling into her heather nest at home. She wriggled to one side, leaving room for Micah.

He squeezed in beside her. "Do you have enough room?"

"Yes." Moth Flight purred as Micah's warm pelt pressed against her.

Dappled Pelt's golden gaze shone through the darkness. "Are you both comfortable?"

"I am," Micah purred.

"Me too." Moth Flight snuggled deeper into the reeds. She yawned, suddenly sleepy. "I hope I remember everything I've learned today."

"You will." Micah shifted beside her, tucking his paws close to his belly.

Moth Flight blinked at him through the darkness. "I don't

think I'll ever forget seeing Drizzle come back to life."

"She was never dead," Dappled Pelt meowed across the den. "She just needed air in her chest instead of water."

Moth Flight suddenly remembered her dream of the blue-gray she-cat. She'd come back to life too. Perhaps she hadn't been dead either. Moth Flight frowned. But no cat had pumped *her* chest, and she hadn't coughed up water.

Beside her, Micah's breathing began to slow and deepen. He was drifting into sleep. Moth Flight rested her muzzle on her paws and watched him. Her fur tingled where his breath stirred her pelt. Gradually, her eyes grew heavy and closed and darkness swirled around her.

A familiar stone tang touched Moth Flight's nose. She opened her eyes as the scent of the Moonstone cave washed her tongue. Leaping to her paws, she gazed around. *How did I get back—*

Before she could finish her thought, two cats padded into the cave. A large, dark tabby, the one she'd seen with the gray she-cat the day she'd come back to life, headed for the Moonstone, his eyes fixed on the dull rock. He glanced at the hole in the roof, the watery starlight reflecting in his yellow eyes.

Moth Flight shivered. There was coldness in this tom's gaze, and a stiffness in his broad shoulders that frightened her. He seemed to be waiting for the moon to light the rock, impatience rippling along his spine.

The gray tom, who'd entered the cave with him, stopped at the dark tabby's side. The tabby jerked his muzzle around, snarling as the gray tom spoke. There was no friendship between these cats. *Then why are they here together?*

The dark tabby sank stiffly onto his belly and touched his nose to the rock a moment before moonlight set it alight.

Moth Flight screwed up her eyes, flinching as brightness blinded her.

The stone beneath her paws turned to squelchy moss. She blinked open her eyes eagerly. Was she back on StarClan's hunting grounds?

Darkness pressed on every side. She turned her head sharply. Trees loomed around her. This wasn't StarClan's land. She recognized the dank scent of rotting wood, sharpened by the smell of pinesap. This was *ShadowClan* territory.

Feline shapes moved among the trees, their shadowy pelts glittering with starlight. *Spirit-cats!* She scanned the starry cats, hoping to see a familiar pelt, but these weren't the StarClan cats she knew. Heart racing, she backed toward a tree, hoping she couldn't be seen. Her fur rippled with fear. These cats moved with solemn purpose and the dark tabby seemed to be waiting for them, his gaze blazing expectantly in the darkness.

His eyes narrowed as a sparkling tom approached him. Moth Flight saw the spirit-cat speak, but she couldn't make out the words. As the tom stepped away, a small ginger she-cat took his place. The she-cat spoke and the dark tabby answered, disdain sparking in his gaze.

Doesn't he respect his ancestors? Moth Flight leaned closer, pelt pricking with interest.

The she-cat reached her muzzle forward and touched the dark tabby's head.

The tabby jerked as though agony flared through him.

This is like the time I saw the blue-gray cat in the cave! Moth Flight remembered her dream. Why did the touch of these spirit-cats seem to cause so much pain?

Moth Flight narrowed her eyes, her breath quickening as one after another, the spirit-cats stepped forward and touched the dark tabby. Each time, he stiffened, his pelt spiking, but he did not give ground. He met each new touch, his eyes burning with hunger.

Finally, the last spirit-cat stepped away and the dark tabby lifted his muzzle. Moth Flight looked into his eyes, searching for some clue as to what the spirit-cats had shared with him, but she saw only pride.

Around him, the spirit-cats' mouths moved. They seemed to be chanting something. Moth Flight pricked her ears, trying to make out the words, but she couldn't. One StarClan tom broke off, his mouth frozen as he stared at the dark tabby.

Moth Flight swallowed as she saw dread darken the spirit-cat's gaze.

She jolted awake, cold with fear.

"Moth Flight?" Micah jerked his head up as she stared, blinking, around Dappled Pelt's den.

The sound of his mew soothed her and she turned and met his gaze.

"Bad dream?" he asked.

As she nodded, he leaned forward and touched his muzzle to her cheek. "Go back to sleep," he murmured softly. "We're safe here."

Obediently, she rested her nose on her paws and closed her

eyes. She felt his tongue lap her ear until weariness muddled her thoughts.

"It was only a dream." Micah stopped and tucked his muzzle beside hers.

These aren't dreams. They're visions. As his breath deepened into gentle snores, worry pulled Moth Flight back from the brink of sleep. *But what are they about? And why do they make me feel so uneasy?*

CHAPTER 20

Early-morning light washed the reed beds. The rain that had drenched the camp for the past two days had finally lifted and sunshine was breaking through the clouds. On the other side of the clearing, River Ripple stretched outside his den. Moss Tail and Dawn Mist were stirring sleepily in their nest while Drizzle and Pine Needle charged across the camp, trying to catch each other's tails.

Dappled Pelt blinked kindly at Moth Flight and Micah. "I've taught you all I know."

Micah whisked his tail. "You know lots!"

"I can't wait to use some of the stuff I've learned!" Moth Flight's pelt prickled with excitement. *I hope I can find goatweed on the moor!* It was one of the herbs Dappled Pelt had shown them. A few leaves, given daily, might lift Slate's grief.

Her paws itched to go home, and yet the thought of leaving Micah made her heart ache.

Micah glanced around the RiverClan camp. "I'm going to miss it here," he murmured. "I was getting used to the sound of the river lulling me to sleep."

I was getting used to the sound of your breathing. Moth Flight glanced at him shyly. Her own nest would seem chilly without him.

Drizzle skidded to a halt between them. "Are you leaving?"

Pine Needle stared at Micah with round eyes. "You can't go yet! I haven't taught you how to fish."

Micah nudged the kit's cheek with his nose. "You need to learn how to *swim* first."

Pine Needle stuck out his chin. "I swam a whole tail-length yesterday!"

Drizzle snorted. "With Dawn Mist holding your scruff!"

"At least I didn't try to swallow half the river!"

"Hush." Dappled Pelt silenced Pine Needle with a look. "Micah and Moth Flight need to return to their Clans."

"Why can't they stay here with us?" Drizzle mewed.

"My Clan needs me," Micah told her.

A twinge jabbed Moth Flight's heart. *I need you.* She pushed the rabbit-brained thought away. "Mine too."

Drizzle's tail drooped. "Okay."

"Will you come and visit again?" Pine Needle asked.

"Of course." Moth Flight swished her tail. "When we have new skills to share."

Dappled Pelt's eyes shone. "I hope it won't be long." Her gaze flitted past them.

Moth Flight turned, following it. River Ripple was heading toward them. She dipped her head as he neared. "Thank you for letting us stay."

"It was an honor."

Micah nudged Moth Flight as the RiverClan leader blinked

at her respectfully. "See what happens when you get chosen by StarClan?" he teased.

"I must get back to my herbs." Dappled Pelt turned toward her den. "They won't sort themselves."

"Thanks!" Moth Flight called as she disappeared inside.

Micah gazed across the reed beds thoughtfully. "Do we have to go home right away?"

Moth Flight shot him a look. "Don't you want to go back to SkyClan?"

"Eventually." Micah leaned close to her ear. "But I like hanging out with you," he whispered.

Moth Flight snatched her gaze away, her pelt growing hot. "I like hanging out with you too," she mumbled.

River Ripple looked away, his whiskers twitching. Moth Flight wondered if he'd heard.

"Perhaps Cloud Spots can teach you about woodland herbs," River Ripple meowed vaguely as he stared toward the forest. "ThunderClan camp isn't far."

Micah blinked at him. "That's a good idea! It'll be fun. And we can tell Cloud Spots what we've learned from Dappled Pelt."

"I'm sure he'll appreciate that." River Ripple kept his gaze on the trees.

Moth Flight shifted her paws self-consciously. "Maybe." She felt guilty about staying away from the moor for so long. *And with Micah.* "But what about WindClan? They might need me."

River Ripple blinked at her. "You've got a whole lifetime to take care of your Clan. Have fun while you can."

She glanced at Micah. If River Ripple thought visiting ThunderClan was okay, then it must be. "Let's do it."

Micah purred. "Great!"

River Ripple's tail twitched. "Do you want me to show you the way?"

And miss walking alone with Micah? "No," Moth Flight told him quickly.

"We'll find it," Micah assured him.

"I thought you'd say that." A teasing glint flashed in River Ripple's eyes. Moth Flight's paws prickled with embarrassment. He *had* guessed they wanted to be alone.

River Rippled turned his muzzle toward the forest. "The camp's in a ravine," he told them. "It's hard to see from the top, so follow your noses."

Micah dipped his head and padded toward the camp entrance. "Thanks."

"Yes, thank you, River Ripple," Moth Flight called as she hurried after Micah.

They followed the trail through the reeds until it opened onto the riverbank. Moth Flight could see the stepping-stones, which crossed to the tree-lined shore beyond. She trotted happily toward them. Dappled Pelt had led her over them so many times in the past few days that she no longer thought twice about getting her paws wet. She knew this stretch of river and the herbs that grew along it as well as she knew the moortop. She beat Micah to the first stone and bounded across, landing at the far side, her chest bursting with happiness.

She purred as Micah landed beside her. "Which way now?"

Micah gazed among the trees, narrowing his eyes as he scanned the shadows. "I don't know this part of the forest."

"Let's explore it together." Moth Flight marched from the shore and hopped over an oak root jutting from the ground. She brushed past a fern, its fresh leaves glowing in the dappled light that glittered through the canopy. Musty scents bathed her muzzle and, for the first time since leaving the moor, she smelled mouse. Her belly rumbled. They hadn't eaten since last night, when Moss Tail had brought them a trout. She longed to taste furry prey again and she scanned the undergrowth, hoping to catch sight of movement among the leaves.

"We mustn't hunt," Micah reminded her. His nose was twitching. "Can't you smell the border scents?"

Moth Flight had been too busy sniffing for prey. She lifted her muzzle and breathed in the scent of ThunderClan cats. "Perhaps we can catch a fish. I'm sure River Ripple won't mind." Her belly growled again.

"Can you swim?" Micah stared at her.

"No." Moth Flight glanced back at the river. "But sometimes they come close to the shore. We might be able to wade in and grab one."

"Or we could wait here for a bird to fly into our paws."

Moth Flight lifted her tail and brushed past Micah, huffily. "It was just a *suggestion*."

He purred and padded after her. "I love your suggestions."

Moth Flight tried not to purr. Micah was so sweet.

He fell in step beside her. "Let's find the camp. Hopefully

ThunderClan will share their prey."

Moth Flight followed Micah, pelt pricking uneasily. Had Cloud Spots warned Thunder that StarClan wanted the medicine cats to share their knowledge? She knew that the ThunderClan leader was Clear Sky's son; did that mean he'd be as suspicious as SkyClan's leader?

They followed a rabbit trail between brambles and bracken as the forest floor rose beneath their paws. It steepened as the trees grew thicker, the shadows deepening around them.

"Do you know where you're going?" she asked Micah hopefully.

"No." Micah scrambled over a rotting log and paused on the other side.

Moth Flight dropped down beside him and gazed between the trees. They seemed to stretch on forever, sunlight piercing the leaves here and there, illuminating spots of woodland with brilliant shafts of light. She pointed her nose toward a thick path of brambles some way ahead. "Do you think that could be the camp wall?"

"Let's check." Micah headed toward it, stumbling as a root tripped him.

Moth Flight steadied him with her muzzle. "I thought you were used to forests," she teased.

"I'm used to *farms*," Micah reminded her. "I don't know if I'll ever stop stubbing my paws on roots."

"Of course you will. You just nee—" Moth Flight yelped as she trod on a patch of young nettles. Pain shot through her paw and she hopped clear, lifting it protectively.

"Wait." Micah glanced at the nettles then began to scan the forest floor, his eyes lighting up. He dashed toward a clump of leaves sprouting beside an ash. Tearing one off with his teeth, he carried it back to Moth Flight.

She stared at it. "What's that?"

"Dock." Micah laid it upside-down on the ground in front of her. "Rub your paw on it."

Moth Flight pressed her throbbing pad to the soft leaf.

"Rub it hard," Micah urged.

Moth Flight squashed the leaf beneath her paw until she felt its juices bathe the sting. To her surprise, the pain eased. "That's great!" She stared at Micah with round eyes.

"I learned it from Cow," Micah told her.

"I wonder if dock grows on the moor," Moth Flight murmured.

A deep mew sounded from between the trees. "If nettles grow there, dock won't be far away."

Moth Flight jerked around, her heart lurching.

Micah flattened his ears warily.

"Don't worry. It's only me." A black tom padded from the shadows.

"Cloud Spots!" Relief washed Moth Flight's pelt.

"Are you two lost?" The ThunderClan medicine cat stopped beside them.

"We've come to visit you," Micah explained.

Cloud Spots sniffed them, his nose wrinkling. "How was your stay with RiverClan?"

"Dappled Pelt taught us so much!" Moth Flight told him

eagerly. "We've come to share what we learned."

Micah lifted his tail. "And hopefully learn some more."

Moth Flight blinked at Cloud Spots. "Will Thunder let us stay?"

"Of course." Cloud Spots flashed Micah a playful look. "He doesn't want SkyClan's medicine cat knowing more than his."

Micah purred. "He sounds like Clear Sky."

"Perhaps," Cloud Spots conceded. "But he also wants to please StarClan."

Micah's whiskers twitched. "I'm not sure Clear Sky cares much about what StarClan thinks. But he cares about his Clan."

Cloud Spots dipped his head. "He's become a worthy leader."

Moth Flight looked toward the bramble thicket. "Are we near the camp?"

"It's not far," Cloud Spots told her. "I'm heading back there once I've collected some borage leaves."

Moth Flight gazed at him blankly. "What's borage?"

"I'll show you." Cloud Spots led them along a winding track through bracken, stopping as the trees thinned. In the patchy sunlight beyond, green plants crowded the forest floor. Their soft leaves looked furry and buds showed at the top of each stem. "By greenleaf, this patch will be purple with flowers."

Moth Flight padded among the stems, breathing in the zesty perfume. She stopped and touched her nose to a leaf, surprised by its softness. "What's it for?"

"The leaves help soothe bad bellies," Cloud Spots told her.

"And relieve tight chests. They can also help nursing queens to make more milk for their kits."

Micah weaved among the stems. "Is someone ill?"

"Milkweed has just had kits," Cloud Spots told her.

Moth Flight blinked. Newleaf seemed to bring kits like it brought fresh leaves. She wondered if any cat in WindClan was expecting.

Micah ran his paw over a borage leaf. "Doesn't she have enough milk?"

"I'm just making sure," Cloud Spots told him. "Milkweed's not as young as she used to be. She had her first litter many moons ago, before she joined the Clan."

"Is Leaf the father?" Moth Flight tipped her head, curious. She'd seen Leaf and Milkweed at gatherings. They'd always stayed close, watching each other with a fondness she'd only seen between her mother and Gorse Fur.

"Yes," Cloud Spots purred.

Moth Flight reached out a paw and tore a borage leaf from its stem.

"The best leaves grow halfway up the stem," Cloud Spots told her. "Not too tough, but old enough to have plenty of sap."

Moth Flight chose another leaf closer to the middle of the plant. "Like this one?"

"That's great." Cloud Spots picked a leaf from the plant beside him and laid it on the ground.

Together they picked enough to make a small pile, then Cloud Spots rolled them into a tight bundle and clasped it between his jaws.

He headed away through the trees. Moth Flight followed, Micah on her tail. They pushed past the brambles and headed across a clearing, Cloud Spots slowing as the forest sloped upward.

He flicked his tail sharply, his ears twitching a warning. Moth Flight halted as the medicine cat stopped and looked down. She followed his gaze, amazed to see the land drop away into a steep ravine.

Spindly trees and bushes crowded the bottom. "Is the camp down there?"

"Yes." Cloud Spots placed his bundle on the ground. "Follow my route down the cliff and watch closely where I put my paws. Some of the ledges are narrow." Picking up the wad of borage, he scrambled down onto a wide shelf, then hopped onto a narrow jutting stone below.

Moth Flight glanced nervously at Micah.

"Trust your paws," Micah told her. "They led you to the Moonstone." Slithering onto the first ledge, he followed Cloud Spots. Moth Flight ignored her pounding heart and jumped down after him.

She landed clumsily and sent grit showering down. "Sorry!" she called as it sprayed Cloud Spots and Micah.

Micah shook the dirt from his pelt. "Don't worry!"

Carefully, Moth Flight leaped down onto the next ledge, unsheathing her claws to help her grip. Fear sparked beneath her pelt as she hopped from rock to rock until at last she saw the ground below. She landed on the smooth earth beside Micah, limp with relief. But there was still no sign of the camp. A large gorse bush blocked their way. She scanned it, searching for an entrance, but it was only when Cloud Spots slid among the dark green branches that she saw it. She followed Micah through, aware of the high cliffs and thick bushes looming on every side. It was different from the airy RiverClan camp.

As she emerged from the gorse, she blinked, surprised to see a grassy clearing. Bushes encircled it, and a wide thicket of bramble crowded one end, while a great rock towered at the other. On the far side, a cliff showed amid burgeoning ferns and, at the other side, a rotting tree lay, bark crumbling around it.

Cloud Spots headed for the brambles, while Micah paused in the clearing.

Moth Flight stopped beside him. She could smell Thunder-Clan scents. They clung to the grass and drifted from every bush, but there was no sign of any cat. "Where is every cat?"

"Hunting!" Cloud Spots called over his shoulder before disappearing among the bramble stems.

"I'm not." A croaky mew sounded from the shadows beneath a jutting branch of the fallen tree. A skinny white tom crept out. Moth Flight recognized Pink Eyes. She'd seen him at her first Gathering. He blinked through sunlight shafting past the thick canopy. *Is he blind now?* The tom was squinting, as though trying to make them out.

"It's me, Moth Flight." She padded closer. "I'm WindClan's medicine cat—"

Pink Eyes interrupted. "You don't need to tell me who you are. The Clan has been gossiping about you since you came back from Highstones, talking of spirit-cats."

Moth Flight hesitated. The Clans *gossiped* about her? She shifted her paws self-consciously as Pink Eyes went on.

"You told Cloud Spots to be our medicine cat, so now he wants me to eat herbs," he muttered peevishly. "He thinks he can cure my aches and pains. But you can't cure old age."

Cloud Spots squeezed out from the bramble. "I can try," he called to Pink Eyes.

"I'd rather you brought me a fresh vole every day," Pink Eyes huffed.

Cloud Spots flashed Moth Flight an exasperated look. "It's my job to take care of you."

A young orange-and-white she-kit who looked about three moons old slid out from the bramble and raced toward the old tom. "Pink Eyes! Shall I fetch fresh moss for your bedding?"

A dappled gray tom-kit chased after her. "I'll help you, Apple Blossom." He stopped as he saw Moth Flight and Micah and blinked at them in surprise. "Are these the visitors you told Milkweed about?" he asked Cloud Spots.

"Yes. Moth Flight and Micah."

"Hi!" Apple Blossom dipped her head, then looked at Cloud Spots. "Can we go and gather moss for Pink Eyes's bed?"

Pink Eyes snorted. "I don't need my nest stuffed with damp moss."

Apple Blossom lifted her tail. "We'll lay it in the sun to dry first." She flicked her muzzle toward the dappled gray tom-kit. "Snail Shell says he found a patch of the softest moss ever."

The tom-kit nodded. "We can fetch it now."

Cloud Spots frowned. "Is it far from camp?"

Snail Shell shook his head. "It's near the top of the ravine."

Apple Blossom blinked hopefully at the ThunderClan medicine cat. "We won't be gone long."

Cloud Spots dipped his head. "Be careful climbing down. It's hard to see where you're putting your paws with a mouthful of moss."

Apple Blossom hared toward the gorse barrier. "We won't fall."

Snail Shell chased after her, disappearing through the gap in the dark green branches.

Pink Eyes rolled his eyes dramatically. "Between swallowing herbs and having my nest cleaned out, I don't get a moment's peace."

Cloud Spots purred. "And don't forget all the kit-watching you do," he teased.

"Kit-watching!" Pink Eyes grunted. "I suppose I feel useful helping out Gooseberry and Yew Tail. Makes the new family feel welcome. But Apple Blossom and Snail Shell hardly need me anymore."

"Shivering Rose, Hazel Burrow, and Morning Fire will, as soon as they're big enough to leave the den."

Moth Flight pricked her ears. *If Apple Blossom and Snail Shell belong to a new family, then the kits Cloud Spots just mentioned must be . . .* "Are they Milkweed's kits?"

Cloud Spots nodded, glancing toward the bramble bush. "Do you want to see them?"

"Yes." Though Moth Flight was more interested in finding

out if Milkweed had eaten the borage Cloud Spots had taken her. She followed the ThunderClan medicine cat toward the tangle of brambles that spilled from one edge of the clearing. As she neared, she saw a small entrance hollowed among the stems.

Cloud Spots stuck his nose in. "Milkweed! Moth Flight's here. May she see your kits?"

"Of course!" A gentle mew sounded from inside.

Moth Flight glanced at Micah, standing in the clearing. "Can Micah come?"

Micah shrugged. "Cow always told me to leave a queen and her kits to themselves. I'll keep Pink Eyes company," he meowed. "He must have plenty of stories to share."

Pink Eyes's tail twitched. "I don't see why a young tom like you would be interested, but okay."

Cloud Spots wriggled through the brambles and Moth Flight followed. She was surprised to find herself in a wide hollow walled by prickly stems. Sunlight speared through gaps in the branches. "How did you make this den?" she asked, gazing around.

"Carefully," Cloud Spots purred.

Three wide nests, woven from twigs and lined with moss, sat on a dry earth floor. A splotchy ginger-and-black she-cat gazed with amber eyes from one. Three tiny kits squirmed at her belly, their eyes closed.

The warm scent of milk touched Moth Flight's nose. One of the kits began mewling as another pushed him away from his mother's soft flank. Milkweed quickly scooped him near with a paw. "That's Hazel Burrow," she purred. "Shivering Rose and Morning Fire are always stealing his milk. But he's going to grow into a handsome tom, just like his father."

"They're all beautiful." Moth Flight gazed at the black-and-white tom-kit, happy now as he nursed at Milkweed's belly. Shivering Rose nuzzled in beside him, her black pelt as fluffy as an owl chick's, while Morning Fire squirmed closer, her dark brown fur camouflaged among the shadows.

Moth Flight glanced toward the empty nest on the other side of the den. It smelled warm. "Is that Apple Blossom and Snail Shell's nest?"

"They share it with their mother, Gooseberry," Cloud Spots told her.

"There's hardly room for them anymore," Milkweed commented. "But there may be more space soon. The third nest belongs to Violet Dawn, and I think she wants to move to Thunder's den."

Moth Flight knew that Violet Dawn was a sleek dark gray she-cat who'd joined ThunderClan several moons ago. Thunder had taken her as his mate.

Cloud Spots narrowed his eyes thoughtfully. "Perhaps they should be building new nests instead of collecting moss for Pink Eyes."

A hoarse mew sounded outside the den. "Do you want me to go scavenging for my own bedding?"

Cloud Spots purred. "Pink Eyes's sight may be weak, but his hearing is as sharp as ever." He nodded toward the den entrance. "Let's leave Milkweed to rest."

"Have you given her the borage?" Moth Flight asked.

Cloud Spots nodded to a pile of leaves beside her nest. "She's had one leaf and I'm leaving the rest in case she needs more."

"Take some for your store," Milkweed told him. "I won't need it all."

Cloud Spots glanced at the kits, suckling happily at her belly, and nodded. "Okay." He grabbed a few leaves from the pile and nosed his way out of the den.

"Thanks for letting me see your kits," Moth Flight mewed gratefully to the queen.

Milkweed purred. "There's nothing better than being a mother."

"I guess." Moth Flight shrugged, wondering what could be better than roaming the moor alone, searching for new plants. She couldn't imagine being responsible for cats too helpless to look after themselves. *But isn't that what a* medicine cat *has to do?* Her belly tightened as she followed Cloud Spots into the clearing. Then she saw Micah. He looked so handsome, a pool of sunshine creeping slowly across his flank. He was lying beside Pink Eyes, his attention fixed on the old tom as he listened.

"The squirrel was near the top of the tree," Pink Eyes rumbled. "But I wasn't going to let it get away. I followed it up. Then, just as I scrambled onto the highest branch, there was—" The old tom broke off and snapped his gaze toward the gorse.

A moment later, the barrier trembled and Thunder padded into camp. Lightning Tail trotted at his heels. The

ThunderClan leader's orange pelt glowed in the dappled sunlight. A rabbit hung from his jaws. Owl Eyes and Leaf followed, carrying prey.

"Good hunting, I see?" Cloud Spots nodded toward the rabbit.

Thunder dropped his catch. "Just wait until greenleaf." His gaze slid toward Moth Flight.

Micah scrambled to his paws and shook out his dusty pelt. "I hope you don't mind—"

Thunder dipped his head to Moth Flight. "We are honored by your visit." He turned to Micah. "How is Clear Sky?"

"He's fine."

Lightning Tail grunted. "Does he still think he's the best cat in the forest?"

"He knows his strengths," Micah answered diplomatically.

Thunder snorted. "I bet he likes you."

"He will," Micah answered. "Eventually."

Leaf was heading for the nursery. "Is Milkweed okay?" he called to Cloud Spots.

"She's fine."

Owl Eyes glanced toward the gorse barrier. "Violet Dawn asked me if you have any chervil. She's had a bellyache all morning."

"Where is she?" Cloud Spots's eyes darkened with worry.

"She stopped to help Apple Blossom and Snail Shell gather moss," Owl Eyes told him.

"I'll get some for her," Cloud Spots meowed. "There's plenty in the forest."

Micah narrowed his eyes. "Don't you keep any in your store?"

Cloud Spots shrugged. "It's better to pick fresh leaves this time of year," he explained. "I'll gather some to dry for my store in late greenleaf, when it's starting to die back."

Paw steps sounded beyond the gorse barrier and Thistle and Clover pushed their way into camp. They were dragging a fat wood pigeon between them.

Thunder swished his tail. "You managed to get it down the cliff!"

Clover sniffed. "Thistle threw it over the edge and we hauled it from the bottom."

Moth Flight glanced at the battered bird, its wings splayed awkwardly. Feathers speckled the ground around it. "It was a good thing no one was underneath."

Thistle sniffed. "Any cat who can't hear a pigeon bouncing down a cliff needs his ears checked."

Micah's eyes flashed with amusement. "It looks like it hit every ledge on the way down."

Pink Eyes padded to the pigeon and sniffed it. "At least it'll be tender."

Cloud Spots nodded toward the ferns. "Do you want to see my den before I go and gather chervil?"

Moth Flight nodded eagerly and followed as Cloud Spots headed across the clearing and pushed through a tunnel of ferns.

Moth Flight glanced at Micah as he stopped beside her. "You go first."

The yellow tom dipped his head and nosed his way after Cloud Spots. Moth Flight followed, padding through the fern tunnel, her belly fluttering with excitement. She could already smell Cloud Spot's herbs. A small clearing opened ahead, edged by a cliff that stretched toward the top of the ravine. Water trickled down the rock, pooling at one edge, and a crack opened in the stone. Moth Flight padded toward it and sniffed, her nose twitching as the pungent herb scents grew stronger. "Do you keep your stores in there?" She peered into the darkness.

Cloud Spots brushed past her and reached into the crack. He pulled out a wad of leaves, neatly bundled and tied with grass. He opened it and spread the herbs over the den floor.

Moth Flight glanced at them, hoping to recognize one. But they were forest herbs, lush and dark and musty-smelling.

"This is comfrey." Cloud Spots pulled the largest leaf closer. "I keep a few leaves in my store in case Pink Eyes is wakened in the night by aches. But the forest is full of it and I like to gather it fresh each day and line his nest with it."

"What does it do?" Micah sniffed the furry leaf.

"It eases the pains in his joints," Cloud Spots told him.

"Can you eat it?" Moth Flight asked.

"Yes, but wrapping sore limbs in the leaves works just as well," Cloud Spots told her. "I've heard it even helps *broken* limbs to heal, though I've not yet had to try it."

The ferns rustled and Leaf padded into the den. "Milk-weed's thirsty," he meowed.

Cloud Spots jerked his muzzle around. "I'm sorry! I

meant to give her fresh moss."

Moth Flight frowned, puzzled. How could moss help thirst?

"I'll take it to her." Leaf padded toward the water pooling beside the rock. He hooked a lump of moss from a heap piled at one edge and dipped it in the water. He let it soak for a few moments, then grabbed it between his jaws and carried it, dripping, toward the fern tunnel.

As he disappeared, Moth Flight blinked. "She laps water from the moss!" Had she seen Reed Tail soaking moss in puddles on the moor? She must ask him when she got back. It was a great idea. Sick cats could stay in their nests and rest instead of roaming the moor in search of a drink.

Cloud Spots gathered up his herbs. "I'd better gather chervil for Violet Dawn. Come with me. I'll show you some other herbs you might find useful."

"Great!" Micah lifted his tail.

Happiness fizzed beneath Moth Flight's fur. She was going to return to WindClan knowing *so* much! Cheerfully she followed Micah and Cloud Spots out of the den.

An owl hooted at the top of the ravine. Moth Flight huddled closer to Micah, searching for a glimpse of the moon through the canopy of trees. Thunder had offered them a nest beside the fallen tree. She could hear Pink Eyes snoring a tail-length away and smell the comfrey lining his nest.

The forest was black with shadow. She was used to the moor, washed silver by moonlight. Countless scents, made richer by a heavy dew, filled her nose. Trying to ignore the pressing darkness, she recalled the plants Cloud Spots had shown them, murmuring their names under her breath. "Coltsfoot, goldenrod, feverfew, catchweed—"

"Can't you sleep?" Micah whispered in the darkness.

"I don't want to forget anything," Moth Flight told him.

Micah nuzzled her ear. "He'll show us again tomorrow," he promised. "You'll remember, don't worry."

I hope so.

"Go to sleep," Micah murmured. "It's been a busy day, and tomorrow might be even busier."

Moth Flight closed her eyes and nestled against his thick fur. It was cozy here. Snail Shell and Apple Blossom had brought back so much moss that there was enough to line their own nest. Micah's warm scent seeped into her thoughts as she slipped into sleep. She purred contentedly. She could easily get used to sleeping beside him every night.

CHAPTER 21

Moth Flight slept. As Micah's soft breath washed her muzzle, she dreamed.

Four kits squirmed between them in a sunny nest. Happily, she nuzzled the strong tom-kit clambering over her flank. "Look, Micah! He's as handsome as you!" She turned to meet Micah's loving gaze, but he'd gone. Alarm spiked through her pelt. "Micah? Where are you?" She was suddenly alone in the nest, cold air flooding around her. "Kits?" Panic surged through her. She leaped to her paws and stared into the shadows closing fast around the nest. Straining to see, she searched for Micah and her kits. "Where did you go?"

"Moth Flight!"

A voice called her name.

"Micah! Is that you?" She struggled awake.

"Moth Flight!"

Bleary with sleep, she struggled free of her dream. She could feel Micah, warm against her. She shook her head, clearing her thoughts. She was in the ThunderClan camp. Soft dawn light crept into the shelter of the fallen tree where they'd made their nest.

"Moth Flight!" Someone was calling her from the clearing.

"I'm coming!" She scrambled onto her paws and hurried out.

Spotted Fur stood in the middle, gazing desperately around. His ears pricked as he saw her. "*There* you are!"

"What's happened?" Fear stabbed her belly. What had sent him here at dawn?

"You said you'd be with RiverClan!" There was reproach in his mew. "River Ripple told me you were *here*." His gaze flicked past her as fur brushed beneath the jutting branch of the fallen tree. "Micah." Spotted Fur's hackles lifted as the yellow tom slid out behind Moth Flight.

Moth Flight flicked her tail impatiently. "What's happened?"

The WindClan tom looked away from Micah. "Rocky's sick!"

Moth Flight frowned. "Is he coughing again?"

"No," Spotted Fur told her. "He's burning hot and he's talking nonsense!"

"Has he been eating catmint?"

"Reed Tail says he's only had tansy," Spotted Fur told her.

Thunder slid from the lichen draping the entrance to his den. "What's going on?" He stared at Spotted Fur.

"We need Moth Flight," Spotted Fur told him.

Around the camp, cats were beginning to stir. Apple Blossom peeked out of the bramble den. Lightning Tail ducked from under a spreading yew, Leaf at his tail.

Lightning Tail narrowed his eyes as he saw Spotted Fur. "How did you find your way into the camp?"

"How do you think?" Spotted Fur snorted. "I followed my

nose, of course. Do you think ThunderClan paw prints don't smell?"

Thunder stepped forward, his ears twitching crossly. "You're disturbing my Clan."

"I'm just here to fetch Moth Flight." Spotted Fur glared at the ThunderClan leader. "One of our Clanmates is sick. We need her."

Heat washed Moth Flight's pelt. Did Spotted Fur have to be rude? Thunder and his Clanmates had been so kind.

Cloud Spots nosed his way from the ferns, a roll of herbs dangling from his mouth. He crossed the clearing and dropped them at Moth Flight's paws. "Take these," he told her. "They're some of the herbs we gathered. They might be some help."

Moth Flight blinked at him gratefully, then dipped her head to Thunder. "Thank you for letting us stay."

Thunder's eyes glowed with warmth. "Send my regards to Wind Runner and Gorse Fur."

"I will." She snatched up the herb bundle and headed for the gorse barrier. Spotted Fur followed.

"Wait for me!" Micah hurried after them.

Spotted Fur glanced at the yellow tom. "We don't need you."

I *do*! Moth Flight grunted crossly, the herb bundle muffling her mew.

"Two medicine cats are better than one," Micah insisted.

Spotted Fur shot Moth Flight a glance. He must have seen the anger in her gaze. "Okay," he snapped, ducking through the gorse barrier. "I guess you can come too."

"Great! See you soon, Cloud Spots!" Micah called over his shoulder. "Take care of Pink Eyes!"

Moth Flight followed Spotted Fur out of camp and stopped at the bottom of the cliff. Spotted Fur was already scanning the rock face. "Follow me." He hopped onto the lowest ledge and began to lead a winding route up the cliff.

By the time they reached the WindClan camp, Moth Flight was out of breath. Her tongue burned with herb juices that had seeped out as she gripped the bundle between her jaws. They'd hared over the last stretch of grass and burst into the hollow as the sun lifted above the distant forest. Sunshine flooded the clearing.

Moth Flight raced toward her den. She could hear Micah's paws thrumming behind her.

Gorse Fur watched them pass, surprise glittering in his eyes. Dust Muzzle and Willow Tail leaped to their paws. Jagged Peak stared from his den, Holly pacing in the shadows behind. Moth Flight felt her pelt prickle as their gaze followed Micah. Why did they look so uneasy?

"Wait!" Wind Runner's yowl sounded across the camp. Moth Flight skidded to a halt.

Her mother was stalking across the tussocks, staring at Micah. "What's he doing here?"

Moth Flight dropped the herbs. "He's come to help!"

"I thought I told you I didn't want him in the camp!" Wind Runner halted.

Moth Flight faced her. "Rocky's sick and Micah's a medicine cat."

Wind Runner didn't blink. "Can't you heal him by yourself?"

"I don't know." Moth Flight held her ground. She fought the urge to drop her gaze as Wind Runner glared at her. Rocky needed help.

Wind Runner's tail twitched ominously "There was an incident while you were away."

Moth Flight tensed. "What happened?"

"A moor rabbit was found in SkyClan's territory," Wind Runner told her.

Micah pricked his ears.

Wind Runner met his gaze accusingly. "Clearly, your Clan is stealing prey from our land."

Micah shrugged. "How do you know it didn't just stray across the border by itself?"

Wind Runner lashed her tail. "Willow Tail said she'd seen SkyClan cats on the moor earlier."

Micah flashed a look at the pale tabby she-cat, who watched through narrowed eyes from beside Dust Muzzle. "That doesn't prove anything."

"It proves SkyClan can't be trusted," Wind Runner snarled.

Moth Flight stepped between her mother and Micah. "I trust Micah!" she growled. "I need his help."

Wind Runner's ears twitched. "One day, you're going to have to stand on your own four paws."

"One day I will. But not today." Moth Flight grabbed the

herb bundle and marched to her den, Micah at her heels.

Inside, Rocky was shivering in his nest. His matted fur clung to his frame. He looked old and weak. Moth Flight's heart quickened.

Reed Tail and Swift Minnow crouched beside him.

"How long has he been like this?" Moth Flight asked Reed Tail.

"He took a turn for the worse last night."

The old tom writhed in the heather, his eyes rolling. "When will leafbare end?" he gasped. "It's so cold!"

How did he get so sick? Is he dying? Thoughts racing, Moth Flight dropped the herbs and thrust her muzzle close to his. Warmth pulsed from his nose. Panic flashed through her. *What do I do first?* Words came. "We need to cool him down." Dappled Pelt had warned her that fevers could be deadly. She turned to Swift Minnow. "Go and find as much moss as you can carry and soak it in a puddle, then bring it back."

"I'm so cold!" Rocky's teeth chattered as Swift Minnow raced from the den.

"What can I do?" Reed Tail asked.

"Go with her."

"Don't you need me here?" Reed Tail frowned anxiously.

"I've got Micah," Moth Flight told him. "We've learned a lot since we left."

Reed Tail nodded and headed out of the den.

Moth Flight hooked a claw through the grass stem that gripped her bundle and snapped it open. The leaves unrolled and herb scents bathed her nose. She stared at them, panic pricking her paws. *Which one is which? What are they for?* Her thoughts whirled as she desperately tried to recall Cloud Spots's training. "Come on," she hissed to herself under her breath. *"Remember!"*

Micah's pelt brushed hers. "Feverfew might help," he murmured.

Feverfew! Of course! But which one is it? She scanned the leaves, her thoughts tumbling over one another. Then she recognized the delicate scalloped leaves that Cloud Spots had helped her pick yesterday.

"Rocky!" She spoke to the tom sternly, hoping he'd understand. "I need you to swallow some leaves, okay?"

He stared at her through clouded eyes, shivering.

"Do you think you can do that?" If Rocky chewed them and spat them out, they'd be wasted. She'd have to return to the forest to fetch more, and there wasn't time.

Rocky stared at her blankly.

Micah leaned forward and rested his muzzle on Rocky's head. "It's just like eating prey," he murmured softly.

Rocky grew still. "Like eating prey," he echoed.

Moth Flight lifted the feverfew to Rocky's lips with a hooked claw. "Just swallow these and you'll feel a bit better."

Micah lapped the old tom's head. "Just a few leaves," he soothed.

Obediently Rocky nibbled the herb from Moth Flight's claws.

"Come on," Micah urged gently. "They'll go down easy."

Relief washed Moth Flight's pelt as Rocky lapped the

leaves down. She stared gratefully at Micah. "Thank you."

"Sick cats are like kits," he told her. "A little gentleness goes a long way."

Moth Flight gazed at Rocky as he slumped deeper into his nest. "What's wrong with him? He's not coughing anymore."

"Listen to his chest," Micah suggested. "Even when Tiny Branch stopped coughing, I could hear him wheezing inside."

Moth Flight leaned into the nest, relieved to feel less warmth seeping from Rocky's pelt. At least the feverfew was working. She pressed her ear to his rib cage and listened. It sounded as though water was bubbling up inside. She sat up, alarmed. "He's drowning, like Drizzle!"

Micah's eyes widened. "He can't be. He hasn't swallowed any water."

"There's water in his chest!" Moth Flight gasped. "I can hear it."

Micah leaned down and listened, his eyes dark with worry as he straightened. "There must be infection inside."

Moth Flight's belly felt hollow. "What can we do?" She stared desperately at Micah. Then she remembered what Cloud Spots had told them on their way home from the Moonstone. "The tree!" She stared at Micah. "The one with the oozing sap! On your territory!"

"Of course!" Micah lifted his tail. "Cloud Spots said it'd cure any cough. Surely it would cure Rocky's chest infection!"

"Do you know where it is?"

"Yes!"

"You're brilliant!" Moth Flight pressed her muzzle against

Micah's cheek, purring. She drew back. "Where is it?"

He nodded. "I took Acorn Fur looking for it. It wasn't hard to find. Its sap smells as strong as pine, but sweeter."

"We must go there now!" Moth Flight's paws itched.

"We?" Micah hesitated. "Perhaps I should go alone. Wind Runner won't want you going to SkyClan territory."

"I'm coming with you!" She had to see where the tree was. One day her Clan might depend on it. And Rocky needed it *now*. She lifted her chin. Wind Runner wasn't going to stop her from being the best medicine cat she could be. "We won't tell Wind Runner where we're going. Let's hurry." She glanced at Rocky, who was worryingly still, his flanks hardly moving.

Micah followed her gaze, then nodded. "Come on." He hared out of the den. Moth Flight raced after him. They crossed the clearing in a few bounds.

"Where are you going?" Dust Muzzle's mew echoed after them as they headed through the entrance.

"We won't be long!" Moth Flight called back evasively.

They raced down the moorside, Moth Flight taking the lead and burning trails through the heather. She reached the SkyClan border, her chest on fire. "Which way?"

Micah pelted past her. "Follow me."

Moth Flight chased him through the wall of ferns and around a clump of brambles. He cleared a rotting log in one bound. She scrambled over it and kept running, digging in her paws to catch up as he disappeared over a rise. She followed, her heart lurching as the ground opened into a ditch. Her forepaws slipped over the edge. She pushed hard with her hind legs and soared over the gap. Landing heavily, she sent leaves swirling behind her. Micah was still running and she chased after him, determined not to lose sight. He swerved past an ancient oak and followed a gully that cut into a glade. The trees thinned and sunlight streamed in. Bluebells misted the ground, turning the forest floor purple.

"This is it!" Micah slowed and circled a tall tree at the bottom of the glade. "The bark at the base is too old," he meowed. "I'll have to climb to the top where there are tender stems."

Moth Flight scrambled to a halt, her heart pounding. "It's so tall! Can you climb trees?"

"I don't know! I've never tried." Micah peered up through the leafy branches. "It can't be harder than the barn ladder."

"It's a lot higher." Anxiety wormed beneath Moth Flight's pelt. She'd never climbed a tree. On the moor, prey lived among the gorse and heather.

"Once I get to the first branch, I'll be okay." Micah reached up with his forepaws and hooked his claws into the bark. Shards flaked away and showered around him.

"I'm coming with you." Moth Flight was not letting him try this alone.

"No. I need to concentrate. If you climb up, I'll be distracted because I'll be worrying about you." Micah looked at her. "You stay here and I'll drop the bark down to you."

Moth Flight blinked at him uncertainly. "Are you sure we can't just scrape the bark away here?" She nodded toward the peeling wood.

"It's as dry as a bone." He leaped up, digging his hind claws in and scooting toward a branch jutting a few tail-lengths above his head.

"Be careful!" Moth Flight called, her breath quickening as she watched him scramble higher.

Grunting, he hauled himself onto the lowest branch. "This is easy!" he called down.

Moth Flight screwed up her eyes as crumbs of bark drifted down like snowflakes. "Don't forget you're not a squirrel!"

"I won't." Micah craned his neck, peering up toward the next branch. Reaching up, he clung to the trunk and hauled himself higher.

Moth Flight paced the bottom of the tree. *Be careful!*

Ferns swished behind her. She glanced over her shoulder.

"What are you doing here?" Clear Sky stalked into the glade, his broad shoulders rippling. An angry snarl curled his lip.

"We need medicine for Rocky," Moth Flight explained. "He's really sick."

"Don't you have herbs on the moor?" Clear Sky stopped a whisker from her nose.

She backed away, shocked by the menace in his mew.

"We need sap from this tree." She glanced toward Micah. Leaves shivered around him, high among the branches.

Clear Sky jerked his muzzle up. "Is that my medicine cat?"

Yellow fur showed between the leaves as Micah climbed higher.

"He's helping me," Moth Flight explained.

"Get off my land," Clear Sky hissed at her.

Moth Flight stiffened. "I'm not hunting!"

"WindClan seem to think that borders only work one way!"

"That's not true." Moth Flight's hackles rose. "It's SkyClan who's been stealing moor prey!"

Clear Sky's blue gaze turned to ice. His pelt lifted along his spine.

Moth Flight froze, wishing she hadn't spoken. She backed away feeling suddenly vulnerable. "I'm just a medicine cat," she mewed. "I only want to get sap to cure Rocky! As soon as Micah finds some bark, I'll take it and leave."

"You're not taking anything from SkyClan territory," Clear Sky snarled.

"But Rocky might die without it!"

"That's not my problem!"

Moth Flight couldn't believe her ears. How could any cat be so cruel?

"Moth Flight?" Micah's mew sounded from high among the branches. "Are you okay?"

Clear Sky glanced upward. "She will be. If she goes home."

Leaves shivered on a branch and Micah stuck out his head. "Clear Sky? What are you doing here?"

"It's my territory!" Clear Sky yowled. "Or had you forgotten?"

Micah blinked at him. "Of course not, but we need to get some sap for R—"

Clear Sky cut him off. "Stop playing the hero for your little WindClan friend. Your loyalty is to me. Get down from there!"

"I'm a medicine cat," Micah called back. "It's my duty to cure cats."

"It's your duty to cure your Clanmates," Clear Sky hissed. "Not every cat you meet."

Anger flared in Moth Flight's belly. "We can't let cats *die,* just because they belong to a different Clan!"

Clear Sky narrowed his eyes. "Are you telling me how to lead my Clan?"

"Someone needs to!" Moth Flight snapped. "You're a fox-heart!"

Eyes flashing with rage, Clear Sky lashed out and raked her muzzle.

Shocked, she recoiled.

"Leave her alone!" Micah began to climb down.

"I will if she gets out of here," Clear Sky snarled.

"Stay where you are, Micah!" Moth Flight dug her claws into the earth. She forced her mew not to tremble. "Rocky needs the sap. I can't let him die."

Brown fur showed at the top of the glade. *Red Claw!* Moth Flight spotted him with a spark of relief. Perhaps he could talk some sense into his leader.

The SkyClan tom padded down the slope and stopped beside Clear Sky. "Is WindClan trying to start another fight?" His gaze swept Moth Flight, cold with disdain. The hope Moth Flight had felt at his arrival dimmed.

Above, a branch shook. "I'm coming down!" Micah called.

"No!" Moth Flight ignored the fear sparking beneath her pelt. "Rocky needs the bark." She narrowed her eyes, glaring defiantly at Clear Sky. "You can do what you like to me. I'm not leaving."

Red Claw glanced uneasily at Clear Sky. "She's hardly more than a kit."

"There's no need to hurt her." Clear Sky lifted his gaze to Micah. "Stop him from getting the bark. She can return to her camp, but she'll go with empty paws."

Red Claw nodded and raced for the tree. Leaping, he clung to the bark and pulled himself onto the first branch.

"Watch out, Micah!" Moth Flight wailed. "Red Claw's coming!"

A growl rumbled ominously in Clear Sky's throat. "I knew I should never have taken him in."

Moth Flight blinked at him. "But he cured your kit!"

"Acorn Fur could have cured Tiny Branch."

"No she couldn't!" Moth Flight spat back. "She knew nothing about healing until Micah came and taught her."

Clear Sky's gaze didn't move from the tree. He was watching Red Claw scramble through the branches. Micah was still climbing, close to the top now.

Moth Flight's chest swelled with rage. "You're lucky to have a cat like Micah in your Clan!" she growled. "He's the bravest and cleverest cat I've ever met."

"*You're* the clever one," Clear Sky snarled. "You're *here*, with your paws safely on the ground. He thinks he's got wings."

Moth Flight lifted her chin. "You've never given him a fair chance!" she growled. "He left his friends to help your Clan, and you treat him like a prisoner! You've made Acorn Fur spy on him! I wish he'd leave you and join WindClan!"

Clear Sky turned on her. "No one leaves my Clan without permission!"

Brambles trembled at the top of the slope. Willow Tail burst out, her pelt bushed. "What's going on here?" She bounded down the slope, pushing herself between Moth Flight and Clear Sky.

Clear Sky stared at her. "*Another* WindClan cat! Can't you smell boundaries?"

Willow Tail nudged Moth Flight away and faced the Sky-Clan leader. "I was worried about Moth Flight when I smelled her trail cross the border. I wanted to make sure she was okay."

"I'm fine," Moth Flight told her. "It's Micah who's in trouble." She nodded toward Red Claw, who was only a few tail-lengths behind Micah. "He's trying to stop Micah from getting the bark we need to cure Rocky!"

Willow Tail's eyes blazed with anger. "Red Claw! I might have known. He was trouble when we were rogues together and he's still trouble now." Pelt bushing, she raced for the tree and scooted up it, as nimble as a squirrel. Leaves showered down as she scrambled up the trunk.

As she disappeared among the leaves, a lower branch trembled and Micah stuck his head out. A long strip of bark hung from his jaws. Scrambling onto the next branch down, he leaped for the trunk and dropped tail-first toward the ground. Landing lightly, he hurried toward Moth Flight and laid the bark at her paws. It glistened in the sunshine, sap oozing from its flesh. "I got it!"

Delight fizzed beneath her pelt. "Thank you!" She pressed her nose against his cheek.

Clear Sky hissed. "How dare you!" Tail lashing, he kicked the bark away.

"No!" Moth Flight leaped after it, trying to rescue it before leaf litter soiled the precious sap.

Clear Sky faced Micah, ears flat. "I actually believed that you might become one of the Clan," he spat. "But you can't be trusted." His gaze flicked to Moth Flight. "How can you steal for WindClan?"

"It's not stealing!" Micah faced him. "Herbs belong to all cats."

A screech sounded above them.

"Murderer!" Willow Tail's cry rang out across the forest.

"Thief!" Red Claw shrieked back.

High up, the leaves exploded around the fighting cats.

Micah jerked his muzzle up. "They'll kill each other!" Spraying earth behind him, he leaped toward the tree and hauled himself into the branches. "Take the bark to Rocky!" he called back to Moth Flight.

Moth Flight froze. *I can't leave!* Not until Micah was safe. "Come back!" she wailed. *Let them kill each other if they want!* Guilt flared through her. She was meant to protect cats, not wish them dead! Her paws were rooted to the ground as Micah's yellow pelt flashed among the leaves. He swarmed upward, toward the trembling branches where Red Claw and Willow Tail fought.

Brown fur crashed through the leaves. Red Claw swung

from a branch for a moment before scrambling back on. Willow Tail balanced farther along, her hind paws trembling as she lashed out, blow after blow, with her forepaws. Red Claw backed away, the end of the branch only a tail-length behind him. It dipped perilously as he retreated from Willow Tail's punishing swipes.

"Stop!" Micah's mew rang out behind them.

Moth Flight strained to see him. She could make out his yellow pelt among the green leaves. He was moving slowly along the branch. "Stop!" he ordered again.

Willow Tail glanced at him. "Stay out of this," she snarled. "It's not your battle."

"It's not *any cat's* battle!" Micah called. "I've got the bark. Moth Flight's taking it to Rocky. There's no point in fighting now."

Red Claw stopped near the end of the branch, his tail thrashing wildly as he fought to keep his balance. "Let's at least fight like cats, not crows! On the ground where cats are meant to be!"

Willow Tail narrowed her eyes. "You always were a mouse-heart!" She advanced slowly toward the SkyClan tom.

"Stop!" Micah followed her along the branch, lifting a paw to grab for her tail. He wobbled, fear flashing in his eyes.

Moth Flight gasped. "Be careful!"

Micah dug his claws into the branch, clinging like a vine.

The branch creaked beneath him. Dry bark fluttered down like dust.

Fear flared through Moth Flight as she noticed that the leaves around Red Claw were withered and brown. With a jolt, she realized that the branch they were on was dying. "Get back!" she cried. It creaked again. "The branch is rotten!"

Beside her, Clear Sky backed away.

A crack split the air. The world seemed to slow as the branch bent, then snapped, the wood screaming as it tore away from the tree and dropped.

She saw Red Claw fall, flailing. Willow Tail dropped beside him, her legs thrashing the air. Red Claw caught hold of a branch and swung, forepaws clinging hard. Willow Tail hit the bough below, yowling with shock as she scrambled to cling on.

The rotten branch hurtled down and smashed onto the ground, shards of wood strafing Moth Flight's flank. She screwed up her eyes, scrabbling away as the world seemed to explode around her.

Then silence fell.

A moment later, leaves rustled overhead and Willow Tail huffed high above.

"Micah?" Moth Flight blinked away the splinters and gazed into the branches. Red Claw had hauled himself onto his paws and was trembling. Willow Tail lay frozen, her paws wrapped tightly around the bough that had broken her fall. Moth Flight scanned the leaves around them, trying to glimpse Micah's pelt.

A low moan sounded from below the tree.

Moth Flight dragged her gaze toward the fallen branch.

Among the shriveled leaves and shattered wood, she saw yellow fur.

Dread hollowed her belly. "Micah?" Her throat tightened.

Trembling, she crept closer. *Don't let it be him.* Once more, she looked up, hoping to see Micah gazing down from the tree, his eyes bright with relief.

The moan sounded again.

Moth Flight felt sick. She forced herself closer, until she could make out Micah's twisted body, his hindquarters crushed beneath the splintered wood.

His head moved.

He's alive! Hope soared in her chest.

Then his pain-wracked gaze sought hers and held it. She could see his hopeless agony. Grief tore at her heart as she crouched beside him. "What can I do?" she whispered hoarsely.

"Let me feel your breath on my cheek." His mew was so weak that she had to lean closer to hear. He sighed as her muzzle touched his. "Moth Flight, I don't want to leave you."

"Then don't!" Desperation filled her plea. "We can drag you out."

"No, Moth Flight. My spine is crushed."

"You don't know that!"

"I can feel only pain." He reached for her gaze again, his eyes clouding.

A sob choked her mew. "I can wrap you in comfrey. Cloud Spots says it can mend—"

"Moth Flight." Micah interrupted, gasping. "Thank you for letting me come with you to Highstones. And for bringing me to the Clans."

Horror pressed at the edge of Moth Flight's thoughts.

"Don't say that!" He was talking like this was the end.

"I'm glad I spent this time with you."

"No!" He mustn't die! He *couldn't*!

"You made sense of my life," he rasped. "You showed me my destiny."

"This can't be your destiny!" Moth Flight fought for breath, her thoughts spiraling into panic. "It's not fair!"

"I love you."

"Then don't leave me!"

"I'll see you again." His eyes flickered. "Next half-moon maybe."

Moth Flight felt a wave of relief. But then she realized what he meant: *Next half-moon. He means he'll see me from StarClan!* "No!" The ground swayed beneath Moth Flight's paws. She thrust her muzzle against Micah's, longing to feel his warm breath. But she felt nothing. Jerking away, she saw his gaze light for a moment, then grow dull, as though dusk had swept through the forest and swallowed the sunshine.

"Micah." Collapsing, Moth Flight pressed her cheek to his. "Don't go. I love you!"

CHAPTER 22

Moth Flight lifted her head blearily, not sure if she'd slept. Dawn light filtered through the trees above. "I forgot about Rocky," she said, but her voice came out hoarse and creaky. "I didn't take the bark to him."

"Reed Tail took it," Wind Runner's voice replied. "Rocky's doing okay. Don't worry about anything, Moth Flight."

She smelled Wind Runner's scent and realized that her mother's warm flank was pressed against hers. Swift Minnow was on her other side. Moth Flight wondered how long they'd been there. A chilly mist swirled around the forest floor.

Dread swelled at the edge of her thoughts and she wondered, for a moment, why. Then she remembered.

Anguish struck her like a wave. She struggled to breathe.

Micah's muzzle was still a whisker from hers, cold and stiff.

She blinked at it numbly. Grief had dragged her through the long, dark night. Foxes had screeched from the depth of the woods. Owls had glided, curious, through the glade, the breeze from their silent wings the only clue they had passed. Paws had scuffed the forest floor as cats came and went, dipping their head in respect to Micah, exchanging sympathies in hushed mews.

"It's time we buried him." Wind Runner's mew cut through Moth Flight's grief like claws.

Panic seized her. "No." They couldn't lay him deep in the earth and cut him off from sunlight forever. "I need to see him."

Wind Runner got to her paws and touched her muzzle to Moth Flight's head. "Foxes will come for his body if we don't."

Moth Flight blinked at her. Why was her mother being so cruel?

Swift Minnow shifted beside her. "Burying him will show our respect."

Wind Runner nodded. "He'll be safe in the earth."

Anguish slammed into Moth Flight. "But what about me?" *I need him.*

"You still have your family," murmured Wind Runner.

"And your Clanmates," Swift Minnow added.

Moth Flight leaped to her paws and glared at them. "I don't want *you!*" she hissed. "I want *him!*"

They exchanged looks, then Wind Runner signaled to some cat with her tail. Gorse Fur padded toward them, with Nettle, Blossom, and Acorn Fur following close behind. The splintered branch had already been cleared away, leaving Micah's body exposed to the brightening day.

Nettle thrust his gray muzzle beneath Micah's flank, heaving him onto his back. Gorse Fur and Blossom crowded beside him, helping to take the weight of Micah's body. Acorn

Fur slid among them, pressing her shoulder beneath Micah's hindquarters. Together, they carried the body from the glade.

Moth Flight watched them wade through the bluebells, the purple blossoms sweeping Micah's matted pelt.

Wind Runner nudged her gently forward. "Come and say good-bye."

Moth Flight's paws felt as heavy as stone as she followed the cats out of the glade. Daylight was beginning to glimmer among the leaves overhead as the sun lifted higher. At the top of the rise she saw cleared earth and a hole dug deep into it. Clear Sky stood at its head, Star Flower at his side. SkyClan gathered around them as Nettle and Gorse Fur paused at the edge of the hole.

Moth Flight blinked at the solemnity in Clear Sky's gaze. Didn't he realize that he'd caused this, with his fox-hearted craving for borders?

Acorn Fur's eyes were misted with grief. She pressed against Birch while Quick Water, Alder, Fern Leaf, and Thorn stared bleakly at Micah's body. Red Claw hung back behind Clear Sky, his gaze fixed on his paws. Moth Flight felt anger flash in her belly, eclipsing her grief for a moment. *You killed him! You and your stupid fight!* She glanced around, wondering if Willow Tail had dared come.

The pale tabby she-cat was watching half hidden behind Dust Muzzle. Moth Flight glared at her, anger seething beneath her pelt. "Don't skulk behind my brother!" she spat. "Come and see what you've done." She jerked her muzzle toward Micah, lying stiffly on Nettle's back.

Moth Flight felt Wind Runner's pelt brush her flank. "It was an accident," she murmured.

"It didn't have to happen! If they hadn't been fighting"— Moth Flight glared at Red Claw—"Micah would still be alive."

Clear Sky caught her gaze and returned it steadily. "Micah died because he was brave. It was a noble death."

"He didn't die because he was brave!" Moth Flight stared at him, stunned. "He died because *you* sent Red Claw after him."

Clear Sky didn't blink. "He chose to climb back up the tree," he meowed simply. "He could have stayed on the ground."

Moth Flight's mind whirled. Was Clear Sky blaming *Micah?*

Star Flower stepped forward, her emerald gaze round with sympathy. "You are angry," she mewed. "A cat you loved has died. But what is the point of blaming Clear Sky? Or Red Claw or Willow Tail? The tree was rotten. Do you blame the tree?"

"Yes!" Moth Flight's pelt bristled. "And Rocky's cough for sending us there! And Clear Sky! And Red Claw and Willow Tail!" Her thoughts seemed to whirl as rage flared. "And *Micah* for being so dumb!"

Star Flower blinked at her. "Would *Micah* have blamed anyone?"

I'm glad I spent this time with you. His dying words echoed in her mind. Shame washed her pelt. *He could have hated me for bringing him here . . . but instead, he was grateful.* She felt the eyes of the other cats fixed on her and backed away, grief welling once more in her chest as her anger withered.

Wind Runner brushed her cheek with her muzzle. "Let's

say good-bye to Micah kindly."

Nettle crouched and let Micah's body slip from his shoulders. It dropped into the hole with a thud. Clear Sky stepped forward and looked into the darkness.

No! Moth Flight closed her eyes and pictured Micah on the stepping-stones, the river sparkling around him. That night, as they'd curled in their nest in Dappled Pelt's den, he'd asked her to be his mate. While Dappled Pelt slept they'd planned a future in soft whispers. They'd told each other that StarClan would find a way for them to be together; they could be medicine cats to both Clans, traveling between them, but always at each other's side.

Moth Flight felt her mother's flank pressing against hers. She watched as Clear Sky pushed a pawful of earth into the hole. Would either leader have let them live that way? Would *StarClan?*

She'd never know now.

Her throat tightened. A wave of sadness flooded her, so strong that the ground swayed beneath her. Wind Runner pressed harder against her. Gorse Fur padded to her other side and pushed his shoulder beneath hers.

Clear Sky lifted his muzzle. "I had doubts about taking Micah in," he meowed. "When he cured Tiny Branch, I regretted my promise to let him stay. He was a farm cat, sleek from easy living, too sure of himself to be trusted. I didn't think he had any place in a Clan."

Nettle nodded. Quick Water murmured in agreement.

Clear Sky went on. "But I was wrong." He gazed sadly into

the grave. "He devoted every thought and every moment to his Clanmates." His gaze flitted from Nettle to Quick Water. "All of us who doubted him came to respect his intelligence and value his kindness." The SkyClan cats nodded solemnly.

Star Flower moved closer to the SkyClan leader as he continued. "I respected Micah. He stood up to me. He did what he thought was right, not what would please me. He died doing what he thought was right." He looked at Moth Flight. "He *had* to climb back into the tree; he was being true to himself. He died as he lived—caring about others, bravely and without hesitation. We were lucky to have known him, even for so short a while."

The forest seemed to spin around Moth Flight. She felt Wind Runner and Gorse Fur press closer, supporting her as her paws buckled beneath her.

Clear Sky's gaze was still on her. "Will you speak for him?"

"I can't—" Moth Flight faltered. Grief seemed to be tearing her heart in two. The other cats stared at her expectantly. She glanced into the hole, glimpsing a flash of Micah's pelt where the rising sun's rays pierced the depths. "May StarClan light your path."

She blinked, surprised at herself. The words seemed to appear in her mouth and roll from her tongue as though she had spoken them countless times before.

"May you find good hunting, swift running, and shelter when you sleep."

Murmurs of approval rippled around the other cats.

Moth Flight backed away.

Wind Runner was watching her, eyes bright with worry.

"I'm okay," Moth Flight breathed. "I just need to be alone." She turned and fled back to the glade, skidding to a halt as she saw the scattered remains of the splintered branch. She turned, her gaze flashing wildly around the forest, unsure where to go.

"Moth Flight." A gentle mew sounded from the trees behind her.

Pebble Heart padded over the rise. "I came to pay my respects."

Moth Flight glanced past him, toward the grave, hidden beyond the crest of the hollow. "Are they burying him?" She pictured the earth tumbling over Micah's poor, beautiful, broken body.

"He is safe now." Pebble Heart stopped beside her. "You should go home and mourn."

"No!" Alarm jolted through her. She didn't want to be like Slate, moving around the hollow like a shadow, pitied by her Clanmates. She didn't want to see her den. Micah had been there. They'd been so excited when they'd remembered the tree bark. Her breath quickened. Rocky would still be there. How could she take care of him? How could she take care of any cat? Her thoughts tumbled, confused. She'd never be able to remember any herb. Every cat would be depending on her. She struggled for breath.

"Moth Flight." Pebble Heart's soft mew sounded through the roar of blood in her ears. "Eat this." An aromatic scent touched her nose. The ShadowClan medicine cat had laid a sprig of tiny leaves at her paws. "It's thyme. It will calm you."

Blindly, Moth Flight leaned down and grabbed the sprig, chewing it as the world seemed to spin around her. Its pungent flavors bathed her tongue, pulling her thoughts away from the spiraling terror that filled her mind. Slowly she felt her heart begin to slow. She blinked, the blurred bluebells brightening around her.

"Come back to my camp," Pebble Heart murmured. "Reed Tail can look after WindClan for a while. You can have peace to grieve until you feel strong enough to return to your Clanmates."

Moth Flight blinked at him, soothed by his amber gaze. "Will Tall Shadow let me stay?"

"Yes. If I ask her," Pebble Heart told her.

Wind Runner's mew sounded at the top of the glade. "Will Tall Shadow let you stay where?" She hurried down the slope, ears twitching.

"I want Moth Flight to spend some time with Shadow-Clan," Pebble Heart told her calmly.

"Why?" Wind Runner bristled. "She should be with her kin."

Pebble Heart returned her gaze. "She needs to be away from responsibility until she's strong enough to bear her grief."

Moth Flight looked at Wind Runner, expecting her mother to argue, but saw worry darken her yellow eyes.

"Is this what you want?" she asked Moth Flight.

Moth Flight nodded, strangely calm. She guessed the thyme must be soothing her. She leaned against Pebble Heart, gratitude washing her pelt.

Pebble Heart dipped his head to Wind Runner. "I'll take her to my camp."

Wind Runner shifted her paws. "I'll send Dust Muzzle to check on her soon."

"Not too soon," Pebble Heart told her. "She'll be in good paws. I'll take care of her until she's strong enough to take care of herself."

Gorse Fur called from the top of the slope. "We should get back to the moor, Wind Runner. The Clan will be unsettled. They'll need you."

Wind Runner touched her nose to Moth Flight's cheek. "Take care."

Moth Flight nodded dumbly as her mother bounded up the slope, and then Pebble Heart began to guide her across the glade. He nudged her gently up the far slope, steering her toward a rabbit trail that cut between the brambles.

With every paw step, grief jabbed at Moth Flight's heart. She was walking away. She would never again see Micah in the forest or on the moor. She was leaving him behind, alone beneath the earth.

Pebble Heart led the way into the ShadowClan camp, ducking through a gap in the vast bramble hedge into a wide, pine needle–strewn clearing.

Juniper Branch looked up from a mouse she was gnawing and blinked sympathetically at Moth Flight. The tortoiseshell queen was looking plump, her belly swollen. Her mate, Raven

Pelt, glanced toward Moth Flight, catching her eye before awkwardly snatching his gaze away.

Mouse Ear, sitting on a sun-dappled patch of grass at the edge of the clearing, leaned closer to Mud Paws and murmured into his friend's ear. "I heard she was in love with the farm cat."

Moth Flight fixed her gaze ahead. *What do you know?* She felt unreasonably angry. Micah was dead and these cats would never know him. It wasn't fair.

"Moth Flight." Tall Shadow padded from the head of the clearing, her eyes soft with sympathy.

Moth Flight stopped and stared at her paws. "Pebble Heart said I could stay," she mumbled.

Pebble Heart padded past her and leaned close to the ShadowClan leader. "I thought she'd grieve more easily here, away from anything that will stir memories."

Everything stirs memories! The sky! The wind! The sun! Moth Flight braced herself against a fresh wave of grief.

Tall Shadow dipped her head. "Of course you can stay."

A black tom padded from a small den woven into the camp wall. "Moth Flight?" He padded closer, his ears twitching nervously. "Are you okay? Sparrow Fur brought us the news. I'm so sorry. I wish I'd known Micah better. Pebble Heart says he had the heart of a Tribe cat and the courage of a Clan cat."

"Thanks, Sun Shadow." Moth Flight met his amber gaze. It was a relief to hear someone say Micah's name. So long as cats spoke of him, he would never be forgotten. "Micah shouldn't have died." She flashed a look at Tall Shadow, wondering whether she was like Clear Sky and Wind Runner. Did she value borders more dearly than the lives of cats?

Tall Shadow's expression was unreadable as she gazed at Sun Shadow. "May Moth Flight have your den?"

"Of course." Sun Shadow glanced over his shoulder toward the brambles. "Should I fetch some fresh moss for the nest?"

"Don't bother." Moth Flight brushed past him. She didn't care where she lay, just so long as it was away from the prying gaze of the other cats. She ducked into the shadows, relieved to find the den cozy. Its bramble walls encircled a nest woven from pine sprigs. She climbed into it, feeling silky needles beneath her paws. It was surprisingly soft to curl into and she settled deep inside, letting the pine and bramble muffle the murmuring of the cats outside.

"Will she be here long?"

"Why did she come *here*?"

Then everything fell quiet. Moth Flight imagined that Tall Shadow had silenced her Clanmates with a stare. "She came here for kindness."

A moment later, Pebble Heart nosed his way into Moth Flight's den. He was carrying a leaf bundle in his jaws. As he dropped it beside Moth Flight's nest, it unfurled to reveal a few tiny poppy seeds. "Dappled Pelt brought these for you. She says they'll help you rest."

"She's here?" Moth Flight peered toward the den entrance.

"She didn't stay," Pebble Heart told her. "She says you need peace more than sympathy right now."

"How did she find me?"

"She was taking these to the moor and met Wind Runner and Gorse Fur."

Moth Flight felt her heart prick with gratitude for her medicine cat friends. *Except Micah isn't one of us anymore.* She closed her eyes, frightened even to think. Each thought seemed to remind her of Micah. She wanted to block out every memory and pretend that he was still alive in the forest, tending to his Clanmates and thinking of her. She leaned over the side of her nest and lapped up the poppy seeds.

Pebble Heart stiffened. "She said just two or three."

"I want to sleep until the pain stops." Moth Flight gazed at him wearily.

"I'll sit with you."

"No. I need to be alone."

"Then I'll check on you in a while."

Moth Flight tucked her nose onto her paws and closed her eyes. Blackness came as a relief. She flattened her ears, blocking out the calling of the birds overhead and the sound of paw steps outside the den. She wished the darkness would swallow her completely and quench the pain blazing in her heart and scorching deep in her belly.

Her thoughts began to slow as the poppy took hold. She heard Pebble Heart's fur brush the den entrance as he left, then felt herself drifting into sleep.

She opened her eyes to find herself back at the Moonstone. *No! Not again.* Weariness dragged at her bones. Grief weighed in her heart like a stone. *I don't want to dream.*

Paw steps brushed rock as two cats entered the cave. A small dark gray she-cat whose brilliant blue eyes sparkled in the gloom, and a flame-pelted tom.

Moth Flight stared at them blankly. She didn't even try to speak. They'd never hear her. This was just another dream, like the dream of the other blue-gray she-cat, and the dark tom who'd shown such scorn for his ancestors. She glanced up at the hole in the roof, unsurprised to see the edge of the moon nudging into view. In a few moments the Moonstone would light up and the spirit-cats would come. The flame-pelted tom crouched before the Moonstone and touched his nose to it. The gray she-cat stepped away and Moth Flight narrowed her eyes, preparing for the explosion of moonlight.

When it came, she hardly flinched as the light blinded her. As it faded, she gazed around. Trees had replaced the stone walls of the cave; but this wasn't ShadowClan's forest. She was in the Fourtrees clearing. The flame-pelted tom stood at the foot of the great rock, his gray companion hanging back as stars swirled overhead.

Moth Flight watched them whirl against the night sky, spiraling down toward the clearing.

The flame-pelted tom backed away, his pelt bristling with alarm. Didn't he know that these were the spirit-cats come to share with him?

The stars spun, melting into one another as they neared the ground, until they blazed like white fire.

Moth Flight blinked as cats emerged from the silver flames, their starry pelts more brilliant than ever. As they padded across the clearing, the white fire faded behind them.

The flame-pelted tom blinked at them, his eyes lighting in recognition. He lifted his tail and Moth Flight saw joy warm his gaze.

A golden tom padded forward, his thick fur like a mane around his head.

The flame-pelted tom greeted him. They exchanged words Moth Flight could not hear. Then the golden tom reached out his starry muzzle and touched the tom's head.

The tom jerked as though fire seared him.

This is just like the others.

Moth Flight frowned. Why did she keep dreaming this, and always with different cats?

A red bushy-tailed tom approached the flame-pelted cat next, sending another spasm through him as he touched his nose to the tom's head. Then a beautiful silver-pelted she-cat took his place. A lithe tabby tom followed. His touch set the flame-pelted tom's fur rippling as though he were running through wind.

Why do I keep seeing this? Moth Flight's paws itched with frustration. *What does it mean?*

Four more cats approached, each one's touch scorching through the tom as though it had sparked lightning. And yet, as each spasm ended, the tom stood stronger, his chin higher.

He met the gaze of the last cat with eyes suddenly misted with emotion.

Moth Flight froze as the pretty tortoiseshell padded closer. *Micah looked at me like that.* She recognized love in the tom's bright green eyes. The tortoiseshell's amber gaze reflected it back with such intensity that Moth Flight's breath stopped in her throat.

Grief swamped her. *He's in love with a dead cat!* As shock jolted through her, she searched the starry ranks. Was Micah here? Would she have a chance to share such a look with him?

She recognized no cat.

Please come! Why couldn't she make her dreams do what she wanted? She could only stand by, unheard and unseen, and witness what she could not understand.

It's not fair!

Her throat tightened as she saw the tortoiseshell stretch her muzzle toward the flame-pelted tom.

He met her gaze, his eyes burning with joy and grief.

Her touch made his pelt glow, as though filling him with moonlight. He leaned in to her, unflinching.

Stop! Moth Flight backed away. She couldn't bear to watch a moment longer. This all meant nothing! She didn't know these cats! Why should she care? All she wanted was to see Micah, but she couldn't!

Hissing, she lashed out a forepaw and slashed through the vision of the tortoiseshell. It was like raking starlit water. The light shattered into countless ripples and faded from view.

A wail welling in her throat, Moth Flight struggled into consciousness. Heart burning with loss, she blinked open her eyes into Sun Shadow's hollow den.

CHAPTER 23

Moth Flight felt a paw push her shoulder. She struggled awake, her mouth dry, her eyes sticky with sleep.

"Moth Flight?" Pebble Heart sounded worried. "Are you okay?"

She lifted her head groggily and blinked at the dawn sunshine filtering into the den. "I'm . . ."

Pebble Heart's shoulders relaxed. "I'm not used to giving poppy seeds," he admitted. "I was worried you'd sleep for days."

Moth Flight looked around, surprised by the dark brambles enclosing her nest. Where was the gorse?

A sick feeling hit her belly like rotten prey. "Micah's dead." She stared at Pebble Heart, a tiny spark of hope flickering beneath her pelt. Perhaps she'd dreamed it all.

But the medicine cat's amber eyes glistened with sympathy. He leaned down and picked up a wad of dripping moss and laid it on the edge of her nest. "I thought you might be thirsty."

Sadness swamped Moth Flight as she remembered the pool in Cloud Spots's den. Micah had still been with her then.

She lapped at the moss, her tongue welcoming the moisture.

"I brought you food too." Pebble Heart draped a mouse over the side of her nest. It was still warm, freshly killed.

Moth Flight wrinkled her nose. "I'm not hungry."

"But you must eat," Pebble Heart reasoned.

"Why?" Moth Flight snorted rebelliously. "If I starve, I can join Micah in StarClan."

"You mustn't say that!" Pebble Heart's eyes widened.

"Why not?" Anger rolled deep in Moth Flight's belly.

"What about your Clanmates? And the other Clans?" Pebble Heart stared at her fiercely. "StarClan shared the secret of the Moonstone with you. You're *important!*"

"And Micah's not?" Moth Flight growled.

Pebble Heart stared at her sadly. "Perhaps he's *supposed* to be with them."

"His *destiny*," she muttered bitterly. She pictured the rolling meadows of StarClan's hunting grounds. Was Micah going to spend forever chasing spirit-rabbits while she worked her paws to the bone taking care of her Clanmates? "What about *me*? Does StarClan *want* me to be lonely? Is that *my* destiny? Am I just here to carry out their orders? I can't even get a good night's sleep because they haunt my *dreams!* Can't they give me any peace?"

Pebble Heart's eye flashed with curiosity. "They haunt your dreams?" he echoed. "How?"

"I dream of spirit-cats doing some dumb ceremony," Moth Flight snapped. "The same thing, over and over again, but to different cats."

Pebble Heart leaned closer. "What cats?"

"Why should I care?" Anger prickled beneath Moth Flight's pelt.

Pebble Heart nudged the dripping moss with his paw. "Drink some more."

"Stop trying to make me feel better, because you can't!"

"I know," he soothed. "But I want to know more about these dreams. They might be important."

"Of course they're important!" Moth Flight snapped. "But StarClan won't tell me why. They just keep making me dream the same dream." She lapped at the moss crossly.

"Perhaps, if you describe the dream exactly, we can work out what it means," Pebble Heart urged.

Moth Flight swallowed back her anger. "I wake up at the Moonstone. And two cats come into the cave."

"Do you recognize them?"

"No." Moth Flight narrowed her eyes as the dream grew more vivid in her mind. "One of the cats sits at the Moonstone and, when the moonlight strikes it, the spirit-cats come."

"StarClan?"

"I guess," Moth Flight told him. "They have starry pelts but I don't recognize any of them."

"Go on." Pebble Heart's pelt twitched along his spine.

"The starry cats approach the living cat and, one at a time, they touch his head with their muzzle." She shuddered. "It seems to hurt a lot. The real cat jerks like he's been hit by lightning, but he doesn't flinch away. He's not scared. He just lets the spirit-cats touch him, one after another and at the end, he looks stronger. Kind of proud, like he's been given a special gift."

"Is it always a tom?"

Moth Flight shook her head. "The first time, it was a she-cat. I'd seen her before in a different dream. She was dead and then she came back to life."

Pebble Heart shifted his paws, his gaze clouding with thought. "What gift could StarClan give a living cat?"

Moth Flight shrugged. "I just know it looks painful. I don't think *I'd* want it."

"Really?" Pebble Heart's ear twitched. "But *you're* the cat who went to Highstones and found the Moonstone. You're the bravest cat I know. I think you'd endure *anything* if StarClan wished it."

Moth Flight returned his gaze, her heart twisting. "I can't endure losing Micah." Her mew cracked.

Pebble Heart got to his paws. "Why don't you come and visit Juniper Branch with me? She's expecting Raven Pelt's kits and I promised to check on her. She's been having pains."

"When are the kits due?"

"Not for another half moon." Pebble Heart flicked his tail. "Join me. This will be the first litter I've helped with. We can both learn a lot."

Moth Flight frowned. Pebble Heart was clearly trying to distract her from her grief. "No." She dug her paws deeper into the nest. "I'm staying here."

"Some fresh air might help you feel better."

"I don't *want* to feel better." She crouched in the nest,

glaring at him stubbornly.

Pebble Heart tipped his head sympathetically. "Okay. You rest. I guess there's no rush."

Moth Flight watched him duck out of the den, uncertain whether she wanted to be alone. *But what use am I to anyone like this?* She tucked her nose between her paws and closed her eyes. Sadness washed over her, wave after wave until she pushed every thought away and sought sanctuary in sleep.

She opened her eyes into another dream. She was standing in a wide meadow. The grass was wilting and the flowers had died. Mist swirled across the ground and swallowed the sky. She glanced around, anxiety creeping beneath her fur as she strained to see through the murky fog. What was hiding there? Her heart quickened as she saw a shape. Broad shoulders, pricked ears, a long tail. It was a tom.

"Hello?" Moth Flight tasted the air warily.

Micah's scent washed her tongue.

"Micah!" She raced toward the shadowy figure in the mist, the scent growing stronger as she neared. "It's me! Moth Flight!"

The tom didn't turn but kept moving, swinging his head from side to side as though searching.

"Micah!" She was only a tail-length away. Surely he could hear her! She caught up with him and dodged in front of him, trying desperately to catch his eye.

He walked through her as though she were part of the mist.

Her heart dropped like a stone. "No!" Rage swept through

her. Why was she so powerless in her dreams? Helplessly, she watched Micah move through the mist, heading one way, then the other, his ears pricked, his mouth open. *Is he looking for me?* Pain stabbed her heart. *Micah, I'm here!*

She woke, trembling, and jerked up her head.

Sun Shadow was sitting beside her nest. "You were dreaming."

Moth Flight blinked at him, the mist from her dream still fogging her thoughts. "What are you doing here?" She pushed herself to her paws. "Do you want your nest back?"

"No." His whiskers twitched. "I thought you might want something to eat."

"Pebble Heart brought me something earlier." She scanned the edge of the nest but the mouse had gone.

"I gave it to Mouse Ear," Sun Shadow told her. "He likes mice best."

Moth Flight's belly rumbled. She hadn't eaten since Micah died. "Did you bring me something?" She looked hopefully over the side of her nest, surprised to feel hungry. Guilt flickered beneath her fur. Her stomach was acting like nothing had changed.

"Come hunting with me." Sun Shadow nodded toward the den entrance where afternoon sunlight was turning the brambles golden. "You can catch your own prey."

Moth Flight shifted in her nest, realizing suddenly how stiff her legs were. Perhaps she should listen to the needs of her body. "I guess I could try." She stood up and stretched. "I've never hunted in a pine forest before."

"I know a stretch where there's hardly any undergrowth," Sun Shadow told her.

"Is that good?" Moth Flight wondered where the prey hid.

"There are plenty of ditches, which means we're bound to find a frog or two."

"No, thank you." Moth Flight wrinkled her nose. "I've eaten toad."

Sun Shadow snorted. "Frogs taste way better." He leaned closer, eyes narrowing. "Why would you eat a *toad*?"

Moth Flight's pelt pricked self-consciously. She hopped out of her nest and headed for the entrance. "It's just something I tried once." She sniffed as she ducked out of the den.

Outside, Tall Shadow was talking with Mouse Ear and Mud Paws in the clearing. The ShadowClan leader snapped her muzzle around as she caught sight of Moth Flight. "How are you?" she called cheerily.

Moth Flight blinked in the sunshine, feeling suddenly furless. Was everyone expecting her to act like she was okay now?

Sun Shadow brushed past her and nodded to Tall Shadow. "Moth Flight's agreed to go hunting with me. We won't be gone long." He nudged Moth Flight toward the camp entrance as Tall Shadow dipped her head silently.

Moth Flight slipped out of camp, relieved to be away from the curious gazes of ShadowClan. Juniper Branch had watched her pass, stretched on a soft patch of grass. Raven Pelt had been sorting through the prey pile, glancing up to see her duck through the entrance.

"This way." Sun Shadow headed past a stretch of mossy

ground and hopped over a fallen tree. One of the spindly twigs jutting from the trunk scratched Moth Flight's belly as she leaped after him. She winced as she landed.

"Are you hurt?" Sun Shadow halted.

"Just a scratch." Moth Flight didn't care. Grazed flesh hurt far less than the loss of Micah.

"Get Pebble Heart to look at it when we get back." Sun Shadow started walking again.

"I might find some horsetail and dock while we're out. That should stop it getting infected." Moth Flight hesitated as Micah's words flashed in her mind. *If you chew dock leaves and horsetail stems into a paste, you can smear it deep into a wound.* Fresh grief swept over her.

Sun Shadow paused at the top of a pine needle–strewn slope and glanced over his shoulder. "Are you coming?"

Moth Flight shook out her fur. "I want to go back to my nest."

"You can." He disappeared over the rise. "After we've caught a frog."

Moth Flight hurried after him.

Tall pines towered around her, shielding the sky. Sunlight glimmered between the branches, but the forest floor was cold and damp. She bounded down the other side of the slope and caught up with Sun Shadow as he reached a stretch of shady woodland rutted with ditches. He paused at the first and she stopped beside him.

"I know what it's like to lose the cats you love." He kept his gaze fixed ahead.

She jerked her muzzle toward him. "You *do*?"

"I came from the mountains to find my father." Sun Shadow appeared to be scanning the ditches, his eyes narrowing as he searched for movement. "He was dead when I got here and the cat I traveled with—Quiet Rain—died shortly after we arrived."

You didn't lose your mate, though. Moth Flight shifted her paws.

He went on. "Suddenly I was alone, far from my home and from the cats I'd grown up with."

"Tall Shadow's kin, isn't she?" He wasn't entirely alone.

"She's kin," Sun Shadow conceded. "But she wasn't like my kin back in the mountains. She'd become a forest cat. Everything was so different here from what I'd known. Most of the cats couldn't even imagine what it was like to hunt the peaks. Or to never be warm." He turned and met Moth Flight's gaze. "I felt like a stranger. Like no one knew how I felt. It was like being trapped beneath ice, mouthing words to cats who couldn't hear what I said."

Moth Flight blinked at him slowly. Did he actually understand the pain in her heart? "Do you still feel that way?"

"No." Sun Shadow's solemn gaze lit up. "It got better as time passed. I've grown to love it here. My Clanmates feel like kin now. We quarrel sometimes, but we look out for each other no matter what. And the hunting is good and, when newleaf comes, and the oak woods turn green and the wind from the moor brings the scent of heather blossom, I am glad I came. And I feel I have gained more than I've lost."

Moth Flight's shoulders drooped. "I'll never feel like I've

gained more than I've lost."

"Maybe not." Sun Shadow leaped the ditch and padded forward. "But you will come to value what you still have, and what you may have in the future."

Could that ever be true? Moth Flight followed him, the forest floor turning spongy beneath her paws as pine needles gave way to moss. Water squelched between her claws.

"Wait!" Sun Shadow dropped his voice, signaling to her to halt with a flick of his tail.

She followed his gaze and saw a green shape hopping along the edge of a ditch a few tail-lengths ahead. A frog.

"Do you want to catch it?" Sun Shadow whispered.

"I'm not the greatest hunter," she admitted.

"If you miss this one, we'll find another."

Moth Flight glanced at him, suddenly aware of how comfortable she was in his company. "Micah would have liked you," she murmured.

"I think I would have liked him too." His eyes glowed as he returned her gaze.

She turned toward the frog and dropped into a hunting crouch. *Lift your tail.* Gorse Fur's words rang in her ears. She crept forward, pleased that the soft moss absorbed her paw steps. A tail-length from the frog, she paused and fixed her gaze on its glistening green body. She forced herself not to shudder. The frog hopped another muzzle length and paused. *They're dumber than rabbits*, Moth Flight thought. *Can't it smell me?* She wondered if the pine-scented air was disguising her scent.

"Hurry up!" Sun Shadow hissed. "They're not as slow as they look!"

Moth Flight kneaded the moss with her hind paws, preparing to jump. Then she leaped, her paws slapping the moss a whisker behind the frog. It jumped, tracing a high arc across the ditch. Moth Flight blinked as it soared away. Bounding over the ditch, she tried to catch it again, her paws sending up water-spray as she splatted the ground half a tail-length behind it. It jumped again, changing direction. Moth Flight spun and tried to knock it from the air, but it had swerved and she landed flat on her belly.

Black fur flashed past her as Sun Shadow flew across the ditch and landed expertly on the frog. He held it down as it squirmed, its flippers churning desperately. "Do you want to give the killing bite?"

Moth Flight screwed up her nose. "No, thanks."

Sun Shadow ducked and killed it, snapping its spine with a crunch. As he straightened, she saw his whiskers twitching with amusement.

"What?" She ruffled her fur.

"You looked funny, that's all," he purred. "I can tell you've never hunted frogs before."

Moth Flight sniffed. "I bet *you* couldn't catch a rabbit."

"Probably not," he meowed warmly. "But you still looked funny, like a kit chasing its tail."

Moth Flight purred, pleasure rising in her without warning. *I must have looked pretty dumb.* Then she stiffened. Her purr dried in her throat.

Sun Shadow watched her, his gaze darkening. "Come on," he mewed briskly. "Let's take this back to camp and you can taste it."

"I'm not hungry." Moth Flight turned toward the camp.

"A mouthful won't hurt." Sun Shadow picked up the frog between his jaws and padded after her.

They padded back to camp in silence. *How could I have purred?* Guilt ripped her belly. *It's like I'm already forgetting him.* Suddenly she wanted to cling to her grief. It was all she had left of Micah now. She ducked first through the bramble entrance.

"You caught one!" Tall Shadow greeted them, lifting her tail happily as she crossed the clearing toward them.

Sun Shadow dropped the frog. "Moth Flight doesn't want to taste it."

Tall Shadow padded around her. "We can't send you back to your Clanmates without having tasted *frog*," she meowed. "What will you have to boast about?"

Moth Flight lifted her gaze wearily to the ShadowClan leader. "I don't want food." She padded across the clearing and nosed her way into Sun Shadow's den. Curling deep into her nest, she closed her eyes and let sadness sweep over her. So what if Sun Shadow had gotten used to his new home? How could she betray Micah by getting used to life without him?

CHAPTER 24

She woke into a misty meadow and knew at once that she was dreaming. "Micah?" She scanned the swirling fog, straining to catch a glimpse of him.

"Moth Flight?" His voice echoed from the murk.

Her heart leaped. Joy surged beneath her pelt. "Micah! Can you hear me?"

"Moth Flight, are you there?"

Moth Flight darted forward, searching for him, but there was no sign of him. Only his scent. "Can you *hear* me?" she repeated, panic rising.

"Moth Flight?" His voice echoed back, sounding lost. "I need to tell you something."

He doesn't know I'm here!

"It *will* be okay." His mew was tight with worry. "I know you're sad. I miss you too. I love you. I'll always love you. Don't let sadness change you. You have to keep going!"

"Micah!" Her cry turned to a wail of frustration. "I need to *see* you!" Why couldn't he show himself, like Half Moon and the others?

She glimpsed his eyes sparkling through the mist on the far

side of the meadow. They seemed to stare right through her, anxious and searching. She raced toward his gaze, his scent enfolding her as she neared.

"Keep going!" he called.

"I'm coming." She raced harder, pushing against the dewy grass.

"Don't give up. You have to be strong. Not just for yourself but for—"

A paw buckled under her and she stumbled, rolling onto the grass. Pain jerked her awake. "My leg!" Her forepaw was twisted clumsily under her chest. She pulled it free, kneading her paw against the bottom of the nest to ease the cramping. "Dumb leg!"

Shadow surrounded her nest. It was still night. She growled crossly. *Micah was trying to tell me something important!*

As the pain eased, Moth Flight thrust her paws under her muzzle. Perhaps she could finish her dream. She screwed her eyes shut, trying to ignore the pounding of her heart as irritation pricked beneath her pelt. With every waking moment, her dream would be fading, and Micah with it.

Be strong! Not just for yourself but for— What was he going to say?

Outside, an owl screeched through the pines. A ShadowClan cat was snoring somewhere in camp. Wind swished through the branches high above her.

I'll never get back to sleep. Heart sinking, she lifted her head. As her eyes grew accustomed to the moonlight that filtered dimly through the brambles, she wondered if dawn was near. She opened her mouth and let the night scents wash her tongue. The dewy air tasted of dusk, not dawn. *I'm sorry, Micah.* Guilt pricked at her belly. She'd let him down. He'd tried to speak to her and she'd woken up.

Why was he still roaming the murky meadow? Why wasn't he in StarClan's hunting grounds yet? He'd be safe there, with Half Moon and the others. *Do farm cats join StarClan?* Her fur lifted along her spine. What if she never saw him again? She stared, frozen. The brambles seemed to close in around her. *I'll never be with him. Ever.*

She lost track of time, her thoughts spiraling in and out of panic. *I should take a walk.* There was no chance of sleep now. But her paws seemed rooted beneath her, her body heavy with dread.

When dawn comes, it'll seem better, she told herself. *But how long until dawn?* Her heart pounded in her chest as she watched though the endless night.

She must have slept eventually, because Pebble Heart woke her.

"Moth Flight!"

She lifted her head sharply. There was fear in his mew.

"I need your help!"

She leaped to her paws, her heart lurching. Dawn light showed at the den entrance. "What's wrong?"

"Juniper Branch started kitting in the night."

"But she's not due for—"

"I know!" Pebble Heart's eyes were wide. "The kits are stuck. She's pushing, but they won't come. I'm scared they might die. That she might di—"

Moth Flight cut him off. "We won't let them." She bounded from her nest and ducked through the entrance. Scanning the camp, she tasted the air. The sour scent of fear pulsed from an opening in the brambles beyond the patch of long grass. She headed for it, Pebble Heart at her heels. She nosed her way through a gap in the branches, surprised by the size of the den inside, hollowed from the thick bramble wall.

Juniper Branch lay beside her nest, her eyes wild with pain. Raven Pelt crouched beside her, his pelt spiked with fear. He glanced at Moth Flight as she slid in beside him, his hackles rising. "What are you doing here?"

"I've come to help."

"It's okay." Pebble Heart padded past her. "She's a medicine cat too."

"She's young." Raven Pelt eyed her warily. "Does she know anything about kitting?"

"Do *you*?" Pebble Heart returned sternly.

Moth Flight pressed her cheek to Juniper Branch's belly. "They're still moving." She could feel the kits squirming inside. "They want to come out."

Juniper Branch moaned. "I'm trying!" Her body convulsed and she shrieked as pain rippled through her.

Moth Flight darted behind her and checked to see if there was sign of a kit. The ground was bare. "Could something be blocking them?" She glanced at Pebble Heart. The den was dark, but enough light filtered through the brambles to see his face.

He looked grim.

"Raven Pelt." She turned to the dark tom. "I want you to fetch moss and soak it in water. Juniper Branch will be thirsty."

Raven Pelt glanced at Pebble Heart questioningly.

"Get it," Pebble Heart told him.

The tom headed from the den.

Juniper Branch stared at Moth Flight, eyes dark with fear. "But I need him with me."

"He's not going far." Moth Flight crouched in Raven Pelt's place and rested a paw on the queen's belly. The squirming was stronger. "Pebble Heart and I will help you." She exchanged looks with Pebble Heart. *I hope.*

"Why won't they come?" Juniper Branch wailed.

Moth Flight narrowed her eyes, her thoughts quickening. Either something was blocking their way, or they weren't ready to be pushed out. "They aren't due for a half-moon," she murmured to herself. Could Juniper Branch's body be pushing them out too soon?

Another spasm gripped the queen. Her belly convulsed.

"Don't push!" Moth Flight ordered sharply.

"But I *have* to." Juniper Branch began to pant.

Moth Flight leaned closer. "Keep panting. Focus on that. We need to stop your body pushing and let your kits find their own way out in their own time."

Pebble Heart blinked at her. "She can't be like this for a half-moon!"

"She won't need to be," Moth Flight told him. Calmness swept over her. She remembered heading into the Highstones tunnel for the first time. She was gripped by the same quiet certainty she'd felt then, as though she *knew* what to do. "What happens when you stub your paw?" she asked Pebble Heart.

"It hurts?" He stared at her, puzzled.

"What else?"

"It swells up."

"Exactly." Moth Flight rested her paws low on Juniper Branch's belly. Heat pulsed from the queen's fur. Something was inflamed. "Her body's not ready yet. I can feel where she's swollen. And each time she pushes, it gets worse. The swelling is blocking the kits' way out. She has to stop pushing long enough for it to go down."

"So they'll have room to come out!" Pebble Heart's eyes widened with understanding.

Juniper Branch growled. "Another pain is coming."

"Keep panting!" Moth Flight darted out of the den and scanned the clearing. Her heart leaped as she saw a thick pine twig lying at the edge. Racing to it, she snatched it between her jaws and headed back to the den. She thrust the twig into Juniper Branch's jaws. "Bite on this when the pain comes. Put all your energy into biting, not pushing."

Juniper Branch screwed up her eyes. A low moan rolled in her throat. The wood cracked between her jaws as she bit down hard.

"We're going to need more sticks," Moth Flight told Pebble Heart.

He nodded and ducked out of the den.

Moth Flight lapped Juniper Branch's belly with her tongue, relieved to feel no spasm reach the kits. "Don't worry, kits," she murmured between strokes. "We'll have you out of there before long."

Juniper Branch fell limp.

Moth Flight jerked her muzzle around and stared at the queen. Her eyes were glazed with exhaustion, but the spasm had clearly passed. The crushed pine twig lay on the ground next to her. "Well done!" she meowed. "You didn't push that time."

Juniper Branch drew in a deep breath and closed her eyes.

"This is going to be difficult," Moth Flight told her. "You need to stop yourself from pushing for a while longer. Just until there's enough space for the kits to get out."

"It's hard," Juniper Branch moaned.

"I know." Moth flight felt a wave of sympathy for the queen. "But you have to do it. For your kits." *And yourself.* She held Juniper Branch's fearful gaze. "We are going to help you."

As she spoke, Pebble Heart slid into the den. He dropped a fresh twig on the ground. "Mouse Ear and Mud Paws are scouring the forest for more."

"Have you got any poppy seeds?" A pang of guilt jabbed Moth Flight's belly. Had she eaten his whole supply that first night?

"Dappled Pelt brought two leaf wraps," he told her.

"Fetch what you've got," Moth Flight ordered. "We need to ease her pain."

"I'll bring thyme as well. It'll calm her."

"Good idea." Moth Flight met his gaze, relieved they were facing this together.

As Pebble Heart disappeared again, Juniper Branch began

to moan. "Here comes another one."

Moth Flight grabbed the fresh twig and slipped it between Juniper Branch's jaws. "Remember. Focus on your breathing. The pain will pass before you know it."

She rested her paws gently on Juniper Branch's belly as the queen stiffened with the effort of not pushing. *No!* The small movements inside were weakening. *Hang on, kits. It won't be long now.* She hoped she was right.

Spasm after spasm gripped the queen. Moth Flight soothed her as she fought each one. Pebble Heart returned with poppy seeds and thyme. Juniper Branch swallowed both and, when Raven Pelt brought water-soaked moss, she lapped at it thirstily.

"Is she going to be okay?" Raven Pelt gazed fearfully at his mate.

Pebble Heart nosed him toward the den entrance. "We'll do the best we can," he promised.

As the black tom let himself be guided out, Mud Paws stuck his head inside and dropped a bundle of pine twigs.

"Thank you!" Moth Flight nodded gratefully to the tom and quickly thrust one of the twigs between Juniper Branch's jaws. Another spasm was coming. She pressed her paws low on the queen's belly. The kits were hardly moving inside. But there was no heat pulsing from her fur. Had the swelling gone down? She caught Pebble Heart's eyes as he came back in. "Feel this."

She moved away and let him place his paws where hers had been. "Less swelling, right?"

He nodded slowly, eyes narrowing with alarm. He lowered his voice to a whisper. "But I can hardly feel the kits moving."

"I know." Moth Flight leaned close to his ear. "She needs to start pushing now or we'll lose them."

"But what if it's too soon?"

"It'll be too late if we leave it longer."

Pebble Heart gazed at her darkly. "I agree." He pulled his paws away and ducked down beside Juniper Branch's head. "When you get the next spasm, we want you to push."

"Really?" Relief sparked in Juniper Branch's gaze. She gasped, her body stiffening.

Moth Flight swapped looks with Pebble Heart. *StarClan help us.*

As a fresh spasm swept Juniper Branch, the queen moaned with effort and pushed. Moth Flight placed her paws on the queen's belly and felt her bear down.

Pebble Heart crouched at the queen's tail. "I see something coming!" Excitement edged his mew.

"Keep pushing!" Moth Flight urged.

Juniper Branch's moan turned to a growl as she gritted her teeth with effort.

Pebble Heart gasped. "It's here!"

Moth Flight darted to his side and stared at the tiny shape beside the queen's tail. A membrane covered it and Moth Flight instinctively reached out and sliced it open with a claw. Fluid spilled out as the wet kit struggled free, mewling as it gulped its first breath.

Juniper Branch lifted her head, straining to see. Moth

Flight grabbed the kit by its scruff and placed it beside her muzzle. As she reached to lick it, her eyes shining with joy, another spasm seized her.

"Push!" Moth Flight told her sharply. She rested her paws on Juniper Branch's belly once more, feeling it convulse.

"Another one!" Pebble Heart's mew was jubilant. Moth Flight rushed to see. He'd split open the membrane by the time she reached it. A purr throbbed in her throat as the kit wriggled and mewled. Lifting it gently, she placed it beside the first.

"How many more?" Juniper Branch asked.

Moth Flight ran her paw over the queen's belly, feeling movement inside. "Another one at least." As she spoke, Juniper Branch jerked with pain. She shuddered, panting as she pushed.

"It's coming," Pebble Heart urged.

Juniper Branch pushed again, yowling. The kits squealed and wriggled blindly beside her cheek.

"I think it's the last one." Moth Flight glanced at Pebble Heart as Juniper Branch fell limp. The movement inside her belly had stopped. "We did it!"

The ShadowClan medicine cat was staring down, his eyes dark.

"What's wrong?" Moth Flight darted to his side.

"It was a she-kit," he mewed softly.

The kit lay on her split membrane, motionless.

Moth Flight's heart lurched as she stared at the limp body. She thought of Emberkit, who'd died moments after he'd been born. *StarClan, help it!* She reached out a paw and touched the lifeless kit's pelt. She was smaller than her littermates, her pale gray fur slick beneath Moth Flight's pad. She leaned down and sniffed her tiny muzzle. "She's not breathing," she whispered. "Like Drizzle!"

Pebble Heart blinked at her. "What do you mean?"

Moth Flight touched a paw to the tiny kit's ribs. "She might have water inside her chest!"

Pebble Heart looked confused. "Do you know how to help her?"

Moth Flight rolled the kit onto her back and placed her paws on her chest. "I think so. But she's so small!" The kit felt as fragile as a sparrow. How hard dare she push?

She began to pump, gently at first, and then, as she felt the easy resilience of the kit beneath her paws, harder.

"What's happening?" Juniper Branch was reaching her muzzle around to see, her eyes wide.

"Take care of the other two," Pebble Heart told her. "We'll take care of this one."

"Is it dead?" The queen's mew was thick with fear.

"We don't know." Pebble Heart moved, blocking the queen's view as Moth Flight kept working on the kit.

"What are you *doing* to it?" Alarm edged Juniper Branch's mew. She tried to struggle to her paws, but fell back, weak with exhaustion.

Raven Pelt darted into the den. "What's going on?"

Moth Flight didn't look at the black tom, but kept pumping the kit's chest. *Am I doing the right thing?* Was Half Moon watching? *Breathe! Please breathe!* Fear sparked beneath her pelt.

Raven Pelt shouldered his way past Pebble Heart. "What are you doing?" He stared at Moth Flight, his eyes round with horror.

As he spoke, the kit jerked and water bubbled at her lips. Moth Flight flipped her over quickly and began to massage her back as the kit spewed up liquid. Then it mewled a loud, desperate mewl.

Moth Flight sat back on her haunches, joy lighting her like sunshine. Trembling, she met Pebble Heart's gaze.

"You saved her." Pebble Heart's eyes shone.

The kit flailed its paws and mewled again.

"I think she wants her mother." Moth Flight backed away and let Raven Pelt scoop the kit up by her scruff.

He placed it beside the others and gazed proudly at Juniper Branch. "They're beautiful."

Moth Flight suddenly realized how weary she was. Juniper Branch must be exhausted. "We should get her into her nest," she murmured to Pebble Heart.

"I'll see to that," Pebble Heart told her. "You look worn out."

Moth Flight blinked at him gratefully. "I am." Her gaze drifted to Juniper Branch and Raven Pelt. They were gazing at their kits, and then each other, with eyes warm with love. Moth Flight's heart twisted, grief stabbing her so suddenly it took her breath away. She and Micah would never share such joy. Weak with sorrow, she heaved herself onto her paws and padded out of the den.

Behind her, the kits mewled while Raven Pelt and Juniper Branch purred. The happiness Moth Flight had felt as the kit had come to life beneath her paws disappeared like mist in the wind. *Oh, Micah. I miss you so much.* Loss hollowed her heart once more. She longed to stop grieving, but how could she? She could never have the life she'd planned with Micah— only emptiness and long days alone. She felt as though all her dreams had died with him.

CHAPTER 25

Moth Flight scanned the nettle patch. She loved this part of the pine forest. Gaps in the canopy let narrow strips of sunshine reach the mossy forest floor and nettles thrived in the rare light. Pebble Heart was waiting for her between the ditches that rutted the ground beyond the rise. She'd been with ShadowClan for nearly a moon now and lately had begun helping him gather herbs for his store. She was used to the gloom, although the tang of pinesap had begun to make her queasy.

But she wasn't ready to go home.

She stretched her muzzle forward and nipped through the base of a fat-looking nettle stem. Then she dragged it over the rise, careful to stay clear of the shivering leaves.

"I think we have enough." Pebble Heart stepped out of the way as she neared the ditch, leaving room for her to drop it over the edge.

It landed on top of the others and began to wilt slowly into the muddy water.

"Are the ones we soaked yesterday finished?" she asked.

Pebble Heart leaped the next ditch and reached his paw

into the next. "Yes," he called over his shoulder. "No sting left."

Moth Flight shook out her fur. "I wonder if *drying* the nettles would get rid of the sting?"

"Drying herbs is easy on the moor," Pebble Heart hauled up a dripping stem and laid it on the ground. "There's plenty of wind and sunshine up there. It's too damp to dry herbs here."

"How are you going to get through leafbare without a store of dried herbs?"

"Dappled Pelt asked me the same question last night." Pebble Heart glanced at her as he hooked another stem from the ditch.

Moth Flight felt a flash of guilt. She'd missed the half-moon gathering at the Moonstone. "What did you tell her?"

"I asked if she could dry some herbs for ShadowClan." She realized that he was looking at her hopefully. "Would *you* dry some too? When you return to the moor?" There was a question in his eyes.

Do you want me to leave?

Pebble Heart must have seen worry darken her gaze. "I mean, when you're ready."

Will I ever be ready? The ShadowClan cats asked nothing of her. They brought her prey and dipped their heads respectfully, and talked about everyday things, like how the prey was running, or how soon greenleaf was coming this year. Being among them was easy.

Her own Clanmates would be more inquisitive. They'd ask

about Micah. And they'd expect her to return to her medicine cat duties. Moth Flight's belly tightened. She wasn't ready to look after anyone yet.

When she didn't answer, Pebble Heart glanced down at the nettle stems. "We missed you at the Moonstone last night."

"I wanted to come with you." She had. She knew deep in her belly that being a medicine cat was her destiny. And helping the ShadowClan medicine cat was renewing her confidence. She had a sense of purpose once more, and satisfaction in her work had distracted her from her grief. Since Juniper Branch had kitted, she'd kept a close eye on the kits. She'd taken Pebble Heart to the edge of the oak forest to gather borage to make sure that Juniper Branch had enough milk for them. But she'd felt so weary in the past moon; she crept, exhausted, to her nest every night. The thought of the long trek to Highstones had been daunting. And, if she was being honest with herself, perhaps she wasn't ready to see Micah among the StarClan cats. *That means he's really gone.* "I was tired."

"I understand." Pebble Heart's gaze flickered over her belly. Had he noticed that her days of resting—eating prey, which other cats had caught—had begun to show in her swollen flanks? Perhaps it was time she pulled herself together and went back to her Clan. Her grief had lost the raw power that had silenced her for days at a time, but she still woke trembling in the night, her longing for Micah so strong that her heart roared in her ears.

"I'm not going to stop being a medicine cat," she reassured him.

"I didn't think you would." He began to straighten the nettle stems.

"The other medicine cats know that, don't they?"

"Of course." He plucked a stringy old grass stem from the edge of the ditch and threaded it under the bundle he'd made. "They told me to tell you not to worry about missing the meeting. They understood."

"Did StarClan visit with you?" Moth Flight had been avoiding the question since Pebble Heart returned at dawn. Had Micah been there? She didn't want to know. If he had, having missed him would break her heart all over again. If he hadn't, she'd worry that he would never be part of their ranks. But she had to know if StarClan had a message for her.

"Half Moon came alone," Pebble Heart told her. "She only stayed long enough to tell us to look after you."

Moth Flight blinked at him. Hadn't she said anything about Micah? "Was that all?"

"Yes." Pebble Heart wrapped the grass stem around the bundle. "Acorn Fur was disappointed. She'd been expecting to see her ancestors."

Moth Flight stiffened, irritation prickling beneath her pelt. "*Acorn Fur* was there?"

Pebble Heart threaded the grass around the stems again, pulling them tightly together. "She's SkyClan's medicine cat now."

"She's a spy!" Moth Flight snapped. "Clear Sky told her to watch Micah because he didn't trust him."

"That might be true." Pebble Heart looked up. "But Micah

taught her a lot. She knows more about healing than any other SkyClan cat. And she likes it. Besides—" He paused, avoiding her gaze. "I've had dreams about her healing her Clanmates."

"You *knew* she'd become their medicine cat?" Outrage flared in Moth Flight's belly. "Why didn't you warn me?"

"I never *knew*," Pebble Heart corrected her. "I have *lots* of dreams. They don't all turn out to be visions." He met her gaze steadily. "Seeing Acorn Fur giving herbs to sick cats isn't the same as knowing Micah would die. Even if I'd guessed he would die, would you really have wanted to know?"

"I could have—"

He cut her off. "What? Changed his destiny? Loved him more?"

Moth Flight stared at him, wordless. If she *had* known, would she have done anything differently? Her time with Micah had been wonderful. Would she really have wanted the shadow of his death looming over those perfect days?

Pebble Heart's mew softened. "I was worried you didn't come to the Moonstone because you blamed StarClan for letting him die."

She blinked at him. "I did blame them," she admitted. "But that's not why I didn't go."

"Do you still blame them?"

Moth Flight shook her head. "Even if they'd known his destiny, they might have been powerless to change it. And you're right: What would I have done if I'd known?"

As she spoke, Pebble Heart's gaze flicked past her shoulder. She stiffened as she saw his hackles rise. Opening her mouth, she tasted the air. Cat scents were billowing behind her.

She turned, flattening her ears.

Two cats padded from among the trees.

"Moth Flight!" A plump black-and-white farm cat called out to her.

The brown tom at her side swished his tail. "We thought we'd never find you!"

"Cow!" Moth Flight hurried toward them, her heart quickening with delight. "Mouse!"

Cow's gaze was rimmed with sadness. "We heard about Micah."

Mouse's tail drooped. "Did he suffer?"

Moth Flight stopped in her tracks, her mew catching in her throat as she remembered Micah's last moments. "Not for long," she managed to mew.

Cow weaved around her, her soft pelt brushing warmly against Moth Flight's fur.

Mouse dipped his head to Pebble Heart. "I hope you don't mind us coming," he meowed. "We crossed the moor, looking for Micah. A cat named Gorse Fur told us about the accident."

Cow held Moth Flight's gaze, her eyes brimming with sadness. "He said you were with him at the end."

Moth Flight wondered for a moment if they blamed her for taking Micah away. But Cow wrapped her tail over Moth Flight's spine, her gaze warm with sympathy. "It must have been hard for you."

"At least I was with him." Her throat tightened as she remembered. She swallowed back grief, noticing their dusty pelts. "You must be tired. It's a long journey from the farm."

Pebble Heart padded forward. "Come back to the camp and rest." He glanced at the bunch of stems. "I need to get these back before they start to rot."

Cow stared at the sodden bundle. "Why are you gathering wet nettles?"

Mouse glanced around the shadowy pine forest, puzzled. "Isn't there any prey here?"

"There's plenty," Pebble Heart purred. "I'm collecting nettles in case one of my Clanmates gets sick."

Cow blinked. "Will stinging them help?"

Moth Flight's whiskers twitched with amusement. "They don't sting, now that we've soaked them. They'll help soothe wounds and, if you eat them, they ease aching bones."

"You seem a lot smarter than when we first met." Cow winked at Pebble Heart. "She tried to cross a field while the farm dog was herding sheep."

Moth Flight purred, remembering. "Micah saved me."

Cow caught her eye. "You must miss him."

"I do," she answered huskily. "We were mates."

Cow pressed her muzzle to Moth Flight's cheek.

Pebble Heart flicked his tail toward brambles showing among the pines. "The camp's not far." He picked up one end of the grass stem between his teeth and began to drag the nettle bundle across the forest floor. Mouse hurried to grab the trailing end.

Cow fell in beside Moth Flight. "How long since Micah died?"

"A moon," Moth Flight told her softly.

They walked on, sharing their grief in silence.

As they neared the camp, Raven Pelt padded from the entrance, tasting the air. His gaze flashed toward them, narrowing as he saw Mouse and Cow.

Moth Flight hurried to meet him. "They're friends," she explained. "They lived on the same farm as Micah."

Tall Shadow slid out of camp, her nose twitching. "Do we have visitors?"

Cow dipped her head to the ShadowClan leader. "We came to see Moth Flight."

"Come in and share some prey," Tall Shadow told her. "It's running well at the moment. There's more than we can eat."

She led Cow into camp, the scent of fresh-kill heavy in the air. Moth Flight and Raven Pelt followed at her heels, while Mouse and Pebble Heart dragged the nettles after them.

Three kits looked up from the long grass where Juniper Branch was resting.

The biggest, a black tom with an orange tail, blinked at them. "Look, Dusk Nose!" He nudged the she-kit beside him. "Visitors!" He dashed across the clearing.

Dusk Nose, a black-and-orange tortoiseshell, followed. "Who are you?" she called to Cow.

"Are you a Clan cat?" Another tom-kit hurried after them, his dappled brown pelt perfectly camouflaged against the shady forest floor.

Moth Flight purred. "This is Cow," she explained. "She and Mouse were friends of Micah."

"I'm Dangling Leaf." The orange-tailed tom scrambled to a halt in front of Cow.

"I'm Dusk Nose," his sister mewed.

The dappled brown tom stopped beside them. "I'm Shade Pelt."

Dangling Leaf tipped his head. "Do you know Micah's dead?" he asked Cow.

Moth Flight flinched, but Cow returned his inquisitive gaze steadily. "Yes."

Dusk Nose nudged her brother. "You can't ask questions like that, Shade Pelt. It's rude."

"Raven Pelt says we can ask anything we like," Dangling Leaf mewed back.

Shade Pelt sniffed. "He also says we have to know when to be quiet, or we'll never be good hunters." He blinked at Moth Flight. "Do *you* mind us talking about Micah?"

Moth Flight ignored the sadness pricking in her chest. "No." It wouldn't change anything to pretend Micah had never existed. It wouldn't hurt any less.

Dangling Leaf was still staring at Cow. "Why did you come, if Micah's dead?"

"We came to see Moth Flight," Cow told him.

Dusk Nose lifted her chin. "Are you *her* friends too?"

"Yes." Cow gazed around the camp. "This looks very cozy."

Behind them, Mouse was helping Pebble Heart hoist the nettle stems high into the bramble wall of the camp to drain. The nettles dangled from the prickly branches and dripped muddy water onto the ground.

"I have my own den," Moth Flight told her.

"You've got *Sun Shadow's* den," Shade Pelt corrected her.

Moth Flight shifted her paws. "That's true. Sun Shadow's letting me use his den until I go home."

Cow blinked at her. "Isn't *this* your home?"

Tall Shadow answered for her. "She lives on the moor."

Cow glanced at Moth Flight's belly. "Will you go home to have your kits?"

Moth Flight stared at her. "I'm not having kits!"

"Are you sure, dear?" Cow tipped her head sympathetically.

Moth Flight froze. *Could I be having kits?* Surely she'd know? Then she remembered: her tiredness, her queasiness . . . She glanced at Tall Shadow, shock pulsing through her pelt.

The ShadowClan leader dropped her gaze.

Pebble Heart padded closer, his ears twitching. "We thought you knew."

Moth Flight's paws seemed to root into the ground. The camp swam around her. "I didn't think!" Her mind whirled. "I've never had kits before." She'd thought that her easy life in ShadowClan was making her fat.

Tall Shadow blinked. "We thought you were happy to have something left of Micah."

Micah's kits. Moth Flight's heart seemed to turn in her chest. She was carrying *Micah's* kits.

Cow purred loudly. "They'll be as handsome and brave as their father."

Kits! Growing inside her! "I can't!" She backed away, shocked. She could hardly take care of herself! How could she be responsible for new lives? Her thoughts flashed back to Slate's kits, lost on the moor because of her. Then she remembered Juniper Branch's kitting. *The pain!* The ground seemed to sway beneath her paws.

Cow pressed against her. "It's the most natural thing in the world."

Moth Flight's thoughts swirled. "I need to go home." The need tugged deep in her belly. "I have to see Wind Runner." Suddenly she wanted to nestle among her kin and shelter in their warmth.

Tall Shadow dipped her head. "Someone must escort you," she meowed firmly. "You shouldn't travel alone."

"I'll be fine," Moth Flight answered, still dazed from the shock.

Pebble Heart stepped forward. "I'll take her."

Moth Flight looked at him blankly. "Can we go now?" Her gaze flitted distractedly to Cow and Mouse. "I'm sorry to leave you. You've only just arrived. But—"

Cow's eyes rounded with sympathy. "We understand."

Tall Shadow flicked her tail. "We'll make sure they are fed and rested before they head home."

Moth Flight hardly heard the ShadowClan leader. Her thoughts were already racing toward the moor, where her Clanmates were waiting for her. How could she have stayed away so long? "I've been so selfish," she murmured to herself as she headed for the camp entrance.

Pebble Heart caught up to her and fell in step beside her. "Perhaps you should have some thyme before we go," he suggested quietly. "You seem shocked."

"I'm okay." Moth Flight kept her gaze fixed ahead. It didn't matter if she was shocked. She had to be strong now. She was carrying Micah's kits. Nothing was more important than that.

CHAPTER 26

Moth Flight struggled for breath as she walked beside Pebble Heart.

"Let's slow down," he urged.

She shook her head. "I want to get home." She padded from the pines and stopped beside the Thunderpath. The stone trail was deserted, but the stale stench of monsters made Moth Flight feel sick. "I've become so weak!"

"I think it's because you're carrying kits." Pebble Heart paused on the grass verge. "Juniper Branch could hardly cross the clearing without panting by the end."

"But I've another moon to go!" Moth Flight hurried onto the smooth stone, not wanting to be reminded of the queen's long and painful kitting.

Pebble Heart followed her, tactfully changing the subject. "Your Clanmates will have missed you."

"Do you think?" She turned as she reached the far side. Would they feel she'd been disloyal by staying away for so long?

"They'll be glad you're home." Pebble Heart bounded up the short, steep slope onto the moorside.

Moth Flight struggled after him, stopping at the top to

catch her breath. She gazed across the heather. Its blossom had turned the moorside purple. Wind swept around her, lifting her fur. She closed her eyes, relishing the sensation. The dank pines had shielded her for too long. "I should have come home earlier."

"You waited until you were ready." Pebble Heart headed upslope.

Moth Flight followed, surprised by the silkiness of the grass beneath her paws. One day her kits would run here. Excitement flickered in her chest. Was she really going to be a mother? To *Micah's* kits! Joy swamped her. Grief would no longer be her only link to him. Soon she'd have his kits; she'd watch them grow. She'd tell them about their brave and handsome father. He would live on through them.

I'll have to raise them alone. The idea daunted her, but the closer she got to home, the more she felt she would be okay. *Wind Runner always knows what to do.* She glanced at Pebble Heart, his gray pelt ruffled by the breeze. "Thank you for being so kind to me."

He slowed to let her catch up. "I didn't do anything really."

"Yes, you did." She remembered all the times he'd brought her prey; how often she'd woken to find water-soaked moss on the side of her nest; how gently he'd encouraged her to help gather herbs and mix poultices. Thanks to him, she'd lost none of her skills; indeed, he'd taught her so much. He was such a wise, serious cat—a dreamer in his own way, but not as easily distracted as she was. She admired him and had grown fond of him. He was almost like a Clanmate.

As her thoughts drifted, movement caught her eye. She looked down the grassy slope and saw cats stalking along the SkyClan border. Their pelts showed among the trees, moving slowly through the ferns. She halted, narrowing her gaze as she recognized Thorn, Birch, and Nettle. "I wonder what they're doing?" she called to Pebble Heart.

Pebble Heart followed her gaze. The three cats had stopped. Birch was marking a tree with his scent. "It's a border patrol."

Moth Flight blinked at him. "A what?"

"Clear Sky's given orders that his borders are to be checked daily and fresh markings left."

Anger flared in Moth Flight's belly. "Does he *still* insist on borders?" She could hardly believe any cat could be so rabbit-brained.

"He says cats belong in their own territory," Pebble Heart murmured.

"So Micah died for nothing!" Moth Flight flattened her ears. "Doesn't he realize that Micah would never have died if he hadn't been so bothered about his borders?"

Pebble Heart avoided her gaze. "He says Micah would never have died if you hadn't crossed the border with him."

Moth Flight trembled with fury. "How dare he?"

"Don't let it upset you," Pebble Heart begged. "If Clear Sky wants to fuss about his borders, then let him." His gaze slid past her.

She jerked her muzzle around, following it, and saw Willow Tail and Eagle Feather watching the SkyClan patrol from a distant, rocky outcrop. "Don't they have anything better to do?" she snapped. "They should be feeding their Clan, not watching borders!" She broke into a trot, heading for the hollow.

Pebble Heart hurried after her. "Let Wind Runner worry about it," he told her. "You're a medicine cat, not a hunter. Borders aren't your problem."

As he spoke, a gray-and-white pelt showed against the heather upslope.

Moth Flight recognized it at once. "Swift Minnow!" The sight of her Clanmate distracted her from her anger.

Swift Minnow squinted at them, lifting her tail suddenly and breaking into a run. "Moth Flight! Is that you?" She sprinted toward them, meowing happily, and skidded to a halt a tail-length away. She stared, her eyes rounding as she saw Moth Flight's swollen flanks. "You're expecting kits!" Joy lit up her gaze. "Are they Micah's?"

"Yes," Moth Flight purred.

"We were beginning to think you were never coming home." Swift Minnow cast an anxious glance toward the hollow.

"I needed time to grieve," Moth Flight explained.

The heather rustled behind Swift Minnow, as Slate padded out. She pricked her ears as she saw Moth Flight. "You're back!"

Moth Flight felt a rush of happiness. The grieving queen looked well, her eyes brighter than they'd been in moons. "How's White Tail?" she called. "Have Silver Stripe and Black Ear been behaving themselves?"

"They're all fine!" Slate hurried toward them. "You'd hardly recognize them! They've grown so much." She slowed, her ears pricking. "You're expecting!"

Swift Minnow plucked at the grass excitedly. "They're Micah's kits!" she told her friend.

Slate wove around Moth Flight purring happily. "Have you come home for good?"

"I want my kits to grow up on the moor," Moth Flight told her.

"Hurry up!" Swift Minnow ducked into the heather. "Let's get back to camp!"

Moth Flight noticed Pebble Heart hesitate.

"I'll go home, now that I know you're safe," he meowed shyly.

"Are you sure?" Moth Flight gazed at him fondly.

"Yeah." He flicked his tail and began to head downslope. "Take care. Send for me when the kits come!"

"Bye, Pebble Heart!" Slate was nudging Moth Flight toward the heather. "Wait until Gorse Fur sees you! He's been so worried."

Moth Flight followed Swift Minnow's trail, zigzagging between the bushes until she emerged onto the stretch of grass outside the camp entrance.

As the scents of home swept over her, her pelt rippled with pleasure.

Swift Minnow had already disappeared inside and Moth Flight followed, her heart beating loudly in her chest.

"Moth Flight!" Dust Muzzle was the first to come bounding

across the tussocky clearing. Spotted Fur and Fern Leaf hurried after him, their eyes bright.

They scrambled to a halt in front of her, staring at her belly.

"I'm expecting Micah's kits." She glanced anxiously at Spotted Fur. Was he still jealous?

Spotted Fur blinked at her, then purred. "Congratulations!"

Relief washed over her.

Fern Leaf purred and murmured "How exciting!" as Dust Muzzle pressed his nose to her cheek. "I'm glad you're home."

Gorse Fur was crossing the clearing toward them, Rocky lumbering behind.

Moth Flight felt a flicker of worry as she saw the old cat. "Are you better?" she called. She should have been here, taking care of him.

"I'm as healthy as a fox," he rumbled.

Gorse Fur stopped beside her. "I knew you couldn't stay in that dark old forest forever." He weaved around her while Rocky stared at her proudly.

"I'm glad you're back," the old tom rumbled. "Reed Tail won't let me have catmint."

Moth Flight stiffened. Had Rocky been exaggerating? Was he still sick? "Do you need some?"

Rocky glanced at his paws. "I don't *need* it, but sometimes I get a sore throat and a little catmint always makes me feel better."

Reed Tail was stalking toward them, his ears pricked. "The only reason you get a sore throat is from snoring so loudly!"

He padded past the old tom and greeted Moth Flight with a nod. "Thank StarClan you're back. I'm run off my paws trying to find herbs, and if Silver Stripe ever makes it through a day without getting a scratch or a graze, I'll be amazed."

Moth Flight's whiskers twitched with amusement. "Where are the kits?" She gasped as she saw three young cats bounding toward her. She recognized their pelts, but they were so big! "Silver Stripe! Black Ear!" They looked old enough to hunt! "White Tail, you've grown so handsome!" The gray-and-white kit had his father's broad shoulders and Slate's soft amber gaze.

"*Black Ear's* handsome too!" Silver Stripe told her proudly.

"Of course he is!" Moth Flight looked admiringly at Black Ear before purring at Silver Stripe. "And you're as beautiful as your mother."

"Who cares if I'm beautiful?" Silver Stripe stuck her nose in the air. "Beauty doesn't help with hunting, and I'm going to be the best hunter in WindClan."

"I can believe it." Moth Flight nosed her way through her Clanmates and headed across the clearing. "How's my den? I hope no rain's gotten in. My herbs should be good and dry by now. Although I need to pick fresh ones. Cloud Spots says fresh herbs work better."

Reed Tail fell in beside her. "I've been using your den," he confessed. "It seemed best, since I was being medicine cat while you were away."

Moth Flight caught his eye, gratitude flooding her. "Thank you so much," she mewed earnestly. "I'm sorry I left you responsible for everything. I just couldn't face . . ." Her mew trailed away as a sudden wave of grief slapped against her like cold water. The familiar faces and scents had carried her back to a time before Micah had died. She swallowed.

Reed Tail shot her a look. "You'll feel at home again in no time," he promised.

"Yes," she answered huskily. She stopped outside her den, her Clanmates watching from beyond the tussocks. They looked so pleased to see her. Her heart swelled with thanks. Then she spotted two pairs of eyes staring from the shadows of Jagged Peak's den. Her fur prickled anxiously. Holly and Jagged Peak hadn't wanted her to leave. She'd stayed away for a whole moon. Taking a deep breath, she headed toward them.

Jagged Peak ducked outside first, his ears twitching.

Holly followed, her gaze cool. "A grieving cat should stay with her Clan," she muttered.

Jagged Peak glanced at Moth Flight's belly. "Are you carrying *his* kits?"

"Micah's?" Moth Flight narrowed her eyes. "Yes. And I'm proud of it."

"He was a SkyClan cat," Jagged Peak grunted.

Moth Flight glared at him. "He was a farm cat too! Does that make it better or worse?"

"Jagged Peak!" Storm Pelt charged across the clearing. He stopped in front of his father and mother and blinked at them. "You should be happy she's come home."

Holly sniffed. "Why did she bother? She's been away from

WindClan so long, she doesn't even smell like a WindClan cat anymore."

Dew Nose slid from the den and stopped beside her brother. "Moth Flight was born WindClan and she'll always be WindClan."

Storm Pelt lifted his chin. "She's the one who found the Moonstone. Aren't you proud she's our Clanmate?"

"Will her kits be our Clanmates too?" Holly muttered. "Even though they carry SkyClan blood?"

"And farm-cat blood," Jagged Peak added.

Storm Pelt faced his mother, pelt prickling. "*You* weren't born WindClan!" His gaze flashed toward his father. "And *you* were a mountain cat who left his tribe."

Moth Flight shifted her paws uncomfortably. She didn't want to cause an argument between kin.

Holly eyed her kits doubtfully. "How do we know she won't leave again?"

"I won't," Moth Flight promised.

"Moth Flight!" Her mother's mew rang across the clearing. She turned to see the WindClan leader bounding toward her.

Wind Runner skidded to a halt and thrust her muzzle against Moth Flight's chin. "You're home at last!" A sigh shuddered through her. She drew back, her gaze darkening. "Did you travel here by yourself? I hope you were careful near the SkyClan border. They've been raiding the moor for rabbits again. Of course, Clear Sky denies it but—" She stopped and stared at Moth Flight. "You're expecting kits!"

Moth Flight sat down, letting her belly bulge. "They're due in a moon."

"Micah's?" Wind Runner tipped her head.

"Of course." Moth Flight purred. Did her mother think they could be anyone else's?

"Let's hope they take after you." Wind Runner lowered her voice. "Micah was a little too sure of himself."

Moth Flight met her mother's gaze calmly. "And you're not, I suppose."

Wind Runner's eyes widened with surprise. Then she purred. "My little kit has grown claws."

Moth Flight glanced down at her belly. "I need to," she mewed. "I've got my own kits to protect."

Wind Runner swished her tail, pride warming her gaze. "You must be tired after your journey. Let's get you settled in your nest."

Moth Flight got to her paws, suddenly realizing how weary she felt. She snatched a look at Jagged Peak and Holly, hoping that they'd be less prickly once they saw that she was here to stay. They avoided her gaze, their pelts ruffled.

Wind Runner nudged her toward her den. "I'm so glad you're back."

Moth Flight purred. It felt good to be home and Wind Runner was pleased to see her. The warmth in her mother's mew reassured her that, from now on, everything was going to be fine.

Moth Flight rolled a wad of borage leaves into a bundle and slotted them into a small gap in the gorse at the back of her den. She relished the coolness here. Outside, early greenleaf sunshine was scorching the camp.

The scent of herbs washed over her and she thanked StarClan that she'd stopped feeling queasy. The kits were due any day and her belly was so swollen that she felt as clumsy as a toad. She sat back on her haunches and looked approvingly at the array of herbs poking out from between the branches. "We've done well." She blinked at Reed Tail.

The silver tabby tom sat down and tucked his tail over his herb-stained paws. "You've taught me so much."

In the moon since she'd returned to the WindClan camp, Moth Flight had shared with him all she'd learned from the other medicine cats. When the kits came, she guessed that there would be times when she'd be too busy to tend to her Clan and she wanted him to be prepared to take her place. And so, she had spent nearly every day with him, scouring the moor for herbs, and teaching him their names as they gathered them for her store.

She glanced at her nest now, wondering when the kits would come. She had woven extra heather to make it larger, and lined it thickly with moss. She shifted as a twinge in her belly made her wince.

Reed Tail stiffened. "Are you okay?"

"I'm fine," Moth Flight told him. "The kits are just fidgety today."

As she spoke, fur brushed the gorse entrance.

Rocky padded into the den, blinking as his eyes adjusted to the gloom. "My chest is feeling a bit tight." He looked at her hopefully. "Can you spare some catmint?"

Moth Flight heaved herself to her paws and crossed the den.

She pressed her ear against his flank and listened for bubbling inside his chest. He was breathing clearly. She looked at him sternly. "You're as fit as a flea. I can't waste catmint on healthy cats. I'd have to travel to Twolegplace to fetch more."

"I could fetch some for you," Rocky offered. "I know Twolegplace well. I used to live there, remember?"

"That's a kind offer." She wouldn't put it past the old tom to travel to Twolegplace in search of catmint. "But let younger cats fetch the herbs. Your paws are too stiff to climb the wooden walls."

Rocky's eyes brightened. "Does catmint help stiff paws?"

Moth Flight's whiskers twitched with amusement. "No, but I can give you some comfrey. Reed Tail and I picked some fresh leaves this morning."

Rocky wrinkled his nose. "No, thanks. The stiffness doesn't bother me that much and I—"

Moth Flight didn't hear the rest of his words. Pain pulsed through her as a spasm gripped her belly. She gasped, swaying.

"Are the kits coming?" Reed Tail raced to her side.

"I think so." She curled her claws into the ground, bracing herself against the pain. "Send someone to fetch Pebble Heart," she puffed. "He knows what to do."

Reed Tail hared from the den and left Rocky staring at her nervously.

"Do you want to lie down in your nest?" he asked hesitantly.

"No!" Moth Flight glared at him as another spasm crushed her belly. She began to pace, a growl rolling deep in her throat. *Focus on your breathing.* She remembered the advice she'd given

Juniper Branch and tried to concentrate on each breath. What if she wasn't ready? What if the kits got stuck? What if they died like Emberkit? Her thoughts began to whirl. She stopped and stared at Rocky, panic sparking through her pelt.

Rocky blinked at her. "I'll get Wind Runner." He ducked out of the den.

Moth Flight moaned, shocked by the pain gripping her belly. She began pacing again, not sure what to do with herself. She couldn't bear the thought of sitting still. Moving distracted her. But she felt weak with the pain. She lay down as another spasm shuddered through her body. Then she scrambled to her paws, frightened at feeling so helpless.

"Moth Flight!" Wind Runner's mew sounded at the den entrance. Her mother hurried into the den and pressed her muzzle to Moth Flight's cheek. "Don't be scared," she murmured. "Everything's going to be okay. Dust Muzzle's on his way to fetch Pebble Heart. And Slate will be here in a moment. We're going to look after you until Pebble Heart arrives."

Moth Flight leaned against her mother, relief swamping her. "I don't know what to do," she whimpered.

"Just keep pacing until you need to lie down." Wind Runner drew away and looked into Moth Flight's eyes. "You're not the first cat to have kits. You will be fine."

"But it hurts!" Moth Flight was startled by the intensity of the pain.

Wind Runner's eyes glistened with sympathy. "You won't remember it afterward, I promise."

"That doesn't help me now!" Moth Flight snapped back.

Another spasm was coming. She closed her eyes as it swept over her. When it had passed, she gazed blearily at her mother. "How long will it take?"

"Not long," Wind Runner soothed. "Not long at all."

Paw steps sounded at the den entrance and Slate hurried into the den. "How's she doing?" she asked Wind Runner.

The Wind Clan leader shot her an anxious look. "The kits will be here before Pebble Heart," she breathed.

Moth Flight stiffened as she heard her mother. "How do you know?"

Slate didn't give Wind Runner time to answer. "Are the spasms *that* close together?" She turned to Moth Flight. "Lie down and let me feel your belly."

Wincing as another spasm pulsed through her, Moth Flight lay down. She growled with pain, hardly feeling Slate's paws on her belly.

Slate nodded briskly. "Your kits feel strong. I think they're eager to come out and meet you."

Pain scorched through Moth Flight. Stronger than before. "Wind Runner!" She reached a paw toward her mother.

"It won't be long now." Wind Runner crouched beside her.

"I need a stick to bite on," Moth Flight panted as she fought the urge to yowl with pain.

"I'll get you one." Slate ducked out of the den.

She returned a few moments later with a tough heather stem.

Moth Flight took it from her, relieved as she bit down hard with the next spasm. The wood crunched between her jaws and she moaned as her belly convulsed with such power that she thought she would die. *Micah!* She focused her thoughts on him, determined to stay strong. The image of his steady gaze shone in her thoughts. He seemed to be silently urging her on. Groaning, she pushed with all her strength.

"Here's the first kit!" Slate ducked behind her and lifted a small squirming bundle.

Moth Flight blinked at it, surprised, and spat out the stick. "Is it okay?"

"It's a *he* and he's fine." Slate laid the tom-kit beside Moth Flight's muzzle. His warm scent filled Moth Flight's nose and she nuzzled him, her heart swelling as he squirmed against her cheek.

Her body convulsed again.

"Another one!" Slate sounded jubilant.

As a spasm seized her once more, the world seemed to blur around Moth Flight. She was aware only of pain and the muted voices of Wind Runner and Slate. In her mind, Micah's green gaze glowed steady and strong. The heady scent of her new kits washed her muzzle and then, suddenly, the pain stopped.

"Four kits." Wind Runner's proud mew broke through the fog.

Moth Flight turned her head, blinking, and saw four squirming bundles beside her. Instinctively she pulled them close to her belly, reaching down to lap them dry. Two of the kits had yellow splotches on their soft white pelts. One was striped yellow all over, just like his father. "His fur!" she looked up at her mother. "It's the same color as Micah's!" The fourth was white, like Moth Flight. "I wonder what color their eyes will be." The kits wriggled against her, their eyes still closed.

"You'll have to wait a few days before you know." Wind Runner's mew was barely a whisper as she leaned down and lapped Moth Flight's cheek. "Well done. I'm very proud of you."

"Is she okay?" Pebble Heart's anxious mew sounded at the den entrance. He nosed his way into the den, puffing to catch his breath. Heat radiated from his pelt.

Slate stared at him. "Did you run all the way?"

Pebble Heart was gazing at the kits. "I'm too late?"

"I'm afraid so," Wind Runner told him apologetically. "But I'm glad you came. You can make sure Moth Flight and the kits are okay."

"They look fine." Pebble Heart's eyes glowed.

Dust Muzzle stuck his head through the entrance. "He outran me!"

Moth Flight blinked fondly at the ShadowClan medicine cat. "I did it!" Pride pulsed through her, stronger than any she'd felt before. "Aren't they beautiful?" She hugged the kits closer, joy washing over her as she felt them warm against her belly. Micah's green gaze flashed once more in her mind. *Thank you, Micah.*

"They're lovely," Pebble Heart agreed. He leaned down and sniffed them. "They seem strong and healthy."

Wind Runner tipped her head, her eyes glittering with worry. "Will you stay tonight, just in case?"

"Of course," Pebble Heart promised. "And I've spoken to

Dappled Pelt and Cloud Spots. They've agreed to visit Wind-Clan regularly in case anyone is injured or sick while Moth Flight's recovering."

Moth Flight lifted her head. "That's kind, but there's no need. I've shared everything I know with Reed Tail. He'll be able to look after WindClan."

Pebble Heart blinked. "You've been busy!"

"I just wanted to be prepared." Moth Flight suddenly realized that, for the past moon, she'd been thinking about the future again. The grief that had dragged her into helpless despair after Micah's death had finally eased as she planned a new life around her kits. And now they were here, each one perfect, and her heart felt as full of love as it had been when Micah was alive. She purred loudly, joy leaping in her chest as her kits purred with her. She suddenly remembered her conversation with Sun Shadow.

I will never feel like I've gained more than I've lost.

Maybe not. But you will come to value what you still have, and what you may have in the future.

She looked at Pebble Heart. "When you go home, tell Sun Shadow he was right."

CHAPTER 27

Moth Flight dreamed.

Warm wind tugged her fur as she raced upslope and the coarse grass grew soft beneath her paws as she neared the moortop. She stopped as she reached the crest. Meadows rolled below her, stretching toward forest, and a river sparkled in the distance as it disappeared among the trees.

Where am I? This wasn't the moor.

The scent of prey washed her muzzle. A rabbit was grazing calmly on the grass a few tail-lengths ahead. Moth Flight imagined carrying it home to her kits. They were almost old enough for their first taste of fresh-kill. She swallowed back a purr as she imagined Bubbling Stream's eyes lighting up at the sight of it. Spider Paw would be first to beg for a taste. Blue Whisker would hang back shyly, but Honey Pelt would make sure she had a piece before he'd take a bite.

Her heart ached with love for her kits as she thought of them. They were perfect. Even Spider Paw's extra toe, which he'd been named for, was adorable.

She dropped into a hunting crouch and began to stalk silently through the grass. The rabbit didn't even twitch as she neared. *This is going to be an easy catch.*

Yellow fur flashed at the edge of her vision. Moth Flight jerked her muzzle around, her breath stopping in her throat as she saw Micah padding toward her. The rabbit, still blissfully unaware, hopped lazily away. Moth Flight let it go, her gaze fixed on Micah.

"Can you see me?" She hardly dared speak. No one ever heard her in her dreams. The last time she'd dreamed of Micah, he'd been wandering in mist, unable to see her. But this time Micah's eyes were fixed on her, sparkling green in the bright sunshine and filled with love.

As he neared her, he quickened his pace until his scent bathed her. She closed her eyes, her heart pounding. Was she really going to speak with him? His whiskers grazed her cheek as he reached her.

"I have missed you so much." His words were soft in her ear.

She purred, rubbing her cheek fiercely against his. "I thought I'd die without you."

"I'm glad you didn't." He drew away and looked at her, his eyes shining. "I've seen the kits. I've watched you with them. You are a wonderful mother."

Joy surged beneath her pelt. "Aren't they gorgeous? They remind me so much of you. Honey Pelt even washes his paws the same way you did."

"Keep an eye on Blue Whisker," he fretted. "She's so shy. Don't let the others push her around."

"They won't," Moth Flight promised. "They're protective

of her. Especially Spider Paw. He won't let Slate's kits near her because she's scared of them."

Micah frowned. "They haven't hurt her, have they?"

Moth Flight purred. "No, of course not. But she can't understand why such big cats act like kits. I keep telling her they're *still* kits. I don't think she believes she'll be that big too in a few moons."

Micah's green gaze darkened. "I wish I were there." Grief edged his mew.

It caught hold of Moth Flight, twisting her heart. "So do I." She hadn't felt anger since she'd left ShadowClan's camp, but rage flared in her belly now. "It's not fair! Why did you have to die? In a dumb *accident*!"

Micah sighed and rested his muzzle against hers. "It was my destiny."

She pulled away, blinking at him. "Did you know all along?"

"No, but I see that our destinies were only ever meant to cross for a short time." His eyes glistened with love. "Aren't we lucky they did? Now you have our kits."

"But I want you too!" Moth Flight couldn't push away her resentment.

Micah gazed at her gravely. "You must travel alone from here on. This is your path. But I will always be with you."

Her vision swam with grief. "How?"

"I will be in your thoughts and your heart and your dreams," he murmured. "You will see me in the kits and if you need me, you only need to close your eyes."

Moth Flight's throat tightened. *Is that enough?* She touched her nose to his softly. It would have to be.

Around her, the meadows began to grow hazy. Micah's pelt grew pale, light showing through.

"Don't go yet!" she begged.

"You'll see me again," he promised, his mew growing faint.

"Micah!"

"Someone is coming to visit you." She could barely hear his mew as it faded into echo. "You must help her. I'm depending on you."

"Who?" She spoke into darkness as the dream faded.

Jerking awake, she lifted her head. The kits fidgeted at her belly, asleep in the starlight that filtered through the gorse.

Moth Flight's heart ached with longing, but warmth enfolded her. *I will always be with you.* As she remembered his words, his scent lingered on her tongue. With a gasp, she recognized the meadows in her dreams—StarClan's hunting grounds! *He's in StarClan.* A purr rumbled in her throat. *Now I know that we will never be far apart.*

"Go faster!" Bubbling Stream's fur spiked with excitement as she clung to Storm Pelt's shoulders.

Storm Pelt bounded across the tussocks and Bubbling Stream mewled with delight.

"Be careful!" Moth Flight watched with wide eyes from the sunny patch of grass outside her den.

Beside her, Slate purred. "She'll be fine," she reassured Moth Flight.

"She's only a moon old!" Moth Flight worried. "Aren't badger rides dangerous?"

Blue Whisker nestled tighter against her belly. "I don't ever want a badger ride," she breathed, staring in alarm at her sister as she bobbed on Storm Pelt's back.

Moth Flight tucked her tail over Blue Whisker, relieved that at least one kit was staying close.

Spider Paw was crouching in the sandy hollow. Silver Stripe crouched beside him, while Black Ear paced in front, advising him on his stance.

"Hindquarters lower," the black-and-white tom-kit told him. "And keep your tail still or the prey will hear you coming."

Silver Stripe fidgeted impatiently. "Can we jump yet?" she begged.

"Not until you've got the perfect crouch," Black Ear told her sternly.

"Is *this* right?" Spider Paw pressed his chin closer to the ground and stared fiercely ahead.

"*Quite* good," Black Ear conceded. "Pull your hind paws in tighter, or your takeoff will be clumsy."

Where's Honey Pelt? Alarm flashed through Moth Flight. She scanned the camp, relief swamping her as she caught sight of his yellow pelt as he burrowed under the heather wall on the far side of the camp.

White Tail was beside him, squeezing under the branches.

Moth Flight frowned. Keeping an eye on four kits seemed far more exhausting than it should be. "What are those two doing?"

"White Tail promised to show him all the secret ways out of camp," Slate told her.

"I hope he's not thinking of sneaking out." Moth Flight remembered hauling Silver Stripe out of the rabbit hole all those moons ago. How had she been so calm? Dread gouged at her belly as she imagined one of her own kits stuck on the moor and wailing for help. She pushed the thought away. She wasn't going to let her kits out of her sight.

She felt a wave of gratitude toward her Clanmates. Among them, someone was always keeping an eye on Bubbling Stream, Honey Pelt, Spider Paw, and Blue Whisker. Even Holly, who was watching Bubbling Stream now, her eyes narrow with disapproval, always knew where they were and what they were up to.

Reed Tail nosed his way out of the den that Eagle Feather and Dew Nose had hollowed from the heather wall of the camp. They had grown too big to share Jagged Peak and Holly's den and had moved into their own with Storm Pelt.

Reed Tail padded across the clearing and paused in front of Moth Flight. "Dew Nose has wrenched a paw," he told her. "She slipped in a rabbit hole while she was hunting. Shall I use up the comfrey from your herb store or pick fresh?"

"Use what we've got for now and pick some fresh later," Moth Flight told him.

He nodded and ducked into the gorse den behind her. Reed Tail had been busy taking care of the Clan's cuts and sprains over the past moon. Moth Flight had tried to keep an eye on her Clanmates' well-being, but every time she left the den to check how a scratch was healing or a sore belly was responding to the chervil Reed Tail had given, one of her kits would start mewling with hunger or squeal for help as they climbed the den wall and got stuck among the branches. It seemed that the moment she set paw in the clearing, a desperate wail would call her back.

"You need to be tougher," Slate had told her many times. "Let them wail. They're safe in camp. They'll survive while you check on your Clanmates."

But Moth Flight couldn't relax. *They've lost their father!* She couldn't bear for them to be without their mother as well.

"They have a whole Clan to raise them," Slate had insisted.

I don't want to be like you, Moth Flight had thought. She ignored the truth that Silver Pelt, Black Ear, and White Tail had grown into happy young cats despite their grieving mother. The Clan had indeed raised them, giving Slate's kits all that kits ever needed: warmth, kindness, food, and protection. *My kits are special,* Moth Flight told herself. *No other cat can give them the love that I can.*

And so she let Reed Tail care for the Clan and told herself that in another half-moon, she'd be ready to return to her duties as medicine cat.

Slate nudged her from her thoughts with a paw. "Look!"

Wind Runner and Jagged Peak had padded into camp. Dappled Pelt and Acorn Fur walked between the WindClan cats, glancing at each other with puzzled looks. Wind Runner's expression was grim. Jagged Peak's ears twitched uneasily.

Moth Flight sat up, alarmed.

Gently moving Blue Whisker aside, she got to her paws. What were Dappled Pelt and Acorn Fur doing here, and why were Wind Runner and Jagged Peak escorting them like prisoners? She crossed the clearing, meeting Wind Runner among the tussocks. "Is something wrong?"

Her mother's eyes were dark.

"I found these two wandering across the moor," she growled.

"We weren't wandering," Dappled Pelt objected.

"We were coming to see Moth Flight," Acorn Fur chipped in.

Moth Flight glanced at the SkyClan medicine cat. Resentment tugged at her belly. *You've taken Micah's place.* She swallowed back her bitterness and met her mother's gaze. "Why shouldn't they cross the moor?"

Jagged Peak lashed his tail. "How can you ask that after everything Clear Sky's done lately?"

Moth Flight faced the tom. "What *has* he done?"

"He keeps sending hunting patrols onto *our* land!" Jagged Peak bristled.

Wind Runner growled. "Willow Tail and Jagged Peak found more rabbit remains on the border this morning."

"Willow Tail spends too much time checking borders," Moth Flight snapped. "She should be hunting for her Clan, not searching for gossip."

Wind Runner flattened her ears. "Prey theft is more than gossip!"

Acorn Fur's tail twitched crossly. "Clear Sky hasn't sent hunting patrols!"

Jagged Peak curled his lip. "Then why do we keep finding signs of fresh-kill on the moor?"

Acorn Fur stood her ground. "How do you know *SkyClan* left them?"

Moth Flight's paw prickled with anger. What a dumb argument! Greenleaf was only just beginning. No cat was hungry. Who cared whether prey was left on one side of a border or another? She glared at Wind Runner. "This has nothing to do with Dappled Pelt and Acorn Fur!" she snapped. "They are medicine cats, not hunters." Blue Whisker scrambled across the clearing. "Moth Flight!" she mewed as she reached her mother. "Why does Wind Runner look so cross?"

Jagged Peak glared at Acorn Fur. "Because SkyClan cats are thieves and liars."

Blue Whisker looked at Jagged Peak with round, anxious eyes. "Micah was a SkyClan cat. Did he lie too?"

Jagged Peak stared at the kit, his pelt rippling uneasily. "I never knew him," he mumbled.

Wind Runner shifted her paws. "Perhaps we should save this discussion for another time."

"Perhaps we should not have it at all!" Moth Flight snapped. She dipped her head to Acorn Fur and Dappled Pelt. "I'm sorry about my Clanmates. They think borders are worth fighting over." She glanced at Blue Whisker. "Go back to Slate, dear. I have to speak with our visitors."

Blue Whisker blinked at her mother. "Will you be long?"

"No," Moth Flight promised. She guided Dappled Pelt and Acorn Fur toward the stones beside the entrance. She could feel Jagged Peak's gaze burning into her pelt. "Is something wrong?" She lowered her voice as they reached the rocks.

"Nothing," Dappled Pelt assured her. The tortoiseshell's gaze drifted after Blue Whisker as she scrambled down into the sandy hollow beside her brother. "Your kits are beautiful."

Moth Flight followed her gaze, her heart swelling. Beside the hollow, Bubbling Stream was still urging Storm Pelt to go faster. "They remind me so much of Micah."

"They have his spirit."

Acorn Fur's words surprised her. "What do you know about Micah's spirit?" Moth Flight questioned.

Acorn Fur dropped her gaze, flinching as though Moth Flight had raked her muzzle. "I worked with him," she mewed quietly. "He was my friend and I miss him."

"We *all* miss him," Moth Flight snapped pointedly. Jealousy bristled through her pelt.

"He spoke about you all the time." Acorn Fur lifted her gaze cautiously. "He loved you very much. I'm sorry that you lost him."

Moth Flight blinked, surprised by the warmth in Acorn Fur's mew. *It's too late to be nice!* She wasn't going to forgive the SkyClan cat so easily. "You spied on him!"

Dappled Pelt's tail flicked uneasily. "Moth Flight, I think you're being unfair—"

Acorn Fur interrupted. "You're right. Clear Sky ordered me to watch him. But I knew, after the first day, that Micah could be trusted. He cared about his Clanmates right from the start. I enjoyed working with him. And I loved helping. One time, Blossom got a thorn in her paw. It was really deep. Micah had to dig around for ages to get it out. He talked to her the whole time, distracting her with jokes and stories of when he was a farm cat. He showed me that there was more to being a medicine cat than learning herbs. You don't just care about the wound; you must care about the cat." Her eyes rounded. "He said that's why StarClan chose you. Because *you* always knew that better than anyone."

Moth Flight stared at her. She suddenly understood why Micah had liked Acorn Fur so much. She was kind and honest and open. Moth Flight dropped her gaze, her pelt prickling with guilt. How could she have judged Acorn Fur so harshly? She hardly knew her. "Thank you," she murmured.

Dappled Pelt glanced to where Wind Runner and Jagged Peak were crouched beside the camp wall, watching their visitors through slitted eyes. "We came here for a reason," she mewed. "Acorn Fur has learned all she can from me and Cloud Spots. Pebble Heart has shared all he knows. Now it's your turn to train her, just as we trained you."

Moth Flight's ear twitched nervously. "But I have kits now."

"You're still a medicine cat," Dappled Pelt reminded her. She glanced back at the kits. They were playing happily with their Clanmates, Slate watching them fondly. "It looks like there are plenty of cats to take care of them while you're busy."

Worry jabbed Moth Flight's belly. "I need to take care of them. They don't have a father."

Acorn Fur shifted her paws before she spoke. "Micah wants you to train me."

Surprise rippled along Moth Flight's spine. *Someone is coming to visit you.* Micah's words echoed in her mind. *You must help her. I'm depending on you.* He'd meant Acorn Fur! "How do you know?" she demanded.

"I dreamed about him," Acorn Fur told her. "He told me to come to you and that you would teach me all I needed to learn."

Moth Flight blinked at her. Acorn Fur must be SkyClan's rightful medicine cat if StarClan visited her dreams. "But what about Wind Runner and Clear Sky? Will they want a WindClan cat training a SkyClan cat?"

Acorn Fur shrugged. "They don't need to know."

Dappled Pelt nodded. "They don't understand the bond between us. They are hunters, not healers. They only understand prey."

Moth Flight dipped her head. Micah wanted her to train Acorn Fur, and he was part of StarClan now. She couldn't go against StarClan's wishes. And she didn't want to disappoint Micah. "Okay." She glanced longingly at her kits. Blue Whisker had returned to Slate's side and curled up against her. Bubbling Stream had slid off Storm Pelt's back and was helping Spider Paw catch imaginary prey in the sandy hollow. Honey Pelt was chasing White Tail toward another gap in the heather wall. They could manage without her for a while. "We might as well start now."

"Where have you been?"

Wind Runner's accusing mew took Moth Flight by surprise as she padded into camp. The sun was sinking toward the horizon and shooting long shadows across the clearing.

Moth Flight dropped the bundle of comfrey she'd gathered. "Training Acorn Fur." *I'm not going to lie about it.*

"Why *you*?" Wind Runner's hackles lifted. "Surely you understand that SkyClan cats are no longer our friends."

"Why not?" Moth Flight demanded.

"They've been stealing our prey." Wind Runner narrowed her eyes. "And I'm sending patrols across their border to hunt."

"*What?*" Moth Flight stared at her. Did her mother want to cause a *war*?

Wind Runner lifted her chin stiffly. "It's important that we show them they can't steal from us without consequences."

"Has anyone actually *seen* SkyClan stealing our prey?" Moth Flight demanded.

"Willow Tail says she saw Red Claw carrying a rabbit over the border yesterday."

"And you believe her?" How could her mother be so naive? "Willow Tail *hates* Red Claw."

"That doesn't make her a liar!" Wind Runner lashed her tail. "It's not just Willow Tail who's seen evidence. Fern Leaf caught Red Claw's scent on our territory. Slate and Jagged Peak have seen bones too. Are *they* liars?"

Of course not. But even if SkyClan cats caught a rabbit or two on WindClan territory—who *cared*? Still, Moth Flight swallowed back anger. She didn't want to get drawn into her mother's argument with SkyClan. Her duty was to heal cats, not fight with them. "I'm going to teach Acorn Fur what I know," she mewed stubbornly.

Wind Runner's pelt prickled. "I'm just worried about you,

Moth Flight. If Clear Sky catches you with one of his cats, who knows what he'll do? I've known him a long time. He's capable of more cruelty than you can imagine."

"Then it's important that his medicine cat is well trained," Moth Flight argued. "If she can earn his respect, she may be able to guide him."

"No one has ever managed to guide Clear Sky before," Wind Runner pointed out.

"Acorn Fur has StarClan on her side. *They* want me to train her."

"They spoke to you?"

"Micah did," Moth Flight told her. "He spoke to Acorn Fur too."

"Micah's not StarClan!"

Moth Flight's throat tightened. "He is now."

Wind Runner gazed at her helplessly. "Then you're going to keep on training her?"

"Yes." Moth Flight scooped up the comfrey and headed for her den. If Micah wanted her to train Acorn Fur, then nothing would stop her.

As the days lengthened, Moth Flight kept her word. Each afternoon, she'd leave Slate in charge of her kits and slip out of camp. She was aware of Wind Runner's gaze following her, dark with worry. But she ignored it, racing to the patch of grass on the moorside where she met Acorn Fur.

This afternoon, clouds hid the sun and a thin drizzle misted the moor. Moth Flight fluffed out her pelt, hoping

Slate would keep the kits in the den. The air was warm, but a wet pelt could mean a chill. She was getting used to being away from them, but she enjoyed their welcome each time she returned home, when they'd clamber over her, purring and begging for badger rides or a game of chase-tail.

She blinked away raindrops and scanned the moorside. There was no sign of Acorn Fur and no scent either. She glanced at the darkening sky, wondering whether, with the sun hidden, the SkyClan medicine cat had lost track of time.

Acorn Fur was a quick learner, just as Micah had said. And she seemed to have a deep understanding of suffering as well as a burning need to ease it. Teaching such a willing apprentice had been fulfilling and, in going over her knowledge in such depth, Moth Flight had renewed her own delight in her healing skills. Was it time she relieved Reed Tail of some of his duties? She frowned. She already felt that she spent too much time away from her kits.

She gazed toward the forest, impatience fizzing beneath her pelt. *Where are you?* It wasn't like Acorn Fur to be late. She was usually pacing the hillside, waiting, by the time Moth Flight arrived.

Unease jabbed her belly.

Perhaps Acorn Fur *couldn't* come.

Her fur tingled with worry. Had Clear Sky found out about their meetings?

He can't stop her from learning! She headed downslope as the rain thickened, heading for the SkyClan border. *Does he think his wishes are more important than StarClan's?* Anger pulsed through her paws as she crossed the wet grass.

The pungent scent of SkyClan markers washed her muzzle as she neared the ferns that edged the trees. She pushed through the dripping fronds. Padding into the shelter of the woods, she glanced around, wondering where SkyClan's camp lay. She had to know where Acorn Fur was. If Clear Sky was stopping her, someone needed to explain to the rabbit-brained leader how important it was for his medicine cat to learn everything she could.

Sniffing the ground, she smelled paw prints and began to follow them. They must eventually lead to the camp. She trailed around a bramble and between two fallen trees. Ducking beneath a branch, she smelled more paw prints. She must be getting close. She could see a glade ahead where rain dripped through the canopy.

I hope he hasn't hurt her. She suddenly remembered her mother's warning. *He's capable of more cruelty than you can imagine.* Moth Flight pushed the words away. She wasn't going to be bullied. She had StarClan on her side.

As she slid through a clump of ferns, a hiss made her freeze. Tortoiseshell fur flashed at the corner of her vision. Something hard slammed into her flank and knocked her, sprawling, to the ground.

Panic flared beneath Moth Flight's pelt as she scrambled to her paws. The scent of a SkyClan she-cat filled the air. Jerking around, she saw Sparrow Fur glaring at her, hackles raised.

"What are you doing on SkyClan land?" The tortoiseshell's eyes flashed with suspicion.

"I'm Moth Flight!" she growled.

"I *know* who you are," the tortoiseshell returned.

"Then you know that I'm a medicine cat! I can walk where I please."

"No one walks in this forest without Clear Sky's permission!" Sparrow Fur growled.

"Since when?"

"Since he said so!"

Frustration surged in Moth Flight's belly. "I've come to find Acorn Fur." Perhaps if she explained that she was worried about her Clanmate, Sparrow Fur would understand.

"Acorn Fur is in camp, doing what she's supposed to do."

"Which is?" she demanded.

"Taking care of her Clanmates!"

"But I haven't finished training her!"

Sparrow Fur's tail swished ominously. "She's had all the training she's going to get."

Moth Flight didn't understand. "Don't you want her to be the best medicine cat she can be?" Just because Clear Sky was a rabbit-brain, didn't mean his whole Clan had to act dumb!

"What *I* want doesn't matter," Sparrow Fur snarled. "Clear Sky is my leader. I follow his orders. And his orders are that no cat should cross our border. Especially not a WindClan cat."

Fury scorched Moth Flight's belly. "I'm not here to *hunt*! StarClan ordered me to train Acorn Fur and that's what I'm going to do." She headed past Sparrow Fur.

The SkyClan she-cat dodged ahead of her.

She glared at the tortoiseshell angrily. "Get out of my way! I have to—" She stopped, surprised to see worry clouding Sparrow Fur's gaze.

"You have to leave!" Lowering her voice, Sparrow Fur glanced nervously over her shoulder.

"Why?"

"Clear Sky will rip you to shreds if you reach the camp," she warned. "And then he'll rip *me* to shreds for letting you."

Moth Flight halted. "He hasn't *hurt* Acorn Fur, has he?"

"No!" Sparrow Fur looked indignant. "But he's angry that she's been sneaking onto WindClan land to train with you. How can he prove that we don't cross the border if she trails SkyClan scent all over the moorside?"

"But you *do* cross the border!" Moth Flight accused. "Willow Tail's seen you."

"She hasn't seen *me!*" Sparrow Fur snapped. "SkyClan cats don't hunt on other Clans' land. Not like *WindClan*. We found Jagged Peak's fur caught on a bramble this morning. And fresh-kill blood less than a tail-length away."

Moth Flight growled under her breath. Wind Runner must have sent him to teach Clear Sky a lesson. She'd only made the situation worse.

"But I'm a *medicine* cat!" she insisted. "We need to be able to travel in each other's territory. How else will I get catmint from Twolegplace? And how can Acorn Fur get to the Moonstone without crossing the moor?"

"That's not my problem." Sparrow Fur began to guide Moth Flight toward the border.

"What if something happens to Acorn Fur and you need my help?" Reluctantly, Moth Flight let Sparrow Fur steer her back along the trail. The tortoiseshell clearly wasn't going to let her pass without a fight, and she didn't want to get her into trouble with Clear Sky.

"Nothing's going to happen to Acorn Fur so long as she stops training with you."

Moth Flight blinked at the tortoiseshell as they reached the border. "This is the dumbest decision ever!"

Sparrow Fur flicked her tail toward the moor. "Just go home!"

Moth Flight saw doubt in her gaze. "You think he's wrong, don't you?"

Sparrow Fur looked away. "He's my leader," she growled and stalked back into the forest.

Blood roared in Moth Flight's ears. If the Clans started guarding their territory like this, how could the medicine cats share their knowledge? Half Moon's word rang in her mind. *Every Clan's destiny depends on you, though they don't know it yet.* Why didn't Clear Sky understand? His medicine cat had to go where she was needed. *There will come a time when they will listen to you and you alone. I can tell you this, but it's up to you to earn their respect.*

How? Helplessness swamped Moth Flight. She had to persuade Wind Runner and Clear Sky that cats' lives were more important than borders. *StarClan, what can I do?*

Chapter 28

Moth Flight threaded among the rustling bracken stems, following her Clanmates into Fourtrees, where the full moon blanched the clearing.

The scents of RiverClan and ThunderClan swirled on the warm evening breeze. She scanned the cats below, recognizing Thunder and River Ripple moving among the gathered cats, dipping their heads in greeting, while their Clanmates clustered in groups, heads close as they shared gossip.

Silver Stripe and Black Ear stampeded past Moth Flight, White Tail leading, their tails flapping excitedly. It was their first full-moon Gathering. They'd been restless all day, excited at the thoughts of seeing new faces and smelling new scents.

"Slow down!" Slate hurried at their heels, her fur rippling anxiously along her spine as her kits burst into the clearing.

Eyes flashed in the moonlight as muzzles jerked around, clearly surprised by the commotion.

Slate dodged in front of White Tail, hissing sternly. "Calm down. I don't want RiverClan and ThunderClan thinking I raised a pack of foxes!"

As the bracken thinned around her, Moth Flight's thoughts

flashed to her own kits back in camp. Rocky had promised to watch them and make sure they were tucked in their nest by the time she returned. Spotted Fur and Holly had also stayed behind with Eagle Feather, Fern Leaf, Reed Tail, and Storm Pelt. With border tensions running high, Wind Runner had not wanted to leave the camp unguarded and, for once, Moth Flight was grateful for her mother's caution.

Not that she believed SkyClan would attack. But if a stray dog or hungry fox found their way into camp, she knew her kits would be well protected.

This was her first Gathering in moons, and the first time she'd see the other medicine cats together since the last time she'd traveled to the Moonstone with Micah. She quickened her pace, falling in beside Dust Muzzle. Her Clanmates flanked them, moving wordlessly through the bracken. There was tension in their hunched shoulders and flicking tails as they neared the bottom of the slope. Wind Runner led the way into the clearing, her eyes narrowed. Moth Flight knew that her mother had come to settle scores, and anxiety wormed in her belly. *Please let her remember the full-moon truce.*

She glanced at the brambly slope at the other side of the clearing, looking for signs of SkyClan. But Clear Sky hadn't arrived yet and the woods beyond were eerily silent.

"Moth Flight!" Following Dust Muzzle from the bracken, she recognized Dappled Pelt's mew. The RiverClan medicine cat was hurrying toward her, Cloud Spots at her heels.

As Dust Muzzle followed Wind Runner into the throng of cats, Dappled Pelt stopped in front of Moth Flight. Her eyes shone. "How are the kits?"

"They're well," Moth Flight told her. In the moon since they'd been born, they'd grown more boisterous each day. Even Blue Whisker had started exploring the camp with her littermates. Only that morning, the yellow-and-white she-kit had climbed the stones beside the camp entrance and called to Moth Flight from the top, her fur fluffed with delight.

Cloud Spots jerked Moth Flight from the memory, flicking his tail happily. "Dappled Pelt says they have Micah's coloring."

"Honey Pelt looks just like him," Moth Flight told him proudly.

Cloud Spots purred. "I'm sure Micah's watching them from StarClan."

He is. Happiness surged through Moth Flight as she remembered her dream.

Silver Stripe's excited mew sounded behind her. "Please can we talk to the others?"

She turned to see the pale tabby pacing around her brothers. Black Ear was staring wide-eyed at the gathered cats, while White Tail gazed around thoughtfully, his nose twitching.

"RiverClan cats smell funny," he commented.

"Hush!" Slate lowered her voice. "They smell a bit fishy, that's all."

"I want to ask them if they really swim!" Silver Stripe whispered.

Moth Flight nodded toward a pair of RiverClan cats. "Go and talk to Drizzle." She'd spotted the gray-and-white she-kit—a young cat now—standing beside her brother.

Pine Needle had grown; his shoulders were broader and his black pelt was as sleek as an otter's. He stared around the clearing, his eyes round. Moth Flight wondered if it was his first Gathering too.

Silver Stripe padded impatiently around Slate. "Can we?" she begged.

But Black Ear was already crossing the clearing toward the young RiverClan cats.

Slate's ears twitched. "Of course."

Silver Stripe hared after her brother, White Tail at her heels.

"Don't forget to be polite!" Slate called after them.

Dappled Pelt watched the young cats race away. "Gray Wing would have been proud of them."

Slate blinked at her sadly. "He always wanted kits of his own," she murmured. "I just wish he'd had a chance to watch them grow up."

Moth Flight swept her tail along Slate's spine. "He's probably watching them right now." *Just like Micah watches over our kits.*

Wind Runner's angry mew rang across the clearing. She faced Thunder, her eyes flashing accusingly in the moonlight. "I knew you'd defend him."

River Ripple padded between the two leaders. "We should wait and let Clear Sky speak for himself."

Wind Runner scowled. "We've heard enough lies from him."

As she spoke, grass swished at the top of the hollow. Lithe

bodies swarmed down the far slope.

Clear Sky? Moth Flight stiffened. Would Wind Runner manage to keep her temper? Would she openly accuse the Sky-Clan leader of sending hunting patrols onto their land? And what would happen when Clear Sky accused her in return?

ShadowClan scent washed over her and she recognized Tall Shadow's pelt, hardly more than a shadow in the long grass.

Dappled Pelt eyed Moth Flight anxiously. "Are there still hunting disputes between WindClan and SkyClan?"

"Yes." Moth Flight's pelt prickled. "Clear Sky has banned any cat from crossing his borders."

Cloud Spots blinked. "How will you fetch catmint from Twolegplace?"

Dappled Pelt didn't give her a chance to answer. "What about Acorn Fur? Did you finish training her?"

Moth Flight dropped her gaze guiltily. "I tried, but Clear Sky won't let her leave and I can't get past the border to see her." She watched the ShadowClan cats weave among the waiting cats, greeting them with nods and flicks of their tail. Murmured gossip hummed in the evening air.

Shattered Ice gazed grimly at Mud Paws. "Clear Sky's patrolling his borders again."

"Pebble Heart was turned away when he tried to gather borage," Juniper Branch told Milkweed.

Moth Flight saw pelts ripple with apprehension. Milkweed glanced nervously toward the bramble-covered slope where SkyClan usually made its entrance. Dawn Mist moved closer to Drizzle and Pine Needle.

Pebble Heart reached the medicine cats, his eyes round with worry. "I thought the prey dispute would have blown over by now, but it's gotten worse."

Moth Flight's ears twitched uneasily. "Clear Sky has stopped me from training Acorn Fur," she told him. "He won't let any cat cross his border. He's been sending hunting patrols onto our land again."

Pebble Heart's gaze darkened.

"Sparrow Fur and Acorn Fur both say that Clear Sky *hasn't* sent hunting patrols onto our land but Willow Tail swears she's seen Red Claw taking WindClan prey across the border." Moth Flight glanced at Willow Tail. The pale tabby stood in a circle of ThunderClan and RiverClan cats, her eyes flashing with malice as she talked. Moth Flight's belly tightened. Why was she so determined to stir up trouble? She lowered her voice. "Wind Runner's started sending hunting patrols onto SkyClan land to teach Clear Sky a lesson."

Pebble Heart's tail twitched. "This needs to stop now before it gets serious." He glanced up the slope hopefully. "Perhaps when Clear Sky arrives we can talk some sense into him and Wind Runner."

Moth Flight's heart lurched. "Do you think they're ready to listen to us?" She glanced at Cloud Spots and Dappled Pelt. How much influence did any of them have over their leaders?

Cloud Spots swished his tail. "We speak for StarClan."

Dappled Pelt frowned. "From what I've heard, Clear Sky has no time for StarClan."

Pebble Heart glanced at the stars, sparkling high overhead.

"They're his ancestors as well as ours."

"We should hold the meeting without him!" Wind Runner's angry mew rang once more across the clearing. As Moth Flight turned, the WindClan leader shouldered her way through the crowd and leaped onto the great rock.

Wind Runner glared at Thunder, River Ripple, and Tall Shadow. "Why should *we* show him respect by waiting when he shows us none by being late?" She lashed her tail, her brown pelt pale in the moonlight. "He probably won't come at all! That's how little he values us."

Tall Shadow weaved past Juniper Branch and Milkweed, glancing at Sun Shadow before jumping up beside Wind Runner. River Ripple followed slowly, his pelt ruffled. Thunder hesitated, checking the SkyClan slope once more before leaping onto the rock.

Wind Runner's gaze swept the Clans as the cats crowded closer and raised their muzzles to their leaders.

"We must treat Clear Sky as he has treated us!" she yowled. "If he wants to stop all cats from crossing his land, then we must turn our tails on *him*!"

Thunder stared at her, ears twitching. "What do you mean?"

"From now on, SkyClan is not one of us," Wind Runner showed her teeth. "They do not exist. They must survive alone."

"No!" Thunder bristled. "Clear Sky must have closed his borders for a good reason. *You* say he's being hostile. For all we know, he's simply defending his land. *You* claim that SkyClan has stolen prey from you! But where's your proof? They're not even here to defend themselves."

River Ripple nodded. "Clear Sky should at least be given a fair hearing."

"Why?" Tall Shadow narrowed her eyes. "He hasn't even shown up. Clearly, he doesn't consider himself one of us. Of course you defend him, Thunder; he's your father. But why should we doubt *Wind Runner's* word? She has never lied before. Clear Sky has been lying since he was a kit. Have you forgotten his treachery to Gray Wing? He started the Great Battle! We have been patient with him long enough! We will be stronger without SkyClan."

Stronger without SkyClan? Outrage surged in Moth Flight's belly. Didn't these cats realize that banishing a Clan would be like pulling a woven twig from a nest? Each twig made it strong. Once you began to unravel it, the whole nest might collapse. "We cannot turn our tails on another Clan!" She was shocked to hear her own voice ring loudly across the clearing.

Eyes flashed toward her.

Dappled Pelt lifted her chin. "We came from the mountains together. We share blood and memories."

"Unite or die!" Cloud Spots yowled. "Don't you remember the Great Battle? The spirit-cats told us afterward that we could not live without each other."

"Unite or die!" Thunder stepped to the edge of the rock. "If we are to survive, we must act *together*. This dispute must be ended with words, not deeds."

"*Words?*" Wind Runner spat. "Since when did Clear Sky

ever resolve anything with words? He only knows how to use his claws and this is the only way we can avoid battle. We must shun Clear Sky, before he starts another war."

Moth Flight stared at her mother. "What about the rest of SkyClan? It's they who will suffer if we abandon them."

Willow Tail called from among the crowd. "*How* will they suffer? They won't starve. They have enough prey in the forest."

Shattered Ice lifted his muzzle. "Clear Sky has always caused trouble for the Clans. Without him, we can have peace."

"But their medicine cat hasn't finished her training!" Moth Flight whisked her tail angrily. "Who will care for their sick? And what if they need herbs that only grow beside the river, or on the moor? Do we turn them away and let their Clanmates die?"

Juniper Branch spoke up. "The Clans must work together. I only survived my kitting because Moth Flight helped Pebble Heart. Now I have three healthy kits!"

Muted murmurs of agreement rippled through the Clans.

Willow Tail silenced them. "A few moons ago, we didn't even *have* medicine cats! We survived then. We'll survive now!"

Moth Flight swung her gaze toward the she-cat. "StarClan ordered us to care for our Clans. Would you go against StarClan?"

"Why not?" Willow Tail snapped. "They're dead! They know nothing about the living."

"That's not true!" Moth Flight lashed her tail. "They watch over us."

River Ripple nudged past Thunder, his eyes glittering with starlight. "StarClan brought peace. They see things we cannot." He stared at Willow Tail. "Do you think you know better than they do?"

Willow Tail looked away, her pelt rippling.

Thunder glanced gratefully at the RiverClan leader. "We cannot make hasty decisions without speaking to Clear Sky."

Wind Runner growled. "It's not *your* border that Clear Sky has crossed. It's not *your* prey he's stolen. It's clear that he wants to push us into war. I am only suggesting a way that a battle might be avoided. By cutting him off, we are sending a strong message: We won't fight with him. We will patrol our borders and protect our land, but we will not fight. He is on his own." She glared suddenly at Moth Flight. "And that means medicine cats too. You will not share your knowledge with Acorn Fur. You must go to the Moonstone without her. She is forbidden from your meetings."

Moth Flight's hackles lifted. *You don't have the right to decide that!* She opened her mouth to object but Wind Runner pressed on.

"This is the best way to stop Clear Sky. You've seen him drag us into war before. Help me stop him from doing it again."

As her gaze swept beseechingly over the Clans, yowls of agreement filled the still night air.

"Cut him off!"

"Forget SkyClan!"

Moth Flight blinked at her mother. Was she really going to deprive SkyClan of help and healing? What would StarClan say? She glanced around her Clanmates, disappointment weighing in her chest. Dew Nose and Swift Minnow were joining in with the cheering.

Gorse Fur lifted his muzzle. "It's the only way to avoid war!"

Moth Flight stared at her father in disbelief. Wind Runner was hotheaded, but Gorse Fur had always tempered her rashness with reason. Why was he going along with this madness?

A yowl sounded at the top of the hollow. The Clans fell silent, their eyes flashing as they turned to see who had called.

Sparrow Fur was haring down the slope. "Help!"

The gathered cats parted and let her race to the center.

The tortoiseshell gazed around, her eyes wide with horror. "Where's Moth Flight? Pebble Heart?" She scanned the Clans desperately.

Moth Flight pushed her way through the cats, Pebble Heart at her heels. "What's happened?"

Sparrow Fur stared at her. "Tiny Branch is hurt! He got his paw trapped! There was a fox. We fought it off but Tiny Branch—"

Dappled Pelt burst from the crowd. "Was he bitten?"

Sparrow Fur nodded, her eyes wild. "It's bad. We've carried him back to camp, but he's unconscious."

"Fox bites cause infection." Cloud Spots nosed his way past Dappled Pelt. "They must be treated at once."

Sparrow Fur was trembling. "Acorn Fur can't stop the bleeding."

Moth Flight's heart lurched. Tiny Branch was less than six moons old. If the blood loss didn't kill him, the shock might. "Come on." She began to race for the side of the hollow.

Wind Runner's snarl made her stop. "Where are you going?"

"I have to help Tiny Branch!" She skidded to a halt and glared at Wind Runner.

"I told you! SkyClan is on their own!" Wind Runner's eyes blazed with fury.

"*You* decided that!" Moth Flight hissed. "I'm a medicine cat. I won't stand by and let cats die."

Shocked mews sounded around her.

"She can't go!"

"She must!"

"What about the kits?"

"That's Clear Sky's problem!"

Shattered Ice blocked her path. "Clear Sky must learn that he can't push the other Clans around."

Moth Flight flexed her claws. "Get out of my way."

A low growl rumbled behind her. Dust Muzzle stalked past and faced Shattered Ice. "Let her pass. Tiny Branch shouldn't have to pay for his *father's* mistakes." He looked meaningfully at Thunder.

Thunder dropped his gaze. "Let her go, Shattered Ice."

Shattered Ice glared at Thunder, hackles raised. "You're not my leader."

"But I am." River Ripple stepped forward. "Let her pass."

Growling, Shattered Ice backed away.

Moth Flight glanced at Dust Muzzle. "Thank you." Breaking into a run, she pelted up the slope. Sparrow Fur charged after her, Cloud Spots, Dappled Pelt, and Pebble Heart at his heels.

Sparrow Fur dodged in front of her as they reached the top of the slope. "Follow me!"

Zigzagging past brambles and leaping logs, she blazed a winding trail through the thick woodland. Moth Flight's chest burned as she raced to keep up. Behind her, she could hear the thrumming paw steps of Cloud Spots, Dappled Pelt, and Pebble Heart.

As the forest floor began to slope down, she recognized the glade where Sparrow Fur had stopped her and sent her home only a few days earlier. The tortoiseshell crossed it and headed for a thick clump of brambles. Ducking through a small gap at one edge, she disappeared. Moth Flight narrowed her eyes against the prickly stalks and followed her through, surprised to find herself emerging into a small hollow edged by trees and lush ferns.

Clear Sky stood in the center. Star Flower trembled beside him. The rest of SkyClan ringed around them, their horrified gazes fixed on a blood-soaked scrap of fur lying at Clear Sky's paws.

Tiny Branch!

Moth Flight scrambled to a halt and crouched beside the kit. She could hear her own heart pounding in her ears as she swiftly scanned his body. There were deep teeth wounds on his flank. His hind paw was twisted and bloody, as though it had been yanked from a thorn bush. His eyes were closed, flickering slightly. His muzzle was clumped with dried blood.

She smelled the sharp tang of horsetail and marigold rising from Tiny Branch's wound. Dried green pulp showed on his bloody fur. Acorn Fur had clearly been trying to treat him for some time. Moth Flight glanced at Clear Sky. "Where's Acorn Fur?"

"She went to find cobwebs." Clear Sky's mew was tight.

Moth Flight pictured the SkyClan medicine cat struggling alone to help Tiny Branch. Sympathy pricked at her heart. She wasn't trained to deal with injuries as bad as this. She must be terrified. "She should have sent for help sooner."

Clear Sky's tail twitched. "SkyClan doesn't ask for help unless there's no choice."

Did you stop her? Moth Flight angrily swallowed back the words. Picking a fight with Clear Sky wouldn't help Tiny Branch.

Star Flower didn't wrench her gaze from her kit. "Will he be okay?"

Moth Flight didn't answer. "Where's her herb store?"

Clear Sky stared at her blankly. "I don't think she has one."

Red Claw stepped forward. "She's been gathering herbs for a while," he told his leader.

Moth Flight turned to the dark red tom. "Where are they?"

Red Claw began to lead the way to a short steep slope where the roots of an oak snaked into the earth.

As Moth Flight straightened to follow, she felt Dappled Pelt's nose on her shoulder.

"I'll go with him."

"Bring every herb she's got," Moth Flight told her. She glanced at Pebble Heart. "What can we do?" She wasn't sure which wound to treat first.

Pebble Heart crouched beside Tiny Branch while Cloud Spots shooed the Clan backward, making room on the kit's other side.

Pebble Heart pressed his paws on the brightest wound, where blood was still welling. "We need to stop this bleeding first. It's the worst injury."

Moth Flight slipped her paws under his. "I'll press the blood back while you check the rest of him." Warmth oozed under her pads. Fear flashed beneath her pelt, but she ignored it.

Cloud Spots sniffed Tiny Branch's mangled hind paw. "This needs wet nettles to take down the swelling."

Moth Flight looked toward the slope, relieved to see Dappled Pelt hurrying back, a wad of leaves in her jaws.

"Are there any nettles in there?" Moth Flight asked as Dappled Pelt dropped the herbs beside her.

"No." Dapped Pelt began to sort through the pile. "It's mainly chervil and borage."

Moth Flight stiffened, frustration flaring through her. If only she'd been allowed to finish training Acorn Fur! Her store would be fully stocked. She avoided Clear Sky's gaze, swallowing back anger. *Tiny Branch is his kit.* This wasn't the time to argue about borders.

"There's some thyme here." Dappled Pelt mewed hopefully.

Moth Flight frowned at the unconscious kit. "He can't chew anything."

"We could put a sprig under his tongue," Pebble Heart suggested.

"That's better than nothing." Moth Flight pressed harder on the wound as Pebble Heart slipped a claw between Tiny Branch's lips and very gently levered his jaws open.

Alarm sparked in her belly. The kit's breath was so weak she could hardly feel his flank move. He was as limp as dead prey.

She watched, her mouth dry, as Pebble Heart slid a thyme stalk beneath the kit's tongue.

"You're here!" Acorn Fur burst into camp. Moth Flight saw relief glistening in the SkyClan medicine cat's gaze. Cobwebs swathed her forepaws and she hurried over and peeled them off.

Pebble Heart took them from her and began stuffing shreds into the bloodiest wound. He nodded to Acorn Fur. "Put your paws here."

As she pressed the cobwebs deep into the bloody flesh, Pebble Heart ripped the remaining wad into two and gave one half to Cloud Spots. Between them, they wrapped every graze and bite they could see.

Moth Flight leaned down and listened to Tiny Branch's chest. There was no bubbling inside, but his heart was fluttering like a trapped bird, weak with exhaustion. Her belly tightened.

She glanced at Star Flower.

The golden tabby she-cat must have seen the despair in her gaze. She recoiled, pressing her muzzle into Clear Sky's shoulder.

Clear Sky's dark gaze swept the medicine cats, then fixed on Moth Flight. "He'll live, won't he?"

Tiny Branch suddenly whimpered. His eyes flickered open for a moment. Then he jerked, and fell still.

Clear Sky stared at him, his mouth open.

Moth Flight pressed her ear to Tiny Branch's chest once again.

Nothing.

Her thoughts raced to her own kits. Were they safely tucked up with Rocky? What if a fox had gotten into the camp? What if one of them had wandered alone onto the moor? Panic tugged at her belly. She needed to see them. She had to *know* they were okay. But first she had to tell Clear Sky his son was dead.

She looked at the SkyClan leader, pity twisting her heart. "I'm so sorry."

His eyes clouded. Pain flared in their blue depths. Moth Flight was startled to see the tough Clan leader sway on his paws. Star Flower rocked beside him, her nose buried deep in his pelt.

Their Clanmates began to move around them. Blossom tugged a clump of damp moss from between the roots of a tree and carried it to Tiny Branch's body. Gently she began to wipe the blood from his fur. Thorn and Quick Water pressed against Star Flower, supporting her as Clear Sky stepped away and crouched beside their dead kit. He rested his nose softly on the kit's head. "I should have been there, my son. I should have saved you."

Moth Flight glanced at Acorn Fur.

The SkyClan medicine cat was staring bleakly at her leader. Moth Flight got to her paws and pressed her nose to the brown she-cat's cheek. "I don't think any of us could have saved him," she murmured.

"If only I'd had more cobwebs in my den," she mewed thickly.

Pebble Heart straightened. "It would have taken more than cobwebs."

"He's with StarClan now," Dappled Pelt gazed sympathetically at Acorn Fur. "You did all you could."

The tugging in Moth Flight's belly grew stronger. "I have to see my kits." Guilt flashed through her as Clear Sky jerked up his nose and stared at her. "I'm sorry—" She began to apologize, but he cut her off.

"Go to them," he growled hoarsely.

She backed toward the entrance, grief tearing at her heart. "I wish we could have come straight away."

Clear Sky's gaze hardened. "Why didn't you?"

Moth Flight froze. She felt the anxious gazes of the other medicine cats flashed toward her.

Sparrow Fur stepped forward. "Wind Runner didn't want her to come," she mumbled. "She said that SkyClan was on its own."

Clear Sky straightened, the muscles in his broad shoulders rippling.

Star Flower padded forward shakily. "She was going to let a kit die?"

"It's not that simple." Fear flashed through Moth Flight. She only wanted peace. "You need to speak with Wind Runner."

Star Flower's green eyes brimmed with pain. She turned away.

Clear Sky blinked at Moth Flight. "You should go," he growled. "Your kits need you."

Her heart pounding, Moth Flight turned and raced out of camp. The scent of Tiny Branch's blood lingered on her tongue. *My kits!* She had to know they were safe. She hared through the forest, her paws skidding on fallen leaves as she swerved among the brambles and ferns. She broke from the forest and pelted onto the moor. She needed to smell her kits and feel their warmth against her muzzle. Her gaze fixed on the distant hollow, she pushed against the coarse grass, racing breathlessly upslope. Bursting into camp, she bounded over the moonlit tussocks and ducked into her den.

Rocky lifted his head sleepily and blinked at her. The kits were curled against his belly. "I told you I'd have them tucked up by the time you got home."

Peace enfolded Moth Flight as she gazed at her beautiful kits. Spider Paw stirred in his sleep, stretching a paw to rest it on Bubbling Stream's muzzle. Bubbling Stream pushed it off and rolled over, a tiny whimper escaping as she snuggled against Blue Whisker's pelt.

Moth Flight padded closer, breathing in their milky scent. She closed her eyes and lifted her muzzle. *Thank you, StarClan, for keeping them safe.*

CHAPTER 29

❧

"Slate!" Moth Flight called across the clearing. "Will you keep an eye on my kits while I check on Rocky?"

Honey Pelt slid under her belly. "We don't need anyone to watch us! We're nearly two moons old."

Moth Flight smoothed his ruffled fur, sweeping her tail along his spine. "I just want to know someone's looking out for you."

Spider Paw sniffed. "What can happen to us in camp?"

Bubbling Stream was rolling in the sun-warmed earth of the sandy hollow, like a sparrow taking a dust bath. Blue Whisker watched her from the edge, her pelt pricking as though the thought of getting dusty horrified her.

Slate looked up blearily from where she'd been dozing in the early morning sunshine. "I'm coming." She got stiffly to her paws.

Moth Flight guessed that last night's Gathering had left the she-cat sleepy. Her thick, gray fur looked matted, as though she hadn't even washed. Moth Flight felt a flash of guilt. Perhaps she should let Slate rest. But Rocky had come to her den, just as Spotted Fur and Reed Tail were leaving for the dawn patrol. He'd been awake all night with aching joints. She had to help him.

She glanced at Honey Pelt, her heart pricking as she remembered Tiny Branch. She wanted to gather her kits to her belly—as she had when they were newly born—and keep them safely wrapped against her. But they were growing. They wanted to run and explore.

Rocky needs me more right now.

Fighting to save Tiny Branch's life had reminded her how important her duties were to her Clan. Leaders talked of border patrols and battles; medicine cats were the ones who had to heal the wounds afterward. Unease itched beneath her pelt; could she have saved Tiny Branch? What if Clear Sky had let Acorn Fur call her sooner? What if Wind Runner hadn't delayed her at Fourtrees? *What if I knew more?*

There was so much to be learned. She was determined to devote her life to her skill. It would help every cat.

"Moth Flight?"

She half heard Spider Paw's mew. She looked up as he repeated her name.

"*Moth Flight!*" He was plucking at the grass outside their den. "Why *can't* we go onto the moor?"

Moth Flight blinked at him, still half lost in her thoughts. "What, dear?"

"Why can't we go out onto the moor?" Spider Paw repeated crossly.

"There are buzzards out there that might carry you off," Moth Flight reminded him. "And foxes and Twoleg dogs. It's not safe until you're big enough to run or fight."

Honey Pelt dropped into an attack pounce, wriggled his hindquarters, and leaped onto his brother. "We can fight!" he squeaked as Spider Paw struggled beneath him. They rolled, wrestling, across the grass.

"Be careful!" Moth Flight flinched as she saw Spider Paw's unsheathed claws. "When you're play fighting, remember to pull in your claws!"

Slate was padding across the clearing, her shoulders drooping.

She looks so tired. Moth Flight frowned. *I hope she doesn't fall asleep while I'm gone.*

She glanced around the camp, hoping to find another cat willing to watch her kits while she tended to Rocky. But the clearing was deserted. Wind Runner had assigned patrols for the day. Gorse Fur had taken Storm Pelt, Dew Nose, and Swift Minnow to flush out rabbits from their burrows on the moortop. Dust Muzzle and Fern Leaf had led a patrol toward the gorge to find lapwings, while Jagged Peak and Holly had gone to gather heather for new nests. Only StarClan knew where Willow Tail was. The pale tabby hardly seemed to be in camp at all these days.

Spotted Fur and Reed Tail were sharing prey at the far end of the camp. Moth Flight blinked at them hopefully, but they were deep in conversation, lying in the long grass, relaxing after their dawn patrol.

Wind Runner lay, stretched on the rocks, beside the entrance. Moth Flight narrowed her eyes. There was no way she was asking her mother for help. They hadn't spoken since the Gathering the night before. Slate would have to do.

Moth Flight watched the gray she-cat settle awkwardly beside the sandy hollow. "Call me if you need me," Moth Flight told her, hoping she wouldn't. She ducked into her den and pulled a wad of comfrey from her herb store. She'd gathered it yesterday and it was nicely wilted. It would be easy to wrap around Rocky's stiff joints. She'd gather more later and line Rocky's nest.

She was about to grab the bundle between her jaws when she hesitated. Glancing back at her stores, she grabbed a few extra leaves and rolled them up with the comfrey. Then she padded into the sunshine and crossed the tussocks to Rocky's den.

She was pleased that her Clanmates had woven a shelter for the old tom. Holly was an expert at threading gorse and brambles into roofs and walls. Moth Flight had been dimly aware of the building work while she'd nursed her kits. She'd heard Holly's mew issuing instructions and ordering her Clanmates to find more stems and sprigs for the den. She'd even made sure any gaps had been filled with moss and leaves, so that, as Moth Flight padded inside, shadow swept her sun-warmed pelt.

Rocky blinked at her through the gloom. "Moth Flight?" His mew was tight. He must be in a lot of pain.

"I'm sorry I've been so long," Moth Flight dropped the comfrey guiltily beside his nest. "I had to find someone to watch my kits."

Rocky grunted. "I wish I could watch them for you."

"You can, once these herbs start to make you feel better." She unrolled the bundle and hooked out the extra leaves she'd tucked among them. "Eat these." She laid the leaves on the side of his nest.

Rocky's eyes gleamed. "Catmint."

"I thought it'd help."

Rocky purred, lapping them up.

As he closed his eyes contently, Moth Flight leaned into his nest and began wrapping his hind legs with the comfrey. "Once the sap seeps through your fur, the pain will start to ease," she promised. "We need to make sure that your nest is lined with comfrey in the future. Now that White Tail, Silver Stripe, and Black Ear are old enough to go onto the moor, I'm sure they'll be happy to gather fresh leaves for you." *Soon they'll be old enough to become apprentices,* Moth Flight thought, wondering which of the older cats would be chosen to teach the adolescents the finer points of hunting and caring for the Clan. It seemed like just yesterday she was helping fish Silver Stripe out of the tunnel. *It's amazing how fast the kits grow.*

"Mmmmm." Rocky was still purring.

Pleasure warmed Moth Flight's pelt. Last night, as she'd fought to save Tiny Branch, she'd felt powerless. Now satisfaction moved deep in her belly as she eased her Clanmate's pain.

"Moth Flight!" A pained shriek sounded outside.

She dropped the comfrey and darted from the den. Beside the tall rock, at the head of the sandy hollow, Slate crouched over Blue Whisker.

The kit was lying motionless on the ground.

Spider Paw and Honey Pelt pressed around Slate while Bubbling Stream hung back, her eyes wide with shock.

"What happened?" Moth Flight raced to Blue Whisker's side. The kit was unconscious.

Slate blinked, her gaze cloudy. "I'm not sure. I just closed my eyes for a moment and—"

Honey Pelt cut in. "She wanted to climb to the top." He looked up at the tall rock. "She wanted to stand where Wind Runner stands when she talks to the Clan."

Moth Flight sniffed Blue Whisker's pelt, feeling for heat that betrayed swelling.

Blue Whisker blinked her eyes open. "Moth Flight?"

Moth Flight's throat tightened. "Where does it hurt?" she asked sharply.

"Nowhere." Blue Whisker's breath was shallow.

"Are you sure?" Moth Flight ran her paws over the kit's white-and-yellow pelt, feeling for injuries.

Blue Whisker struggled to her paws, swaying slightly. "I'm okay," she whispered.

Slate stared at the kit. "She was just winded."

"Are you sure you're okay?" Moth Flight's heart pounded in her ears.

Blue Whisker met her gaze. "I'm sure."

Relief flooded Moth Flight. She jerked her muzzle toward Slate. "Why weren't you watching?"

Slate coughed. "I'm sorry. I'm not feeling too well."

"Why didn't you say anything?" Frustration sparked in

Moth Flight's fur. Was she supposed to do everything? Take care of Rocky *and* watch her own kits? She swallowed back anger. Perhaps she should have asked Reed Tail to tend to Rocky. Or swallowed her pride and asked Wind Runner to watch the kits.

Angrily, she turned on Blue Whisker. "What were you doing climbing the rock? Didn't you realize it was dangerous?"

Honey Pelt padded in front of his sister. "She saw me do it yesterday," he told her.

Moth Flight blinked. "*You* climbed it yesterday?"

"I did too," Spider Paw lifted his chin.

"And me," Bubbling Stream told her.

Moth Flight stared at them. Why hadn't she noticed?

"It was while you were at the Gathering," Honey Pelt told her, as though reading her thoughts.

"Did Rocky let you?"

"He said we were too timid. And that Micah would have had us hunting on the moor by now." Spider Paw glanced guiltily toward Rocky's den. "He promised to catch us if we fell."

Bubbling Stream padded closer. "He wouldn't let Blue Whisker climb. He said she wasn't ready."

"So she decided to try it today." Moth Flight glared at Blue Whisker.

Blue Whisker's eyes glistened. "I'm sorry," she whimpered.

Honey Pelt puffed out his chest. "I didn't see her climbing, or I'd have stopped her."

But you didn't! Moth Flight shifted her paws. *Why should you?*

He was only a kit. He wasn't responsible for Blue Whisker's safety. *I am!*

"Is she okay?" Her mother's voice took her by surprise. Moth Flight glanced over her shoulder and saw Wind Runner stalking across the hollow. Reed Tail and Spotted Fur hurried after her.

"She's fine," Moth Flight told them. "Just winded." As she spoke, she was suddenly aware of heat pulsing from Slate's pelt. She sniffed at the she-cat, and smelled the sour scent of fever. "You should go and rest in your den," she told her softly, guilt pricking beneath her pelt.

Slate didn't argue, but padded slowly away.

Moth Flight jerked her muzzle toward Blue Whisker. "Go and play with your littermates." She watched her kits head away, tails drooping.

Spotted Fur trotted after them. "Why don't we have a game of moss ball!" he called.

Honey Pelt turned, his gaze brightening. "Can I be on your team?"

"*I* want to be on Spotted Fur's team!" Bubbling Stream raced toward the golden tom and clambered onto his shoulders.

Spider Paw glanced at Blue Whisker. "You can be on my team," he purred. "We'll beat them easily."

Moth Flight dragged her gaze away, gratitude soothing the tension in her belly. *Thank you, Spotted Fur.*

Reed Tail's mew pierced her thoughts. He was watching Slate disappear into her den. "What's wrong with her?"

"I think she's caught a chill," Moth Flight guessed, still distracted by her kits.

"I'll check on her," Reed Tail offered.

Moth Flight flicked her tail toward Rocky's den. "Will you finish putting comfrey on Rocky's joints first? I've given him catmint to lift his spirits, but he's still in a lot of pain."

"Of course." Reed Tail padded away.

Moth Flight looked at Wind Runner.

Her mother had sat down and was staring at her. "It's not easy, is it?"

"What?" Moth Flight stiffened. A snarl edged Wind Runner's mew.

Her mother eyed her coldly. "Making sure every cat is safe and well."

Moth Flight prickled. "What are you trying to say?"

"You think I'm wrong for rejecting SkyClan. But I'm doing it because I think it's best for all of us."

"It wasn't best for Tiny Branch." Moth Flight lifted her chin. "He *died.*"

She saw Wind Runner flinch, but the WindClan leader didn't soften her gaze. "I presume you tried to save him."

"Of course!"

"But you couldn't."

"I might have, if Clear Sky had allowed Acorn Fur to ask for help earlier." Moth Flight flattened her ears. "Or if *you* hadn't tried to stop us from going to help."

"*Really?*" Wind Runner narrowed her eyes.

"I don't know!" Moth Flight snapped. "I never will. And neither will Clear Sky."

"That's how it feels to be a leader," Wind Runner growled. "You make the best decision you can. But you can't be sure how it will turn out. I've seen what Clear Sky is capable of. I fought in the Great Battle. Not because I wanted to fight, but because *not* fighting would have destroyed the Clans."

"How?" Moth Flight didn't understand. How could peace hurt any cat?

"Clear Sky was hungry for power. We would have lived like prey if we hadn't stood up to him." Wind Runner's tail twitched. "No cat should live like prey."

"Clear Sky's changed."

"How do you know?"

"I watched him grieve for his kit."

A low growl rumbled in Wind Runner's throat. "I've grieved for kits. Do you think it softened me?"

Moth Flight glared at her mother. "I wish it had!"

Wind Runner thrust her muzzle forward, rage blazing in her yellow eyes. "Every decision I make is for the good of the Clan. You may think I'm wrong, but *never* dare to question me again!"

Moth Flight ducked just in time to avoid her mother's lashing tail as the WindClan leader turned and stalked away. Moth Flight watched her go, her belly hollow. How could Wind Runner stand by her decision to shun SkyClan? A kit had died! She curled her claws into the sandy earth. *I'd do the same again and again. A leader might let a cat die, but I'm not a leader; I'm a medicine cat.*

She glanced across the clearing and guessed that Reed Tail must still be dressing Rocky's aching joints. She'd see to

Slate herself. She padded toward the she-cat's den and ducked inside.

Slate was alone, lying in her nest, eyes closed. Moth Flight leaned close, shocked by how much heat pulsed from the she-cat's pelt.

Slate's eyes flickered open, then she coughed. Jerking, she struggled to her paws, the cough taking hold of her and shaking her body. Moth Flight reached out a paw to steady the she-cat as she rocked. How had Slate grown so ill so quickly? Moth Flight widened her eyes, adjusting to the gloomy den, and saw stains darkening the moss beneath Slate's chin.

Blood!

Moth Flight backed away, heart lurching.

Fur brushed the gorse entrance and she turned to see Reed Tail slide in.

"That cough sounds bad." The tom blinked at her, stiffening as he read her gaze. "What is it?"

"Redcough," Moth Flight breathed.

Reed Tail glanced at Slate, stiffening. "Do you have any bark left from when Rock—"

Moth Flight didn't let him finish. Her thoughts were whirling. "The sap dried up and flaked off a moon ago. She needs fresh."

"But how do we get it?"

"I'll go."

"But it's in SkyClan territory."

"So?" Moth Flight looked at him. "Last night I tried to save Tiny Branch's life."

"But he died."

"I *know* he died!" Moth Flight snapped. "But Clear Sky saw us trying to save his kit. That must count for something. Even to a Clan leader!" Bitterness rose in her throat. She pushed past Reed Tail. "Look after Slate. I'll be back as soon as I can."

She raced from the den and charged across the tussocks.

"Moth Flight!" Spotted Fur called from outside her den.

She skidded to a halt, impatience burning in her paws. *"What?"*

Honey Pelt and Bubbling Stream were wrestling on the grass while Blue Whisker and Spider Paw poked through the freshly stocked prey pile. Gorse Fur, Storm Pelt, Dew Nose, Fern Leaf, and Swift Minnow were back in camp. They lounged at the edge of the clearing, sharing a rabbit.

Spotted Fur headed toward her. "Where are you going?"

Moth Flight scanned the camp for Wind Runner before answering. There was no sign of the WindClan leader.

"You look worried." Spotted Fur stopped in front of her.

"Slate's got redcough," Moth Flight told him. "I'm going to get some of that bark I got for Rocky when—" She stopped, her breath catching in her throat. She swayed on her paws. *When Micah died.* She'd been so worried about Slate, she hadn't thought about it until now. Grief wrenched her heart.

"I'm coming with you." Spotted Fur brushed against her flank, steadying her.

Moth Flight looked at him, feeling suddenly sick. *I can't go back there.* "Wind Runner will be angry if we cross the border," she murmured numbly.

"So will Clear Sky if he catches us." Spotted Fur's gaze didn't waver. "We just have to make sure we don't get caught."

Moth Flight stared into his amber eyes. Her thoughts slowed. She steadied her breath. She *must* get the bark. Slate needed it.

She lifted her chin. "Are you ready?"

"Yes." Spotted Fur turned and called to Swift Minnow. "We need to gather herbs! Can you look after the kits?"

Swift Minnow stretched languidly. "Of course!"

Gorse Fur clambered to his paws, kicking the remains of the rabbit toward Storm Pelt. "I'll watch them," he offered. "I can show them some hunting moves."

Bubbling Stream looked up from the prey pile excitedly. "Will you take us up to the burrows?"

"Not today," Gorse Fur purred.

Moth Flight's heart was fluttering like caught prey. *Micah!* How could she go back there? Panic spiraled in her mind. "Come on." She needed to run before fear crippled her. She raced for the camp entrance and burst onto the moorside.

Spotted Fur's paws pounded behind her as she raced down the slope and shouldered her way into the heather.

"Moth Flight!" Spotted Fur called. "Use the trails!" She headed blindly for his voice, crashing through the purple branches until she glimpsed him. Ducking behind, she followed as he swerved among the stems.

As she exploded onto the grass, she pushed hard against the earth, her gaze fixed on the forest where the SkyClan border edged the moor. She was panting by the time they reached it, her pelt spiked by the wind.

"Slowly!" Spotted Fur pulled up.

Moth Flight spun, her paws skidding on the smooth grass.

"Let's be careful," Spotted Fur warned.

"Nothing's going to stop me from getting the bark!" Moth Flight glared at him. *Micah* would understand how she felt! He'd been with her last time she'd made this trip. Her heart swelled with fresh grief.

Spotted Fur glanced along the border, his nose twitching as he scented for patrols.

He stiffened, his gaze flashing toward striped fur showing amid the ferns. "Wait," he hissed. Crouching, he pulled himself toward the tabby pelt.

Moth Flight watched him, frustrated by the delay.

Suddenly his shoulders loosened and he straightened. "It's only Willow Tail."

As he spoke, the WindClan she-cat padded from the fronds.

"What are you doing here?" Spotted Fur asked her.

Willow Tail sniffed. "I'm just making sure those prey-stealers haven't crossed the border again." She narrowed her eyes. "What are *you* doing here?"

"We've come to get bark for Slate." Moth Flight marched past her. "She's got redcough."

"I'll come with you." Willow Tail sounded excited.

"Wait." Spotted Fur ducked in front of Moth Flight, blocking her path. "We can't all go rushing onto SkyClan's land. They'll think it's an invasion." He tipped his head, his gaze resting on Willow Tail. "We need you to wait here. If we don't come back, fetch help."

Willow Tail's eyes widened eagerly. "Good idea."

Moth Flight headed through the ferns. *Well done, Spotted Fur.* The last thing she needed was another cat under her paws. A pointless mission would keep Willow Tail busy.

She headed through the forest, forcing herself to remember the route Micah had taken last time they were here. She recognized a fallen log and scrambled over it, her heart twisting inside her chest as she pictured Micah leaping it with ease.

"Are we going the right way?" Spotted Fur hissed under his breath. The golden tom's ears were pricked, his mouth open for warning scents.

"Yes." Moth Flight pushed on, each paw step feeling heavier than the last until the trees thinned and she saw the hollow where Micah had died.

Her paws turned to stone. She stopped and stared down, grief swamping her. A few shards of splintered branch still flecked the ground.

Spotted Fur's pelt brushed hers. "Slate needs that bark," he murmured.

She dragged her gaze toward the highest branches of the tree at the center of the glade. "Up there," she murmured hoarsely. "We need to get it from the top, where the bark is the softest."

"You wait here." Spotted Fur bounded down the slope and leaped for the trunk. Heaving himself into the branches, he disappeared among the leaves.

Moth Flight watched the tree tremble as he climbed. Her heart seemed to beat in her throat. Sorrow—as suffocating as the day Micah had died—pressed in her chest. She stood motionless, as though her paws had sprouted roots and fixed her to the earth.

She shook out her pelt. *Mourning Micah again won't change anything. He'd be proud I came here.* This felt like *his* tree now.

The leaves rustled and Spotted Fur's pelt showed beneath them. A moment later, he was scooting down the trunk, strips of bark clasped between his jaws. He hurried toward her. The tang of sap sent thorns of pain jabbing through her heart. It was the scent she'd smelled as Micah died.

Spotted Fur nudged her from the glade. His eyes were half closed, streaming from the pungent scent. Moth Flight led him through the woods, staying close to guide him past stray brambles and rutted earth.

As they neared the border, she scented heather and quickened her pace.

Paw steps scuffed the earth behind them. Moth Flight froze.

"Where are you going?"

A hostile mew made her turn. Nettle was staring at her across a patch of blueberries. Birch and Alder flanked him, their eyes narrowed aggressively.

Spotted Fur spat out the bark, his hackles lifting. He pushed in front of Moth Flight and faced the SkyClan cats. "She's come to get medicine for a sick Clanmate."

"I thought Wind Runner didn't recognize SkyClan

anymore." There was a sneer in Nettle's mew. "Yet you still come to steal from us."

Moth Flight stepped forward. "We're not stealing! We're taking bark, not prey! Just let us go. Slate might die without it!"

Alder curled her lip. "No one is allowed to help SkyClan, but SkyClan must help you?"

"We should all help each other!" Rage pulsed beneath Moth Flight's pelt.

Birch tipped his head, his eyes glittering with curiosity. "Don't you agree with Wind Runner?"

Of course I don't agree! Moth Flight held her tongue. She wasn't going to betray her mother, or her Clan.

"Just pretend you haven't seen us," Spotted Fur reasoned. "It makes no difference to you whether we take the bark or not."

Birch narrowed his eyes. "I'm sick of WindClan telling us what to do."

Alder padded closer. "You'll come back to camp with us. And don't try to run. Clear Sky will only send a bigger patrol to fetch you. He'll want to know what you're doing on our land."

"But my Clanmate's sick!" Moth Flight fought the urge to rake the gray-and-white she-cat's nose.

"Let's go with them," Spotted Fur breathed softly in her ear. "Don't forget that you tried to save Clear Sky's kit. He might be more understanding than these fox-hearts."

Nettle glared at him. "Stop whispering and get moving."

The SkyClan cats fell in beside them and began to herd

them deeper into the forest.

Moth Flight glanced at the bark left behind on the forest floor. Its precious sap would be leaking into the earth. But, if she explained everything to Clear Sky as quickly as she could, there might be enough left to take back to Slate.

She quickened her pace.

"You seem to be in a hurry," Alder snarled.

"I just want to sort this out and get home," she snapped back. She spotted the bramble barrier on the slope ahead. Birch had to break into a run to duck through the gap before her.

As she emerged into the hollow, faces turned to stare.

Sparrow Fur got to her paws. Blossom blinked from the shadow of a yew.

Moth Flight's gaze flashed toward the earth where Tiny Branch had died last night. Leaves had been scattered over it, but dark bloodstains still showed between.

She felt suddenly weary, her paws as heavy as stone. All she wanted was to help the cats around her, but every paw step seemed to lead her into another nettle patch.

"Clear Sky's in his den." Alder jerked her nose across the clearing. "Spotted Fur can wait here while you speak to him." She steered Moth Flight up the short, steep slope and through the trees beyond. "Clear Sky?" She paused and called into the shadows.

The SkyClan leader padded slowly out.

Moth Flight blinked. Clear Sky's eyes were hollow. His pelt was matted and slicked against his broad frame. He looked as though he'd been dragged from a river.

Star Flower followed him. Grief glistened, still fresh, in her eyes. She stared blankly at Moth Flight. "What's she doing here?"

"We found her on our land," Alder told the she-cat. "She was with a Clanmate."

Clear Sky padded closer, confusion clouding his stricken gaze. "No cat is allowed on SkyClan land," he mumbled.

"I had to come," Moth Flight told him. "I need bark from the tree where Micah died. It's to cure a sick Clanmate. She's got redcough. She might die." She waited for Clear Sky to understand. But he only stared at her.

"No cat is allowed on SkyClan land," he repeated.

"I need the bark!" Moth Flight glared at him. "I know you're grieving and I hate to disturb you. We don't *want* to disturb you. We just want to take the bark and go."

"No." Clear Sky slowly lifted his head, his gaze clearing. "Last night, you tried to save Tiny Branch, and I will always be grateful for that. But if Wind Runner hadn't tried to stop you from coming, my kit might still be alive. Wind Runner has to realize that there are consequences for her actions. She has to admit her mistake."

Cold fear rippled along Moth Flight's spine. There was darkness in the SkyClan leader's words. *He is capable of more cruelty than you can imagine.* "What are you going to do?"

"To you?" His ear twitched. "Nothing."

Moth Flight heard paw steps. Pelts moved at the edge of her vision. She smelled the scents of Alder and Red Claw as they closed in behind her.

Clear Sky went on. "You will simply be our guest until Wind Runner comes to fetch you."

"She won't come here!" Panic flashed through Moth Flight. *She* can't *come here. It's not safe!*

"She must." Clear Sky sat down heavily. "She has accused us of stealing prey. She has stolen prey herself. And why?"

Moth Flight stared at him. Did he expect an answer?

He went on. "She has listened to the word of a rogue and believed it over the word of a mountain cat." He glanced at Star Flower. "It's hardly surprising. Wind Runner was a rogue herself once."

"What are you talking about?" Moth Flight felt lost. "What rogue?"

"Willow Tail."

Moth Flight shifted her paws uneasily. "What do you mean?"

"I've been talking to Red Claw," Clear Sky told her. "He and Willow Tail go back a long way. Willow Tail has been lying for moons. She's been spreading half-truths and stirring up trouble just to settle scores that have nothing to do with the Clans."

Moth Flight shifted her paws nervously. She had no idea if what Clear Sky was saying was true. But she could see a way out. "Why don't I go and tell Wind Runner this?" *I can take the bark back with me.*

"No!" Clear Sky snarled. "You will stay here until Wind Runner comes to me, admits her mistake, and banishes

Willow Tail from her Clan."

"She'll never do that!" The words burst out before Moth Flight could stop them. Wind Runner was far too proud to come groveling to Clear Sky. And too proud to banish Willow Tail. By banishing Willow Tail, Wind Runner would be admitting she had made a mistake by letting the she-cat join her Clan. It simply wasn't something Wind Runner would do.

"She will," Clear Sky meowed. "We just have to wait."

"How long are you going to keep me *prisoner*?" Moth Flight snarled. Her thoughts skipped from Slate to her kits. How dare he keep her from them? They *needed* her!

"For as long as it takes."

Moth Flight glared at the SkyClan leader. "You can't do this!"

His tail twitched menacingly. "This is my territory," he growled. "I can do anything I like."

CHAPTER 30

✤

"What do we do now?" Spotted Fur paced the den.

"We can't stay here!" Moth Flight stared angrily from the entrance. The tiny cave, hollowed from the bramble close to Clear Sky's den, still carried the stale scent of Star Flower. Clear Sky's mate must have slept here at one time. Her ragged nest looked as though it hadn't been used in moons. It would probably crumble into dust if any cat climbed into it.

Moth Flight thought of her own nest at home. She could almost smell its heathery scent and the warmth of her kits rising from its thick moss lining. Anxiety twisted in her heart. And what about Slate? She needed the bark. "We have to escape."

"How?" Spotted Fur jerked his muzzle toward Alder, who sat, as still as a rock, a few tail-lengths from the entrance.

"We could burrow through the back," Moth Flight suggested.

Spotted Fur grunted, glancing at the prickly stems, so thickly woven that no light filtered through. "If we had paws made of wood."

Moth Flight whisked her tail crossly. "Why do Clan leaders make life so difficult?"

Spotted Fur blinked at her. "Who knows?"

Moth Flight tipped her head. "Do *you* think Willow Tail has been stirring up trouble?" she asked. "Slate and Jagged Peak have seen the bones, too."

Spotted Fur shrugged. "But she *is* usually the first one to make accusations." He frowned. "And she's the only one who's actually seen SkyClan stealing prey. If she is really as bad as Clear Sky says . . . she could have planted the bones."

Planted *the bones?* It seemed crazy to Moth Flight. She crouched and drew her paws tightly under her. "Doesn't she realize that she might cause a battle?"

"Perhaps that's what she wants." Spotted Fur stared at her grimly.

"No!" Moth Flight refused to believe it. "Why would any cat want to cause suffering?"

Spotted Fur didn't answer. His gaze flicked back toward Alder. The gray-and-white she-cat still hadn't moved. "Even SkyClan cats have to eat, surely?"

"If she goes, another cat will take her place." Moth Flight wondered how long they'd been here. The sun glimmered through the distant branches, low enough to show through the den entrance. Her kits would start wondering where she was. Yearning tugged in her belly, as sharp as hunger. "Do you think Willow Tail has realized that we're not coming back?"

"She's probably on her way to camp now."

Moth Flight stiffened. "I hope not." How would Wind Runner react to news that her daughter had gone missing in SkyClan territory? "What if she sends a patrol looking for us?"

"Isn't that what Clear Sky wants?"

"He wants her to apologize." Moth Flight stared at him, dread worming beneath her pelt. "Doesn't he know Wind Runner at all?" She remembered her mother's warning. *You may think I'm wrong, but never dare to question me again!* She was far too stubborn ever to apologize to Clear Sky.

Spotted Fur's ears twitched. "Do you think she'll fight him?"

"Of *course* she'll fight him!"

"But she says she wants peace between the Clans."

"Not enough to admit she was wrong."

"We need to get to her before Willow Tail does. We can explain why Clear Sky's so mad." Spotted Fur began pacing again. "Perhaps I can distract Alder and you can make a run for it. Or you could distract Alder and I could make a run—"

Paw steps cut him off. He jerked his muzzle toward the entrance.

Moth Flight followed his gaze, her heart quickening as she saw Acorn Fur approach Alder. The SkyClan medicine cat held dripping moss between her jaws. She dipped her head to Alder, who nodded toward the den.

"Thank StarClan you're here!" Moth Flight hurried to meet Acorn Fur as she padded inside.

The chestnut brown she-cat dropped the wet moss on the ground and blinked anxiously at Moth Flight. "Are you okay?"

"We're fine," Moth Flight assured her. "But we've got to get back to camp before Willow Tail!"

Spotted Fur crouched to lick thirstily at the moss. "If she

tells Wind Runner we're missing," he told her between laps, "in SkyClan territory, we're worried it'll start a war."

"We have to get out of here." Moth Flight stared at her urgently.

Acorn Fur backed away. "I can't help you escape." She glanced at Alder, lowering her voice. "They're my Clanmates. I can't betray them."

Spotter Fur narrowed his eyes. "We only need to get past Alder."

Moth Flight nodded. "I can pretend I'm ill and you can fetch Alder, and Spotted Fur can slip out while she's—"

"No!" Acorn Fur looked stricken. "I want to help. But when Alder sees you're okay and Spotted Fur's gone—"

"She'll think I tricked you!" Moth Flight interrupted.

Acorn Fur stiffened. "She *knows* that you trained me. She'll suspect me. Every cat will suspect me! How can I heal my Clanmates if they stop trusting me?"

Spotted Fur glanced at Moth Flight. "She's right. We can't ask her to betray her Clan."

Moth Flight's thoughts flashed to her kits. They'd be terrified if Willow Tail raced into camp telling everyone that she and Spotted Fur had gone missing in SkyClan territory. Her heart began to pound. "You could fetch the others!" She blinked at Acorn Fur.

"The others?" Acorn Fur echoed.

"The other medicine cats," Moth Flight explained. "Bring them here. *They* can reason with Clear Sky."

Acorn Fur tipped her head. "It *might* work."

Spotted Fur shrugged. "It's worth trying."

"Go now!" Moth Flight nosed Acorn Fur toward the entrance. She lowered her voice as Alder turned, ears pricking. "Run as fast as you can!"

"Take care," Spotted Fur murmured under his breath as Acorn Fur trotted past Alder and disappeared down the slope.

Moth Flight blinked at him. "Do you think she'll bring them in time?"

Spotted Fur's tail twitched. "Even if she could, I'm not sure Clear Sky will listen to medicine cats."

"He *has* to!" Moth Flight began pacing again. Too much was at stake. Slate needed the bark. Her kits needed to know she was safe. And Wind Runner—

She flinched from the thought. What if the WindClan leader chose war? *No cat should live like prey.*

"Moth Flight." Spotted Fur's mew was soft in her ear. She met his gaze, surprised to see warmth there.

"What?"

"I just wanted to tell you how sorry I am."

"Sorry?" She didn't understand.

"About Micah," he murmured. "About him dying. I know I was jealous when you brought him back from Highstones with you. I always thought I'd be your mate."

Moth Flight shifted her paws uneasily.

"This probably isn't the best time," Spotted Fur told her quickly. "But it's so hard to get you alone these days. You're either with your kits or busy with your medicine-cat duties. I just wanted you to know that I understand how much you loved Micah. And I'm glad you got to spend time with him before he died. And the kits . . ." His mew trailed away.

Moth Flight saw sadness in his gaze. "Thank you," she mumbled self-consciously. "I'm sorry I hurt you, but I had to follow my heart."

"And I must follow mine." His gaze lingered on her, glowing.

He still loves me. Moth Flight looked away. "You're a good friend, Spotted Fur. And the kits love you but—"

A shriek ripped through the trees.

Moth Flight raced to the den entrance.

Alder was leaping into the hollow, her pelt bushed, as the forest rang with the yowls of battle.

"WindClan!" Moth Flight's heart lurched. "They're attacking the camp!"

CHAPTER 31

Spotted Fur beat her out of the den. Moth Flight hared after him, skidding to a halt at the top of the hollow. Pelts swarmed from the bramble barrier. Wind Runner was leading the charge, Willow Tail and Gorse Fur at her heels. Behind them raced Dust Muzzle, Fern Leaf, Swift Minnow, Holly, and Storm Pelt. Jagged Peak trailed at the rear, his lame hind leg slowing him down.

Star Flower yowled, her eyes blazing, and dragged her kits, Dew Petal and Flower Foot, beneath a yew at the edge of the clearing. She crouched in front of them, eyes slitted, a low growl rumbling in her throat.

SkyClan cats streamed from their dens and met the invaders with outstretched claws. Wind Runner crashed into Nettle, and they fell, squirming like snakes, onto the ground. Swift Minnow's gray-and-white pelt flashed beneath Sparrow Fur's as the tortoiseshell knocked the she-cat's paws from under her and leaped onto her back. Blossom jumped from the roots of an oak. She landed on Dust Muzzle's back and sank her jaws into his neck.

Moth Flight flinched. "Dust Muzzle!" The yowl of battle swept away her panicked cry.

Fern Leaf shouldered her way through the battling cats and attacked Birch with a flurry of blows while, behind her, Quick Water leaped at Holly as she crossed the hollow.

Moth Flight heard a yowl of rage behind her and turned to see Clear Sky racing for the clearing. Fury glittered in his eyes. Flattening his ears, he leaped from the short, steep slope and hurled himself at Spotted Fur.

Moth Flight felt panic rising. "Stop!" Her wail was lost in the shriek of battle. "You mustn't fight!"

Pale tabby fur caught her eye. Willow Tail had halted beside the barrier and was watching Red Claw through slitted eyes. The glossy red tom was fending off Gorse Fur with strong forepaw swipes.

"Look out!" Moth Flight saw Alder streak toward Willow Tail. The pale tabby whipped around and lifted her paws as the SkyClan she-cat slammed into her. Staggering for a moment, Willow Tail kept her balance and hooked her claws into Alder's pelt. With a hiss of fury, she hauled Alder onto her belly.

The tang of blood touched Moth Flight's nose. Her heart seemed to burst in her chest. "Wind Runner! Stop! Clear Sky only wanted to talk!"

Wind Runner held Nettle down, raking his belly with her hind claws. She didn't even look up. Moth Flight felt as though she were in a dream, unable to make herself heard.

Thorn slid from the ferns crowding the other side of the hollow. His blue gaze narrowed on Fern Leaf. The Wind-Clan she-cat was pinned to the ground by Birch. Her hind legs churned desperately as she fought to loosen Birch's grip. Thorn dropped into an attack crouch and showed his teeth.

That's not fair! Moth Flight leaped from the top of the slope, landing heavily on the soft earth of the hollow. She had to help Fern Leaf! She dodged out of the way as Swift Minnow and Sparrow Fur rolled toward her. "Fern Leaf!" Rearing, she strained to see over the jumble of pelts.

She was too late. Thorn was on Fern Leaf's back, his hind-legs scraping lumps from the young she-cat's pelt while Birch aimed vicious blows at her muzzle.

She froze. *What do I do?* A medicine cat was meant to heal, not harm, but she couldn't watch while her Clanmate was attacked.

Suddenly, gray fur flashed beside Thorn. *Dust Muzzle!* Moth Flight watched her brother plunge toward Thorn and rip him away from Fern Leaf. Fern Leaf's eyes flashed with triumph as, freed, she reared and slashed Birch's nose.

Blood sprayed the ground. The tang grew stronger, bathing Moth Flight's tongue.

I'm going to need supplies! She stared around the camp. *Where's Acorn Fur's den?* Why had she sent the SkyClan medicine cat away? She'd never manage all these injuries alone.

Cobwebs. The thought flashed in her mind. If she could gather enough to staunch any bleeding, it would do until she had time to tend to the wounds properly. She slid between Blossom and Red Claw and scrambled out of the hollow. Hurrying among the trees, she scanned their trunks for cob-webs. Her heart leaped as she saw the roots of an elm swathed in a gray mist of web. She scraped it away, wrapping as much around her paws as she could and turned back toward the hollow.

"What are you doing?" Blossom faced her, eyes glittering with rage.

Moth Flight bristled. "I'm trying to help!"

"Help who?" Blossom padded closer.

"Any cat who's injured." Moth Flight lifted her paw to show the cobweb. "This will stop bleeding."

"You're wasting your time," Blossom snarled. "We're going to make WindClan bleed so badly, all the cobwebs in the forest won't save you."

Moth Flight blinked at her. "Can't you just stop fighting and *talk*?"

"You invaded our camp!" Blossom padded closer, a menacing gleam in her eyes.

"I'm not fighting you." Moth Flight lifted her chin. "I'm a medicine cat. It's my duty to heal. Get out of my way so I can get on with it."

Blossom showed her teeth. "You *have* to fight."

Moth Flight held her ground. "No, I don't."

Blossom reared and slashed a paw across Moth Flight's muzzle.

Pain sliced through her. *StarClan! What do I do?* Rage pulsed beneath her pelt. Her claws itched to rip the fur from Blossom's spine. She narrowed her eyes as Blossom lifted her paw again.

Gray fur flashed behind the SkyClan she-cat. *Jagged Peak!*

The lame tom flung himself at Blossom, snarling viciously.

Blossom gasped as he sunk claws into her shoulders and hooked her hind paws from under her with a sharp kick.

Moth Flight blinked gratefully at her Clanmate as he pinned Blossom to the earth. She started for the hollow. "Don't hurt her," she hissed as she passed him.

Surprise flashed in his eyes. "This is a battle, not a Gathering!" he called after her as she leaped into the clearing.

Fern Leaf was staggering at the far edge, blood welling from a gash on her flank. Birch was backed against the ferns, flailing at Dust Muzzle as the WindClan tom swiped at him with vicious blows. Moth Flight skirted the battle and skidded to a halt beside Fern Leaf.

The black she-cat was panting, her eyes cloudy with pain. Moth Flight unwrapped a swath of cobweb from her paw and padded the open wound. Fern Leaf winced, but didn't flinch. "This will stop the bleeding," she told her.

"Good." Fern Leaf leaped to her paws.

"You can't fight again!" Moth Flight blocked her way. "You must rest or it'll start bleeding again."

Fern Leaf met her gaze. "If one of my Clanmates dies while I'm resting, I will never forgive myself."

Moth Flight stared at her wordlessly.

Fern Leaf snatched her gaze away and fell in beside Dust Muzzle. The two cats reared together, sending well-aimed blows at Birch's nose until the SkyClan tom backed deep into the ferns.

Moth Flight scanned the battle for more injuries. Nettle

staggered beside Red Claw, who was wrestling with Gorse Fur. Swift Minnow struggled beneath Sparrow Fur, her whiskers dripping with blood.

"Let her go!" Moth Flight shrieked at Sparrow Fur as the tortoiseshell pressed Swift Minnow's muzzle into the earth. "She's hurt!"

Claws hooked Moth Flight's scruff and jerked her backward. Gasping, she struggled. A deep-throated snarl sounded in her ear. *Red Claw.* "If you don't want to fight, get out of the battle."

"Get off!" She thrashed helplessly. "I need to help!"

Red Claw let go and she turned on him.

"You have to stop them from fighting!" she wailed. "This won't solve anything!"

"Really?" Sneering, Red Claw pushed past her and grabbed Holly. Dragging her from Quick Water's back he hurled the black she-cat to the ground. Then he reared and slammed his paws into her chest.

Rage surged through Moth Flight. *This is rabbit-brained!*

Suddenly Wind Runner's tabby pelt flashed at the edge of her vision. The WindClan leader was racing toward Clear Sky.

"Stop!" Moth Flight chased after her, skidding to a halt as Wind Runner leaped at the SkyClan leader. Clear Sky turned as quick as a fox. Lashing out with a forepaw, he slashed Wind Runner's neck. Blood sprayed the clearing. Wind Runner staggered, her eyes rounding with shock.

Moth Flight raced toward her, her heart in her throat.

Wind Runner batted her away, her gaze fixed on Clear Sky. Blood welled at her throat and dripped from her fur. "You went too far this time." Her mew was husky with pain. "You took my kit hostage."

"And *you* let my kit die." Clear Sky glared back at her.

"Moth Flight *came*, didn't she?" she snarled at the SkyClan leader.

"Not soon enough!" Clear Sky flew at her, his blue eyes cold with fury. He threw another blow at her, cracking her cheek with such force that she staggered and fell. Leaping on top of her, he pinned her to the ground and raked her belly with powerful hind claws.

Horror surged beneath Moth Flight's pelt. She unsheathed her claws, rage burning in them. Her thoughts whirled. She was meant to heal—but she couldn't watch Clear Sky hurt her mother.

Wind Runner twisted, knocking Clear Sky's hind paws clear. She leaped up and raked his muzzle with a powerful blow.

Blood glistened on his nose as he raised his gaze to meet hers. "How dare you attack my camp? My kits are here!" He glanced toward the yew where frightened eyes peered out behind Star Flower. "Are you determined to kill them *all*?"

Rage lit up Wind Runner's eyes. "*You* started this!" Snaking beneath his belly, she pushed hard against his chest and heaved him onto his side. He hit the ground with a thump and she lunged for his throat.

Her jaws snapped thin air as he rolled out of the way just in time. Leaping onto his paws, Clear Sky reared. Wind Runner lifted her forepaws to meet his, but he was quicker and threw a blow at her cheek. She lurched backward, unbalanced. Her hind paw slid over a root. It snagged her and she fell, her leg twisting beneath her.

Moth Flight heard a crack and froze with horror. She'd eaten enough prey to recognize the snap of breaking bone. Her mother's leg bone had broken.

"Wind Runner!" She raced to her mother's side. Wind Runner groaned, her eyes rolling with agony.

At the sound of her groan, Dust Muzzle and Gorse Fur glanced over from the far side of the clearing. They were driving Nettle backward toward a birch trunk. As their attention slipped, the SkyClan tom lashed out. He lunged low and clamped his jaws around Gorse Fur's paw. Dust Muzzle's gaze darted away from Wind Runner and he sliced his claws across Nettle's ears.

Moth Flight jerked her muzzle fearfully toward Clear Sky. Was he going to attack again?

He stood as still as stone, and watched the WindClan leader coldly. Then his blue gaze flitted across the writhing pelts and rested on Willow Tail.

Wind Runner gasped, trying to move, and fell back. Moth Flight dragged her gaze from Clear Sky and looked into her mother's eyes. Was that fear she glimpsed? Fresh blood was still welling at Wind Runner's neck, and her hind leg stuck out at an ugly angle. Moth Flight's chest tightened. She'd never seen her mother afraid before. "You're going to be okay." Forcing herself to think, she remembered the cobwebs on her paw. Quickly, she unwrapped a long strip and wadded it into the deep scratch at her mother's throat. Then she ran a paw along Wind Runner's leg. The WindClan leader flinched.

"I'll be gentle," Moth Flight promised. She could feel the break. Her breath quickened as she felt a jagged edge pressing inside the flesh. The bone was bent like a broken twig. Alarm shrilled through her. Could a bone heal like gashed flesh? She remembered Cloud Spots showing her comfrey, all those moons ago: *I've heard it even helps broken limbs to heal, though I've not yet had to try it, thank StarClan.* She closed her eyes and prayed he was right.

A screech sounded behind her.

Moth Flight spun, her breath stopping in her throat as she saw Clear Sky back away from Willow Tail, his eyes bright with shock.

Willow Tail staggered, a wail rolling deep from her belly. As she swung her head around, Moth Flight gagged.

Long gashes streaked the she-cat's face. Blood streamed from her slashed eyes and dripped from her whiskers. Willow Tail moaned as her paws buckled beneath her. She collapsed onto the ground and stared blankly ahead.

Moth Flight's paws trembled. *He's blinded her.* She gaped at Clear Sky. Around him, the battling cats slowed, letting their paws drop as they turned to look at Willow Tail.

Clear Sky moved away, his pelt rippling along his spine. He lifted his muzzle toward Red Claw at the edge of the clearing. "She's yours now," he growled softly. "Do what you like with her."

Willow Tail dragged herself feebly across the earth while

the Clan cats backed away from her, their shocked gazes darting away. Red Claw unhooked his claws from Swift Minnow's pelt and padded slowly toward the blinded cat.

Her nose twitched. Whimpering, she tried to crawl away, her head jerking one way, then the other, as though she was chasing glimpses of light.

Red Claw stopped beside her. "Why did you have to lie?"

Willow Tail froze. "Don't you know?" Her mew cracked desperately.

"But why did you have to drag the Clans into it?" Red Claw's eyes brimmed with grief. "It was never their argument."

"It was the only way I could punish you!" Willow Tail's pelt rippled along her spine. "You killed my friend!"

Red Claw bristled. "I didn't kill her! The *dogs* killed her!"

"And who led the dogs into our camp?" Willow Tail rasped.

"Do you think I did it on purpose?"

"Of course you did! You lured them there."

"They were chasing me." Red Claw crouched close beside Willow Tail. He was shaking, his mew cracking as he spoke. "I was young and dumb. I ran into a pack of dogs and, when they started chasing me, I ran back to the one place I'd always felt safe. I thought if I got there, nothing could hurt me. It wasn't until the dogs attacked that I realized what I'd done!"

"You ran away!" Willow Tail accused. "You left us to die."

"There was nothing else I could do." Red Claw's shoulders drooped. "I am so ashamed. I've been trying to pretend it never happened."

"But it *did* happen!"

Red Claw hung his head. "I'm sorry, Willow Tail." His mew was thick. "If there was anything I could have done to change it, I would have."

Wind Runner lifted her head and gazed at him. "Was Willow Tail lying about the stolen prey?"

"Yes." Willow Tail rested her chin on the ground, her eyes red with blood. "I killed rabbits and dragged them across the border, then told you that I'd seen SkyClan hunting on the moor."

Clear Sky's gaze flicked sharply toward the WindClan leader. "You believed a rogue over *me*!"

Wind Runner growled from where she lay, pain tightening her words. "She's my Clanmate."

Clear Sky didn't move. "And you are *always* loyal to *your* Clan," he sneered.

Wind Runner didn't flinch. "Aren't you?"

Clear Sky looked away.

Moth Flight felt a surge of pride. Despite Wind Runner's terrible pain, she'd silenced Clear Sky. *Of course* he'd be loyal to his Clanmate. If Willow Tail had been a SkyClan cat instead of a WindClan cat, he'd have stood by her. Moth Flight looked back at Willow Tail, her heart twisting with pity. The pale tabby's flanks were quivering. Her ears were flat. A low moan crackled in her throat.

She's in shock! Moth Flight scanned the edges of the hollow, hoping to see thyme sprouting between the roots and brambles, but there was none. She scrambled toward Willow Tail and swept her tail along the tabby's spine. "It's okay," she murmured. "We'll get you back to camp and take care of you."

Willow Tail began to shiver, her matted fur spiking. She turned her gashed eyes toward Moth Flight. "Will I see again?"

"I don't know," Moth Flight whispered. Helplessness gripped her. She glanced around the watching cats. All she could see were wounds: scratched muzzles, torn pelts, ripped ears. Blood and fur specked the clearing. Fury rose in her chest. "You fought for nothing." She glared at Clear Sky. "Why didn't you let me go home? I could have spoken to Wind Runner. I could have told her what you'd said about Willow Tail and Red Claw. You could have settled this with words."

Clear Sky narrowed his eyes. "I didn't ask Wind Runner to attack my camp."

Moth Flight hesitated. If only Wind Runner had sent a patrol to search for her, not to start a war. "You need to make peace." She got to her paws and stood between her mother and Clear Sky. Looking from one to the other she growled. "This must end here."

Clear Sky's gaze lingered on her for a moment. Then he dipped his head. "It was a dumb fight," he conceded.

Wind Runner took a shuddering breath. "It was never our battle," she rasped.

Paw steps thrummed the forest floor beyond the camp barrier. The brambles shivered as Acorn Fur hurtled in. She skidded to a halt, her eyes widening as she saw the battle-scarred cats. Pebble Heart raced behind her, Cloud Spots and Dappled Pelt on his tail.

They stared.

Dappled Pelt's gaze shot toward Willow Tail. Pebble Heart hurried over to Wind Runner. He sniffed her pelt, peering at the gash in her neck before running a paw along her flank.

"Her leg is broken," Moth Flight told him anxiously. She looked toward Cloud Spots and Dappled Pelt. "We have to help the injured." She blinked at Acorn Fur. "I'm going to need herbs from your herb store."

"Let's go." Dappled Pelt was already climbing the steep bank.

Acorn Fur ran after her.

Cloud Spots whisked his tail. "I'll gather fresh dock and marigold." He ducked out of camp.

Gorse Fur hurried across the clearing, his anxious gaze fixed on Wind Runner. "Is she okay?"

"She's broken her leg," Moth Flight told him.

"*Broken* it?" Gorse Fur's gaze darkened. "Will it heal?"

Pebble Heart answered for her. "Yes. If we wrap it with comfrey." He leaped over Wind Runner and began tugging tough shoots that spouted from the base of the oak. "But first we need to make a support for it."

Gorse Fur hurried to help.

"The bone's twisted out of line." Moth Flight felt sick as she remembered the jagged shape beneath her mother's flesh.

"We can straighten it." Pebble Heart snapped a stiff shoot from the trunk. He showed it to Gorse Fur. "We need more like these," he ordered.

Gorse Fur nodded and hopped over the roots, his eyes scanning the bark.

Moth Flight glanced at Willow Tail. "What can we do to

help her?" she mewed desperately.

Pebble Heart's gaze darkened as he saw the she-cat. She looked like fresh prey, crumpled on the ground, blood soaking into the earth around her. "I think it's too late," he whispered.

Red Claw dropped beside Willow Tail, his eyes wide with horror.

Pebble Heart padded to the tabby's side. He pressed his ear to her flank. Lifting his head slowly, he shook it, his gaze grim. "She's dead."

Swift Minnow limped closer, her eyes glistening with grief. Jagged Peak glared at Clear Sky.

Wind Runner caught the lame tom's eye. "What's done is done," she croaked. "All we can do now is bury her."

Dappled Pelt appeared at the top of the slope, a wad of leaves in her jaws. Acorn Fur leaped past her, carrying cobwebs. The brambles rattled as Cloud Spots returned with marigold, dock, and thyme. The ThunderClan medicine cat glanced quickly around the hollow. As he narrowed his eyes, Moth Flight realized he was assessing the injuries.

"Fern Leaf's got a nasty gash in her flank," she told him.

Cloud Spots headed toward the black she-cat. Acorn Fur weaved between Blossom and Swift Minnow, checking for wounds. Dappled Pelt padded to where Nettle swayed beside the birch tree. Within moments, the three medicine cats were treating the injured—crouching to chew poultices, wrapping bloody paws in cobweb, lapping sap into scratches.

Fur brushed Moth Flight's flank. Gorse Fur was standing beside her, a bundle of oak shoots between his jaws. He dropped them and crouched beside Wind Runner. "Moth Flight will have you well in no time," he promised softly.

Pebble Heart jumped down the slope and laid a wad of lush leaves at Moth Flight's paws. "I found comfrey." He glanced at Wind Runner. "You're going to need something to bite on." He picked the thickest shoot from the pile Gorse Fur had dropped and slid it between her jaws.

Unable to speak, she blinked at him questioningly.

"We have to straighten the bone before we can wrap it." He reached toward a clump of straggly grass and tugged out a few tough strands, then he nodded to Moth Flight. "Put your paws at the top of her leg and, when I give the signal, press down."

Moth Flight obeyed, resting her pads on Wind Runner's fur. Heat pulsed from her injured leg.

Pebble Heart gripped Wind Runner's hind paw between his jaws. Flicking his gaze toward Moth Flight, he gave a tiny nod. Then he tugged.

As Moth Flight pressed down, she felt the bone move and heard the stick crunch between her mother's jaws. An agonized groan sounded deep in Wind Runner's throat.

Stiffening, Moth Flight jerked around and lapped her mother's cheek fiercely. "It's over now," she soothed, suddenly feeling more like a mother than a kit.

Gorse Fur was staring at her, his eyes round with horror. "You hurt her!"

"We had to." Pebble Heart let go of Wind Runner's leg and ran his paw over the break. He blinked at Moth Flight. "What do you think?"

Moth Flight was trembling. She reached out a paw and ran it nervously over her mother's fur. The jagged lump had gone. "You've straightened it!" Relief rushed over her. She purred at Gorse Fur. "Hopefully, it can mend properly now."

"We have to wrap it so it can heal." Pebble Flight hooked up two of the shoots and laid them either side of Wind Runner's leg. He laid several more above and below. Then he wrapped comfrey thickly around them. Moth Flight realized what he was doing and grabbed one of the tough stems of grass. Threading it under her mother's leg, she wound it around the comfrey and the shoots, like bundling soaked nettles. Before long, Wind Runner's leg was tightly encased in comfrey, held straight by the shoots.

Moth Flight blinked at Wind Runner. "How does it feel?"

Wind Runner stared back at her, pain showing in her eyes. "Not bad," she lied.

"I've got poppy seeds in my den," Moth Flight told her. "They'll help with the pain." She suddenly remembered her kits. Who was looking after them? Were they okay? They'd be frightened—wondering where she was. Her heart lurched. She'd been so caught up with the battle and the wounded, she hadn't even thought about them.

Guilt washed over her.

"Moth Flight?" Pebble Heart was staring at her, frowning. Had he seen her gaze darken? "What's the matter?"

"My kits!" she whispered urgently. "I don't know who's looking after them."

Pebble Heart blinked sympathetically. "We can manage here." He nodded toward Dappled Pelt, Cloud Spots, and

Acorn Fur, who were still tending to injured cats. "Go home to your kits. I won't leave Wind Runner's side until she's safely back in camp."

Moth Flight stared at him, her emotions whirling. Could she really abandon her mother and her Clanmates?

"Go!" Pebble Heart urged. "While your thoughts are with your kits, you'll be of little use here."

She backed away, a chill sweeping her. Was that true?

She shook out her fur. *Who cares?* Right now, Honey Pelt, Spider Paw, Bubbling Stream, and Blue Whisker might be wailing for her.

Turning away, she hared out of the SkyClan camp and headed for the moor.

CHAPTER 32

Moth Flight stirred in her sleep, dreaming. She blinked open her eyes into a vision of the moorside. A flame-pelted tom stood below a starless sky. Moth Flight recognized him at once. She'd dreamed of his meeting with StarClan while she'd been with ShadowClan. A brown-and-white tabby she-cat lay on the wind-rippled grass beside him, so still that Moth Flight wondered if she was dead. A third cat twitched her ears, scanning the mists that swirled around them.

Moth Flight padded closer. She knew that the other cats could not see or hear her. *I am here to watch.* The brown-and-white tabby sneezed suddenly and scrabbled to her paws. She glanced at the flame-pelted tom, as though looking for reassurance. He rested his tail-tip on her shoulder and, as he did so, a gray-and-white tom padded from the mist. Droplets sparkled on his pelt like stars. *Is this a spirit-cat?*

The gray-and-white cat exchanged words with the flame-pelted tom. Moth Flight didn't even strain to hear; she knew she'd pick up nothing but the whispering of wind in her ears. Then the spirit-cat touched his nose to the tabby's.

The she-cat jerked with pain.

Moth Flight narrowed her eyes. She'd seen this before. The cat was receiving the agonizing blessing of StarClan. She worked her paws deeper into the coarse grass, her pelt pricking with curiosity as more cats appeared from the mist.

A dark gray tom touched the brown-and-white tabby, and the tabby shuddered again.

Then an older white-and-tabby she-cat stepped forward. *They must be related.* Their markings were similar, and the look that passed between them glistened with affection. *Are they mother and kit?* Moth Flight's thoughts flicked to Wind Runner. In the two days since the battle, her mother seemed to have grown worse, not better. A moan of pain jerked her attention back to her dream. As the older cat touched noses, the young tabby stiffened and jerked, clenching her teeth. She swayed on her paws, but held her ground until the older cat withdrew and began fiercely lapping her cheek, as though sorry for the pain she'd caused. *They* must *be mother and kit.* The young tabby closed her eyes, seeming to relish the moment. Then the old tabby turned and headed into the mist.

The young tabby watched her go, eyes desperate with grief. She opened her mouth to yowl. Though Moth Flight could not hear the words, she guessed that the tabby was begging her mother not to leave.

Grief stabbed at Moth Flight's heart, so sharp it jerked her awake.

She blinked her eyes open. Her den was shady and cool. Through the entrance she could see sunshine scorching the clearing.

Wind Runner lay beside her on a bed of moss and heather, her broken leg jutting over the edge. Moth Flight leaned close. The WindClan leader felt hotter than ever. *What can I do?* Over the past two days, Wind Runner had struggled into consciousness less and less often, sleeping most of the time now. Perhaps it was a blessing. It saved her from the pain. Perhaps it was her body's way of healing. But if that was true, why was Wind Runner's fever worsening? *Perhaps I'm giving her too many poppy seeds? Maybe she needs to feel the pain to fight it.*

Moth Flight frowned. She'd helped Pebble Heart set her mother's broken leg, and felt sure that they'd done the right thing. She'd treated the gash in her throat with dock and horsetail, just as Micah had taught her. And yet, it still oozed blood.

She sniffed the neck wound. Her pelt pricked with alarm. Beneath the pungent tang of herbs, she smelled sour infection. Why hadn't Micah's poultice stopped it from turning bad? Was *this* wound what was making her mother so sick? If Micah's herbs weren't strong enough to heal it, what herbs should she use?

Perhaps she should go and ask Pebble Heart. *No.* After a moon in ShadowClan, she knew his herb store as well as her own. There were no herbs there she didn't have already. What about Dappled Pelt? When she'd visited RiverClan with Micah, the RiverClan medicine cat had only just begun to experiment with the lush plants growing along the riverbank. Perhaps she'd discovered something new, something strong enough to fight Wind Runner's infection.

"Moth Flight?" Honey Pelt's mew interrupted her thoughts. He was peering at her from the den entrance. "Can you come and play yet?"

She'd left her kits in the care of the Clan while she'd tended to Wind Runner.

Honey Pelt's eyes were round with worry. "We miss you."

Guilt wormed in her belly. "I'm sorry," she told him. "I have to look after Wind Runner."

Honey Pelt didn't argue, but turned away, his tail drooping. Moth Flight's guilt deepened.

Another shadow darkened the entrance. She smelled Gorse Fur's scent before she could make out his pelt against the bright sunlight.

"How is she?" Gorse Fur's mew was grim as he padded in. He stopped beside Wind Runner and sniffed her pelt.

"Her fever's getting worse," Moth Flight confessed. "I'm not sure what to do."

A growl rolled in Gorse Fur's throat. "This isn't fair!" he snapped. "After the Great Battle, I thought the Clans had stopped acting like foxes! Can't a new moon pass without bringing us fresh troubles?"

Moth Flight got to her paws and met her father's gaze. "I *will* heal her," she promised. "I'm going to RiverClan to see if Dappled Pelt has any herbs to treat the infection in her neck wound. Will you watch her while I'm gone?"

"Of course."

As Gorse Fur settled close to his mate, Moth Flight nodded toward the wet moss piled beside her mother's makeshift nest. "Drip a little water into her mouth every now and then," she told him. "Send Dust Muzzle or Spotted Fur to get fresh if the old moss dries out."

Gorse Fur's ears twitched. "Will you be gone long?"

"I'll be as quick as I can." Moth Flight ducked from the den, screwing up her eyes against the harsh sunshine. Slate was lying in the long grass outside her den. The gray she-cat was recovering from her cough, but was still weak. Storm Pelt was nosing through the prey pile with Swift Minnow. The other hunting parties were still out on the moor. Jagged Peak had been organizing patrols while Wind Runner was sick, making sure the prey pile was well stocked.

"Moth Flight!" Blue Whisker's excited mew sounded from the sandy hollow. "Have you come to play with us?"

Moth Flight stiffened. "I have to go and speak with Dappled Pelt."

Spider Paw scrambled out of the hollow and stared at her. "But you haven't played with us for days!"

Honey Pelt and Bubbling Stream stopped wrestling beside Blue Whisker, untangling themselves and jumping to their paws.

"Just one badger ride!" Honey Pelt mewed.

"Please." Bubbling Stream blinked at her eagerly.

Moth Flight's belly tightened with frustration. Digging her claws into the earth she met Honey Pelt's gaze. "I'll play with you as much as you like once Wind Runner is well."

Slate heaved herself to her paws. "I'll play with them," she puffed.

"You need to rest," Moth Flight told her sternly.

Storm Pelt looked up from the prey pile and called to Honey Pelt. "Once I've eaten, I'll give you a badger ride."

"And me?" Bubbling Stream scrambled toward the young tom.

"Eagle Feather and Dew Nose will be back from hunting patrol soon," Storm Pelt told her. "Then you can have as many badger rides as you want."

Moth Flight glanced gratefully at Storm Pelt. "Thank you." She headed over the tussocky clearing and hurried out of camp.

The heather was browning after endless days of sunshine. Moth Flight looked at the horizon, hope flickering in her belly as she saw clouds bubbling in the distance. Rain might help cool Wind Runner's fever. The feverfew leaves she'd given her hadn't helped.

She headed downslope. The dry heather jabbed her pelt as she nosed through it. Grass crunched beneath her paws. As she neared the gorge, she heard the faint swish of the river far below. Slowing as she neared the edge, she followed the steep trail that sloped down the cliff and flattened onto the shore. In newleaf, the river churned and frothed between the sheer sides of the gorge, swelled by moons of rain and snowmelt. Now, it swirled smoothly, its deep currents pushing quietly against the bank. Moth Flight stopped to lap water, her throat burning with thirst, then hurried along the bank as it opened onto marshland. She could see stepping-stones ahead and remembered, with a jab of grief,

Micah waiting for her there only a few moons ago.

This time, she would cross them alone.

Micah? She lifted her face to the sky, hoping StarClan could hear her. *How can I make Wind Runner well again?*

The sun glared down at her, stinging her eyes, and she hurried along the bank. If StarClan couldn't help her, maybe Dappled Pelt could.

She reached the stepping-stones and bounded across. The sun-drenched rocks burned her pads and she paused on a low stone to let the river lap over her paws, relishing the water's chill. She scanned the reeds ahead, searching for the opening where a trail would lead her to the RiverClan camp.

Fox scent touched her nose. She stiffened, unnerved by its freshness, and gazed along the river to where the water split the reed beds from the forest. Among the trees, birds chattered in the cool shadows. Wings flitted among the branches. But there was no sign of a red pelt between the trunks. She leaped the last few stones and landed on the marshy bank, pelt pricking as the fox stench grew stronger. She paused, stretching onto her hind legs to peer over the reeds. Was a fox skulking there? She couldn't turn back. She needed to reach Dappled Pelt. Padding along the shore, she pricked her ears. A gap showed in the reed wall beside her. Her heart lifted. It was the trail she and Micah had followed on their first visit. She opened her mouth, letting scents wash her tongue. The fox stench was still strong.

She paused. River Ripple would have smelled it surely? He'd have sent patrols to drive the fox away from his camp. It must be gone by now. She ignored the foreboding in her belly. She'd have to risk it. Wind Runner's life depended on her.

As she ducked into the reeds, squeals sounded behind her. Her heart lurched as she recognized the desperate mewls.

"Spider Paw!"

"Help him!"

"He'll drown!"

She turned and saw Honey Pelt, Bubbling Stream, and Blue Whisker clustered on a stepping-stone in the middle of the river. They huddled, fur bushed, and stared at the water flowing away from them.

Moth Flight followed their gaze, horror sparking through her fur. Her heart lurched as a paw jutted from the water, disappearing again as the current swept it onward.

Lightning seemed to jolt through her. She pelted toward the stepping stones, ignoring the surprised squeals of Honey Pelt and Bubbling Stream.

"Moth Flight!"

"Spider Paw fell in!"

She had already plunged into the water. The chill of it took her breath. Gulping, she struggled for the surface and flailed desperately toward the tiny whirlpool, which was all she could see of Spider Paw. The current grabbed her and spun her, dragging at her fur. Fighting to keep her muzzle above water, she kicked fiercely with her legs, trying to steer herself toward Spider Paw. The river dragged her down, sucking at her pelt. As water closed over her head, she blinked open her eyes, panic sending her thoughts spiraling into terror. *Spider Paw.*

Moth Flight forced herself to focus, straining to see through the stinging water. It clouded around her and dragged her downstream. She kicked out determinedly, pushing herself upward until her head broke the surface long enough to take a desperate gulp. The squeals of Bubbling Stream, Honey Pelt, and Blue Whisker seemed far away. She could hardly hear them as water gurgled in her ears. Reeds blurred at the edge of her vision as the river swept her under again.

Prepared this time, she struck out with her hind legs and scanned the murky water. A pale shape showed ahead, white fur in the spinning current. *Spider Paw!* Blood roared in her ears and she flailed, trying to swim. She shot forward, closing the gap between her and Spider Paw. Reaching out with a forepaw, she felt fur snag between her claws. She grabbed it and fought once more for the surface.

She broke into fresh air, a bundle flailing against her chest. Its scent filled her nose. It was definitely Spider Paw.

Churning her hind paws, she managed to keep her head above water. Dizzy with fear and disorientated by the swirling river, she looked for the bank, her heart sinking as she saw it across a vast stretch of water.

I can make it! Gritting her teeth, she steered herself toward it, fear sparking through every hair as the struggling bundle in her claws grew limp. Grunting with effort, she tried to heave Spider Paw above the surface. "Lift your head!" she ordered sharply. "Breathe!" She shook her paw, desperately trying to rouse him as she struggled closer to the bank.

His muzzle dragged through the water.

Is he dead?

Her hind paws hit stones and she scrabbled to find her footing as the riverbed rose to meet them. Limping, she dragged Spider Paw from the water and laid him on the pebbly shore.

Panic scorched beneath her pelt as she stared at his bedraggled body. His muzzle lolled to one side. His paws flopped onto the stones. "Spider Paw!" Her mind clouded with dread. Her paws froze beneath her.

Moth Flight. A distant voice sounded in her ears. *Remember what Dappled Pelt did.*

"Micah?" Moth Flight gazed numbly around as she recognized his calm mew.

Remember Drizzle.

Of course! Pushing fear away, Moth Flight lifted her forepaws and rested them on Spider Paw's white chest. She began pumping, her thoughts clearing. Juniper Branch's kit! She'd done this before! Spider Paw was much stronger. "Breathe!" she growled, pumping harder.

Spider Paw jerked suddenly beneath her paws and coughed up water.

She rolled him quickly onto his side and massaged his flank. Then she glanced upstream. The river had carried her far from the stepping-stones. She'd climbed out beside the reed beds, on RiverClan's side. She narrowed her eyes, searching for Honey Pelt, Bubbling Stream, and Blue Whisker.

The stepping-stones were empty.

Her pelt spiked with fear as fox scent touched her nose. "Hurry!" She nosed Spider Paw up. "We have to find your littermates and get out of here." Hardly daring to look around, she grabbed Spider Paw's scruff and picked him up. He churned his paws indignantly as she carried him along the bank toward the stepping-stones. *Where are they?* She scanned the far shore, her gaze flitting over the water and toward the reed beds. Her heart lifted. Three shapes crouched at the water's edge, shadowed by the reeds. They'd crossed the stepping-stones and were waiting for her on this side of the river. She raced toward them, scrambling to a halt and dropping Spider Paw beside Honey Pelt.

Fox stench still soured the air.

"Come on!" She began to herd them toward the stepping-stones. "We have to get out of here." Alone, she had been willing to risk meeting the fox, but her kits would be easy prey for it. She had to get them out of danger.

As they reached the crossing, she darted in front. "Wait on the shore," she told them. "I'll carry you across one at a time." She wasn't going to let another kit fall in. Snatching Blue Whisker by the scruff, she bounded across the stones and dropped her on the far shore. Racing back, she scanned the reed beds, her heart pounding as she looked for flashes of red fur among the stems.

There was no sign of fox, only its stench heavy in the air. She grabbed Spider Paw and carried him, dangling, across the river. Bounding back, she thanked Dappled Pelt silently for the many trips across the stepping-stones. Her paws seemed to find the rocks without her looking. She picked up Bubbling Stream and turned, grit cracking beneath her paws. Leaping over the stones a third time, she set Bubbling Stream down beside Blue Whisker and turned back for Honey Pelt.

The yellow kit was already halfway across the stones.

Moth Flight froze, her eyes widening with fear.

"I'm okay!" Honey Pelt paused and met her gaze.

Hardly breathing, Moth Flight watched him bound onto the next stone. His paws skidded on the rock, but he kept his balance and leaped for the next. Two more stones and he reached the shore.

Moth Flight stared at him, anger churning beside pride in her belly. "Why did you come here?" she snapped. "It's not safe!"

Blue Whisker stared at her with round eyes. "But *you* came here," she mewed anxiously.

"I know how to take care of myself." Moth Flight jerked her gaze toward Spider Paw. "I can cross the river without falling in."

Spider Paw looked tiny, his wet pelt slicked against his bones. He blinked at her, his green eyes glittering with guilt.

Moth Flight's heart twisted. She'd nearly lost him! She pressed her muzzle against his cheek, then began lapping the water from his fur.

Honey Pelt nudged her flank. "Shouldn't we go?" he mewed. "I can smell fox."

Moth Flight blinked at him. Then she glanced toward the reed beds. She needed to speak with Dappled Pelt. But first, she had to get her kits out of danger. "Follow me," she ordered. She led the way along the shore, heading for the gorge and the steep trail onto the moor.

As they reached the top, her shoulders loosened. Fresh wind whipped down from the moortop, clearing the stench of fox from her nose. She nosed her kits forward and began to guide them toward camp.

As they neared the hollow, she spotted Gorse Fur and Storm Pelt zigzagging over the grass. Gorse Fur lifted his tail as he saw her and called to Storm Pelt. "They're safe!"

The toms raced to meet her, slithering to a halt as they neared.

"I don't know how they snuck out," Storm Pelt panted. "Gorse Fur was at the entrance."

Honey Pelt lifted his nose. "We used the tunnel White Tail showed me."

Gorse Fur eyed the kits sternly. "You were supposed to stay in camp."

Bubbling Stream glared at him. "We wanted to find Moth Flight."

"She was by the *river*," Blue Whisker told him breathlessly.

"*I* fell in," Spider Paw announced.

Gorse Fur's pelt spiked.

"Moth Flight had to save me," Spider Paw explained.

Moth Flight shook out her dripping pelt. As her fear ebbed, irritation prickled in her paws. She was supposed to be asking Dappled Pelt about herbs for Wind Runner, not escorting her kits home. Her mother's life was at stake. She looked at Gorse Fur. "I have to go back."

Honey Pelt looked alarmed. "But there's a fox."

Moth Flight glanced toward the gorge. "River Ripple will

have sent a patrol to drive it away by now."

Blue Whisker pressed against her flank. "But what if he hasn't?"

Moth Flight ignored her. There wasn't time to worry. "How's Wind Runner?" she asked Gorse Fur.

"She's talking," he told her. "But her words don't make any sense. She opened her eyes for a while, but it was like she couldn't see me."

Moth Flight's heart quickened. Her fever must be worse. She turned away. "Dappled Pelt will know what to do." She raced for the gorge. "Watch the kits!"

"What about the fox?" Storm Pelt called after her.

"I'll deal with that if I have to. Just stay with the kits!" Moth Flight felt the wind whip her words away as she hurtled downslope.

Would Dappled Pelt know? Fear crawled beneath her fur. What if the RiverClan medicine cat couldn't help? She could go to Cloud Spots. Or Acorn Fur. Her mind began to spin. What if none of them knew how to save Wind Runner?

I have to try. She pushed harder against the grass, the wind singing in her ears.

Orange-and-white fur showed at the top of the gorge. Moth Flight slowed, narrowing her eyes. *Dappled Pelt!* The tortoiseshell she-cat was padding toward her.

Moth Flight raced to meet her.

Dappled Pelt's eyes shone with relief as Moth Flight skidded to a halt in front of her. "I smelled your scent beside the river."

"I was coming to see you." Moth Flight caught her breath.

"There's been a fox hunting on our land," Dappled Pelt told her. "I was worried it had hurt you."

"I smelled it," Moth Flight told her.

"River Ripple sent out patrols to chase it off." Dappled Pelt flicked her tail. "Why did you want to see me?"

"Wind Runner's sick," Moth Flight told her. "I think it's an infection in her neck wound. I've tried dock and horsetail, but the wound smells sour and she has a fever. Do you have any herbs I could try?"

Dappled Pelt frowned. "It sounds as though the infection's gone too deep for poultices," she meowed gravely. "I don't know any herbs that can fight it from inside."

Fur lifted along Moth Flight's spine. "Then there's nothing I can do?" She glanced toward the forest, not waiting for an answer. "Perhaps Cloud Spots will know."

Dappled Pelt followed her gaze, her eyes dark. "Perhaps." She didn't sound convinced. "Wind Runner's fate might be for StarClan to decide."

"No!" What if nothing could save Wind Runner? Help-lessness swamped Moth Flight, the ground seeming to shift beneath her paws. "There must be something I can do! I'm a healer!"

Dappled Pelt dropped her gaze. "Some wounds cannot be healed."

Moth Flight's thoughts spun. She stared desperately at Dappled Pelt, but the tortoiseshell was avoiding her gaze.

Suddenly, green wings fluttered at the edge of her vision.

She recognized them at once.

The moth! Turning sharply, she saw it—the beautiful, great moth that had led her to Highstones.

Why had it come back now? She stared at it, energy sparking in her paws. It circled her then flitted upslope, dancing on the breeze as it had all those moons ago, as though it was beckoning her.

Moth Flight glanced at Dappled Pelt. Had she seen it too?

The RiverClan medicine cat was gazing at the moth, her eyes glittering with curiosity.

The moth fluttered farther uphill, and paused again.

"It wants me to follow it," Moth Flight breathed.

Dappled Pelt leaned forward, her pelt pricking. "Then follow it," she murmured.

Hope flickering in her chest, Moth Flight raced after the moth.

Did *it* have the answer she'd been searching for?

Could the green moth show her how to save Wind Runner's life?

CHAPTER 33

☘

As Moth Flight followed the moth upslope, a chilly breeze lifted her fur. She glanced over her shoulder and saw clouds rolling in behind her, darkening the sky over the forest and marshes. Rain was coming.

She ran quicker, skirting the camp as the moth fluttered farther and farther ahead.

Wait for me! Moth Flight suddenly realized how tired she was. The days of tending to Wind Runner and the long run back and forth to the river had worn her out. But she had to keep going. The moth was showing her something.

But what? She paused as she reached the high moor, the ground sloping away ahead of her, rolling down into the valley toward Highstones.

The moth flitted on and Moth Flight followed it over the crest of the slope and raced downhill. *It wants me to go to Highstones again!* Her heart lifted. Perhaps StarClan was waiting there with advice. Were they going to tell her how to cure Wind Runner?

The moth stopped, hovering on the breeze. Then it ducked past Moth Flight, heading back toward the moor.

Moth Flight turned in surprise, skidding on the grass. "Where are you going?" She raced after it and watched it bob downslope toward the camp. It halted again and shivered in midair while she caught up.

Frustration surged beneath Moth Flight's pelt. "Where do you want me to go?" she demanded.

The moth bobbed once more toward Highstones. Moth Flight turned to follow but, the moment she did, the moth headed back toward camp. There, it hung in the air, letting the wind toss it one way, then the other.

"Make up your mind!" Moth Flight froze, her anger melting. Around her the wind grew stronger, sharp with the scent of rain. Her dreams of the Moonstone flashed in her mind. The cats she'd seen there had all been accompanied by a Clanmate. And when they arrived, StarClan had given them something. Moth Flight plucked impatiently at the grass, thinking hard. She knew it must mean something. Something that mattered *now*! That's why StarClan had sent the moth to fetch her.

Not just me! Moth Flight understood. As the first drops fell from the darkening clouds, she blinked at the moth. "You want me to bring Wind Runner!" The moth fluttered closer to the camp, as though agreeing. Moth Flight hurried after it. "You want me to lead her to the Moonstone!"

As she yowled into the wind, the moth fluttered higher, its green wings bright against the gray sky. Deep in her belly, Moth Flight knew she was right. StarClan was waiting to give Wind Runner the same gift they'd given the other cats in her dreams. Would it save her life?

She had to try. Narrowing her eyes against the thickening rain, Moth Flight raced for camp.

Spotted Fur, Fern Leaf, and Dust Muzzle were carrying fresh prey toward the prey pile. They stared in surprise as she passed them. Swift Minnow was nosing Slate toward the shelter of the camp wall, while Reed Tail slid into Rocky's den, a wad of comfrey in his jaws.

Black Ear sat proudly beneath the tall rock, ignoring the rain battering his muzzle. A freshly killed rabbit lay beside him. Honey Pelt, Bubbling Stream, and Spider Paw crowded around him, their pelts soaked. "Look what I caught!" he called to Moth Flight as she bounded past.

She slowed, glancing at the rabbit.

Bubbling Stream was sniffing it, her ears twitching with excitement. "*I'm* going to catch a rabbit soon," she mewed.

Moth Flight paused. "Go and shelter with Slate and Swift Minnow," she told them distractedly. Her attention was fixed on her den. How was she going to explain her plan to Gorse Fur? Could Wind Runner even make it to Highstones? *She has to!*

Bubbling Stream scrambled out of the hollow. "Moth Flight!" Hurt edged her mew as her mother headed away.

"Not now!" Moth Flight called. "I'm busy!"

Spider Paw jumped out of the hollow and blinked at her. "You promised you'd play with us!"

"Shouldn't you be taking care of your kits?" Jagged Peak padded from the shelter of the gorse, his eyes narrow with interest, while Holly watched from the shadows behind.

Moth Flight ignored him. She slid into her den. "I've had a sign from StarClan," she told Gorse Fur.

Her father was crouched beside Wind Runner. He jerked around, his pelt pricking nervously. "Is she going to be okay?"

"I have to take her to the Moonstone." Moth Flight tried to catch her breath.

"Highstones!" Gorse Fur leaped up, eyes blazing. "She can't travel!" He swung his nose toward Wind Runner. She lay sprawled on the bed of heather, her comfrey-wrapped leg jutting awkwardly. Her eyes were half closed, whites showing through the slits.

Moth Flight stiffened, fear stabbing her heart. Was Wind Runner dead? She ducked down beside the WindClan leader, relieved to feel her mother's flanks tremble. Her breath was fast. Heat pulsed from her pelt.

"I'll mix her some herbs to give her strength for the journey." Moth Flight hurried to her store, plucking leaves from between the gorse stems.

"No!" Gorse Fur growled. "You're not taking her anywhere."

Moth Flight shredded a pawful of feverfew and ripped nettle, catmint, and coltsfoot onto the pile. She sprinkled poppy seeds over it, hoping they'd ease her mother's pain without making her sleepy. She had to do everything she could to get Wind Runner to the Moonstone.

Gorse Fur's breath billowed over her ears. "Did you hear me?"

Moth Flight looked at him. "I can't sit and watch her die."

"You can't take her out *there* to die!" Gorse Fur's pelt spiked with fury. "If she's going to die, she should be with her Clan."

"If I can get her to the Moonstone, she *won't* die!" Moth Flight glared at her father. "StarClan is guiding me. I *know* it!"

A shadow moved at the den entrance. Jagged Peak slid in, his pelt wet with rain. "Have you spoken with StarClan?"

Moth Flight met his gaze. "In my dreams, yes!"

"And they told you to take Wind Runner to the Moonstone?" Jagged Peak tipped his head.

"Not exactly," Moth Flight snapped. "But I know that's what they meant."

Jagged Peak narrowed his eyes. "You *think* that's what they meant."

Moth Flight growled. "I *know* it."

Gorse Fur padded to Wind Runner's side and gazed down at her. "She's in no state to travel."

"She will be." Moth Flight grabbed a mouthful of shredded leaves and pushed past him. She spat the scraps onto the heather beside Wind Runner's muzzle. "Wind Runner, can you swallow these?"

Wind Runner moaned softly, but didn't open her eyes.

Panic flashed in Moth Flight's belly.

"Leave her in peace!"

Moth Flight felt her father's claws drag her backward. She turned on him, hissing. "You have to trust me! You have to trust StarClan! When Half Moon made me a medicine cat, she told me that the Clans' destiny would one day depend on me."

Jagged Peak leaned forward, ears flat. "What has *this* got to do with the Clans' destiny?"

"I don't know!" Moth Flight trembled with rage. "But you have to let me find out."

Fur brushed the heather at the den entrance. A gentle mew sounded behind Jagged Peak. "Trust her, Gorse Fur."

Dust Muzzle! Gratitude swept Moth Flight as she saw her brother's solemn gaze. He padded past Jagged Peak and stopped in front of his father. "Has she ever been wrong?"

Gorse Fur hesitated, his eyes glittering with fear. He glanced at Wind Runner, then at Moth Flight. Finally, he dropped his gaze. "No."

"Then let her take Wind Runner," Dust Muzzle murmured.

Gorse Fur began to tremble. "But she'll die."

"Don't be frightened, Gorse Fur." Wind Runner's parched mew sounded from the heather.

Moth Flight jerked around to see her mother blinking up at them.

Gorse Fur turned beside her.

Wind Runner went on. "Every cat must die. But I won't go without a fight. I am WindClan's leader and I must show I have courage. It will give my Clan courage. I will go to the Moonstone with Moth Flight."

Moth Flight's heart leaped. *She trusts me!*

Jagged Peak stared at the WindClan leader, his eyes round

with surprise. "But you're too weak!"

"I'll find the strength." Wind Runner's eyes were clouded with pain.

"Eat these." Moth Flight nosed the shredded leaves closer and Wind Runner turned her head to lap them from the heather.

She swallowed and gazed into Moth Flight's eyes. "I am proud of you, Moth Flight. You are ready to fight for what you believe in."

Joy washed through Moth Flight's pelt. Wind Runner struggled onto her three good paws, grunting with pain as her broken leg trailed on the ground, held stiff by the swaths of comfrey. At once, Moth Flight ducked down beside her and eased the wrappings enough for her to tuck her hind paw beneath her.

Limping on three legs, Wind Runner headed past Jagged Peak.

Gorse Fur hurried after her. "I'm coming with you!"

Wind Runner swung her head around. "No."

Gorse Fur blinked at her, clearly shocked. "But—"

She cut him off. "If I don't make it back, WindClan will need you." She glanced at Jagged Peak. "Gorse Fur will be the next leader." Limping out of the den, she left Gorse Fur gazing after her.

Moth Flight's paws trembled as she saw the helpless grief on her father's face.

"I'll make sure she comes home," she promised desperately. *Please, StarClan. Save her!*

She followed her mother into the clearing. Rain battered her face. It pounded the clearing and pooled among the tussocks. The wide, dark sky glowered over the camp. She felt fur brush her flank as Dust Muzzle stopped beside her.

"We're coming with you." He beckoned Spotted Fur with a flick of his tail.

Spotted Fur looked up from the mouse he was eating beside the drenched prey pile. His eyes rounded, questioningly.

"We're taking Wind Runner to the Moonstone," Dust Muzzle called.

Spotted Fur leaped to his paws and hurried to join them. "Can she walk that far?" His gaze followed Wind Runner. She was padding clumsily through the tussocks.

Holly darted out from the shelter of the gorse. "She's too ill to leave camp!"

Swift Minnow stared after her leader. "Wind Runner! Come back!"

"Where's she going?" Storm Pelt stopped, Spider Paw clinging to his broad shoulders. Honey Pelt and Bubbling Stream stood beside him, their ears pricked.

Moth Flight blinked at Storm Pelt. "I'm taking her to the Moonstone."

"You've only just got back!" Honey Pelt mewed.

Spider Paw shook the rain from his pelt. "Stay with us!"

Moth Flight avoided their gaze. *I can't, my loves. I have to save Wind Runner.* Her heart seemed to crack inside her chest.

Gorse Fur padded from the medicine den. His gaze swept the watching cats. "This is something Wind Runner must do." He nodded to Moth Flight. "StarClan has called her and she must go."

Moth Flight raced back to her father and pressed her cheek against his. "I'll take care of her," she whispered before pulling away and heading after Wind Runner.

"Moth Flight!" Blue Whisker's mew sounded beside the heather wall. Moth Flight turned to see her kit, cowering from the rain. Her wet pelt clung to her tiny frame. She stared at her mother anxiously. "Are you leaving again?"

Moth Flight hurried to her kit and snatched her up by her scruff. Bounding across the tussocks, she dropped her at the entrance to Rocky's den and nosed her inside. "Keep her warm and dry while I'm gone!" Her mew echoed into the heather cave.

Reed Tail stuck his head out.

"I'm taking Wind Runner to the Moonstone," Moth Flight told him. "Take care of the Clan. I'll be back as soon as I can."

"Moth Flight!" Blue Whisker's plaintive mew sounded from the shadows.

Rocky's rumbling purr answered her. "She'll be back soon."

Moth Flight turned away, sorrow weighing like a stone in her belly. Raindrops streamed from her whiskers. *I'm sorry, kits. I have to do this.*

Spotted Fur and Dust Muzzle had already reached Wind Runner. They walked on either side, pressing their shoulders against hers to support her. Moth Flight hurried after them, catching up as they reached the camp entrance.

Outside, the rain streaked the moorside, whipped by the

wind. Wind Runner's face was stiff with pain, her eyes firmly fixed ahead. Moth Flight slid into the lead, choosing the easiest path to the moortop.

She reached the crest first and looked back, stiffening as she realized how far behind Wind Runner had fallen, even with Spotted Fur and Dust Muzzle supporting her. She glanced at the sky, wishing the clouds would clear. She'd been rabbit-brained to hope for rain! *Where's the sun?* Was it slipping toward Highstones yet? They must get there before the moon rose. In her dreams, the Moonstone had blazed with moonlight when the other cats had met StarClan. Wind Runner must be there when it did.

What if the clouds didn't clear? What if moonlight couldn't touch the stone? Her pelt spiked. She pushed away the thought. *Just get her there!* She beckoned Dust Muzzle to hurry, flicking her tail urgently. He gazed at her pleadingly. She knew he was doing his best. They couldn't risk pushing Wind Runner too hard. But they had to get there tonight. Moth Flight guessed that her mother couldn't survive another day's raging fever.

She gazed through the rain to the Thunderpath below. Monsters roared, thundering in both directions, their eyes lit up, spraying walls of water in their wake.

How would they get Wind Runner across?

She hurried down the slope, leaving Dust Muzzle and Spotted Fur to follow with Wind Runner. As she neared the bottom, where the Thunderpath cut through the grass, she slowed. Monster stench stung her eyes and burned her throat.

The ground trembled beneath her paws. She watched the gaps between monsters, trying to judge whether there would be enough time to get Wind Runner between them.

When she glanced back, her heart sank. Spotted Fur and Dust Muzzle were still near the top of the slope. *She'll never be fast enough!* Heart racing, she pelted toward them, circling as she reached them. Wind Runner hardly seemed to focus her gaze. Moth Flight thrust her muzzle close, smelling the rank stench of infection in her mother's breath. Then she saw blood seeping from the wound in her neck. Rain dripped from her fur, reddened by her blood. *I should have brought cobwebs!* Moth Flight cursed herself for being so dumb.

"How's she doing?" she asked Dust Muzzle.

Wind Runner paused and lifted her gaze hazily. "I'm doing okay," she rasped.

It was strange for Moth Flight to see her mother so weak. She'd always seemed stronger than any cat.

Dust Muzzle exchanged a look with Moth Flight. She saw fear flash in his eyes as he glimpsed the busy Thunderpath. "We'll never get her across there!"

"We have to," Moth Flight told him.

Spotted Fur narrowed his eyes. "If we get the timing right, we could just do it."

Moth Flight looked at him hopefully.

"We might have to stop in the middle," he added.

"Stop in the middle?" Moth Flight could hardly believe her ears.

Dust Muzzle was following Spotted Fur's gaze. "There's a

narrow channel where the monsters pass each other. If they don't touch each other, they won't touch us."

Moth Flight's belly twisted with fear as she realized they'd have to try. It was their only chance. "Okay." She turned toward the Thunderpath and headed slowly toward it.

She could hear her mother's breathing as she struggled to keep up. Wind Runner was fighting for every breath. Her injured hind paw was tucked beneath her. Moth Flight couldn't imagine the pain that compelled her to keep it from trailing along the ground.

She fixed her thoughts ahead before fear could overwhelm her. *We're going to do this!*

As they neared the Thunderpath, she began to judge the gaps between the monsters once more. As the rain grew heavier, the monsters seemed to slow, the gaps between them widening.

"Come on!" They had to cross while the rain was at its heaviest. She crouched at the edge of the black stone, screwing up her eyes as a monster hurtled past. Filthy water arced like a wave over her back and sprayed Spotted Fur, Dust Muzzle, and Wind Runner as they caught up.

"Give me a moment to catch my breath," Wind Runner growled. She slumped as Dust Muzzle stepped away, her flanks heaving.

Moth Flight leaned close to her muzzle. "I hope I can be as brave as you one day."

Wind Runner lifted her gaze. "You already are."

"Let's go!" Dust Muzzle nosed Moth Flight away, pressing

hard against Wind Runner. A wide gap had opened between two monsters.

This was their chance. Moth Flight hopped onto the Thunderpath, pausing to make sure Wind Runner was following. Spotted Fur and Dust Muzzle half carried the WindClan leader onto the stone. Wind Runner fought to find her paws. "I can do this!" she hissed through gritted teeth. Shaking the toms away, she limped forward. Moth Flight turned to face the oncoming monster. It pounded toward them, its eyes flaring. Another monster hurtled toward them from the other direction.

"Wait here!" Spotted Fur screeched, throwing himself against Wind Runner. Moth Flight ducked into her mother. Dust Muzzle pressed against them. Moth Flight screwed up her eyes, and her heart seemed to burst as the two monsters screamed past on either side. Foul water drenched her pelt as the ground shook beneath her paws.

"Move!" Dust Muzzle's order was sharp.

Moth Flight opened her eyes and saw that the way to the far side was clear.

Wind Runner straightened with a groan of pain and hobbled toward the verge. Spotted Fur pushed his shoulder beneath her and urged her on. The roar of another monster screamed in Moth Flight's ears. She turned her head, blinded by the glare of its eyes.

"Don't look! *Run!*" Dust Muzzle shoved her forward and she stumbled over the edge of the Thunderpath, collapsing onto the muddy grass beyond as the paw of a monster whisked past her tail. The wind from its passing tugged her dripping fur.

"Wind Runner!" She looked around, fear shrilling through her. Wind Runner was lying on the grass a tail-length ahead.

Spotted Fur half cradled her against his belly. He struggled from beneath her. "I fell," he grunted, shaking rainwater from his fur. Dust Muzzle hurried to help Wind Runner to her paws.

Moth Flight was on his heels. "Are you okay?" She sniffed her mother's broken leg. The swaths of comfrey were hanging from it loosely. Wind Runner flinched as she touched it with her nose.

Moth Flight looked into her mother's eyes, seeing agony spark in their amber depths. Then she looked back at the Thunderpath. Monsters streaked back and forth, picking up speed as the rain began to ease. The gaps closed between them. There was no way back now. They had to keep going.

"Can you do this?" She searched Wind Runner's gaze, praying she'd say yes.

Wind Runner nodded and struggled to her paws. Dust Muzzle and Spotted Fur flanked her.

Moth Flight blinked through the rain, scanning the meadows ahead. Perhaps she'd find some poppy seeds along the way. Anything to ease her mother's suffering.

They crossed the sodden fields slowly. Mud clung to their paws as they skirted meadows and squeezed beneath hedgerows. Every few steps, Moth Flight glanced up at Highstones, hoping each time that they'd loom larger. But it seemed that, with each paw step, the great, dark cliffs were moving farther away. *We'll never make it!* Staring at the ground, Moth Flight trudged on. She could hear Wind Runner swallowing back gasps of agony. Rain thrummed her pelt as the fields around them darkened. She focused on the mud clogging her paws as she tried to block the fear churning in her belly. She flattened her ears against the pained growling of Wind Runner.

Was I wrong? Doubt sliced into her thoughts. What if she'd misunderstood her dreams? What if the moth had nothing to do with StarClan? Moths and butterflies danced across the heather all greenleaf. Why was this one special?

She lifted her head, blinking at Spotted Fur and Dust Muzzle as they helped Wind Runner squeeze beneath a hedge. She could hardly see them in the darkness. Dusk was passing and night rolling in.

Had they come all this way for nothing? She stopped, frozen with fear.

"Moth Flight?" Dust Muzzle's call jerked her from her thoughts. She stared at him as he turned from the hedge and headed toward her. "Are you all right?"

"What if I was wrong?" she whispered.

"You're never wrong," Dust Muzzle told her.

Moth Flight hardly heard him. "Gorse Fur said that if she's going to die, she should be with her Clan. And we've taken her away from them."

"She's with *us*." Dust Muzzle leaned closer, keeping his mew low. "And she's *not* going to die."

Moth Flight looked past him. She could just make out the shapes of Spotted Fur and Wind Runner beyond the hedge.

The WindClan leader was lying on the ground. Moth Flight darted forward, panic spiraling in her chest. She wriggled under the hedge and sniffed Wind Runner's muzzle. Was she still breathing?

"I'm just resting," Wind Runner grunted.

Moth Flight's paws trembled beneath her as relief swept her pelt.

"Did you think I'd give up when we were so close?" She lifted her chin from the muddy earth and looked toward Highstones.

Moth Flight blinked in surprise. They were nearly there! As she gazed up at the sheer cliff face, green wings fluttered above her. She looked up and saw the moth bobbing toward the dark opening in the stone.

Hope flared in Moth Flight's belly. *I must trust myself more!* "Come on!" She nosed Wind Runner gently to her paws. "We have to get there before the moon does."

"Are we racing the *moon*?" Wind Runner glanced at her out of the corner of her eye, amusement flashing through her pain. "I always told Gorse Fur you were a strange one. . . ."

Affection opened like a flower in Moth Flight's chest.

Then Wind Runner coughed, her paws buckling beneath her. Moth Flight smelled the scent of fresh blood. She pressed her shoulder against her mother's as Dust Muzzle slid around the other side. Wind Runner's fur felt warm and wet and Moth Flight guessed that her neck wound was bleeding heavily now. *Please let her make it.* Praying to StarClan, she began to guide Wind Runner onward. *I just hope the Moonstone can save you.*

CHAPTER 34

"You have to wait here." Moth Flight gazed solemnly at Spotted Fur. She nodded to Dust Muzzle. "You too."

They had managed to haul Wind Runner over the stone lip of the cave. Wind Runner leaned against Dust Muzzle, her eyes clouded. She murmured under her breath. "Where's Gorse Fur? Tell him I'm coming."

Moth Flight glanced at her mother anxiously. Wind Runner was clearly lost in a feverish world of pain.

Dust Muzzle peered into the darkness at the back of the cave. "Where's the Moonstone?"

"It's down a tunnel," Moth Flight told him.

"Can you get her there alone?"

"I must." She was their medicine cat. She alone must guide her mother to StarClan.

Spotted Fur shifted his paws uneasily. "We could help her there and then leave."

Moth Flight hesitated. Wind Runner was exhausted. *Do I really have the strength to help her though the tunnel?* Outside, the clouds were clearing, revealing the night sky. Stars stretched to the distant moor. *So much depends on me.* Spotted Fur and

Dust Muzzle were hunters—moor runners who fed the Clan. *My bond with StarClan is special.* Her belly hardened. She met Spotted Fur's gaze. "I must do this alone."

Sliding between Wind Runner and Dust Muzzle, she staggered as she took Wind Runner's weight. "Come on," she whispered, hoping her mother could hear her.

Wind Runner padded forward unsteadily. Moth Flight pressed her paws hard against the stone, trying to keep her balance as she steered the WindClan leader toward the back of cave. As darkness swallowed them, she became sharply aware of her mother's rasping breath and the scuffing of their paws as they limped together into the tunnel. The air grew cold, swirling around them like freezing water. The tunnel sloped beneath Moth Flight's paws. The dank scent of stone was masked by the iron tang of Wind Runner's blood. A droplet smacked the tunnel floor. Moth Flight felt it spray her paws. Another drop fell, the sound ringing around the stone walls.

Moth Flight pushed on faster, heaving her mother forward with every step. *Don't die.* Her heart quickened. Wind Runner's dripping blood spattered her fur. Ignoring the fear that was tightening like bindweed around her heart, she focused on moving forward, letting her whiskers brush the cave wall where she could, carefully following the twisting tunnel deeper into the earth. Every sense was fixed ahead, every thought willing Wind Runner on. *You can do it.*

Her mother's breath was growing uneven—a few short breaths, followed by the desperate drawing in of air. Moth

Flight swallowed. Each breath sounded like Wind Runner's last.

Moth Flight smelled fresh air. It felt warm on her nose after the icy chill of the tunnel.

The cave!

They'd made it.

A few more steps and the walls opened into the Moonstone cavern. Soft starlight filtered through the hole in the roof. The Moonstone rose, still and dark, from the middle of the cave floor. Grunting with effort, Moth Flight heaved her mother forward and let her collapse against it. Wind Runner gasped as she fell, then lay still.

Moth Flight backed away, heart pounding.

Her mother didn't move.

"Wind Runner?" Moth Flight's paws felt rooted to the stone. She stared, terror clutching her chest. Was it too late?

Suddenly the Moonstone blazed into white fire. Moth Flight flinched, screwing up her eyes. Through a slitted gaze, she saw moonlight flooding through the hole in the roof.

She strained to see her mother, and could just make out her body, a dark shadow against the glittering stone.

Please move. Desperately, she willed Wind Runner to twitch an ear, or move a paw. *Show me you're alive!*

A soft mew sounded beside her ear.

Everything will be fine.

Moth Flight froze as she recognized the mew. Her breath stopped in her throat as she smelled a familiar scent. "Micah?"

Fur brushed hers and she snapped her head around,

meeting his gaze a muzzle-length from hers.

Micah blinked slowly at her, his pelt sparkling with star-light. His warmth seemed to melt into her and she realized suddenly how cold and wet she was. She softened against him, letting herself lean into the familiar curve of his flank. He pressed his cheek against hers. "You've done so well." His mew was thick with love.

Joy flared in her chest. "Will Wind Runner be okay?"

"You've done all that you can," he breathed. "Now she belongs to StarClan."

She stiffened. *Belongs to StarClan?* Was she dead?

Micah's breath stirred her ear fur. "One day you will gather the scattered petals of the Blazing Star, but not yet."

She drew away from him and stared into his green gaze. "What do you mean?"

He blinked at her. "Just watch," he whispered. He turned his head toward the Moonstone.

Moth Flight followed his gaze. Around the shimmering rock, pelts were appearing, sparkling as though stars were woven into the fur.

StarClan had come.

Gray Wing stepped from among the ranks of starry cats and stopped beside Wind Runner. He turned to Moth Flight. "You are more like your mother than you imagine," he told her gently. "It took courage to bring her here. And strength. More than you knew you had." He dipped his head. "But it also took something even your mother does not share. You are special, Moth Flight. You can see what is hidden from ordinary cats.

You can read signs and understand their meaning."

Moth Flight glanced at her mother, slumped against the rock. Wasn't Gray Wing going to heal Wind Runner? "Don't waste time!"

Gray Wing's gaze didn't waver. "You must understand the importance of this skill."

"Any cat can follow a moth." Impatience prickled through Moth Flight's fur.

"Few cats would understand which moth will lead their Clan to safety," Gray Wing told her.

"I haven't led my Clan anywhere." Moth Flight's heart began to quicken. She looked for Micah. He wasn't behind her anymore. She glimpsed his pelt among the other spirit-cats. "I only brought you Wind Runner. You're going to save her, right?"

"We can't save this life." His words echoed from the walls, ringing in Moth Flight's ears.

She stared at him, feeling sick. "But you have to!"

Gray Wing stepped back while StarClan moved at the edges of the cave, forming a glittering ring around the blazing Moonstone.

Moth Flight's heart seemed to stop. "Don't let her die!"

"We can only give her our gift." Gray Wing leaned down and touched his nose to Wind Runner's head as she lay against the rock. "Wind Runner, with this life I give you the determination to bring unity to all the Clans."

Wind Runner suddenly jerked, as though sharp teeth had seized her body. She shuddered, her fur bushing.

As Gray Wing stepped away, the WindClan leader lifted her head and blinked. She staggered to her paws and stood unsteadily, staring at the circle of star-flecked cats.

Moth Flight wanted to race forward and press her muzzle to her mother's cheek, but her paws felt frozen, her body too stiff to move. She watched helplessly as another cat stepped forward. Moth Flight recognized Petal from her first meeting with StarClan. The she-cat leaned toward Wind Runner, who blinked at her, confused.

"With this life," Petal told her, "may you learn to love friendship and loyalty above all things." She touched her nose to Wind Runner's and Wind Runner trembled, her ears flattening.

"Please don't hurt her," Moth Flight called. "She's suffered so much already."

Micah's gaze flashed toward her, soft with sympathy. Moth Flight stared at him pleadingly. He blinked slowly, as though reassuring her again that everything would be fine.

Wind Runner swayed on her paws as Petal drew away. Her eyes sparked with fear as Turtle Tail took Petal's place. She recoiled, tucking her broken leg tighter beneath her.

"Don't be afraid, Wind Runner," Turtle Tail soothed. "We are giving you a gift. A gift for all the Clans."

Wind Runner straightened, pushing her injured leg to the ground. Moth Flight's paws turned cold as she saw her mother grimace, as though gritting her teeth against pain.

Turtle Tail reached her head forward. "With this life, I give you stubbornness to keep going in the face of future troubles."

Wind Runner moaned softly as Turtle Tail touched her, the fur lifting along her spine. Moth Flight felt sick. She knew her mother was suffering. She tensed as Wind Runner tensed and, as Turtle Tail stepped away, she felt limp with relief.

Wind Runner turned her head to stare at the star-pelted cats crowding the cave. She blinked as though noticing them for the first time. Then her eyes widened as a gray tom padded toward her. Her ears twitched. "What are you doing here?" There was a snarl in her mew.

Moth Flight tipped her head, curious. Who was this strange cat? She hadn't seen him before.

The tom dipped his head as he stopped in front of Wind Runner. "I know you hate me for leaving you."

Wind Runner hissed. "You're a coward, Branch! You abandoned me before I could even hunt properly! There's nothing I want from you!"

"I didn't mean to leave you."

"Yet you left me all the same!" Wind Runner narrowed her eyes. "It was the kindest thing you ever did for me. If you hadn't disappeared, I'd never have met Gorse Fur. He's a better cat than you could ever be! He has given me love and loyalty, and kits that I'm proud of."

Moth Flight frowned. Who was this? Clearly a cat her mother had known when she was young. As she strained to recall her mother's stories, Branch spoke.

"You deserve a cat like Gorse Fur far more than you deserved me." He leaned forward and touched his nose to her head. "With this life, I give you the confidence to open your heart to other cats. I give you trust."

Wind Runner jerked again, trembling as his touch sent pain searing through her. But Moth Flight didn't flinch. This was like it had been in her dreams. Wind Runner must endure it, just as the other cats had and, when it was over . . . Moth Flight narrowed her eyes. When it was over, then what?

A familiar pelt moved toward Wind Runner. *Willow Tail!*

Clear-eyed and strong, Willow Tail stepped forward. She carried no signs of her injuries from the battle. Chin high, she took Branch's place.

Wind Runner met her gaze, her eyes flashing with anger. "You lied to me."

Willow Tail nodded. "I know. I led my Clanmates into battle for no good reason." As she leaned forward, Wind Runner began to duck away. "I'm sorry."

Wind Runner paused and met Willow Tail's touch with her nose.

"With this life," said Willow Tail, "I give your heart the grace to forgive all cats, however weak or wrong they may be."

Wind Runner hardly flinched. Only her tail-tip shivered.

As Willow Tail stepped away, a kit took her place. Moth Flight's heart swelled with joy as she recognized Morning Whisker.

As the she-kit padded forward, Wind Runner blinked. Her eyes clouded. "Morning Whisker?" Disbelief edged her mew.

Morning Whisker purred loudly. "Hi, Wind Runner."

Wind Runner thrust her muzzle forward to greet her, but Morning Whisker backed away.

"Not yet." The she-kit gazed at Wind Runner, joy shining in her eyes.

Wind Runner's tail trembled. "Are you happy? Are you well?"

Morning Whisker glanced fondly toward her starry Clanmates. "Yes. Half Moon and Gray Wing have taught me how to hunt."

"You *hunt*?" Wind Runner sounded surprised.

"We hunt, and warm our pelts in sunshine and share tongues, just like you."

A delighted purr throbbed in Wind Runner's throat. Then she paused. "Is Emberkit with you?"

Morning Whisker blinked slowly at her mother and then, without answering, reached up and touched her nose. "With this life, I give you resilience, to keep going, whatever troubles life brings." As she finished, Wind Runner's pelt bushed. She stiffened, her claws scraping stone as she braced herself against the pain of her kit's gift. Then her shoulders loosened and Morning Whisker backed away into the shadows.

Emberkit took her place.

Moth Flight leaned forward, her heart pounding. What must it be like to meet a kit you'd never had chance to know in life?

"Emberkit?" Wind Runner's mew was thick with emotion.

"Hello, Wind Runner." Emberkit stared at his mother with round, star-specked eyes.

"It is so good to see you." As Wind Runner's gaze flicked over the young tom-kit's fluffy pelt, Moth Flight swallowed back a purr of pleasure.

"I wish I could have stayed with you longer," Emberkit told his mother softly. "But I'm happy to be with StarClan. There are moors for me to play on. One day I'll show them to you." Before Wind Runner could answer, Emberkit reached up and touched his nose to her muzzle. "With this life I give you love."

This time, Wind Runner did not flinch with pain. Her pelt smoothed. Closing her eyes, she swayed softly. She grew still as Emberkit drew away, her eyes closed as though lost in a dream.

Half Moon took the tom-kit's place, waiting patiently for Wind Runner to drift back into the moment.

When, at last, Wind Runner opened her eyes, she tipped her head as though confused. "Who are you?"

"Half Moon." The slender white she-cat's dark green gaze reflected the shimmering Moonstone.

"Are you *Stoneteller*?" Wind Runner dipped her head. "Gray Wing and Jagged Peak have spoken of you often. Moth Flight too. I am honored to meet you."

"You are the first," Half Moon told her solemnly. "May you carry StarClan in your heart always."

"The first?" Wind Runner narrowed her eyes.

Half Moon stretched her muzzle forward and touched noses with the WindClan leader. As she did, a jolt seemed to race through Wind Runner.

Moth Flight stiffened as her mother jerked wildly. Her paws buckled beneath her and she collapsed to the floor.

"No!" Heart bursting, Moth Flight darted to her mother's side. Wind Runner lay like dead prey on the stone, her flanks still. No breath stirred the cold air. "You killed her!"

She glared accusingly at Half Moon. "I brought her here to be saved!"

Half Moon blinked calmly and stepped away. "Have faith, Moth Flight."

Moth Flight's mind whirled. Have faith? In what? They were meant to *stop* Wind Runner from dying! She stared around the starry cats, appalled at the joy lighting their eyes. Didn't they realize what they'd done?

Why had they brought her here? Had they *wanted* Wind Runner to die?

Desperate with grief and rage, Moth Flight buried her nose in Wind Runner's pelt. How was she going to tell Gorse Fur that his mate had died, far from her Clan and the moor?

Suddenly Wind Runner moved. Moth Flight jerked her nose up, shock sparking through every hair. She stared as her mother pushed herself lightly to her paws.

Wind Runner lifted her chin and shook the comfrey from her hind leg. The once-bloody fur around her throat was clean and soft. Her injured paw pressed against the stone, as strong as the others.

Moth Flight shivered, her thoughts spinning. Had her mother joined StarClan? She scanned her pelt for sparks of starlight, but saw only plain brown fur. "I don't understand." She stared at Half Moon.

"Remember your dreams," the white she-cat told her.

Those cats didn't die! Moth Flight's fur prickled with hope.

Half Moon dipped her head to Wind Runner. "You are the first of the stars that will rise."

The prophecy! *We will split the sky. And later, stars will rise.*

Half Moon went on. "We have given you the gift we will give all leaders: the gift of nine lives. From now on, you shall be known as Windstar."

Joy flooded like starlight beneath Moth Flight's pelt. She remembered her vision of the gray she-cat in the ditch. Suddenly it made sense. Wind Runner could die eight times and still come back to life.

Around her, StarClan began to chant, their voices echoing around the shimmering walls of the cave. "Windstar! Windstar! Windstar!"

CHAPTER 35

"Moth Flight!" Bubbling Stream paced in front of her mother, her stumpy tail fluffed with excitement. "White Tail says I can go hunting with him and Storm Pelt."

Moth Flight was lying in the morning sunshine outside her den. She gazed sympathetically at her kit. "You're too little."

"He says he won't let any buzzards get me," Bubbling Stream argued.

"Storm Pelt's taking White Tail out to teach him hunting techniques," Moth Flight argued. "How can he learn anything if he's protecting you from buzzards?"

Bubbling Stream scowled and stomped away.

Blue Whisker hurried to meet her littermate. "I told you she'd say no."

Moth Flight flicked her gaze past her kits to the sandy clearing below the tall rock. Windstar stood at the head, Gorse Fur beside her, while the Clan milled around her. She was assigning patrols for the day. The bright morning sunshine gleamed on her pelt. As she paced, the WindClan leader showed no sign of a limp. At her neck, there wasn't even a scar where the gash had been.

Jagged Peak nosed his way through his Clanmates and stopped in front of her. "Can I hunt the moortop burrows?"

Windstar shook her head. "We've hunted there too much this greenleaf. There'll be no rabbits left. Take Holly to the ShadowClan border and see what's running there." She nodded toward Dust Muzzle. "I want you to train Silver Stripe. She's fast, but her stalking needs work."

Silver Stripe pricked her ears. "Can we hunt lapwings?" she asked Storm Pelt excitedly.

Storm Pelt padded toward the young she-cat. "Lapwings are hard to catch," he told her. "Let's start with mice."

Black Ear pushed past his sister. "Can you train me as well?"

Windstar cut in. "Spotted Fur can train you."

Black Ear lifted his tail happily as Windstar turned to Spotted Fur.

"Show him the borders and the best places to scent mark," she ordered.

Spotted Fur puffed out his chest proudly as Windstar turned to Swift Minnow.

"You can go to the ShadowClan border with Fern Leaf, Jagged Peak, and Holly. Reed Tail"—she nodded to the tom— "take Dew Nose and Eagle Feather along the moorside. I saw kestrels hunting there yesterday. The prey must be running well."

Moth Flight noticed Reed Tail's gaze flit over Windstar anxiously. "Will *you* be hunting again today?"

"Of course." Windstar sounded surprised. She'd hunted

every day since her return.

Reed Tail was staring at her healed hind leg. "Are you sure you're strong enough?"

Windstar rolled her eyes. "How many times must I explain? I'm fine now. You've even checked my leg. Does it look broken?"

Reed Tail's ear twitched. "It's just hard to believe StarClan has such power."

Moth Flight understood his bewilderment. She could hardly believe what she'd seen. And yet it was true.

When they had returned from the Moonstone a few days ago, reaching camp in the early dawn light, Gorse Fur had been waiting at the entrance, his eyes widening with shock as Windstar padded toward him. He'd run to meet her, circling her in disbelief.

"StarClan healed you!" he gasped.

Windstar met his gaze steadily. "They did more than that. They gave me this life back, and eight more lives to lead WindClan through endless moons."

Gorse Fur halted, his pelt rippling along his spine. He glanced toward Moth Flight. "Nine lives? How can that be?"

"I'm not sure." Moth Flight shifted her paws. She was still awed by StarClan's power. "But it's true. I've seen it before in my dreams. It's a gift they will give to all leaders."

In the days that followed, Moth Flight had traveled to each camp, sharing her news with Acorn Fur and Clear Sky, Cloud Spots and Thunder, Pebble Heart and Tall Shadow, Dappled Pelt and River Ripple. River Ripple had seemed the least surprised; Clear Sky the most excited. Moth Flight was sure he'd have traveled with Acorn Fur by now to receive his nine lives. She hoped all the Clan leaders had visited the Moonstone by now. She'd find out tonight at the half-moon gathering.

Windstar's mew jerked her from her thoughts. "Honey Pelt, get down!"

Moth Flight looked up to see the tom-kit scrambling onto the ledge halfway up the tall rock.

Swift Minnow and Reed Tail had leaped from the hollow. Reed Tail reached up with his forepaws, stretching until he was high enough to pluck Honey Pelt from the ledge by his scruff. He placed him on the ground.

Honey Pelt fluffed out his fur grumpily. "I'm not allowed to have any fun!"

Windstar stared at him sternly. "Go and play with your littermates." She nodded toward where Bubbling Stream and Blue Whisker were chasing Spider Paw's tail as he darted among the tussocks, whisking it over the grass.

Frowning, Honey Pelt padded toward them. His Clanmates streamed past as they raced for the entrance, heading for the moor. Above the camp, the sky stretched, clear and blue. Heather scent mingled with prey scent, rolling into camp on a light breeze.

Spider Paw halted and stared wistfully after Windstar and Gorse Fur as they followed the others through the gap in the heather wall.

Bubbling Stream bounced around him. "Let's play

hunting!" She ducked low, pressing her belly against the grass. Blue Whisker crouched beside him. Honey Pelt scrambled onto a tussock and reached his forepaws into the air. "I'm hunting buzzards!"

"Has a cat ever caught a buzzard?" Blue Whisker blinked at Moth Flight.

Moth Flight padded toward her. "I don't think so. But when Gray Wing used to tell stories of the mountains, he said they caught eagles."

"Who's Gray Wing?" Blue Whisker asked.

Before she could answer, Rocky padded from his den. The old tom blinked at her sleepily. "Do you want me to watch the kits while you gather herbs?"

Moth Flight hesitated. Her stores had been low since Windstar's sickness. She ought to restock them. But, in the days since she'd returned from the Moonstone, she'd felt a desperate need to be near her kits.

Rocky stared at her. "Yesterday, you said you need to fetch more catmint," he reminded her. "You said your store was so low—"

Honey Pelt interrupted. "Can I have a badger ride?" He leaped from the tussock and landed on Moth Flight's shoulders. She staggered, struggling to keep her balance.

Rocky padded closer. "I can do badger rides."

Bubbling Stream bounded toward him. "Me first!"

Moth Flight padded forward, Honey Pelt wobbling on her back. Her thoughts drifted and unease twisted beneath her pelt. Windstar had nearly died. Spider Paw had nearly drowned. Torn between the needs of her Clan and the needs of her kits, Moth Flight felt herself veering between indecision and panic. She wasn't being the best medicine cat she could be. Her medicine cat-duties threatened her kits' safety. Her duties as a mother threatened the good of her Clan. How could she give her full attention to both?

I'm a medicine cat.

Half Moon's words rang in her mind again and again. *This is your destiny, whether you want it or not. You have no choice but to follow it. Every Clan's destiny depends on you.*

Rocky gazed at Moth Flight questioningly. "Are you going to collect herbs?"

Moth Flight winced as Honey Pelt dug in his tiny claws. "Tomorrow," she told Rocky. "I want to spend today with my kits."

Moth Flight followed Pebble Heart through the tunnel. Cloud Spots padded behind. The scents of Acorn Fur and Dappled Pelt hung in the chilly air. "They must be waiting for us," Moth Flight murmured, half to herself.

Pebble Heart's tail stirred the air ahead. "It smells like they've just passed this way."

Cloud Spots's mew echoed against the damp stone. "I hope the clouds clear soon. The moon is rising."

Fresh scents swirled around Moth Flight's muzzle as the tunnel opened into the cave. In the watery light, she could just make out Acorn Fur and Dappled Pelt, sitting beside the Moonstone. Dappled Pelt's face was raised toward the hole in the roof. Cloud shielded the stars.

"No moonlight tonight," Dappled Pelt murmured.

Cloud Spots padded to the Moonstone and settled beside Acorn Fur. "The clouds might still clear."

"Not before the moon passes." Dappled Pelt turned to face him. "How will we share with StarClan?"

"Perhaps they don't want to share tonight," Acorn Fur sniffed. "That's why they sent clouds."

Moth Flight padded across the cold stone and sat down a little way from the others. Her heart felt heavy, her paws weary. She'd spent the whole journey praying that the sky would clear. She needed to share with StarClan. *Half Moon, help me.* Grief tugged at her belly.

Pebble Heart padded to her side and sat down. "StarClan has shared enough this moon."

Acorn Fur tipped her ears toward him. "Did they give Tall Shadow nine lives?"

Pebble Heart nodded. "She's Shadowstar now."

Dappled Pelt's tail swished over the rock. "River Ripple is Riverstar."

"Thunder is Thunderstar," Cloud Spots told them. He glanced at Acorn Fur. "What name did they give Clear Sky?"

"Skystar." Acorn Fur's tail swished over the stone. "I was so scared when I saw how much pain each life caused."

"I don't know how Riverstar stayed on his paws," Dappled Pelt admitted.

Moth Flight gazed blankly at the Moonstone, only half-listening. She wanted to reach out and touch the dark stone.

Perhaps StarClan would share even without moonlight.

"Did they really heal Windstar's leg?"

Moth Flight suddenly realized Cloud Spots was speaking to her.

She shook out her pelt, trying to focus. "It's like it was never broken."

"I wish I could bring Sun Shadow here," Pebble Heart commented sadly.

Moth Flight jerked her muzzle toward him. "Is Sun Shadow sick?"

"He's had redcough," Pebble Heart told her. "He's over the worst of it, but he's taking a while to get his strength back."

Dappled Pelt leaned forward. "Do you think the Moonstone heals any cat?"

Moth Flight stared at the rock, surprised how dull it was without moonlight. "The Moonstone doesn't do anything except let us share with StarClan. It's StarClan that heals."

Acorn Fur dipped her head. "Then let's pray they heal Sun Shadow."

Cloud Spots and Dappled Pelt murmured in agreement.

Pebble Heart glanced at Moth Flight. "How is the rest of your Clan? Have they recovered from their battle injuries?"

"Storm Pelt's ear tip will always be torn," Moth Flight told him. "But I think he's secretly proud of his scars."

Acorn Fur snorted. "Red Claw's the same! He asked me not to treat the scratch on his muzzle. I told him not to be silly. What if it got infected?" She purred suddenly, her eyes glistening with affection. "I didn't realize Red Claw was such a kind cat. He's changed since the battle. I think making peace with Willow Tail has softened him."

A teasing glint flashed in Dappled Pelt's gaze. "You sound like you're in love."

Acorn Fur looked away shyly. "We have been getting close," she admitted. "We've even talked about sharing a nest."

Cloud Spots purred. "It looks like Moth Flight won't be the only medicine cat with kits."

"*No!*" Moth Flight stiffened, surprised at the harshness of her mew.

Pebble Heart blinked at her. Dappled Pelt and Cloud Spots narrowed their eyes.

"What's wrong?" Acorn Fur tipped her head uneasily.

Moth Flight's throat tightened. Grief swelled in her chest.

"Are you worried I'll lose him like you lost Micah?" Acorn Fur pressed. "You were unlucky. Not all relationships end like that. I mean, I'm sorry yours did, but it doesn't mean Red Claw will—"

Moth Flight glared at her. "*You don't understand!*" The walls echoed the sharpness of her voice. The fear and uncertainty that had nagged at her since Windstar had been hurt hit her like an icy blast of wind. She gripped the stone with her claws, bracing herself against the emotion sweeping over her. "No medicine cat should have kits! They shouldn't even take a mate!"

Acorn Fur stared at her. "But *you* did!"

Moth Flight's mouth dried as she gazed back at the Sky-Clan cat. "I was wrong." Her mew cracked.

"What do you mean?" Pebble Heart's eyes rounded with worry.

"I can't be a mother *and* a medicine cat," Moth Flight sobbed. "Spider Paw nearly drowned. I pulled him from the river. He wasn't breathing." She stared at the others wildly. "I was so scared, I didn't know what to do! A medicine cat can't be like that!"

"But you saved him," Pebble Heart pointed out.

"*Micah* saved him!" Moth Flight confessed. "He spoke to me and told me what to do. I was frozen with terror! If Micah hadn't told me what to do, I would have watched my kit die." Her flanks heaved as her breathing quickened. She felt Pebble Heart's tail smoothing her spiked fur, but she went on. "I spend half my time terrified that my kits might die while I'm looking after my Clan, and the other half terrified a Clanmate might die while I'm looking after my kits. StarClan sent me a sign that let me save Windstar. But what if they'd sent it earlier, while I was rescuing Spider Paw? I would have missed it! Windstar could be dead. And we'd have never discovered that leaders should have nine lives."

Cloud Spots lifted his chin. "StarClan would have sent another sign! They'd have made sure you saw it."

"You don't know that! We can't risk it!" Moth Flight's eyes grew hot as she glared at Acorn Fur. "You can't have kits with Red Claw. You mustn't even share his nest. You must live only for your Clan. It's the only way to stay strong."

Acorn Fur's eyes flashed angrily in the darkness. "That's easy for you to say. You've had a mate. You've got kits!"

Moth Flight shifted her paws, the stone walls pressing in around her. "I can't do it anymore!"

Pebble Heart stiffened beside her. "Are you going to stop being a medicine cat?"

"No." Moth Flight gasped as sorrow plunged thorn-sharp claws deep into her heart. "Being a medicine cat is my destiny. It's what I was always supposed to be. The Clans depend on me. Half Moon told me."

Pebble Heart's eyes glowed darkly in the half-light. "What *are* you going to do?"

The earth seemed to tremble beneath Moth Flight's paws. The pain she'd felt at Micah's death seemed to open in her chest, pouring out grief sharper than any she could imagine. "I'm going to give up my kits."

CHAPTER 36

❦

"The oaks are so big!" Honey Pelt's breathless mew echoed across the shadowy Fourtrees clearing. He gazed up through the branches. The sky was turning purple as the sun sank below the distant horizon. Stars began to show, glimmering among the leaves.

Blue Whisker huddled closer to Moth Flight. "Can we go home now?"

Moth Flight's throat tightened. Words dried on her tongue. She couldn't answer. Instead she called to Spider Paw, who was scrambling over an ancient oak root. "Stay close."

He glanced over his shoulder. "But I want to explore."

Honey Pelt marched toward his brother, Bubbling Stream at his heels. "Moth Flight said to come back!"

Blue Whisker started to shiver. "I'm cold."

"It won't be long now." Moth Flight scanned the slopes of the Fourtrees hollow. Were they coming?

Pebble Heart, Dappled Pelt, Acorn Fur, and Cloud Spots had arranged everything. They'd spoken to their leaders and brought news that each Clan would accept one of Moth Flight's kits.

"Are you sure that you don't want them to stay together?" Acorn Fur had asked when she'd visited the WindClan camp the day before.

"No." Moth Flight had been certain. "I want one kit to go to each Clan." She hadn't explained more. She knew she was doing the right thing.

"But if they stay together, they'll be able to look after each other," Acorn Fur had reasoned.

"I'm sure their new Clans will look after them well enough." Moth Flight hadn't met Acorn Fur's gaze. It was hard enough to stop her mew from trembling.

Acorn Fur didn't press her. "Clear Sky and Star Flower are thrilled to be taking Honey Pelt. They still miss Tiny Branch, and Honey Pelt will be a comfort to them."

"Moth Flight?" Blue Whisker's mew jerked her back to the moment. The she-kit was gazing through the branches. Her white-and-yellow pelt glowed in the dusky light. "Is that where StarClan lives? In the sky?"

"A new star is born each time a cat dies," Moth Flight explained.

"Which one's Micah?" Blue Whisker narrowed her eyes, straining to see through the leaves.

"I'm not sure." Moth Flight's mew thickened. "But he's up there watching you."

"Really?" Blue Whisker blinked at her hopefully.

Moth Flight touched her muzzle to the yellow-and-white kit's head. "Really," she promised.

"Get out of the way!" Bubbling Stream's cross mew rang

across the clearing. She was trying to pull herself onto the gnarled oak root beside her brothers.

Moth Flight gazed at them desperately. They were so small, their pelts like pale thistledown against the bark. "Come here," she called. "I need to speak to you."

Honey Pelt leaped from the root and charged toward her. He must have heard the fear in her mew. "What's wrong?"

Spider Paw raced after him. "Are we going home now?"

Bubbling Stream dropped to the ground and hurried behind them. "Why did you bring us here?"

Moth Flight nosed Blue Whisker away from her flank. "Stand beside your littermates." She gazed at her kits as they lined up in front of her, their eyes wide with excitement. "I have to tell you something important."

One day you will gather the scattered petals of the Blazing Star, but not yet. Micah's words burned in her mind. She remembered the stories her mother used to tell of the Blazing Star prophecy, which had separated the cats into Clans.

You will gather the scattered petals.

She was destined to bring the Clans together, one flower made of five petals, just like the Blazing Star flower.

But not yet.

She would bring the petals together, but first, she must scatter them. Her bloodline must flow into each Clan.

She blinked solemnly at her kits. "The leaders of the Clans are coming here tonight."

"Why?" Spider Paw pricked his ears.

Blue Whisker shrank back. "Do we have to meet them?"

Moth Flight didn't answer. She forced herself to go on. "They are coming here to meet you. They want you to go live with them, as part of their Clans. Each of you will go to a different Clan."

Bubbling Stream stuck out her muzzle. "I'm not going anywhere."

Moth Flight steadied her breath. "You will be well cared for and your new Clan will be your home from now on."

Blue Whisker's eyes clouded with terror. "I don't want to go."

"Are you giving us away?" Spider Paw looked confused.

Bubbling Stream frowned. "Did we do something wrong?"

"No!" Moth Flight's heart seemed to crack. She began to tremble. "I love you so much. But it has to be this way."

Honey Pelt's gaze grew hard. "No it doesn't. You *want* it this way."

Moth Flight swallowed. "Yes," she admitted softly. "But not because I don't want you—it's because you are special."

Spider Paw growled. "So special you have to get rid of us!"

Micah, help me! Moth Flight glanced up desperately. *Why do I have to do this alone?* She straightened, determined to be strong. "Your father spoke to me," she began. "He told me that one day I would gather the scattered petals of the Blazing Star."

"What's that got to do with us?" Spider Paw demanded angrily.

"*You* are the petals," Moth Flight told him. "Long before you were born, the spirit-cats came into this clearing—"

"*Spirit-cats?*" Bubbling Stream looked anxiously over her shoulder.

"Are they with us now?" Blue Whisker blinked into the shadows.

"We're alone," Moth Flight soothed. "But they *used to* come here. Before I found the Moonstone. Before the Clans existed. It was the spirit-cats who told us to split into five Clans, like the petals of the Blazing Star flower. The cats had grown jealous. They all wanted land. They fought over who owned the forest and the moor. Many died. So we divided the land fairly among us and became the Clans."

"But the Clans *still* fight each other," Spider Paw pointed out. "That's how Windstar got hurt."

Moth Flight nodded. "That is why you must each join a Clan. You are littermates. Your bond is strong. One day, when you are grown up, that bond will make the Clans into one family once more. You are the petals of the Blazing Star."

Honey Pelt narrowed his eyes thoughtfully. "So we won't fight anymore?"

"Exactly." Pride warmed Moth Flight's pelt.

Bubbling Stream looked unconvinced. "Why do *we* have to join new Clans? Why can't Storm Pelt and Eagle Feather and Dew Nose?"

Spider Paw glanced at his sister. "Because we're special."

Blue Whisker stared at Moth Flight. "I don't want to be special."

Moth Flight hesitated. Her mind whirled back to the moor, all those moons ago. She remembered her father's words. *Dust*

Muzzle will make a fine hunter one day, but Moth Flight is special. How little she'd understood. She thrust her muzzle close to Blue Whisker, her heart twisting. "I need you to be brave, little one. I'm asking you to do something very hard. I know you're scared. But you will be safe. ThunderClan cats are kind. You'll love the forest. It's full of beautiful plants, and it's warmer than the moor. The wind whispers high in the trees so you'll never feel lonely. And the Clan will raise you as its own."

"But I want *you* to raise me." Blue Whisker's breath warmed Moth Flight's cheek. The pain in her heart was almost too much to bear, but she forced herself not to tremble.

Honey Pelt nosed between them. "Come on, Blue Whisker. It'll be exciting. You'll see Moth Flight at Gatherings and the rest of us won't be far away." He looked at Moth Flight. "Which Clan will I go to?"

"SkyClan," Moth Flight told him.

"You see?" Honey Pelt blinked at Blue Whisker. "I'll be living in the same forest as you, and Bubbling Stream or Spider Paw will be in RiverClan."

"Spider Paw is going to live with RiverClan," Moth Flight told him.

Spider Paw's eyes widened with horror. "I'll have to eat fish. And *swim!*"

Honey Pelt nudged him. "At least next time you fall in the river, you won't half drown."

Spider Paw tipped his head thoughtfully.

Moth Flight was still watching Blue Whisker. She had guessed that her shyest kit would take it hardest. But Blue

Whisker's eyes were sparkling with curiosity. "Do Thunder-Clan cats climb trees?"

"I don't know," Moth Flight confessed.

Blue Whisker's gaze drifted upward. "I've always wondered what it's like to look down on everything, like a bird."

Honey Pelt flicked his tail encouragingly. "I bet Thunder-star's always climbing trees. It's probably the first thing he'll teach you."

Bubbling Stream was staring up the slope, where darkness swallowed the forest. "I'll be going to ShadowClan." She sounded uncertain.

Moth Flight's thoughts flicked back to the moon she'd spent there. "It's peaceful in the pine forest. And Juniper Branch's kits are only two moons older than you. You'll have someone to play with."

"You'll have to eat frogs," Spider Paw snorted. "That's even worse than fish!"

Bubbling Stream ignored him. "Are ShadowClan kits allowed out of camp?"

"They're probably allowed to roam anywhere they like," Honey Pelt told her. "Buzzards can't hunt in forests."

Moth Flight blinked at him gratefully. He sounded so much like his father: so optimistic and ready to take on any challenge. She purred. "I will miss you all so much."

Blue Whisker brushed her muzzle along Moth Flight's jaw. Spider Paw weaved around her legs.

Bubbling Stream clambered onto her back. "One last badger ride!"

Moth Flight began to lumber heavily across the clearing, making Bubbling Stream sway on her shoulders until the kit mewled with delight.

Honey Pelt trotted beside her. "Skystar is the bravest leader, isn't he?"

Moth Flight glanced at him, trying not to imagine what sort of guardian Skystar would be. "He's the most confident," she conceded.

Honey Pelt whisked his tail. "I wonder what forest prey tastes like."

"Better than fish," Spider Paw muttered.

"Fish tastes great." Moth Flight halted and blinked at him. "You'll love it."

"Moth Flight." Blue Whisker's anxious mew made her stiffen. The kit was staring at the far slope.

Moth Flight followed her gaze. The bracken stirred as a shape moved through it. She shook Bubbling Stream from her shoulders, opening her mouth and tasting the familiar scent of RiverClan.

The stems swished as Riverstar padded into the clearing.

Spider Paw pressed against her. "I don't want to go."

"It will be all right." Moth Flight lifted her chin to greet the RiverClan leader. "Thank you for coming."

Riverstar dipped his head. "I am honored that you trust RiverClan to care for one of your kits."

As he spoke, paw steps thrummed the slope behind. Moth Flight looked up as Thunderstar bounded into the clearing.

He scrambled to a halt beside Riverstar. "Hi." His gaze

swept the kits, glowing with surprise. "They look so much like Micah!"

Before Moth Flight could answer, more paw steps sounded as Shadowstar followed Skystar into the clearing.

Blue Whisker ducked beneath Moth Flight's belly. Bubbling Stream backed away.

"This must be very hard for you all." Shadowstar stopped in front of Moth Flight, her gaze solemn.

Honey Pelt stepped forward, meeting her gaze. "We're not scared."

Skystar purred. "I can't imagine any kit of Micah's being scared."

Bubbling Stream tipped her head. Blue Whisker crept from beneath Moth Flight. Spider Paw lifted his muzzle.

Thunderstar blinked at them. "Which one is Blue Whisker?"

"I am." Blue Whisker's mew was hardly more than a whisper. She padded slowly forward and stopped in front of the ThunderClan leader. Moth Flight could see her trying not to tremble.

"Violet Dawn has made you a nest," Thunderstar told her.

"I've never slept by myself," Blue Whisker whispered.

"Then you can share a nest with Milkweed's kits." Thunderstar's mew was gentle. "They're not much older than you. Although Milkweed says they fidget like rabbits in a burrow."

"Bubbling Spring fidgets too," Blue Whisker murmured. "So I won't mind."

Thunderstar pointed his nose toward the forest. "Are you ready to leave?"

Blue Whisker glanced back at Moth Flight, her eyes glistening. "Can I stay with you, please?"

Moth Flight hurried forward and pressed her nose into the kit's soft fur. Blue Whisker's warm scent filled her nose. She fought the urge to scoop her close and never let go. "You must go," she croaked. "ThunderClan needs you."

Blue Whisker turned away, her tail down, and began to follow Thunderstar from the clearing.

Bubbling Stream padded toward Shadowstar. "I'm supposed to come with you."

Shadowstar blinked at her. "You must be Bubbling Stream."

"I'm not eating frogs," Bubbling Stream told her bluntly.

Shadowstar's eyes flashed with surprise. "Okay."

Bubbling Stream glanced at Moth Flight. "Will you come and visit?"

"Of course!" Moth Flight hurried forward and pressed her muzzle against Bubbling Stream's.

Bubbling Stream drew away and stared at Moth Flight. Anxiety darkened the kit's eyes, but she blinked it away. "See you soon then." She padded toward the slope.

Shadowstar nodded to Moth Flight. "We'll take care of her like she's one of our own."

Moth Flight dipped her head, unable to speak. Blue Whisker and Thunderstar had vanished over the top of the slope as Shadowstar turned away. At the edge of the clearing, Bubbling Stream nosed her way into the bracken.

Riverstar glanced from Honey Pelt to Spider Paw. "Which one comes with me?" His friendly mew was brisk.

Honey Pelt glanced at his brother. Spider Paw was staring at the RiverClan leader as though Riverstar were a hawk circling prey.

Riverstar swished his tail enticingly. "The cats of River-Clan are looking forward to meeting their new Clanmate."

Spider Paw edged forward. "I'm coming with you," he murmured.

Riverstar blinked at him. "You look like you'll make a good swimmer. You have broad shoulders and wide paws." He nodded toward Spider Paw's extra claw. "Fish are slippery. That claw will make them easier to catch."

Spider Paw glanced down. "I nearly drowned once."

Riverstar snorted. "That's because you didn't have the right swimming coach." He began to head toward the slope. "I haven't lost an apprentice yet. You're in safe paws."

Spider Paw blinked at Moth Flight. "Do I really have to go?"

Moth Flight leaned forward, pressing her muzzle against his head. "It's your destiny," she whispered. "Don't be afraid. StarClan is watching over you."

"I want to be your kit, not RiverClan's," Spider Paw whispered.

Moth Flight met his gaze. "You'll always be my kit." The words caught in her throat and she looked away as her gaze clouded.

When she looked back, Spider Paw was hurrying after Riverstar.

Skystar padded forward. He dipped his head to Honey

Pelt. "Are you ready to join SkyClan?"

"Yes." Honey Pelt lifted his chin.

Skystar glanced at Moth Flight. "Are *you* ready?" Compassion filled his gaze.

Moth Flight reached for words, but could only stare back, her heart breaking.

Honey Pelt touched his nose to her cheek. "I know you have no choice," he whispered. "If this is StarClan's wish, then I'm happy to go."

"Your father will be as proud of you as I am," Moth Flight croaked.

"Don't be sad." Honey Pelt pressed his muzzle deeper. "We'll be fine."

As he drew away, Moth Flight felt cold air touch the fur his breath had warmed.

She watched numbly as Honey Pelt padded after Skystar. "Good-bye," she murmured under her breath.

You've done the right thing. Micah's mew touched her ear fur, as light as the evening breeze.

"Have I?" she whispered.

"You have changed the destiny of the Clans." Micah's voice was clear now. She wondered if Skystar and Honey Pelt could hear it as they climbed the slope toward the forest. But neither cat looked back.

Micah went on. "You were always braver and smarter than you thought. It's one of the reasons I loved you, and why I still miss you. But you have so much left to do. Making decisions is easy; living with them is the true test of courage. Only by being true to yourself and becoming the medicine cat you dream of will you learn how truly special you are."

Moth Flight looked up, staring past the branches to the sky beyond. The stars flashed like flecks of sunlight on rippling water, brighter than she'd ever seen them and too many to count.

"I will do my best," she promised. "I will always do my best."

CHAPTER 37

Moth Flight fluffed out her fur against the chilly air of the Moonstone cavern and looked up. Stars glittered beyond the hole in the roof. Moonlight spilled over the rim. As she waited for it to reach the Moonstone, she listened to the other medicine cats talk.

"I'm glad the clouds cleared in time," Pebble Heart mewed.

"Clouds never last long when it's this breezy," Dappled Pelt answered. "The wind has been tugging at my whiskers all day."

"It brought down the first fall of leaves in the forest," Cloud Spots told them.

Acorn Fur shivered. "I'm not ready for leafbare."

"That's a few moons away yet," Pebble Heart reassured her.

Moth Flight's thoughts drifted from their idle chatter, her mind sifting through everything they'd told her on the journey here. In the moon since she'd given Honey Pelt, Bubbling Stream, Blue Whisker, and Spider Paw away, her heart had felt like a heavy, cracked stone in her chest. She'd curled into her empty nest each night, feeling their absence in the cold moss around her, and each morning she'd awoken expecting to feel their soft pelts nestling against her but feeling nothing but the twitching of her own paws.

"How is Blue Whisker?" she'd asked Cloud Spots as she met him at the WindClan border.

Cloud Spots had told her that Blue Whisker was eating well and had made friends already with Milkweed's kits. "She and Shivering Rose are inseparable."

Acorn Fur had purred as she told Moth Flight that Honey Pelt was following Skystar around camp, asking endless questions. "Skystar enjoys it," the chestnut she-cat had reassured her. "His eyes light up whenever Honey Pelt darts in front of him, begging to know something new. He seems impressed by Honey Pelt's eagerness to learn."

"How's Bubbling Stream?" Moth Flight had asked Pebble Heart as they'd crossed a dusky meadow.

"She's leading Dangling Leaf, Dusk Nose, and Shade Pelt on expeditions outside camp."

Moth Flight's belly had tightened with worry. "Are they safe in the forest by themselves?"

"Someone always tracks them," Pebble Heart had promised her. "Mouse Ear followed them through a nettle patch yesterday. They all came home with stung noses and pads."

Moth Flight's heart had quickened with alarm. "Is Bubbling Stream all right?"

"I had plenty of fresh dock in my store," Pebble Heart had told her gently. "Besides, *every* kit gets stung eventually. Mouse Ear should have known better than to walk through a nettle patch, but he said he didn't want to let them out of his sight."

Moth Flight had felt reassured and hurried to catch up

with Dappled Pelt. "Is Spider Paw settling into RiverClan?"

"He can swim already." There had been a hint of pride in Dappled Pelt's mew.

"Not by himself, surely?" Alarm flashed through Moth Flight's pelt.

"Kits never swim by themselves," Dappled Pelt promised her. "Not until they're strong enough to ride the currents."

Moth Flight's thoughts had flashed back to her "swim" with Spider Paw. She'd felt helpless against the buffeting of the water. She couldn't imagine Spider Paw ever being strong enough to survive it.

"He'll be swimming like a fish before long." Dappled Pelt must have guessed Moth Flight's anxiety. "It's just like running through a gale." She'd glanced sideways. "You've never been knocked off your paws by the wind, have you?"

"No." Moth Flight had been unconvinced. But she had to trust RiverClan.

Dappled Pelt gently changed the subject. "Drizzle and Pine Needle think Spider Paw's great. He's been teaching them how to play moss-ball. He's a great jumper. Drizzle can never get the moss past him."

Moth Flight pictured Spider Paw now, as she gazed at the Moonstone. She could imagine him charging around the RiverClan camp as he'd done in the hollow. Her heart ached. Did her kits miss her? They sounded happy in their new homes. *Happier than with me?* Guilt pricked her paws. She *wanted* them to be happy, and yet she hoped they still kept a place for her in their hearts.

Acorn Fur's mew cut into her thoughts. "I wonder if StarClan has anything important to share with us."

Moth Flight shifted her paws uneasily. Had they known she would give her kits away? Had she done the right thing? Guilt hollowed her belly.

The Moonstone flared. Moth Flight flinched, slitting her eyes as light blanched the cave. Countless stars seemed to blaze before her face. Leaning forward, she touched her nose to the glittering stone.

The floor shifted beneath her paws. Her heart lurched as she felt herself swept sideways, whirling dizzyingly until suddenly she felt soft pasture beneath her paws. She opened her eyes into the half-light of evening. Pebble Heart, Dappled Pelt, Cloud Spots, and Acorn Fur stood nearby, blinking at the rolling meadows and distant forest. They were in StarClan's hunting grounds, on the breeze-blown hilltop, grass rippling around their paws.

Above them, a purple sky deepened to black as it stretched toward the distant horizon. She gazed at it, the stars blurring as she stared at them. They began to swirl like a flock of shimmering birds, spinning toward the ground.

Pebble Heart lifted his chin, his eyes wide in wonder. Dappled Pelt's fur pricked along her spine. Acorn Fur backed away as the stars circled closer. Moth Flight narrowed her eyes against the brightness as the grass sparkled and the stars slowed, coming to rest on the hilltop around them.

Blinking, she saw the light fade until she could make out the shapes of the StarClan cats.

Half Moon stepped from among them, her white pelt glistening. She stopped in front of Moth Flight and dipped her head.

Moth Flight tensed, trying to glimpse the expression in the StarClan cat's dark green gaze. *I scattered the petals of the Blazing Star, just as Micah told me.* She knew what she wanted to say. She had given away her kits and she wanted to tell StarClan that it was the only thing she could have done. But the words she'd planned stalled on her tongue. "I had to!" she blurted as Half Moon met her gaze.

"We know." Half Moon stared at her steadily. "You made the right choice."

Moth Flight glanced beyond the white she-cat, hoping to glimpse Micah. He'd given his blessing to sending their kits to new homes, but she wanted to see him—she needed to read his gaze and truly know that he understood.

Before she could spot him, Half Moon spoke again. "Your greatest loyalty must always be to StarClan and your Clanmates." Her gaze flicked to Acorn Fur. "The only way to ensure this is for you all to promise never to take mates or have kits."

Acorn Fur's eyes flashed indignantly. "That's not fair! I can be loyal to you, *and* my Clanmates, *and* a mate and kits!"

Half Moon didn't answer.

"I *can*!" Acorn Fur insisted.

A starry she-cat padded forward. Snow-white fur flecked her gray muzzle. "How do *you* know what it is like to be a mother?" she challenged Acorn Fur, her eyes flashing.

Acorn Fur snorted. "I've seen Star Flower with her kits. It's not hard!"

The old she-cat's tail twitched crossly. "I am Quiet Rain, mother of Gray Wing, Clear Sky, and Jagged Peak. I stayed behind in the mountains when they left the Tribe. But my heart cried out for them every day they were gone."

Moth Flight shivered. *Will grief torture me forever?*

Quiet Rain went on. "My need was so strong that I spent my final days crossing unknown lands to see them. Only when I was sure they were safe in their new home could I give in to the sickness that made every step heavy with pain."

Acorn Fur stared at her. "I'm not you! *My* kits will stay near me. I won't have to worry about them!"

Quiet Rain gave a hollow purr. "Do you really believe that you'll be able to ignore their cries to treat an injured Clanmate?" She swung her head toward Moth Flight accusingly. "Haven't you warned this foolish cat?"

"She's not foolish!" Moth Flight stepped closer to Acorn Fur. "*I* thought I could be a mother and medicine cat too. I had to *experience* it before I realized how impossible it was to give my heart twice over." She blinked at Acorn Fur. "You must make your choice now, *before* you have kits. You mustn't ever face the choice I faced. It will break your heart." Her eyes prickled with sadness. "Choose *now*. Either care for your Clan, or take a mate. You can't do both."

Pebble Heart swished his tail. "What about us?" He nodded toward Cloud Spots. "We can't be mothers."

Half Moon tipped her head. "But you can be *fathers*. Do you think a father loves his kits any less?"

Gray Wing slid from among his Clanmates. "Pebble Heart," he meowed gently. "Each medicine cat must make the same choice. Live like an ordinary Clan cat and take a mate. Raise a family if you like. But if you do, renounce your medicine-cat duties."

Half Moon's gaze flitted around the medicine cats. "We brought you closer to us than any of your Clanmates. One day your Clan may depend on what we share with you. We need to know you hear us. If you don't, who will suffer?"

Pebble Heart's eyes darkened. "Our Clan."

Half Moon nodded. "Then choose."

Pebble Heart shifted his paws, his gaze lingering on Half Moon's for a moment. Then he spoke. "My greatest loyalty will always be with StarClan and my Clanmates."

Half Moon's ear twitched. "Do you agree you will never take a mate or have kits?"

Pebble Heart nodded.

Half Moon's gaze flicked to Cloud Spots questioningly.

The ThunderClan medicine cat dipped his head. "Me too."

"And me." Dappled Pelt gazed solemnly at Half Moon.

Quiet Rain was still staring at Acorn Fur. "And *you*? Have you decided which you will choose?"

Acorn Fur glanced around anxiously. She caught Moth Flight's eye hopefully, as though hoping for advice.

Moth Flight lowered her gaze. "You must decide for yourself."

Acorn Fur shifted beside her. "Okay," she mewed. "If I

must choose, I choose StarClan."

Quiet Rain narrowed her eyes sharply. "Are you certain?"

Acorn Fur lifted her chin. "I'm certain."

Relief washed Moth Flight's pelt. She knew how hard Acorn Fur's decision must have been. She thought, with a rush of love, of her first moon with Micah. The memory still warmed her. She couldn't imagine her life, never having known such love. Or worse, having known it but knowing she must refuse it.

Softly, she pressed against Acorn Fur. "Tending to your Clan will give you all the joy and warmth and love that you need," she murmured, hoping it was true. "Give your heart to them." She blinked at Half Moon. "It must always be this way."

Half Moon nodded. "In the future, medicine cats may never take a mate. They must never have kits."

Gray Wing swished his tail. "Their loyalty will rest only with StarClan and their Clanmates."

Around them, StarClan murmured with approval, their mews echoing beneath the starless sky.

Watching them, Moth Flight caught sight of Micah at last. His gaze was fixed on her, brimming with affection.

She returned it, her heart twisting with sorrow. *I'm sorry, my love. But while I live, I must give you up.* She had sent her kits away so she could be the best medicine cat she could be. She couldn't share her dreams with Micah any more. Her dreams belonged to StarClan now. Every hair in her pelt, every beat of her heart, every breath belonged to *them*.

TURN THE PAGE FOR AN
EXCLUSIVE MANGA ADVENTURE . . .

CREATED BY
ERIN HUNTER

WRITTEN BY
DAN JOLLEY

ART BY
JAMES L. BARRY

WILL THESE DO?

THAT THEY WILL, SPIDER PAW. YOU CHOSE WELL.

THE NEXT STEP IS TO STRIP THE LEAVES OFF.

MOTH FLIGHT, I MEANT TO ASK YOU BEFORE--WHY DIDN'T YOU COME TO THE GATHERING LAST MOON?

OWL SONG NEEDED ME.

SHE'S...A BIT ANXIOUS ABOUT HER KITTING.

THAT REMINDS ME-- WAS BLUE WHISKER AT THE GATHERING?

HER KITS MUST BE DUE SOON, TOO.

OH, SHE WAS THERE, ALL RIGHT.

SHE'S AS FAT AS A BADGER NOW, BUT YOU KNOW BLUE WHISKER--NO WAY IS SHE EVEN GOING TO MISS ANY GOSSIP.

BLUE WHISKER ALWAYS WAS A CHATTY CAT.

I WONDER... IF BLUE WHISKER'S KITS REALLY ARE CLOSE, MAYBE...

MAYBE I SHOULD VISIT?

THANK YOU. THANK YOU SO MUCH.

BUT, WELL... I HAVE TO WARN YOU. IF ANYTHING, BLUE WHISKER'S ANXIETY IS MAKING HER TALK EVEN MORE THAN USUAL.

OH, THAT'S NOTHING TO WORRY ABOUT, THUNDERSTAR.

I'VE SEEN SIMILAR THINGS WITH OTHER KITTING SHE-CATS.

I'M SO GLAD YOU'RE HERE, MOTH FLIGHT! OUR MEDICINE CAT TOLD ME WHAT TO EXPECT, BUT...

...BUT I'VE NEVER DONE THIS BEFORE AND IT'S ALL SO STRANGE AND I JUST DON'T KNOW IF WHAT'S HAPPENING IS SUPPOSED TO HAPPEN AND I--

BLUE WHISKER, TAKE A BREATH. YOU'RE DOING FINE.

YOU--FETCH SOME WET MOSS.

YOU--GIVE HER MORE PADDING UNDER HER HEAD.

MY KIT OR NOT, WE FALL INTO A FAMILIAR ROUTINE.

WELL, FAMILIAR FOR ME, ANYWAY.

SOON BLUE WHISKER DELIVERS THREE ABSOLUTELY GORGEOUS KITS.

THE EXPERIENCE TIRES HER OUT SO MUCH THAT SHE ACTUALLY FALLS SILENT.

I TRY NOT TO SHOW IT TOO MUCH, BUT...WATCHING MY OWN KIT GIVE BIRTH...SEEING HOW BEAUTIFUL HER KITS ARE...

I DON'T KNOW THE LAST TIME I'VE FELT THIS HAPPY.

IT PUTS ME RIGHT BACK AT MY OWN KITTING...MAKES ME RELIVE THE JOY I FELT, WHEN BLUE WHISKER AND HER BROTHERS AND SISTER ARRIVED.

BUT AT THE SAME TIME, I CAN'T HELP BUT WONDER...

...HOW MUCH DID I MISS OUT ON? HOW MUCH DID I NEVER SEE, BECAUSE I CHOSE THIS PATH?

MOTH FLIGHT?

WHAT? THAT VOICE! IT CAN'T BE...CAN IT?

BUBBLING STREAM!

I CAN'T BELIEVE IT! IT'S...IT'S SO GOOD TO SEE YOU!

BUT WHY HAVE YOU COME? WHY NOW?

I JUST... I SENSED THAT I SHOULD COME HERE TODAY.

AND LOOK AT WHAT I FIND! MY SISTER KITTING, AND OUR MOTHER WATCHING OVER HER! WHO WOULD HAVE THOUGHT?

IT'S NOT REALLY THAT STRANGE, HONESTLY. NOT TO ME.

BUT...WHERE'S HONEY PELT?

HE'S RIGHT OUT THERE! GO TAKE A LOOK!

NO, NO, NO-- YOU NEED TO G CLOSER TO TH GROUND!

THAT WAY YOU GET MORE SPRING IN YOUR LEGS--MORE DISTANCE OUT OF YOUR LEAP!

TYPICAL OF HONEY PELT. A SKYCLAN CAT, BUTTING INTO ANOTHER CLAN'S TRAINING SESSION AND TAKING IT OVER!

HE'S SO MUCH LIKE HIS FATHER. I CAN PRACTICALLY SEE MICAH DOING THAT VERY THING HIMSELF.

BUTTING IN OR NOT, IT'S FANTASTIC TO SEE THE CLANS COOPERATING.

I HEAR SKYSTAR TREATS HONEY PELT LIKE HIS OWN SON.

ALWAYS ASKING HIM FOR ADVICE ON HUNTING AND FIGHTING.

I WONDER, THOUGH...

HE'S SO HANDSOME. GROWN INTO A FINE CAT, JUST LIKE HIS LITTERMATES.

WILL HE BE AS HAPPY TO SEE ME AS BUBBLING STREAM AND BLUE WHISKER?

MOTH FLIGHT?

MOTH FLIGHT!!

AMAZING. TODAY OF ALL DAYS...

...TO HAVE ALL FOUR OF MY KITS CLOSE AGAIN, ALL AT ONCE.

FOR THE FIRST TIME SINCE I SENT THEM ON THEIR WAY. ME AND MY KITS, TOGETHER.

I KNOW IT'S BEEN A WHILE SINCE I'VE SEEN YOU...

...BUT I DIDN'T THINK YOUR FUR HAD TIME TO GET THIS GRAY!

HUSH, YOU! RESPECT YOUR ELDERS!

AND COME--YOUR SISTER JUST KITTED. COME AND MEET THE LITTLE ONES.

HELLO, LITTLE ONES! WELCOME TO THE WORLD.

THEY'RE GORGEOUS, BLUE WHISKER. YOU MUST BE SO PROUD.

ACTUALLY, HONEY PELT, SINCE YOU MENTIONED THE PASSING OF TIME...

...I DO EXPECT TO BE HUNTING WITH MICAH IN STARCLAN VERY SOON.

IN FACT, I'VE BEEN DREAMING ABOUT IT.

BUT...BUT THAT'S RIDICULOUS! I DIDN'T MEAN IT ABOUT THE GRAY FUR--YOU'VE GOT PLENTY OF TIME LEFT! LOTS OF TIME!

DON'T WORRY. I DON'T WANT ANY OF YOU TO GET UPSET OVER THIS. I WILL GO TO STARCLAN A HAPPY CAT...

...BECAUSE I AM SO PROUD OF ALL OF YOU.

I KNOW I MADE THE RIGHT CHOICE, ALL THOSE MOONS AGO--

MOTH FLIGHT?

WHAT'RE YOU LOOKING AT?

WHAT'S WRONG?

I KNOW NONE OF MY KITS CAN SEE THAT MOTH.

IT'S MEANT JUST FOR ME.

LISTEN CLOSELY. NO MOTHER COULD EVER BE PROUDER OF HER KITS.

AND I WANT YOU TO CONTINUE ON THE PATHS YOU'VE CHOSEN. YOU HEAR ME?

...YES.

STAY TRUE TO YOUR CLANS...

HELP AS MANY CATS AS YOU CAN...

A new adventure begins for the warrior Clans.

Read on for a sneak peek at

A VISION OF SHADOWS

WARRIORS

BOOK ONE:
THE APPRENTICE'S
QUEST

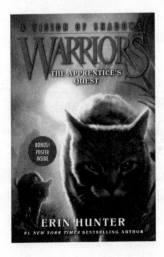

For many moons, the warrior cats have lived in peace in their territories around the lake. But a dark shadow looms on the horizon, and the time has come for Alderpaw—son of the ThunderClan leader, Bramblestar, and his deputy, Squirrelflight—to shape his destiny . . . and the fate of all the warrior Clans.

CHAPTER 1

Alderkit stood in front of the nursery, nervously shifting his weight. He unsheathed his claws, digging them into the beaten earth of the stone hollow, then sheathed them again and shook dust from his paws.

Now what happens? he asked himself, his belly churning as he thought about his apprentice ceremony that was only moments away. *What if there's some sort of an assessment before I can be an apprentice?*

Alderkit thought he had heard something about an assessment once. Perhaps it had been a few moons ago when Hollytuft, Fernsong, and Sorrelstripe were made warriors. *But I can't really remember . . . I was so little then.*

His heart started to pound faster and faster. He tried to convince himself that some cat would have told him if he was supposed to prove that he was ready. *Because I'm not sure that I am ready to become an apprentice. Not sure at all. What if I can't do it?*

Deep in his own thoughts, Alderkit jumped in surprise as some cat nudged him hard from behind. Spinning around, he saw his sister Sparkkit, her orange tabby fur bushing out in all directions.

"Aren't you excited?" she asked with an enthusiastic bounce. "Don't you want to know who your mentor will be? I hope I get someone *fun*! Not a bossy cat like Berrynose, or one like Whitewing. She sticks so close to the rules I think she must recite the warrior code in her sleep!"

"That's enough." The kits' mother, Squirrelflight, emerged from the nursery in time to hear Sparkkit's last words. "You're not supposed to *have fun* with your mentor," she added, licking one paw and smoothing it over Sparkkit's pelt. "You're supposed to *learn* from them. Berrynose and Whitewing are both fine warriors. You'd be very lucky to have either of them as your mentor."

Though Squirrelflight's voice was sharp, her green gaze shone with love for her kits. Alderkit knew how much his mother adored him and his sister. He was only a kit, but he knew that Squirrelflight was old to have her first litter, and he remembered their shared grief for his lost littermates: Juniperkit, who had barely taken a breath before he died, and Dandelionkit, who had never been strong and who had slowly weakened until she also died two moons later.

Sparkkit and I have to be the best cats we can be for Squirrelflight and Bramblestar.

Sparkkit, meanwhile, wasn't at all cowed by her mother's scolding. She twitched her tail and cheerfully shook her pelt until her fur fluffed up again.

Alderkit wished he had her confidence. He hadn't wondered until now who his mentor would be, and he gazed around the clearing at the other cats with new and curious eyes. *Ivypool would be an okay mentor,* he thought, spotting the silver-and-white tabby she-cat returning from a hunting patrol with Lionblaze and Blossomfall. *She's friendly and a good hunter. Lionblaze is a bit scary, though.* Alderkit suppressed a shiver at the sight of the muscles rippling beneath the golden warrior's pelt. *And it won't be Blossomfall, because she was just mentor for Hollytuft. Or Brackenfur or Rosepetal, because they mentored Sorrelstripe and Fernsong.*

Lost in thought, Alderkit watched Thornclaw, who had paused in the middle of the clearing to give himself a good scratch behind one ear. *He'd probably be okay, though he's sort of short-tempered....*

"Hey, wake up!" Sparkkit trod down hard on Alderkit's paw. "It's starting!"

Alderkit realized that Bramblestar had appeared on the Highledge outside his den, way above their heads on the wall of the stone hollow.

"Let every cat old enough to catch their own prey join here beneath the Highledge for a Clan meeting!" Bramblestar yowled.

Alderkit gazed at his father admiringly as all the cats in the clearing turned their attention to him and began to gather together. *He's so confident and strong. I'm so lucky to be the son of such an amazing cat.*

Bramblestar ran lightly down the tumbled rocks and took his place in the center of the ragged circle of cats that was forming at the foot of the rock wall. Squirrelflight gently nudged her two kits forward until they too stood in the circle.

Alderkit's belly began to churn even harder, and he tightened all his muscles to stop himself from trembling. *I can't do this!* he thought, struggling not to panic.

Then he caught sight of his father's gaze on him: such a warm, proud look that Alderkit instantly felt comforted. He took a few deep breaths, forcing himself to relax.

"Cats of ThunderClan," Bramblestar began, "this is a good day for us, because it's time to make two new apprentices. Sparkkit, come here, please."

Instantly Sparkkit bounced into the center of the circle, her tail standing straight up and her fur bristling with excitement. She gazed confidently at her leader.

"From this day forward," Bramblestar meowed, touching Sparkkit on her shoulder with his tail-tip, "this apprentice will be known as Sparkpaw. Cherryfall, you will be her mentor. I trust that you will pass on to her your dedication to your Clan, your quick mind, and your excellent hunting skills."

Sparkpaw dashed across the circle to Cherryfall, bouncing with happiness, and the ginger she-cat bent her head to touch noses with her.

"Sparkpaw! Sparkpaw!" the Clan began to yowl.

Sparkpaw gave a pleased little hop as her Clanmates chanted her new name, her eyes shining as she stood beside her mentor.

Alderkit joined in the acclamation, pleased to see how happy his sister looked. *Thank StarClan! There wasn't any kind of test to prove that she was ready.*

As the yowling died away, Bramblestar beckoned to Alderkit with his tail. "Your turn," he meowed, his gaze encouraging Alderkit on.

Alderkit's legs suddenly felt wobbly as he staggered into the center of the circle. His chest felt tight, as if he couldn't breathe properly. But as he halted in front of Bramblestar, his father gave him a slight nod to steady him, and he stood with his head raised as Bramblestar rested the tip of his tail on his shoulder.

"From this day forward, this apprentice will be known as Alderpaw," Bramblestar announced. "Molewhisker, you will be his mentor. You are loyal, determined, and brave, and I know that you will do your best to pass on these qualities to your apprentice."

As he padded across the clearing to join his mentor, Alderpaw wasn't sure how he felt. He knew that Molewhisker was Cherryfall's littermate, but the big cream-and-brown tom was much quieter than his sister, and had never shown much interest in the kits. His gaze was solemn as he bent to touch noses with Alderpaw.

I hope I can make you proud of me, Alderpaw thought. *I'm going to try my hardest!*

"Alderpaw! Alderpaw!"

Alderpaw ducked his head and gave his chest fur a few embarrassed licks as he heard his Clan caterwauling his name. At the same time, he thought he would burst with happiness.

At last the chanting died away and the crowd of cats began to disperse, heading toward their dens or the fresh-kill pile. Squirrelflight and Bramblestar padded over to join their kits.

"Well done," Bramblestar meowed. "It wasn't so scary, was it?"

"It was great!" Sparkpaw responded, her tail waving in the air. "I can't wait to go hunting!"

"We're so proud of both of you," Squirrelflight purred, giving Sparkpaw and then Alderpaw a lick around their ears. "I'm sure you'll both be wonderful warriors one day."

Bramblestar dipped his head in agreement. "I know you both have so much to give your Clan." He stepped back as he finished speaking, and waved his tail to draw Molewhisker and Cherryfall closer. "Listen to your mentors," he told the two new apprentices. "I'm looking forward to hearing good things about your progress."

With an affectionate nuzzle he turned away and headed toward his den. Squirrelflight too gave her kits a quick cuddle, and then followed him. Alderpaw and Sparkpaw were left alone with Molewhisker and Cherryfall.

WARRIORS : THE NEW PROPHECY

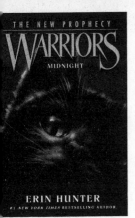

1

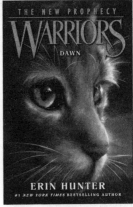

2

3

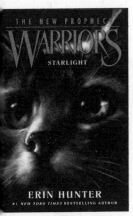

4

5

6

In the second series, follow the next generation of heroic cats as they set off on a quest to save the Clans from destruction.

HARPER
n Imprint of HarperCollinsPublishers

www.warriorcats.com

1

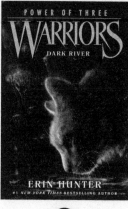

2

3

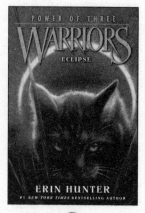

4

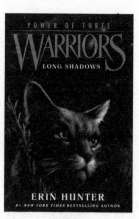

5

6

In the third series, Firestar's grandchildren begin their training as warrior cats. Prophecy foretells that they will hold more power than any cats before them.

HARPER
An Imprint of HarperCollinsPublishers

www.warriorcats.cor

WARRIORS: OMEN OF THE STARS

OMEN OF THE STARS
WARRIORS
THE FOURTH APPRENTICE
ERIN HUNTER
#1 NEW YORK TIMES BESTSELLING AUTHOR

OMEN OF THE STARS
WARRIORS
FADING ECHOES
ERIN HUNTER
#1 NEW YORK TIMES BESTSELLING AUTHOR

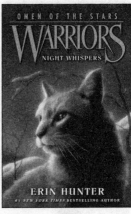

OMEN OF THE STARS
WARRIORS
NIGHT WHISPERS
ERIN HUNTER
#1 NEW YORK TIMES BESTSELLING AUTHOR

OMEN OF THE STARS
WARRIORS
SIGN OF THE MOON
ERIN HUNTER
#1 NEW YORK TIMES BESTSELLING AUTHOR

OMEN OF THE STARS
WARRIORS
THE FORGOTTEN WARRIOR
ERIN HUNTER
#1 NEW YORK TIMES BESTSELLING AUTHOR

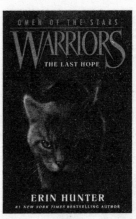

OMEN OF THE STARS
WARRIORS
THE LAST HOPE
ERIN HUNTER
#1 NEW YORK TIMES BESTSELLING AUTHOR

In the fourth series, find out which ThunderClan apprentice will complete the prophecy.

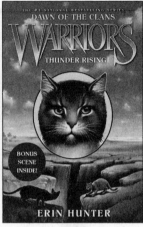

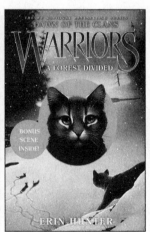

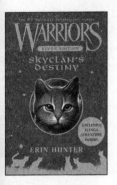
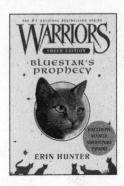

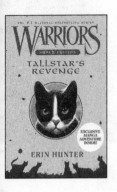

WARRIORS: BONUS STORIES

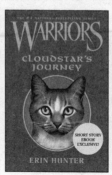

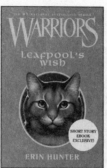

Discover the untold stories of the warrior cats and Clans when you download separate ebook novellas—or read them in two paperback bind-ups!

HARPER
An Imprint of HarperCollinsPublishers

www.warriorcats.co

WARRIORS: FIELD GUIDES

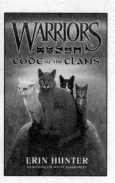

FOR THE ULTIMATE FAN!

Delve deeper into the Clans with these Warriors field guides.

HARPER
Imprint of HarperCollinsPublishers

www.warriorcats.com

ALSO BY ERIN HUNTER:
SURVIVORS

SURVIVORS: THE ORIGINAL SERIES

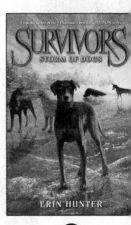

The time has come for dogs to rule the wild.

HARPER
An Imprint of HarperCollins*Publishers*

www.survivorsdogs.co

URVIVORS: THE GATHERING DARKNESS

In the **second series**, tensions are rising within the pack.

SURVIVORS: BONUS STORIES

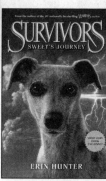

Paperback

Download the three separate ebook novellas or read them in one paperback bind-up!